LIGHTNING

STRIKES

Angels of Ember Trilogy: Book One

by

Joni Mayhan

Cover photograph taken by Leah Vantlin
Cover design by Joni Mayhan

Also by Joni Mayhan

Ember Rain (Angels of Ember trilogy – Book 2)
Angel Storm (Angels of Ember trilogy – Book 3)

Acknowledgments

When I was seventeen years old, an encouraging teacher took my first short story and read it to all of her other classes. Something pretty magical happened in that moment. I decided I was going to be a writer. With that said, I'd like to thank Mrs. Betty Hunt of Poseyville, Indiana, for giving me the first nudge towards a passion I'll pursue for the rest of my life.

I'd also like to thank early readers of this novel. Your comments and ideas helped me transform a melody into a symphony. Thanks go to Janet Halpin, Jerry Bouchard, Evelyn Baczewski, Melinda Hammond, Tina Aube, Marian Luoma, Charlotte York, Harold Stierley, Susie Stierley, Leah Vantlin, Trevor Mayhan, and Laura Mayhan. Much appreciation also goes to Jeff Legere, for walking me through cover design. Thank you to Sandy MacLeod for proofreading, and for encouraging me to eat plenty of pie in diners to keep my strength up. Extra thanks go to my son, Trevor, for helping me work out the ending of this book, and to my daughter, Laura, for her assistance with several key scenes.

Thanks also to my sister, Leah Vantlin, for her outstanding photography skills. If it weren't for her daughter, Lily, I would have never had the inspiration for the character, Elizabeth.

I simply couldn't have done this without the support of my friends and family. Thank you for putting up with me and for encouraging me through all the dark spots.

For my parents, who always believed in me.

1

I was sixteen years old when the world came to an end.

Instead of a breathtaking display of explosions and clouds shaped like grey mushrooms, it came in the form of a virus, something vulgar and vile, something one human being should never do to another. The virus was deadly. It leached into the skin, invisible and probing, and it took people down very quickly. They'd start with a sniffle and end with a gasp, and then pretty soon there'd be one less of us left on the planet.

A sharp crack in the darkening sky brings me into a standing position before I even register the sound. I glance up in time to see lightning streak across the sky like a fracture. It is followed by a roll of thunder that rumbles within the tumbling depths, something that would hurt me just because it could. The energy that surges through the air feels tangible, like something I could scoop with my father's fishing net. It is enough to send me scurrying inside for the safety of my hidey-hole.

My hidey-hole is a hollowed-out cabinet in our kitchen. After our house was hit by lightning several years ago, the entire kitchen had to be rebuilt from the ground up. My father was always a practical person and did most of the work himself. When he ended up with extra space at the place where the cabinets met the wall, he added a hidden door inside one of the lower cabinets, thinking it would be a fun place for my sister to play in. Now it has become the one place in the house where I feel safe.

I climb inside and pull the false door closed behind me as the sound of thunder and lightning grows stronger outside. A powerful gust of wind rushes against the house, making it creak and moan like a living thing. I curl up in the corner and pull my grandmother's quilt around me. Even though the space is barely big enough for one person, Elizabeth and I always slept here together. She would curl against me like a warm extension of my own body, twirling a strand of my hair between her fingers as she fell asleep each night, making me feel safer for reasons I can't explain. Now that she's gone, the space feels too large and too empty. I try to tamp down on the memory, but it is stronger than my will to repress it.

Elizabeth.

Her eyes were wild as she screamed my name, begging me to *do something* as the bad men yanked her away from the front door, wearing only the white cotton nightgown my mother gave her for Christmas. And then I remember the softening silence as the truck filled with angry men disappeared down the road.

Her face floats into my mind, sleepy and soft, blond against cream. My father always called her our little nymph, something that sent me racing to the library to research because it sounded somehow dirty and inappropriate. But, I'd been surprised at how agile the nickname was, how it was so perfectly *Elizabeth*, so true to form.

She'd usually rise from bed as cuddly as a kitten, searching for someone to nuzzle up with for a while, but that morning she'd woken up in a foul mood. She stomped around the house like a three-year-old, mindless of common sense or rational thought.

"I want my mother," she told me as though I could change history.

I tried to put my arm around her to comfort her, but she shook me off. She was an unstable stick of dynamite sometimes, and she terrified me with her moods. If she'd been like any other ten-year-old, I could have reasoned with her until she understood the logic, but Elizabeth could be unwavering in her stubbornness.

"Did you have a bad dream, honey?" I touched her arm, but she yanked it away, her long fly-away hair falling down over her eyes. She glared at me through the pale strands, the blue of her eyes standing out in the shadows, almost glowing in the morning sunshine.

"I want my mother!" she demanded.

"Elizabeth. You know where she is. You helped me bury her." I closed my eyes and felt the familiar sense of hopelessness weigh me down like a rock sinking in water. My parents had spent a lifetime giving in to her, and I wasn't sure I could continue dealing with the consequences.

I took a deep breath and pulled a ribbon from my pocket. I'd found it earlier in the morning in a pile of my mother's sewing supplies. I was going to give it to her when she woke up, in the hopes that she'd allow me to brush the tangles out of her hair. "Mommy does it!" she told me on the few times I tried.

"Look what I found this morning." I stretched it out across my fingers, allowing the morning sunshine to catch the gold gossamer strands in the pink ribbon. My mother seldom sewed, but she had always been unable to walk away from something beautiful. The ribbon had caught her eye on one of our shopping excursions and she'd bought a roll of it, murmuring uselessly that maybe she'd use it to trim a pillow or *something*.

Elizabeth's head tilted up, her hair parting around her face again. The look in her eyes transformed from outright rage to sheer delight and then returned to outright rage again. Before I could react, she snatched it from my fingers and darted away.

3

Joni Mayhan

"That's mine. Mommy bought it for me. She said it was mine!" She ran through the front door, not hearing the sound of tires on gravel at the end of the driveway.

"Elizabeth! *No!*"

She turned and glared at me one more time before running across the lawn. "It's mine and you CAN'T HAVE IT," she screamed at the top of her lungs. Brakes had squealed and the vehicle came to a sliding stop in the loose gravel, sending a hail storm of pebbles against the house.

The men started yelling and the next thing I knew, Elizabeth was running back towards the door.

"Ember, save me! *Do something,*" she'd screamed, her blue eyes wide with fear, the pink and gold ribbon still clutched between her fingers. I'd stared at her for the duration of a heart beat before I did something that would haunt me for the rest of my life. I shut the front door and ran to my hidey-hole, leaving my sister to the wolves that had come for both of us.

I hear another sound outside and strain my ears to listen. At first I think it is the sound of more thunder, but as I listen harder, my blood runs cold. The bad men are back.

I pull the blanket up to my nose and hold my breath, waiting.

The truck charges up the driveway, tires crunching the asphalt gravel and festive music braying from the tinny speakers. They sound as if they are going to a street festival instead of a possible execution. I can hear them laughing over the music, probably telling jokes back and forth between houses. It skids to a stop and the music cuts out in an instant, leaving a perfect silence in its place.

In ten seconds, I will hear the pound of their footsteps on the wooden deck. In twenty seconds, they will make it to the

4

door, their big black guns held in front of them like assassins. In thirty seconds they will be inside the house, looking for me.

My mind races wildly. Have I left anything out that could give me away?

Have I been careful?

I try to walk through my day backwards, trying to find a wobbly place in my routine, a place where I might have slipped up and left something undone. Instead, I find myself starting at the beginning of the day, unwinding it like a ribbon.

When I awoke at dawn, I crawled out of my hidey-hole, listening to make sure it was safe. I am well acquainted with the pulse of the house, the moaning of the walls as they brace against a heavy wind, the creak of the oak tree outside the kitchen window as it sways in the breeze. If someone were in the house, I would know these sounds too. I would hear the huff of a breath, the squeal of a floorboard as someone walked across the wooden floor, not knowing the quiet places to step. Our house hides nothing from nobody. My father said it had something to do with the floor joists, but since I don't how to fix them, I just walk in the places that do not make any noise.

After I was certain the house was empty, I found my way out to the woods, to the place where I watered the plants, as I've come to call it. I always pick a different spot, to prevent the weeds from turning brown and giving me away. I even tossed a handful of fresh dirt over the top of it to mask the immediate smell of my urine.

For breakfast, I ate an apple from the tree out back. Every autumn, my mother and I would pick the apples off the tree and make pies and tarts, producing much more than we could possible ever eat. I close my eyes and a flash of memory returns to me like a movie clip of my mother and me in the kitchen, white aprons tied with long strings around our waists, the sound

of Aerosmith's *Walk This Way* on the radio. We danced as we
sliced and diced apples, swinging our hips and lip synching the
words, pretending we knew the lyrics when we really didn't.
Elizabeth wandered in and out of the room, drawn by our
energy, but not interested in participating in the work. She sat
at the table and played with a long red apple peel until she got
bored and drifted away.

After that, I poked around the house for a while, picking up
objects and allowing them to share their memories with me
while trying not to cry in the process, my grief wrapped around
me like a cloak. In my mother's room I found the robe she
always wore in the summer months. It was silky and blue, mixed
with green and white lotus flowers that were meant to look
Asian and exotic. I try to remember if I put the robe back into
the closet and closed the door. If I didn't, would the bad men
remember this? Do they have every room in every house
committed to memory?

The footsteps grow louder. Twenty seconds have passed
and the bad men have made it to the back door. They are
speaking in a language I don't understand. All I know about
them is what I learned on the television before it died. They are
terrorists from a small, but potent foreign country, the same
men who blew up embassies and hijacked airplanes. They are
bronzed skinned and angry, falling into prayer as often as they
shoot down survivors. Even the other people from their country
are afraid of them. Several months ago, they somehow
stumbled upon the one thing that would bring us to our knees,
despite our weapons and our arrogance, and they used it with a
glee that made me sick to my stomach. They released a virus.

It started north of us and blanketed the entire area within
days. When I first heard about it on the news, I listened with
vague interest, not really paying attention until my last day of

school, when most of the seats had been empty and the teachers were ashen and shaky, trying to hide their bloody tissues from us. By the time I got home, the worst of it was in full swing and the TV was filled with news alerts as everyone tried to figure out what was happening. Just before dinner, my mother came home, sneezing and coughing into the corner of her arm, like she always taught us to do to prevent the spread of germs. I watched her climb the stairs, while the reporter on the television behind me described the symptoms that would soon take her away from us.

The bad men open the heavy kitchen door. The rusty hinges squeal with a sound that runs straight through me. I would like to oil it, but now that they've heard it protest, I'm afraid to change it. I am careful to keep everything exactly the way it was. I always close doors after I walk through them, even though the inside of the house sometimes grows warmer than a hundred degrees during the heat of the day. If I leave them open, then they will have to remain open, even during the winter, and I don't plan on freezing to death after everything else I've survived.

They step across the floor, barely ten feet away from me, and stop talking. My heart pounds wildly. Can they hear me breathing?

I closed my eyes and hold my breath, willing my heart to stop beating so loudly. It thuds like thunder in my head and I can almost see the sound bouncing off the four walls in my little hidey-hole. Did I leave anything out?

After the apple, after the apple, my mind prompts me.

After the apple. I force myself to return back to that point in time, to when I buried the apple core in the woods and then returned to the stream to wash my hands. Then I walked around the house, looking at my mother's robe.

After that, after that?

After that, I walked to my sister's room. Her bed had been unmade, the pink comforter draped across the corner in a way that always made me want to fix it. I imagined pulling it up over the flat of her mattress and tucking it beneath the two pink pillow shams that were lined with blue satin. Then I would collect the stuffed animals from the floor and I'd prop them up side by side along the length of her pillows like a silent audience.

Then what did you do?

I picked up Clementine, the faded ragdoll who looked like the character in my sister's favorite book. My mother's voice returns to me, soft and lilting and I can see her tucked close against my sister, their heads touching, brown against blond.

"Her hair was as orange as a sunny surprise.

She had rosy cheeks and a gleam in her eyes.

She loved sunsets, orange lollipops, and golden birds on a line.

Everyone called her Clementine."

She was the lovey that Elizabeth couldn't sleep without. We once drove all the way back to Boston to retrieve her from a theater seat. I picked up Clementine and I carried her around for a while, holding her close to my face, breathing in the smell of old cotton, catching the slightest hint of my mother's perfume Elizabeth had sprayed her with.

I thought I'd hidden all of my mother's perfume, but Elizabeth must have climbed to the top of the closet and found it. I'd stomped into the room, where she sat holding her doll, flipping through the pages of a book.

"Perfume leaves an odor in the room, Elizabeth! You can't use it. If the bad men come back, they'll smell it and know we're here," I told her in a hushed sort of way.

She shrugged and tucked the doll closer to her, curling her chin over the top of the doll's head protectively, her blond hair falling across her face like a partition, separating us. "I like the smell."

I'd stared at her, exasperated. If we were going to get caught, it would be because of something she'd done. There was no way for me to prevent it. She refused to close doors after she'd walked through them or even cover her own waste in the woods. I couldn't take a nap in the afternoon, worried that I'd awaken to find her dancing in the front yard, in full view of the road. She just didn't understand.

Sometimes I allowed myself a moment of perfect anger and wondered if I'd be better off without her. With this, I sigh inside, the pull of guilt as strong as an ocean tide.

Be careful what you wish for.

The sound of a squeaking floor board brings me back in an instant. The men walk through the kitchen and into the dining room, where the long wooden table sits with a half a load of laundry still splayed out at the end, partially folded. My mother's silk shirts are draped across the back of a chair, something she often did to prevent them from wrinkling until she could get them onto a hanger. Piles of towels have been folded and are stacked like useless pillars along one end, waiting for my mother to come back and put them away.

Did you put the doll away? my mind nags, and I try to remember.

I walked through the house, smelling my mother's perfume on the doll, remembering how defiant Elizabeth could be. She'd get angry if I told her to stay away from the windows, telling me she would do what she wanted to do. And then she'd open a box of crackers I'd been saving for leaner times, leaving the crumbs where ever they fell. Her capture was unavoidable. I

9

couldn't have done anything to have prevented this. I tell this to myself soundly and firmly.

The sounds grow louder and louder. They've come back into the kitchen and have stopped directly in front of my cabinet.

My mind burns red with terror. I must have left something undone, something that has given me away. I imagine a muddy trail of footprints trailing across the worn linoleum floor, leading directly to the cabinet where I hide. I can envision them, one nodding to the other knowingly, holding up a finger to his lips. On the silent count of three they will tear me from the cabinet and carry me to their Bronco, like they did with Elizabeth. Hot tears spring to my eyes and I force them back. I will not cry. Not even if they find me.

I take a deep breath and let it out silently.

Control, Ember. Control.

I move my hand slowly, touching my thigh to where my thread-worn dress presses tightly against my skin. It is growing hot in my cabinet. The air feels like vapor and I become aware of the scent of my own musky sweat. I pull on my dress and realize that a portion of it is caught between the fake wall and the cabinet. If they open the cabinet under the sink, they will see the white triangle of my dress poking out, giving me away.

Adrenaline spikes through me.

One of the men says something and the other responds.

I tug on my dress, trying to work it through the crack, bit by bit.

A cabinet door is opened above the stove. Boxes are shifted.

"Mashed po-ta-toes?" one of the men says, and they both laugh. They have found the box of instant mashed potatoes that I've been saving for winter. I can hear the box being shuffled

10

back and forth, followed by the sound of pouring. I cringe as I realize what they are doing. They are emptying the box of potato flakes onto the floor. The minute I walk out of my hole, I will leave footprints behind.

Another cabinet door is opened, and cans are shifted. I pull on my dress again, trying to match the pulls with the shifting of the cans so I won't be heard.

One of the men says something with a laugh. It is followed by a terrible crash that sounds like glass breaking. There is more laughter and then another crash. I realize what they are doing and my heart nearly freezes. They are pulling the canned foods from the cabinet and are throwing them at the window, damning me to a frozen winter with a window that will never close.

Another cabinet door is opened and then another and another. They are moving through the kitchen, cabinet by cabinet until mine is the last one left. I pull on my dress again, making the tiniest of noises.

The men stop. One of them hushes the others.

My heart pounds as I realize they've heard me.

I feel for my dress with panicked fingers.

Do I have it all?

The cabinet door opens.

I hold my breath and simply go somewhere else in my mind.

2

Elizabeth was three the first time she was struck by lightning.

She skipped across the broad green lawn, pulling a red balloon behind her like a beacon, with my mother's sculptures surrounding her like Greek gods. The barometer began dropping rapidly in a way that made my head feel as though it were being pulled into a vacuum. Clouds had been rolling in for an hour or better, but we'd ignored them for the sake of being children. My mother would have normally noticed and ushered us indoors, but she had been in the midst of an art show, something that consumed her whole and made her forget about everything else in the world, even her children sometimes.

My mother was a sculptress, an artist who spent vast portions of time bent over a block of stone wondering what it could become, what was trapped inside of it asking to come out. The majority of her work lived on our lawn. Large, spatial pieces sat in the middle of her flower gardens, accentuating the mystic creations in a way that seemed to please the gods. My favorite was Aphrodite, the goddess of love. I thought it was amazing that the goddess of love looked exactly like my mother.

Her sculptures now rise from the overgrowth like archeological ruins, appearing strange and stark against the soft grass. Birds land on Aphrodite's outstretched hand and soil her cheeks with their droppings. I sometimes walk among them, admiring them for what they once were, remembering the parties that were once held in their honor.

She would throw tremendous, glittery galas, thinly disguised as art shows, in the gardens at our house. Caterers with white jackets and steaming silver carts would bring tray upon gleaming tray into the huge white tent, where friends and acquaintances sat fanning themselves. A small band would set up on the far end of the lawn, just on the other side of the tent, and their music would drift through the air like perfume, faint and sweet. After everyone finished eating their Cornish hens, she'd shamelessly borrow the microphone and tell them about her latest pieces. By the end of the week, the statues begin to disappear as the work trucks came one by one to pull them from the garden, leaving gaping wounds in the landscaping like places where teeth had been extracted.

None of us saw the lightning. My mother was at the other end of the garden with her group and I had retreated to my swing set, where I pushed myself back and forth on a swing, digging the black paten toe of my shoe into the soft dust, making swirly patterns.

The lightning had slammed into the ground with a boom and lit the world with a terrific splash of white light. Every hair on my arm stood up and I could taste the electricity in the air like ashes on my tongue. Once the light faded, we found Elizabeth sitting in the middle of the lawn, looking dazed but otherwise unharmed. We weren't completely certain she'd actually been struck until the second time it happened, when my father went along for the ride.

One of the bad men says something very close to my hiding spot. The cabinet door is open and all they have to do is push the side wall to find me.

I suddenly want my mother so badly it hurts.

"Mother," I breathe her name and can almost feel her wrap her warm arms around me, telling me that everything will be okay. I've been so strong. I've tried so hard. I know she would be proud of me for keeping my chin up, but I don't know how to keep doing this. I need her so badly. When she first got sick, we had just found out about the virus, didn't fully realize that it would be the last thing to knock her down. After years of

13

fighting breast cancer, after losing both of her breasts and undergoing weeks of painful chemotherapy, where she lost her hair and very nearly her will to live, she fell to this.

This.

She lasted precisely four days and then she was no more. I tried to call 911, but the line just rang and rang. Then I called our closest neighbor and found nothing but silence at the other end of the line. After a few days, Elizabeth and I wrapped our mother in clean sheets and carried her out to the garden where we buried her in front of Aphrodite, in a place she might have chosen herself.

Words are spoken very close to my head again and items are shifted in the cabinet beside me. Will they wonder why the entire left side of the cabinet is empty? I imagine them cunning and feral, the kind of men who could sniff the air and track me by scent.

Finally, the door is slammed shut and I exhale, my pulse thready and wild, pounding beneath my sweaty temples. I open my eyes and stare into the darkness, trying to imagine the men walking out of the kitchen, trying to judge what they are talking about by the tone of their lilting voices. It's possible they are setting a trap for me. They could be standing on the other side of the doorway, waiting for me to climb out of my hiding place. I hold my breath and listen, but I don't hear anything more than the sound of my own heart pounding. After a moment, I hear their engine starting and the pop of tires on gravel.

Anger settles in where fear has left an empty spot and it takes hold of me bit by bit, leaching into my soul like poison. My hands knot into fists and I imagine turning the tables on them and giving them a taste of the same terror they've been serving to me. I don't understand how they can do the things they do.

By the time I find the nerve to crawl out of my cabinet, the sun is embracing the horizon and my stomach reminds me that all I've had to eat all day was the lone apple I'd picked from my father's tree. I stare at the potato flakes on the floor, wondering what I should do about them. If I sweep them up, the men might notice the next time they come back, but if I leave them scattered across the floor, I won't be able to use my cabinet again. My footprints will give me away. It feels like a phrase my mother used to say: between a rock and a hard place. I imagined the hard place being a snap-jawed iron trap and the rock being a jagged boulder.

I might be able to sweep the flakes back a little bit, making it look as though the wind has blown them, but I'm not even sure that will work. For one brief second, I am thankful that Elizabeth is no longer around. She would have tracked the potato flakes all over the house without a second thought. As soon as the thought washes through me, I feel the familiar pull of guilt fill the crevices of my soul. I dig my fingernails into the sides of my arms until my skin nearly bleeds, angry at myself, disappointed to the hollow of my bones. As the guilt fades, the tears try to find me again, but I push them back. I have to stay strong.

I take a deep breath and then tiptoe into the dining room, watching the windows for signs of movements before moving to the living room beyond it. The outdoors seems to be itself again. The only sounds I can hear are the birds chirping and rustle of small animals moving through the dry grass.

I find my way to my mother's garden. Fat tomatoes and juicy yellow squash just beg to be eaten. I pluck a tomato from the vine and eat it where I stand, letting the juices dribble down my chin. I bring the squash into the kitchen, where I will sauté it on the gas stove. As I come back through the dining room, I

15

remember Elizabeth's Clementine doll and I freeze. I am almost certain I left it sitting on the dining room table, but now it is gone.

Did I leave it there or not? I mentally retrace my steps.

I'd walked around the house carrying it in my arms like a baby and then the memory gets muddy. I've become such a creature of habit that I often put things away without realizing I've even done it, but this time I am drawing a complete and utter blank. I freeze as I consider the possibility that one of the men could still be here. He could be hiding, toying with me like a cat plays with a mouse, batting me around a bit before sinking his teeth into my soft underbelly.

I look left and then right, my movements slow and quiet. All I can hear is the swell of adrenaline pounding through my veins. The house is completely silent, the old floor boards giving nothing away.

After a moment I remember to breathe. A trickle of breeze flows through the broken window, making the room smells like dusty summer grasses and sunshine, not the stagnant stuffy air I've grown accustomed to. Dust particles float through the rays of sunlight. The house is as quiet as a tomb.

I search the rest of the rooms, but Clementine is gone. With a sigh, I leave the thought alone because I don't understand what it could mean. Surely the bad men didn't take the Clementine doll? Why would they want it?

I return to the kitchen with the squash. I still have a half bottle of olive oil left in the cabinet and I heave a sigh of relief when I realize that the bad men didn't smashed it through the window along with the other cans of food. I pour a bit of it into the bottom of a Teflon-coated skillet, my fingers trembling from the receding adrenaline. I wonder for a moment about what will happen to Teflon considering all the scientists are now dead. If

16

the men with the masks have their way, we will be returned back to our primal roots, hunting for food with clubs and cooking it over a roaring fire. Teflon and the recollection of it will simply fade away like the memory of the people we once loved. After a while, the word will sound vaguely familiar, but will blend in uselessly with other words like Velcro, Spandex, and Kevlar, until they are foreign and meaningless.

I slice the squash with a steak knife. I'll bring the knife and the pan down to the stream in the woods to wash it as soon as I've finished eating. I've learned to economize my motions, boiling everything down to as few steps as possible. After my mother died, I fell back on the tradition I was familiar with and cooked with several pans, and then served our dinners on plates. After several days of lugging armfuls of plates and pans down to the stream, I realized the uselessness of the effort. Inside me was a need to stay civilized, to remember the way things were and honor them properly, but there was a stronger need to survive, so I adapted and turned it into an adventure for Elizabeth. We learned to eat with our fingers straight from the pan, then walking to the stream to clean up afterwards. It had become the beginning of a game we played nearly every night during the summer, right up until the day she'd been taken away, the day she'd had the tantrum.

3

As darkness descends moment by moment, I sit on the edge of the porch and watch the sun sink into the still waters of the pond. I sigh and try to get a hold of myself. Tears are not safe. They pull you off-guard, make you stop noticing the things that you need to pay attention to and make you weak.

"There wasn't anything I could have done," I say and realize this is the first time I've spoken out loud in days, possibly a week. My voice sounds rusty and alien, like it belongs to someone else altogether.

"They saw her. They saw her run out into the front yard."

If I had tried to save her, they would have caught both of us. Even if we made it to the hidey-hole in time, I wouldn't have been able to keep her quiet while they searched the house. She would have sobbed or kicked at me, still angry about the ribbon. Then we would have both been taken.

A braver person would have run behind the retreating vehicle, hiding behind trees and shrubs as she followed them into town. She would have learned where they were keeping her and broke in during the night to rescue her. I thought about it many times over the following days, but in the end the fear won out. I couldn't imagine a scenario that wouldn't end with me captured as well. Instead, I stayed where I was and prayed for a miracle that never came.

I force myself to think about something else, but my mind isn't always compliant. It latches on the next worst thing and worries it, like a dog with a meaty bone. I think about the day my father died in the lake and feel the tear slip down my face.

It wasn't a good day, from the very beginning. The smoke detector went off in the kitchen while my mother stood at the stove in her blue and green oriental robe, frying bacon. The sound, so startling and frank, screamed through the house like a banshee, waking up my father and then my sister, pulling them from the depths of their dreams by the roots of their hair.

My father stomped into the kitchen and accused my mother of sabotaging his only day to sleep in, his brown shaggy hair falling down over his eyes, making him look like an aging rock star with a Sunday morning hangover instead of a forty-year-old electrical engineer. His dark eyes were nearly lost in the deep shadows under his eyes, making his face seem even longer and thinner than it was. My sister joined him, crying and holding her hands over her ears, pleading with my mother to "make it stop, make it stop!" [to match the same thing on the next page]The moment built to a crescendo as the towel my mother was using to fan the bacon caught fire on the open gas flames. She tossed it into the sink, into the basin full of soapy water, as my sister's sobbing turned to screaming and the smoke detector steadily shrieked.

"GOD DAMMIT! Won't somebody do something, or do I have to do EVERYTHING?" he'd thundered above the other noises.

My mother turned and glanced at us, her face quiet and composed despite what she must have been thinking. Her tumble of chestnut hair had been piled up on her head and secured with a plastic clip, making her look as though she had a plume of brownish feathers on the back of her head.

With a sigh, she turned on the fan above the stove and opened the back door to let some fresh air in, something that always seemed to appease the smoke detector, but it wasn't urgent enough for my father. He stomped into the dining room, yanked the smoke detector from the ceiling and flung it against the wall hard enough to make it bleed batteries and sharp white pieces of plastic. He should have continued through the living

19

room to his study, where he could have calmed down before returning to the three of us who were holding our breath in the kitchen, but he didn't. The effort of ruining the smoke detector hadn't been enough to diffuse his anger.

Elizabeth was still crying, her chorus of "make it stop, make it stop, make it stop" transformed to "you broke it, you broke it, you broke it." He stormed back into the kitchen, his mind latching onto everything that bothered him about Elizabeth.

"I'm sick and tired of you always crying. There's nothing wrong with you. We've had you to every doctor in the goddamned state and they've said there's nothing wrong with you." He turned to my mother, who was draining the steaming bacon grease into an old can. "It's your damn fault for enabling her all these years."

My mother didn't even look up from her pouring, probably knowing better than to wade into the middle of one of my father's foul moods. Once she finished, she returned the hot skillet back to the stove and then began scrambling the eggs in a large white mixing bowl, her gleaming whisk moving a thousand miles an hour around the confines of the bowl.

"Howard, go take a walk outside and cool off before you say something you don't mean," she said.

"Don't give me that shit. If you didn't baby her so much, she'd probably be normal."

My mother poured the soupy eggs into the skillet the bacon had just come from. The eggs hissed in the hot grease, making me jump a little. She tucked a tendril of hair behind her ear. "I haven't done anything you haven't done, Howard. We've both enabled her."

He stared at the back of her head, the fumes nearly radiating off of him in waves.

20

I took Elizabeth's trembling hand under the table and held it, hoping it would calm her down. She had thankfully stopped chanting "you broke it," but she was still sobbing. If the sound grew any louder, I worried that it would draw my father's attention back in her direction, back to someone who wouldn't be able to deflect it as skillfully as my mother could.

"You've gotta freaking be kidding me. Who removed her from of the public school system last year so she could be home schooled?"

My mother sighed and probably rolled her eyes, although I couldn't see her face. "We both did, Howard. The other kids were absolutely tormenting her and she wasn't learning anything."

"Yeah, well... you didn't give me any choice on that. It was either: pull her out of school or listen to you nag me about it every second of the day."

"It was the right dec..."

"...and what about swimming lessons? Whose bright idea was it to pull her out of swimming lessons? We have a goddamned pond out front where she could very easily drown. We agreed to take her to the Y and teach her how to swim, but noooo....some kid must have looked at her cross-eyed and made poor Elizabeth cry, so Mommy pulls her from her classes. I'm SICK AND TIRED OF THIS," he roared, slamming his fists onto the table. His eyes were wild and the blood vessels in his temples stood out from his skin. Elizabeth sniffled and hugged her knees to her chest.

"Stop YELLING!" she screamed into her knees, her face streaked with tears and snot, her yellow hair hanging down into the mess.

Her words simply made my father come unglued. Any resolve he'd had vanished in an instant. He flew across the room and grabbed her arm.

"Come on Elizabeth. You are going to learn how to swim whether you like it or not."

While my mother and I watched, our mouths making soft o's of surprise, he dragged Elizabeth from the chair and pulled her across the kitchen floor by one arm. She tried to grab onto a chair leg, but he yanked her free.

My mother was frozen to the spot, a spatula in her hand, the eggs still spitting and hissing in front of her.

"Mother. Do something," I screamed. She looked down at the eggs and turned off the burner and then drifted out of the room after them. I ran to the kitchen window and watched as my father dragged Elizabeth down to the pond, still dressed in her white summer nightgown, my father still in his navy plaid sleeping pants and white t-shirt. They made footprints in the dewy grass, the golden morning transforming into brittle chaos.

The sky darkened in an instant, covering the warm sun with heavy black blankets as a storm swooped in. The winds picked up, blowing stray leaves and debris across the lawn. One of my mother's blue lawn chairs fell onto its side as the sound of thunder rumbled in the distance.

"Daddy NO!" Elizabeth howled as he pulled her into the cold water.

I could hear her words echo inside my head as though she were speaking to me directly. The sound pierced through me, like a nail through my mind and I pressed my hands to my ears as if to stop it.

They'd barely taken three steps into the lake when the world went white. A loud crack filled the air with the sensation of a thousand bombs, the image burnt onto the retinas of my eyes for long seconds. I heard my mother scream my father's name before I regained my eyesight. By the time I made it down to the pond, my mother was pulling my father's limp body from the water while Elizabeth huddled on the shore, soaking wet.

"I told him no, I told him no, I told him no," she keened over and over again. I took her hand and led her to the house, where I dialed 911 and watched my mother hug my father's body by the water as my sister curled into a corner and shrieked louder than the smoke detector had. Nothing was ever the same after that. In some ways, it was the beginning of the end.

A flash of movement at the end of the driveway catches my eye. I stare into the shadows, trying to separate reality from imagination. It could just be a deer, slipping from the safety of the forest to nibble on the long slender grass that lines the driveway, but it could be something else too.

I kept a vigil after our mother died, watching out the windows for intruders. The outside world became a terrifying place. Besides the bad men who drove up and down the streets in their black Broncos, there were other people to worry about as well, people even worse than the bad men. I feel a cold chill climb my spine just thinking about it.

Before the stations faltered, Elizabeth and I had been glued to the television, trying to piece together the madness. We knew about the virus and the bad men, but there was so much more we didn't know. We occasionally saw people wandering down the road, looking lost and alone, their minds no longer coherent, but we had no idea what had happened to them. Some of them were angry, kicking mailboxes and screaming obscenities into the sky, but others just seemed drained of their personalities.

As the stations began fading to static, I managed to catch one of the last news clips. They were talking about the virus survivors. I called my sister into the room and we watched with rapt attention. What we learned chilled us to the bone.

The newscaster reported that while most people died within days of contracting the virus, not everyone died. Some of them, like my sister and I, suffered no visible consequences, but others didn't fare quite as well. The virus attacked their brains and turned them into feral versions of themselves. Some of them became angry, walking around with permanent snarls on their faces. Others, who'd gotten a stronger dose, raged down the streets, screaming like mad men, looting stores and beating anyone who got in their way. Some of them hit the jackpot of craziness, though. They became cannibals.

When I heard it, my blood ran thin. I saw the word *cannibal* rise in my mind, complete with pictures of primitive men tearing bloody flesh from bones with their long sharp teeth. I couldn't imagine a human being who hunts and eats other human beings. I didn't think there could be any worse way to die than to know that you would also be eaten after your heart stopped beating. Cannibals were something you saw in old movies, not something that happened in real life, but there it was in full color.

They played a clip of a man walking calmly down the street in downtown Cincinnati with what looked like a severed woman's arm in his hand, a silver watch still attached to her wrist. The television stations went off the air later that day as the bad men came into town.

I stare harder into the shadows. If it's a deer, I will watch it for a moment to make sure it stays away from my mother's garden, but if it is a cannibal, I'll need to retreat back into my hidey-hole with the biggest knife in the kitchen. After a few minutes, I see a brown body disappear back into the undergrowth and I relax a little bit. It's probably just a deer, but I'm still not taking any chances. I head inside.

Twilight has almost fully transformed into night. A rose light radiates from the horizon, filling the room with a dusky glow. I change out of my white dress and slip into a pair of black jeans and my favorite black Rolling Stones t-shirt. A chill is in the air, so I shrug on my black hoody, happy to find my flashlight still tucked in the jacket pocket. I turn it on, but only a weak yellow beam filters from the end. It would be bright enough to read by, but not bright enough to shine into the bushes if something made a noise. I have used every last battery in the house, even pulling them from all the remote controls and Elizabeth's old toys. I am now down to mere minutes of light. I settle down on the living room couch and stare out the window, watching the shadows gather close to one another.

I am afraid of the dark. When the last of the evening sunset fades, I can see the possibilities for terror as though they are written in the air above me. I imagine bad men tip-toeing through my house, ghosts floating above my bed, roaches skittering between my toes. When I finally try to drift off to sleep each night, I press my eyes closed very tightly because there is no clear remedy without electricity, batteries, or candles to chase them all away. I long for my night light nearly as much as I long for my family.

I turn the flashlight over in my hands, wishing it whole again. I will only use it if I really, really need to see something. The thought gives me a shiver. Usually when you really, really need to see something, it's already too late.

A breeze trickles through the house, finding its way in through the broken kitchen window. I'm not sure what to do about it. Now that the bad men have broken it, it will need to remain broken. In the summer, this is a good thing, but winter

25

will be a different story. I might be able to camp out in the basement, but it won't be much warmer. Without a fireplace, I'll freeze to death either way. As much as I hate to, I'll need to relocate somewhere else.

The thought of leaving my house terrifies me to the tips of my toes. The world outside my window has gone insane. Mad men and bad men wander the streets, specifically looking for people like me. When the bad men came and shot my closest neighbor, a cannibal had come along later to take care of the remains. They didn't shoot Elizabeth though, which gives me hope. I have to wonder why.

Several theories have burbled up in my mind and I'm not sure which one to believe. They could be using her for testing, to find out why she didn't get the virus, or they could be using her for something worse. I've thought long and hard about it and the only thing I can come up with is the fact that children are more obedient. Adults would fight back and would always be looking for a means of escape, but children could be molded. They could work the farms the bad men will need to create, to take care of daily tasks and also to repopulate the new civilization. I think of Elizabeth being used as a breeder and my throat tightens up.

"She's only ten," I whisper to myself. They'll need to wait a few years for that. The need to find her temporarily rises above my fear of leaving and for one shining moment, I imagine getting up from the sofa and heading to town to find her. I am actually pulling myself to my knees when I see a flash of movement in the dining room window.

I turn my head just in time to see a man peering in, his eyes wild with wanting.

I gasp, my mind falling numb with terror.

I only see him for a second, but it is enough to recognize him. It's Mr. McFarley, our former school janitor. The kids always gave him a wide berth in the hallways, slinging taunts at him as though they were spit balls.

There was something about him that initially struck a nerve with me. I might have just felt sorry for him. He was tall and thin with wiry brown hair and a long, hang-dog face. His eyes always looked so sad, so lost. He reminded me of those men you saw in pictures from the Great Depression.

My parents always told me to practice what you preach, so I started saying hello to him when I passed him in the hallway. I figured that it was a harmless gesture that might make him feel better about himself, maybe even bring him out of his shell a little. The first time I greeted him, he turned and scrutinized me as though I were going to follow it up with something sarcastic, but when I didn't, he nodded. The second time, he was a little warmer and said hello back. The third time, he actually smiled, and I felt very good about the situation until my best friend, Annie, saw me do it and made me stop. She said he was a pedophile, a druggie, and probably had fleas as well and that if I didn't stop talking to him, he might follow me home and hide under my bed. That had been enough for me. When I heard that he'd been fired for making lewd advances towards a freshman, I was thankful for her advice. And now he's at my window trying to get in.

I slip off the couch and onto the floor, crouching low so I can't be seen. It's possible he's just looking for food and shelter, but I can't trust that. He could also be infected. Tremors run down my arms. He could be a cannibal.

As the thought rings through my head, I hear the tinkle of glass raining down on the kitchen floor. He's trying to get inside through the broken window.

I scurry backwards until I'm on the other side of the couch, my heart beating a mile a minute. I hope he hasn't seen me. If he hasn't, I might be able to sneak out the front door and across the lawn to the driveway. I hear another tinkle of glass, which is followed by the sound of the window sliding open.

Oh, God. Please don't let this be happening to me.

I creep backwards on my hands and knees, the terror washing over me in waves. I imagine him turning in my direction, seeking me out by smell alone and smiling an evil smile, knowing there's nothing I can do about it.

I am only ten feet away from the front door.

He steps over the window sill. His feet thump heavily on the linoleum floor.

I shift backwards until I am at the end of the couch. The room is growing dark, but it is at least fifteen minutes away from being full dark. If he looks in my direction, he might see me.

He takes a step further into the kitchen and his shadow snakes across the floor, nearly touching the place where I hide. He stares into the kitchen, his face a perfect blank. He is probably noticing the opened cabinets, wondering what had happened here. My heart hammers.

I wait until he looks the other way and begin inching closer to the door. I hear his footsteps behind me as he walks further into the kitchen. If he takes two more steps into the room, he won't be able to see me as I make my way to the door.

Please, please.

I hear the footsteps and I bolt the door before I remember the unoiled hinges. It sounds like a thousand angry banshees when it is pulled open. The only other door is in the kitchen, but I'd have to walk past him to get to it. I take a deep breath. I

28

could slip up the stairs and hide in one of the bedrooms, but I discount that quickly. If he comes upstairs, I'll be trapped.

I have to just run for it. It's my only chance.

I steady myself and then grab the doorknob. I pull it open and grimace at the sound.

"Hey!" the man calls.

My mind goes numb as I stumble across the porch and onto the dimly lit lawn, trying to find my footing in the tall grass. I don't try to find the bare spots. I just put one foot in front of the other and run, mindless of anything except putting distance between us. The sound of his footsteps behind me pound like thunder.

He's coming after me.

4

Silvery rays of dusk linger on the horizon. The moon is nothing more than a sliver in the sky, hiding me from clear view. I try to remember the layout of my own yard, but the details escape me as I run for my life. I stumble over the bushes lining the sidewalk and nearly fall into the tall grass as my toe catches the corner of the sidewalk.

I scramble to my feet and give my mother's grave a wide berth, barely glancing at her statue, with its arms held high to Heaven. I run past the garden and stop short at the edge of the wide front lawn, knowing that I will be vulnerable and very visible out in the open. All he will have to do is look in my direction and he will know where I'm going.

The grass looks navy blue in the moonlight and is as still as the sky above it. I can smell the mossy warmth of the lake in the valley below. A bullfrog makes a deep belching call and then leaps into the pond with a resounding plop as though everything were normal. I take a deep breath and bolt out onto the lawn, my feet flying beneath me like wings. Footsteps pound behind me.

I cross the patch of lawn and find the stone driveway beyond it. As my feet make contact with the loose gravel, I nearly slide to a fall before I catch myself. I take another step and the crunch of gravel punctuates the quiet night like a small explosion. I dart a glance over my shoulder. There's no way he didn't hear me.

I don't see him behind me, but I don't stop. I head down the driveway where the trees make a dark spot. The driveway makes a lazy bend towards the valley below and as I climb down the steep decline, I slip on the loose gravel. I throw my hands up in front of me to buffer my fall, but the sharp stones dig into my palms and tear at my knees. I can hear him reach the gravel, twenty yards behind me. Tears well up in my eyes.

Not like this.

After everything I've been through, it can't just end like this. If I die, Elizabeth is on her own. There will be no one else to save her.

"Hey little girl," he calls behind me, his voice sing-song and delirious. It is enough to propel me to my feet. Not like this.

My father always told me to always have a plan and I find one quickly. There is an old culvert ahead. He dug it years ago to keep the driveway from flooding out. It is barely five feet in diameter and runs under the driveway, allowing the stream to flow beneath. This time of the year the water level will be low and I might be able to hide there until he goes past. I slip off onto the grass beside the driveway and tiptoe down towards the stream.

Water burbles gently through the muddy banks, trickling over rounded stones and moss-covered logs. I have played here hundreds of times, trying to catch the crayfish as they come out of their mud tunnels to hunt for minnows and water bugs. I find the stream and step into it, feeling the cold water seep into my shoes and numb my feet in an instant. The stones are slippery beneath my feet and I struggle to maintain my balance as I follow the stream back to the driveway. I pause at the beginning of the tunnel as I am confronted by the screen covering. My mind nearly freezes. I forgot about the screens.

My father bolted screens onto both ends to keep debris from clogging it up. I find the edge and pull on it, feeling the rusted metal bend with the pressure. I pull with all my might and manage to bend an edge backwards, making a small doorway for myself. I push through, trying to ignore the horrible stench that drifts up from the muck.

31

The culvert smells like rotten leaves and death. Something must have found its way inside and died, trapped by the screens. I only hope I don't step in it. At the thought, bile rises up my throat and I force it back down with a fervent swallow. *Not now.*

I close my eyes for a second, trying to regain my composure. I will be okay. There's no way he will find me here. He will keep on walking until he reaches the road and then he will walk back into town. I will be able to slip back into my house and be back in my hidey-hole in fifteen minutes tops. I just need to wait here for a little bit longer. I can almost see it in my mind.

I wish my father were here to protect me. In the days after his death, I felt his absence in bits and pieces. He was no longer in the places he used to be. In the mornings, he was no longer at the coffee maker asking me if I'd like a "cup of Joe," in his fake Irish brogue that I had always found annoying. He wasn't there in the evenings at the dinner table, asking me about my day at school and teasing me about boys and he wasn't here now, to save me. I will have to save myself this time.

I move away from the entrance. I have barely made my way halfway down the tunnel when I hear the sound of him on the road above me. I gasp, despite myself. He is much faster than I thought he would be.

"Come out, come out, where ever you are," he calls. His voice is like nails down a chalkboard, grating and high. He has to have been infected. I can hear it in his voice. I cower down, my feet covered in water, and bury my face in my knees.

This can't be happening to me.

He pauses on the driveway directly above me, his feet shifting on the loose gravel as he comes to a stop. He is so close; I can hear the sound of his jagged breaths. I imagine him staring down the driveway, wondering where I went. I press my eyes tightly together and pray to any God who will listen to me.

Please don't look down.

If he looks down, he will know where I am in an instant. The metal culvert bulges above the driveway, making a bump that my mother always slowed down to pass over. I imagine him scratching his head, knowing I couldn't have made it to the road already.

Please move on. Please.

I mentally will him to take a step forward off the culvert, to keep walking ahead until he reaches the road, but he does something else instead. He kneels down and rubs some of the gravel off of the culvert, probably making a clean spot. By the sounds alone, I can imagine him as clearly as if I were seeing it. After a moment, he chuckles. He knocks on the metal and the sound echoes around me with a resounding boom. I tighten myself into a ball. *Oh God.*

He knows where I am.

I look at the other end of the tunnel. Another screen blocks my exit.

I consider moving toward it, to see if I can find a loose spot, but I'm afraid to move. What if he comes in from that end instead?

"Hmmmm," he murmurs with amusement. "I wonder where she went."

I hold my breath as my heart beats wildly.

Seconds feel like hours before he shifts again on the gravel. He is playing with me, enjoying the hunt. He is silent for so long the crickets begin to chirp again in the darkness and I begin to wonder if he's managed to walk away without making any sounds. Cobwebs dangle from the ceiling, tickling my neck and I resist the urge to brush them away because I know without knowing that he is listening for me. I can't hold my breath any longer, so I take a breath. The gravel shifts above me and I jump at the sound. I close my eyes tightly as he walks to the edge of the culvert. He pauses again and then climbs down the bank to the entrance. His feet rustle in the tall weeds.

I open my eyes to find him standing at the end of the tunnel, backlit by the moonlight.

I gasp despite myself.

He has blocked my exit. The only way out is through the other end and it is covered with screen.

"Marco...," he calls out as if expecting me to answer "Polo".

A scream finds its way past my lips before I clamp my hand over it.

He bends the screen and joins me in my tunnel.

I find my feet and scramble to the other end. My legs nearly collapse beneath me as I kneel down in front of the screen, my knees landing in something soft and decaying. I pull at the screen, my fingers wild and uncontrollable as he comes further into the tunnel.

If he catches me, he will kill me. I know this.

Daddy, help me.

I imagine him putting the screen onto the culvert, grimacing as he loops the wire mess over the bolts. He would have made it easy to remove in case he needed to clean out the debris. I put my shoulder against the screen and push with all my might until I feel it give and then I push harder until the wire snaps free from the bolts. As I slip through the gap, I feel the cannibal touch my arm, his fingers slipping as I move away from him.

I don't think, I just move, my feet finding purchase on the slippery bank. When I reach the driveway, I run with all my might, putting feet and then yards between us. By the time I reach the road, my lungs nearly explode, the air coming in gasps. I don't stop running until I reach the crossroads and then I slow to a walk before I collapse.

I put two miles between us before I calm down enough for rational thought. The McDonald's farm appears ahead of me, barely visible in the moonlight. Sometimes when we passed it on our way to town, my mother would break into song.

"Old McDonald had a farm…e-i-e-i-ohhhhh."

An old farm truck sits beside the road, looking like a dinosaur in the shadows.

The windows of the farm house are dark and I try not to think about all the horrors that could be inside, but I can't help myself. I imagine dinner plates still sitting on the oak farm table, of the sink full of water that had once been sudsy and warm, but is now cold and coated with scum, and of the bodies fermenting in their beds. Despite all that, I would like to run inside and find a place to hide, but I don't want to take the chance. It is so obvious. It will be the first place he looks. I pull my gaze from the windows of the house and try to focus on the road ahead of me. I need to put more distance between us.

My shoes make a squishing sound with every step. I glance behind me at the empty road. He could be trailing behind me in the shadows, running from tree to tree so I can't see him. I pick up the pace, my heart still pounding.

I wonder if there were any other survivors, if anyone else managed to avoid both the virus and the masked men. I imagine finding a group of them, huddling behind the door of a house, pulling me to safety. There must be some people left, but they will be difficult to find. If I walk into a house looking for them, the risks are far greater than the prospects for reward. If I don't

35

find dead bodies, I might very well end up shot or stabbed by a terrified survivor. It just isn't worth the effort.

Something brushes my pant leg and I look down to find a fallen branch on the side of the road, half expecting to see my mother's dog beside me instead

Desmond.

He was a small black and white rat terrier, my mother's constant companion. He was spotted like a cow, with the personality of a much larger dog, following us everywhere we went, yapping happily at everything and at nothing at all. Sometimes I can think I can feel him at my ankles, following me through my day, possibly blaming me for his death. I shake my head, as if to dislodge the thought. Of all the things I feel guilty for, Elizabeth tops the list, but Desmond is a very close second.

He was a strange little dog, always sniffing at the edges of his world, head down and serious about his role in life. He'd nearly run headlong into walls while in pursuit of the perfect scent and then look up, startled that someone had the audacity to plant something in his path. If he hadn't been such a vocal little guy, he would have been the perfect companion. I glance down at the space where he would be, hoping he knows how sorry I am for what I had to do to him.

I slip onto the road and walk at the edge, keeping my eyes open for the next available hiding spot in case a vehicle comes around the corner. I pass the dark houses, each having a million memories attached to them, each one as dark as the next.

5

In the days after my father's death, our household became unnaturally quiet. The funeral came and went and we visited his grave frequently, placing fresh flowers on the mound of dirt and thinking, but not speaking of the incident that led to it.

I knew that Elizabeth had something to do with it. I think about how clearly I heard her voice in my head just before the lightning hit and I wonder about it more than I think about the lightning. I'd heard the same voice as the bad men carried her away. There was more to my sister than what meets the eye.

If my mother thought about the lightning, she didn't talk about it. I tried to bring it up once, but she just looked at me with empty eyes and walked away, letting me know it was better to just to think of it a freak accident than to consider the implications.

Nearly an hour later, I come to the edge of town.

The town of Purlow sits at the base of the Berkshire Mountains in the western part of Massachusetts. It was always a sleepy town, filled with enough drug stores and coffee shops to keep the six thousand or so residents properly medicated and caffeinated, but was still small enough to maintain a sense of being a small town. The downtown area consisted of several blocks of stores, lined up one after another, with residential housing surrounding it like a halo. Being the county seat, the town was host to a white courthouse and several municipal buildings. It would be an ideal location for the bad men to set up a camp, but I was pretty sure it wasn't the only draw.

I'm pretty sure they came for the chemicals.

I glance towards the hill where Gordon Plastics sits, silhouetted against the soft night sky like a monolith. My father had been an engineer there for over twenty years and spoke often about the dangerous chemicals that were used in the production of plastic. One of them was phosgene.

I didn't know a lot about it, but I knew enough about phosgene to make my stomach curl. It was an important component for making plastic and was one of the deadliest gases on the face of the planet. One single breath of it would turn your lungs to jelly, causing you to drown in your own fluids. In World War One, the German army used it against the British, wiping out entire populations. My father always said if there was ever an accident at the plant, the phosgene could easily wipe out the entire town. He said it smelled like musty hay, so I always kept my nose to the wind, searching for it.

As I stare into the distance, I can see the glow of fire at the edge of town. Lightning must have struck a house. I glance back and forth between the fire and the chemical plant. Several miles separate them, but the fire could easily jump from house to house and make its way up the hill. If that happened, we'd all be dead in a matter of days, if not hours. The ground is still moist from a rainstorm, which will slow it down, but it is very feasible. Hopefully it will burn out, but I can't find a lot of reassurance in that thought

As I come into town, I feel as though I've walked into an alien landscape. The quaint, tree-lined street that was always so carefully maintained lies in total ruin. The rows of perfect maple trees that were always lit with sparkling white lights at Christmas are nearly unrecognizable. The majority of them have been burnt to stubs. The ones that aren't scorched are broken and splintered, their leafy branches resting on the trash-littered sidewalks. I remember the year they were planted. I'd been eight and my sister was still small enough to ride in a stroller. My mother brought us to the Fourth of July parade and we'd marveled at how nice it looked.

Many of the familiar buildings are nothing more than charred structures, blackened beams spilling out onto the street like severed appendages. A burned-out car rests on its roof in the middle of the street. The smell of death drifts through the air with every steady gust of the breeze, bringing with it the vision of bloated, bullet-riddled bodies lying amid the destruction. I stop despite my need to continue and just stare for a moment, tears stinging my eyes.

I have avoided this truth by hiding in my parent's house, eating stale crackers and drinking from the burbling stream, and it comes to me with a blast of utter reality. Nothing will ever be the same again. It is all gone. All of it.

I allow the image to sink deeply into my soul before I move forward. With trembling legs, I pick my way down the sidewalk until I come to the small grocery store, where my mother used to shop. She preferred the smaller family-owned store to the big chain stores on the north side. She said they made her feel more welcome, even if their prices were twice as high. The building is still standing, but all of the windows have been smashed. The shards of glass glint in the moonlight, scattered before me like broken diamonds.

I stand in the shadows and try to compose myself. So much has changed in the past three months. I'm no longer certain where to go or what to do. The memory of the cannibal returns to me and I turn to look behind me, relieved to find the street as empty as it was before.

I cock my head and listen to the sounds of the night, trying to detect human sounds from the constant hum from the crickets and the wind raking through the leaves on the remaining trees. I close my eyes for a moment and rest my temple against the cool brick of the building. I don't know what to do. The feeling of helplessness is so strong, I nearly crumple into myself.

Where could Elizabeth be? I don't have any idea where to even start. A trickle of courage rises inside me, growing stronger than the fear that lingers in my mind and as a result, the need to find my sister becomes so powerful I can no longer ignore it. When I was home, hiding in my cabinet, it was easier to pretend that she was okay, but now that I've seen more of the madness, I cannot imagine her being out here alone. If I don't find her soon, the phosgene might. I don't have a lot of time to waste thinking about it.

Where would they bring her?

I think about this for a moment. If I could live in any house in town, where would I live?

The answer comes to me as a twig snaps directly behind me.

I turn with an involuntary gasp and find nothing but darkness behind me.

"Who's there?" I hiss. I am answered by a long stretch of silence.

Has the cannibal found me?

I want to bolt in the direction that I came from, but I can't. If he is following me, he'll just follow me back home. I can barely breathe; the panic is so full and ripe.

Calm, calm, calm, I chant in my head, trying to find my center in the pattern of the words.

With a deep breath, I step over the knee-high window frame of the grocery store and slip into the darkness. I find a solid wall between the front door and the broken windows and put my back against it for a moment, allowing my eyes to adjust. The only sounds I can hear are the crickets chirping outside and the sound of my own pounding heart. I turn slowly and look behind me at the empty street to see if anything moves.

The street is still quiet, but I don't take any comfort in it. If the cannibal is following me, he could be hiding, just like I'm doing.

A piece of paper blows, end over end, down the middle of Main Street, before catching on the stop sign post at the corner of Main and South Street. I have the terrible feeling that someone is watching me, but I can't tell if it's real or imagined.

"Get a hold of yourself, Ember," I whisper under my breath. I take another deep breath and study the store in front of me.

I take a tentative step forward, cringing as my foot lands on a piece of broken glass. It crunches loudly beneath my foot and I freeze, waiting for the tell-tale sounds of someone following me. When nothing happens, I take a few more steps and make my way to the first row of shelves. I sweep my hand out in front of me, hoping for batteries or a bottle of water, and find nothing but empty metal.

I have a quick mental flash of the store in happier days and remember the long aisles filled with household items, like bread, cereal and potato chips. The sound of Oldies 108 drifted through the ceiling speakers as the fluorescent lights flickered softly overhead. Somewhere in the back, Mr. Hardy would be singing along in his off-key baritone, stopping mid-song to greet customers. As fast as the image comes, it disappears, leaving me in the ruins of the memory. An empty pallet sits in the middle of the aisle, depleted of its product. A sign rests on the empty crate advertising forty-pound bags of dog food.

I walk down an aisle and see nothing but more dusty shelves. I flick on my flashlight, hoping to find a good hiding spot, but the weak beam barely makes it two feet. Something even worse could be hiding in the shadows.

My heart beats with a frantic rhythm. I try to calm myself down, but the effort is futile. I've never felt so lost and all alone. I am so unprepared for this. I've never had to do anything more difficult than stand in front of my class and give a speech. Even living through the death of my father is nothing compared to this devastation. The tears choke in my throat and I swallow them away. I wish I had someone's hand to hold.

I think of my best friend, Annie. She'd know what to do. The yearning is so strong, I can nearly taste it. We'd sit on her bed with her Magic 8 Ball between us and ask it question after question and then dissect the answers.

"Will Adam Larkin ever notice me?" Annie would ask.

I flipped the ball over. "Yes, definitely," but Annie hadn't been enthusiastic about the answer.

"Oh it says that about half the time. I think they made that side lighter so it floats to the top more often." When it was my turn, Annie usually had a better solution than the Magic 8 Ball, which was good, considering. Listening to a ball full of water probably wouldn't have been the smartest method of solving my problems. Now that Annie and everyone else are gone, I almost wish I had the ball back. At least it would be something.

I listen to the silence for several long moments, not hearing anything. I try to shrug off the feeling of panic. If I'm going to survive this, I need to stay focused.

I look around, hoping to find supplies to help me through. I need batteries for my flashlight, as well as food and water. I find an empty backpack sitting on a shelf and slip it over my shoulders. If I find any provisions, I will need something to carry them in. I glance down and see a lone package of gum on the floor, near the end of the candy aisle. I pick it up with a sigh. It's

42

not batteries, but it's better than nothing. I put it in my pocket for later. I reach the door and pause to listen.

A soft wind ripples through my hair, carrying with it the smell of leaves and motor oil from the gas station across the street. My mother used to have her oil changed there and I remember the acidic tang that permeated the building like a personality. I imagined the men, with grease under their fingernails, going home with the same smell attached to them, absorbed into their pores like a second skin, and I wonder how long it will take before the odor becomes a distant memory. Without the right people, there will be no more cars or gasoline, or anything for that matter. We will go back to the days of the pioneers, where everything is manual and difficult and cold. I step out of the building and head down the street, keeping to the edges where there are plenty of places to hide.

I pass the burned-down remnants of the post office, remembering all the times I stood in line with my mother, waiting to purchase stamps or mail a package. The Laundromat next door is in the same shape, the white husks of washers and dryers gleaming through the soot and debris. Something is hanging out the window and I stare hard at it until I realize it is a dead body and then I look away quickly.

The odor of death is strong in town and I try not to consider all the other decaying bodies lying behind closed doors. I tiptoe past a parked car and the smell nearly knocks me over. I don't have to look through the windows to know that it has become someone's coffin. I hold my breath and keep my eyes firmly on the ground in front of me until I'm safely past.

I dart a glance over my shoulder. The street behind me is still dark and empty. If the cannibal is following me, he is nowhere to be seen.

I see the police station across the street from me, hiding in the shadows. I stare into the darkness at it, noticing that the windows have been smashed to shards on the sidewalk. It probably would have been the first place the bad men looted, looking for weapons and ammunition to power their mission. I try not to envision the bloody scene inside, of the bodies draped over desks, shot full of holes, but the image assaults me anyways, giving me a good look at what might have happened. I continue on, breathing through my mouth to avoid smelling any dead bodies as I pass the fire department. I come to the library. It is one of the few buildings in town that looks exactly like it did before the virus. I pause on the sidewalk, taking in the looming brick structure and wonder if I should go inside or just keep walking.

Something about the library is very calming to me. My mother brought me here as a toddler to listen to the kindly old assistant librarian read during story hour, and I've come on my own since grade school. The building is perpetually cool and quiet, a necessary refuge against the chaos of my normal, everyday life. I could use a few books on first aid and canning vegetables. If nothing else, I need five minutes of normal.

I step inside and stand for a moment, letting my eyes adjust. The building is long and narrow, with only one other exit at the very end of the building, which feels like miles away in the thick darkness. Long, thin windows rib the side walls, letting in a hazy glow of moonlight. The room smells musty and stale as though the air hasn't been stirred up or refreshed in months.

The librarian's desk is coated with an inch of dust. I swipe my finger down the top, leaving a long swirly streak, before wiping it clean with the heel of my hand. Mrs. Gibson must be rolling in her grave. She always walked around the library with a dust rag in her pocket, taking pride in the cleanliness of the

44

library. If we even thought about leaving a book out on the reading table, she'd materialize behind us with narrowed eyes.

I hook a left and find the long outside wall. As I pass each row, I stare down the length of it and study the deep shadows for any signs of movement before I continue on.

The aisles are so dark; I can only see the outlines of the bookcases. My imagination begins playing tricks on me. A librarians cart becomes a crouching cannibal and I nearly jump out of my skin as I bump into it. I can imagine bad men hovering around the corner, guns held low. I hear a moan come from the back of the building and I hold my breath, feeling the adrenaline race through my body.

I swivel softly on the balls of my feet and turn in a slow circle. Everything is very still. I creep to the edge of the aisle. Maybe it's just the building settling.

The main aisle seems to stretch for miles in the darkness. I stare down the length of it, watching the shadows for signs of movement. I hold onto the straps of my backpack to keep them from jingling and dart across the opening. I know the library like I know the back of my hand and find the self-help section quickly. I turn on my flashlight and shine it across the rows of books. It seems brighter than it should be, and I am quick to shield it with my other hand, directing it solely on the shelf in front of me. *Sewing, knitting, crafts for kids.* I run my fingers down the spines, not finding the books I need. They have to be here somewhere. I nearly scream as I hear another noise.

I crane my head, trying to figure out where it came from. It sounded whispery and fleeting, like paper scuffing against paper. It could be the wind or maybe a mouse rustling through some loose papers.

45

The reedy thread of my pulse thumps in my temples. I press the button on the flashlight again and shine it further down the shelf, finally finding the books on canning food.

A grab the first book on canning I find and slip it into my backpack, anxiety growing steadily by the second. The longer I am inside the building, the more dangerous it becomes. I can nearly feel it sprouting arms and legs and sharp ragged teeth. I hear another thump and turn around, expecting to find someone standing directly behind me, but the aisle is empty.

I need to get out of here. I hurry to the aisle where the first aid and survival books are located and stuff two or three into my pack.

I am halfway to the door when I hear a sound that turns my blood to ice.

It is not the groan of a building settling or a paper blowing in the wind. It is a sound that only another living breathing creature can make. It is a sneeze.

I freeze in my tracks and the fear simply overcomes me.

6

"Who's there?" I call softly into the darkness. I imagine rapists and murderers lined up, shoulder to shoulder, along the entire back wall, knives and hangmen nooses held firmly in their hands. I am surprised when a tiny timid voice answers back.

"It's me, Teddy. Who are you?"

I nearly wet myself in relief and press my hand against my pounding heart to keep it contained inside my chest. Teddy.

I walk towards the sound of his voice, the anger and injustice setting in, step by step. It is not fair. It just isn't. I think of all those old lines where one person says to another, "if you were the last person left on Earth, I still wouldn't like you." He is and I don't.

Teddy is Annie's little brother, the demon-spawn who cut the hair off of all our dolls and told her mother when we were playing with her makeup. He once woke us up on a Sunday morning with a squirt gun filled with sticky lemonade and often super-glued quarters to the floor to watch people try to pick them up.

"It's me, Ember," I tell him, and he groans in return. The retaliation for the lemonade squirt gun bath was an ongoing project. The next weekend, I wrote "I am a skuzzy pecker head" on his forehead with permanent marker while he was sleeping and then let him walk around half the day unknowing. He had promised to get back at me, but never got the chance, until now. I supposed his simply being alive is retaliation enough.

We meet in the middle of the aisle. Even though it is only Teddy, he is a human being all the same and I forget the lemonade and the tattle-tailing. I pull him into a hug and nearly cry at the feel of another person's touch. I hold him for an eternity until a bubble of thought pops into my mind. I push away from him, thoughts of Annie so powerful I can almost believe them.

"Is Annie still alive?" I imagine her in the next building, foraging for supplies.

Teddy looks down at his feet and my hopes grow anchors.

"No, nobody is. My mom and Annie got the flu and my dad never came home from work." He looks back up, his expression sad yet accepting. We've both been through hell. It gives us permission to allow the sadness some distance. You can only cry so much before you just have to stop.

"I'm sorry," I tell him.

He looks at me and arches his eyebrows. The question he wants to ask is prevalent on his face. I'd love to be able to tell him something good, but there isn't anything good left in my world. I simply shrug one shoulder and tell him everything I need to say in that one gesture.

His shoulders slump forward and he hangs his head for a moment, looking at the ground. His sorrow is so real I can almost see it shimmering around him like an aura. He has grown over the past few months. He is around thirteen or fourteen, I can't remember his exact age, only that he is several years younger than his sister. He'd always been short and plump, with iron red hair and a splattering of freckles across the bridge of his nose. Now, he is nearly as tall as I am, thinner than he'd been before.

Teddy's family lived at the edge of town close to the chemical plant, in a huge Victorian with five bedrooms and a turret his mother used as a reading room, and it occurs to me that he must have been all over town. I want to grill him about all that he knows, but first I need to know how safe we are right here, right now.

"Is it safe here? Have the bad men been here?"

48

"I think we're okay here. They're set up across town at the Cooper House," he says, and I nod. It makes sense that they'd set up their camp at the largest house in town. It is where I would go if I could live in any house in Premont. It might be where they are keeping my sister.

"Have they been there long?"

"For a month or so. They started out at the police station and then more of them came to town, so they moved to the Cooper House. They usually don't go out too much at night, so we're probably okay."

We hear a rumble of machinery outside and I realize I still have the pen light turned on. The light is low, but it could be reflecting through the window. Even the faintest of glows could be deadly for us, so I turn it off and pull Teddy back into the shadows.

"So much for them not going out much at night," I whisper.

The truck drives past the building, going very slowly, slow enough to make me wonder if they might have seen us. I am dying to peer out the window, to see where they are and to see if they are staring at our building, but I resist the impulse. A face at the window would be worse than a light. It would be a certain death sentence for both of us. As the thought comes to me, I realize that I am now thinking in the plural again: us. My stomach clinches. It is a commitment I'm not certain I'm ready for.

"Follow me," Teddy says, pulling me towards the back of the library.

"Hang on a second." I run back to the section where I'd been when he'd sneezed and retrieve my backpack. Teddy follows me, making no effort at being quiet.

"What are you doing?" His voice is louder than I am comfortable with. If someone were standing outside, they could have heard him clearly. I think about the cannibal and shiver.

"Sssshhhh." I press a finger to my lips and then slide my arms through the straps on the back pack. I consider the child in front of me, who is still watching me. "We have to be quiet. Always whisper."

"It's okay. They're gone." He points to the window, his hand nothing more than a shadow in front of the dimly illuminated window. "I've been living here for two months. I know when they're here and when they're gone. Lighten up."

"Lighten up? Lighten up?" His words pierce through me. After everything I have been through and everything I have witnessed, I will never, ever do something as foolish as lighten up. It is a death sentence. It is something one fool says to another shortly before taking a bullet between the eyes. I grab his arm and press my fingers tightly into his skin.

"Let's get something straight. I've survived for two months now too. The bad men have been to my house twice. The only reason why they haven't gotten me is because I've been careful. I've been cautious."

He tries to squirm out of my grasp, so I tighten it.

"Let go, Ember. You're not my mother. You can't tell me what to do."

I relax my hold. "You're right, Teddy. I'm not your mother and I don't need you. Why don't you go back to wherever it was you were hiding and just leave me alone?"

The anger presses hot tears into my eyes and I turn, intending on just leaving the rotten brat there. The last thing I need is another obstacle to drag around behind me. It was bad enough with Elizabeth, and she was my sister. Teddy means nothing to me – less than nothing. I could leave him and not feel a thing.

I stomp towards the door.

"Ember, don't go. I'm afraid," he says in a small voice.

I stop in my tracks, his words pouring through me like water through sand. I count to ten in my head, then turn slowly to look at his silhouette in the aisle. If he'd said anything else, anything, I probably would have kept on walking, but the fact that he is afraid is something I can't ignore.

"Me too," I whisper. I join him in the aisle.

He stares up at me, his eyes hopeful. I remember him as a small boy, always gooey-faced from eating something messy, his hair a red tumble of curls. Annie was convinced that Teddy was the child her parents had always wanted. "I was just a practice baby until they finally got it right," she'd say, narrowing her eyes.

I take a deep breath and let it out with a long sigh.

"We have to set some ground rules if we're going to hang out together."

He looks down at his feet and I realize he is barefoot. I imagine all the dangers he's endured and all the stupid risks he's taken. There must be hundreds of empty shoes in this town and he's risking his life by walking around barefoot.

"First of all, we're going to get you some shoes."

He starts to protest, but I put a hand on his chest.

"Second of all, I am in charge. You will listen to me." I give him a chance to soak in what I've said before I smile. "And third of all, I really, really have to pee. Can you help me find a safe place to go?"

He nods in the shadows and then leads me out the back door, where the moonlight feels like a spotlight after being in the dark library. The air is fresh and fragrant, smelling like green

51

leaves and honeysuckle. It tickles the thin line of sweat that is dripping down my temple, making me realize how hot it was inside the library. I take a deep lungful and allow it to wash through me, cleansing me.

We slip around the side of the building, where a thick row of evergreen bushes hugs the foundation. It is a place where kindergarteners hide from their mothers and where boys bring girls to kiss them deeply. It is also a great place to water the bushes.

"Don't worry, I won't look." He turns around and puts his back to me, letting me know that above everything else, he is a gentleman. Possibly, he's also just a tiny bit afraid of me. Either way, he's not looking, so I take the opportunity.

I've become a master at urinating on the ground after months of practice. The first time I'd tried it, I'd misjudged the power of my stream and had peed on my shorts, but I don't even think about it anymore, the process is so automatic. When I am finished, I pull my pants up and fish the bottle of hand sanitizer from my pocket.

"Want some Fred?" I ask him, and he turns with a frown.

"Fred?" He has forgotten the day at the department store, when our mothers brought us back-to-school shopping. He'd found a hand sanitizer mounted on the wall and ran back to show his sister.

"Look, I have a new pet. His name is Fred," he'd said, and his sister had slapped the bottom of his hand, making the gooey puddle fly skyward. He'd looked appropriately horrified. "You killed Fred," he'd said, and we'd laughed, nearly splitting our guts open. We'd called it Fred ever since.

"Don't tell me you've forgotten about your pet?" He frowns for a moment and then smiles, suddenly and almost beatifically.

"Oh yeah. Fred." He holds out his hand and it occurs to me that this is probably the first time he's washed his hands since it happened. Water isn't very easy to find and when you do find it, you drink it. Washing has become a true luxury.

"When is the last time you've washed your hands?"

He shrugs. "I dunno. Why are you using hand sanitizer?" he asks, making the words sound like something you'd find on the bottom of your shoe.

"Because the last thing I want to do is get sick. Just because I didn't get the virus doesn't mean I'm not going to get anything else. The hand sanitizer helps me stay healthier and I want you to start using it too. Okay?"

He nods, rubbing it into his skin. He is being agreeable, but I'm afraid it won't last. After he gets used to the thought of me, I'm fearful the real Teddy will eventually emerge again.

"So what now?' he asks me.

I look down the street, at the cave of darkness shrouded with a heavy canopy of tree cover that used to be Main Street. Time is of an essence, so I want to start at the most obvious places first. "I'd like to check out the Cooper House," I say and manage to suppress the shiver that lingers near my spine.

Teddy nods. "That's where they brought Elizabeth."

The wind is nearly knocked from my lungs. I blink several times, letting the words truly sink in, and then I lunge forward and grab his arms.

"You saw them bring her there?"

"Let go of me, Ember. You're hurting me."

I glare at him, wishing the moonlight were brighter so he could see the murder in my eyes. "Why didn't you tell me that already? Why did you wait until I asked about the Cooper House?"

He wriggles free of my grasp and then rubs his arms dramatically as though I truly hurt him. It might have had an impact if one of our mothers saw it, but out here, it was as useless as light bulbs.

"I was going to tell you...geeze, Ember. Stop being so mean to me."

I sigh and turn away from him. I count to ten again and try to find my center. When I turn back around, I am calmer by a fraction. It is a small fraction, but it is precisely enough to prevent me from wrapping my fingers around his pudgy little neck.

"Okay. Stop whining and tell me what you know about Elizabeth." I have a mental picture of them dragging her into the house, kicking and screaming, and of him, hiding in the bushes outside watching, his jaw dropping open as he recognizes her.

He opens his mouth to speak and then stops, his eyes wide with sudden terror.

"We have to hide," he whispers, already moving back towards the doorway of the library.

"Why? What's wrong?"

As he pulls me through the doorway, he whispers four words, and they are enough to make my blood turn to ice. "The cannibal is coming."

54

7

We race breakneck through the dark library, nearly knocking down displays and carts full of books on our way. Teddy has such a tight grip on my hand, I am helplessly pulled along in his wake, reminding me that he is no longer the child I remembered. He is nearly as strong as a man, which both scares and surprises me at the same time.

The sliver of the moon appears in a window, and then reappears in the next window like a strobe light. My breath is sharp, etching against my lungs and racing against my pounding heart. Panic nearly floods my mind with blackness and it's all I can do to stop myself from screaming. I glance behind me, certain to find cold skinny arms reaching out for me, but the darkness is quiet and unassuming.

How did he find me? Had he been behind me all the time?

Footsteps pound behind us, echoing loudly through the building.

Teddy pulls me to a doorway near the front that leads to a narrow set of stairs. I know where he is taking me, but I cannot fathom the reason why. The microfiche room isn't a great place to hide. It is a small rectangular room filled with low shelves, each packed with heavy cartons of film. Moving one will require a tremendous amount of effort. We'll never have enough time to move it and then hide behind it.

As we come to the bottom of the stairs, the darkness is so perfect I cannot see my hand in front of my face. Teddy slows down and grasps my hand a little tighter. I imagine him swiping the air with his other hand, feeling for the wall. Behind us comes the sound of laughter.

"Wait here for a second," he says.

"Teddy. What the hell? He's coming."

He ignores me and continues back up the stairs, returning seconds later, breathless from the effort.

"Okay. Come on." He grabs my hand and pulls me through the doorway.

Once we get on the other side of the door, he pauses, listening.

"I don't think he knows where we went."

"He was at my house tonight," I tell him.

"Do you think he followed you here?"

I think back to the noises I'd heard as I'd first come into town. "I don't know. Maybe."

I am so scared. I want to jump out of my skin. "We need to hide or get out of here, Teddy. We can't just stand here and wait for him to come eat us."

"I know, I know. Just follow me." He pulls me down a hallway filled with doors.

"Where are we going?"

"To my hiding place in the microfiche room. I moved some boxes so the bottom shelf is empty inside...hollowed out," he says. I don't respond, but instead consider all that he's gone through to become this version of Teddy, the one who has managed to keep himself alive for two months even though he is only fourteen.

The only Teddy I've ever known is the one who cried at the dinner table because his mother made him eat broccoli. He was such a baby. He wouldn't eat anything except peanut butter and jelly sandwiches on toast. He'd never had to do anything he didn't want to do. While Annie was in charge of mowing the grass and doing the laundry, Teddy would sit on the family room sofa, playing video games with a big bag of chips propped between his meaty thighs. I cannot imagine how he's managed to survive, at least not outside of an abandoned Dorito factory.

56

"Okay. We're here. Just stand there for a second and then when I tell you, follow me inside."

I can hear the sound of a box moving and Teddy's heavy breathing as he struggles with it. After a few seconds, the sounds cease, except for his ragged breathing.

"Okay. You can come in now," he says, and I kneel down and crawl through the opening, following the sound of his voice. I crawl until I run into another box and then hear the sound of the box being moved back into place. The space is as big as the floor of my closet, which isn't saying much. We are pressed so closely together, I can smell Teddy's fetid breath, along with the stronger acrid stench of unwashed fourteen-year-old. He obviously hasn't been as fixated with his personal hygiene as I have been. After a moment, I can hear him fumbling around with something. I pull my shirt up over my nose and mouth and attempt to breathe through the fabric.

"What are you doing?" I whisper.

"You'll see." A second later, a light flickers on and I can see him, grinning at me in the eerie green glow from a lantern.

I nearly panic in my need to extinguish the light. "Turn it off. He'll see us!" I reach for it, ready to tackle him if necessary.

He dangles the lantern outside of my reach, his smile eroded by my panic.

"No he won't. Look, Ember." He points to the inside of the boxes that are now covered with black cloth. "I covered them with the black curtains from the reading room. I've checked. You can't see any light."

"But why take that chance?" My voice is nearly hoarse with fear.

I close my eyes for a second and just allow myself to calm down. Being panicked isn't healthy. It makes me careless and impulsive, jumpy and agitated

57

My mother's face rises in my mind. She would push me in directions that scared me silly, signing me up for a small role in a town play to help me get over my fear of public speaking and making me place our orders at every drive-thru window. At the time I thought she was just being cruel, but now that I have put some distance from it, I see that it was actually very practical, a sign of her love. If she hadn't cared about me, she would have just let me continue to build the fears, like a collection of black, ugly things, until they consumed me whole. I put my finger on my wrist and count my heart beats, imagining myself relaxing with every beat like she also taught me to do so long ago. After a moment, I am calm enough to talk.

"Have you seen him here before?" The scary image rises to my mind again and I shiver. At no time in my life have I ever had to deal with so many new evil things. Cannibals were almost laughable. They were something you saw on old television shows, not something that attacked the public library patrons in the self-help aisle.

Teddy rests the lantern on a pile of books in the corner. "No. I've never seen him come into the library, but I've seen him around town. One night a woman was walking down the street and he jumped out and grabbed her and dragged her into the bushes. She screamed really loud, but then it got really quiet." He holds my gaze steady as he speaks, the fear written strongly on his features, making him look far older than fourteen. "I went back the next morning and looked at the bushes to see if she was there...you know, dead."

"Was she?"

"No...I mean, I don't know. All I found was a lot of blood and one of her shoes. I don't know if he ate her or not, but he definitely killed her."

I shudder at the thought.

58

"You should probably turn the light off," I say, much calmer than I feel. I don't care if Teddy swears on his mother's grave that the light can't be seen from outside the boxes. If I hear someone coming down the stairs, the light will be extinguished even if I have to extinguish Teddy first.

He takes a deep breath. "Don't worry, Ember. I booby-trapped the basement. If anyone comes down those stairs, you'll know about it pretty quickly." He smiles proudly as he says this, leaning back against the wall.

"What did you do?" I imagine trip-nooses, which would catch my foot and hang me up by the ceiling, or concealed pits that I might fall into with sharp spikes at the bottom, but he is quick to dispel my fears.

"Nothing dangerous. I just put some tin cans in the doorway when we came down the stairs. If he comes through, he'll knock them down and we'll hear him, plain as day." He shrugs, proud of himself, but not wanting to look too proud. I can see it in the way he puffs his chest out, but keeps his eyes focused firmly on the blanket beneath him.

"That's good. Good thinking, Teddy."

"I also locked the other door, the one that leads outside from the basement. Nobody can get in without a key." As he says this, he pulls a key out of his pocket.

"Where did you get that?"

"I got it out of the librarian's desk. I couldn't find the one that goes to the main doors, or else I would have locked it too."

I look around me for the first time and notice all the supplies he's gathered. Besides the lantern and a stack of borrowed library books, there is a pillow and a blanket, a small supply of boxed crackers, canned fruit, and several bottles of spring water. An IPod sits next to a ragged-looking brown teddy bear, one that probably came from his bed at home.

59

"Where did you get all this stuff?"

"Most of it came from my house. I stayed there for the first couple of weeks, but the bad guys kept coming around so I moved here. They don't seem to like the library too much."

"Yeah, they've been to my house a few times too."

He drops his gaze. "I figured that when I saw Elizabeth."

"How do you know they took her to the Cooper House?"

"I heard them drive by with her." I watch him, wanting very badly to pounce on him and demand more information, but force myself to be patient. I'm not sure why I am feeling so charitable, but I am. Maybe I'm just tired. I don't know. I just remember Elizabeth and Teddy playing together when our mothers had coffee. Once, Annie and I married the two of them in our back yard and then sent them to the playhouse for their honeymoon, disappointed that they didn't do anything more than read comic books once they were there. "Aren't they going to kiss or anything?" Annie asked, disgusted and disappointed.

"I was out scouting for supplies when they went by with her," he says, looking up to meet my eyes for brief seconds before looking back down at the blanket under his legs. "I heard her half way down the block. She was screaming..." He stops, too embarrassed or possibly too worried to continue.

"What was she screaming, Teddy? It's okay. You can tell me."

He sighs. "She was screaming your name, like you were going to come for her."

As he says this I melt into myself, the emotion as raw and potent as it had been that day. Gone, very suddenly, is any sense of anger I've ever had for her, for her inexcusable laziness and the defiance she lobbed at me at every turn, for the way she stomped and cried when she didn't get her way. I only remember her, soft and smiling, her long silky blond hair

60

blowing across her tanned shoulders, her blue eyes flashing with childlike wonder. She probably waited for me for several weeks, having every faith in the world that I would come rescue her. I don't know how I'll ever explain to her why I didn't come right away. How can you explain terror?

I wonder when she finally gave up on me. The tears come hot and fast, swelling in my eyes like lava. I bury my face in my hands and cry silently without making a sound, as I've learned to do. After a few moments, I feel Teddy's warm, slightly sticky hand on my arm.

"She seemed okay," he tells me. "I followed the truck to the Cooper House and I've gone back a few times to see if I could get her. I heard her at night sometimes, yelling at them."

I look up to find he has scooted closer to me in his effort to touch my arm. I am almost afraid to ask him the next question, the one that must be spoken, no matter what.

"Is she still there?"

He shrugs. "I don't know. I haven't been there in a few days, but I know what they normally do. They drive around all day looking for people. When they find them, they shoot the grownups and they bring the kids back to the Cooper House and then they haul them off somewhere else. I've seen the trucks. They use these big green Army trucks."

I think about this for a moment. If they are keeping the younger survivors alive, it's a good sign for Elizabeth.

"Did you recognize anyone else?"

Teddy shakes his head. "I'm not sure. I didn't really get close enough to see their faces..." he starts to say, but is interrupted by the distinct sound of cans tumbling down stairs. He puts his fingers over his lips and then shuts off the light, leaving us in the darkness.

The cannibal is coming.

61

8

We press tightly against the far wall, trembling against each other. The cans tumble down the stairs like bombs exploding. I imagine the cannibal standing there, watching the cans tumble, knowing they were placed there deliberately, and knowing there must be some monumental prize at the bottom. It will be like an Easter egg hunt for him. He just has to search for us.

He begins down the stairs, his footsteps loud and deliberate. The sound alone terrifies me. He isn't afraid of making noise. The bad men must have given him a pass, letting him roam freely, maiming and torturing the survivors. Maybe he brings them scalps at the end of the day and they reward him for it.

"Fe – fi – fo – fum," he calls in a lilting, high-pitched voice.

The hair on my arms stands up with gooseflesh and I am paralyzed with fear.

When I was five-years-old, a man tried to lure me into a corner of the library. He'd been smiling at me from across the room for several minutes, giving me a jaunty little wave and smiling with small weasel teeth.

"Come here, little girl. I have something for you," he had called.

I had looked around for my mother and realized with a jolt of panic that she had walked away. I'd gotten up from my pillow on the floor, tucking my book beneath my arm, bent on finding my mother.

"Come here, little girl. Don't you want to see my pet worm? He's right here on my lap. If you are really, really good, I'll let you pet him. I think he will like you."

I'd taken a step forward, entranced by his promise of a pet worm. I hadn't known what the worm really was, but something inside of me had warned me, flashing like a red light in my mind. I turned and ran, yelling for my mother. He grabbed me and I sank my teeth into the soft flesh of his wrist until he let go. By the time my mother and the librarian returned to the reading room, the man was long gone.

Even though I know who the cannibal is, I imagine him being the same man from my childhood. I can see him standing there in the moonlight, his short little weasel teeth glimmering as he smiles. "Come here little girl," he will call and I will simply wither and die right there.

The cannibal reaches the bottom of the stairs and stops at the doorway to the microfiche room, his feet scuffing the concrete as though he has stopped short. I imagine him staring directly at our hiding place, smiling and rubbing his hands together. It is suddenly so obvious; I want to scream for allowing myself to crawl into the death trap. There is no way out except for the way that we came in and he is blocking the doorway. All he will have to do is figure out where we are.

"I know you're in here," he whispers in a voice that is like sandpaper.

Teddy stiffens beside me and I wonder if he has a knife. He has grown stronger, but I don't think he would even know how to use one if he had one. I wish fervently I'd taken that self-protection class down at the YWCA like my mother wanted. "You never know when it will come in handy," she'd said.

I hear the distinctive sound of a cigarette lighter flicking, followed by a deep low moan. I close my eyes and try to count my heartbeats, but they are coming too closely together, like a drum roll.

"You might as well just come out," he says.

Teddy trembles beside me and I nearly die in my mind.

"It's not like I'm going to eat you or anything," he says, and then laughs. "Well, maybe I might eat a little bit of you."

I press my eyes closed tightly and hold on to Teddy's hand.

I reach deep into my soul for more courage and find that my reserves have dried to dust. There is nothing left. I am empty inside, except for the fear.

I squeeze Teddy's hand tighter.

"Come out, come out, where ever you are," he calls. He is now just inches away. I brace myself against the wall.

A box shifts in the darkness, allowing a thin trickle of light through the opening. He peers in, his face long and looming, haunted by shadows. His hair is long and shaggy, hanging down on either side of his face in grey tangles. He smells like an unwashed dog. The fumes waft off of him in waves. My blood turns to ice. I have no weapons, no way to escape. I am ready to try anything.

"Mr. McFarley? You must remember me. I used to say hello to you in the hallway. Do you remember me?" I ask, trying to appeal to the human side of him, but he gives no indication that he has even heard me. There is a wild look in his eyes, something I've never seen outside of a horror movie, and I shudder, knowing that if I survive this moment, this image will be burned in my mind for all eternity. He is the hunter and we are the prey and there is no doubt in my mind that not only will he eat us once he's killed us, but he will draw it out and make it last as long as possible.

Without warning he grabs Teddy's leg and begins pulling him towards the crack.

Teddy scrambles onto his stomach and reaches out for me. His fingers graze mine and then slip away.

"Ember, help me!"

I grab Teddy's arm and pull as hard as I can.

64

"Leave him alone!'

"Just give into it, boy. It's no use fighting me," he says.

I pull harder on Teddy, trying to keep him from being tugged through the opening.

"You're just a janitor!" I scream at him. "You're nothing but a rotten, stinking janitor!"

My words hit their mark. The expression on his face changes in a second, the hatred and anger wiping the smirk away. He lets go of Teddy without a second thought. He shoves aside the box as though it were filled with air and climbs through the opening, coming after me with murder in his eye.

Teddy scrambles to the side and attempts to push another box away to create an emergency exit, but the box is too heavy. He fumbles in his blankets and pulls out a hunting knife.

"I'll cut you!" Teddy screams, his voice high and girlish.

The cannibal laughs, leaning through the opening with the lighter in his hand. It sends long, flickering shadows against the boxes, making the boxes appear to leap back and forth.

I look at Teddy's knife and feel doubt spread through me. I'm not sure he even knows how to use it.

"Don't even bother," the cannibal says, and grabs my leg. Before I can kick him away, he pulls me towards him. I turn to look at Teddy, who is paralyzed with fear, the knife pressed between his two hands like a prayer.

"Teddy, throw me the knife!"

He stares at me blankly.

"Teddy!" I dig my fingernails into the wooden floor, but the cannibal still has a strong grip on me. He pulls me forward, close enough to smell his hot, rotten breath. One more tug and he'll have me out of the shelving.

"Teddy!" I scream again, but he just stares at the cannibal.

"Dammit, Teddy! Throw me the knife YOU LITTLE TWERP!" I scream.

Teddy's eyes focus as though he's been slapped. He tosses the knife to me and I catch it with one hand, already moving in the direction of the cannibal. I don't have time to aim. I just slice it forward and it sinks soundly into the cannibal's arm.

He screams and pulls away, the craziness in his face replaced by a look of pure horror.

I pull the knife out of his bleeding wound, ready to strike again, but he pulls away. I can hear the sound of his footsteps as he races back up the stairs.

I scramble back to where Teddy huddles and we listen until we can't hear his footsteps any longer. Blood drips down my knuckles and I toss the knife down with disgust. I wipe my hand on the floor, trying desperately to rid myself of the cannibal's blood.

Teddy grabs my other hand and squeezes it tightly.

"It's okay, Ember. He's gone."

I take a deep breath and count to ten. After a moment my heartbeat slows, beat by beat, until I am nearly normal again.

I squeeze his hand back, finally.

"Thanks buddy."

We listen until there is nothing more to listen to and then we count our blessings, one by one.

9

We wait until we are sure the cannibal is truly gone before we climb out of hiding place. I stand up and my legs protest with pins and needles. I have a very strong need to get outside. I can feel the walls closing in on me and cannibals lurking around every corner. The darkness has grown eyes and needle sharp teeth. I shudder and nearly fall over from the drop in adrenaline.

"Come on. Hurry up," I tell Teddy. I find myself longing for my own hidey-hole in my kitchen again. The feeling is so strong; I can clearly picture the warm wood beneath my fingers and the smell of my mother's kitchen surrounding me like a soft, time-worn blanket. A certain knowledge comes to me with a gasp. Now that the cannibal has seen me in my house, I can never go back. I've left my home forever. The only place I can go is forward into a future full of terrifying unknowns. The thought gives me a chill and I wrap my arms around myself to ward it off.

Teddy spends an eternity stuffing his possessions into a nylon backpack. The sound of his zipper is like the shot from a starting gun. I grab his arm and I am off like a racehorse at the starting line. I do not want to be here if the cannibal comes back.

"Wait," Teddy says as we get to the stair well.

He shines his flashlight around. The stairs are dark and windowless, so the risk is worth the effort. It is one place I wouldn't want to be surprised by a boogeyman. It would be a perfect place for someone to hide. Instead of trying to pull us from our boxes, he could just fool us by pretending to leave and then wait for us in the darkness. It would be like shooting fish in a barrel, a phrase my father used incessantly.

The pale light flickers up the pale green walls, bouncing off the picture of Ellis Boundbury, the founder of the library, his scary Jesus-eyes following me like they did when I was a child.

"Nobody's here," Teddy announces, as though I've lost my eyesight.

I step over the litter of tumbled cans at the bottom. Teddy starts to collect them, but I touch his arm and he understands how futile the effort is. We can never come back now that the cannibal knows where we've been. It's another place that is scratched off my list.

We reach the library's back door without pausing, navigating easily through the wide aisle until we find the rectangle of moonlight, gleaming at us like a beacon.

We step out and the air is so sweet and chilled, I want to drink it like a glass of pure nectar. I breathe deeply, holding the air in my lungs until I must let it go again. Teddy guides me to the side of the building, near the spot where I stopped to urinate earlier. He touches his finger to his lips, indicating that I should be quiet, and then leads me into the cover of perfect darkness. We climb behind the bushes, where we can see out but not be seen, and allow our eyes to adjust.

The last of the adrenaline filters through my body, leaving me weak and shaky in its wake. I press my hands against the cool bricks of the building and try to calm myself. The cannibal is probably miles away by now.

"You okay?" I ask.

"Yeah, I guess so. I'm just glad he's gone."

"No kidding."

We fall back into a comfortable silence, neither of us willing to push forward for the moment. The wind rustles through the leaves of the trees above us, shuffling them together with the sound of paper against paper. Somewhere down the street a dog barks and then is joined by the voice of another barking dog. In the distance, another joins in until it is a symphony of barking, deep barks mixing with yappy barks, mixing with howling. A shot rings out and the dogs all fall into silence. I jump to my feet, ready to flee.

"It's okay, Ember. It's just the bad guys. They probably just shot a dog." Teddy says.

"What do you mean?"

"They shoot dogs. I don't know why. I've seen them do it a few times."

I shift against the brick wall, feeling too vulnerable where we are. "Maybe we should get moving if they're that close."

"They're always close, Ember. It's just something you get used to after a while," he says, sounding forty instead of fourteen. "Besides, I need to rest for a minute. My stomach is all cramped up." He wraps his arm around his middle and makes a sour face.

After a moment, the crickets begin chirping again. It is a comforting sound. It is nature's burglar alarm because if the insects didn't feel safe, they wouldn't sing. I lean back against the building, feeling the solidness of the bricks holding me up. Teddy's right, I need a moment to catch my breath too. My fingers are still trembling, so I shove them in my pockets to keep them still.

Teddy shifts and then sets his heavy backpack on the ground beside him. It makes me realize how heavy my own backpack is, but I'm not comfortable enough with my surroundings to do the same.

"Why do you think people become cannibals? Is it the virus or did they just go crazy?" Teddy asks.

"I'm not sure. I saw something on the news about it. The news said it was the virus, that it affected some people's brains. I guess they are everywhere."

We both shudder simultaneously. Hopefully there aren't more in town.

It doesn't seem fair. Not only do we need to stay away from the bad men, but we also need to worry about the survivors. It has become an ocean full of big fish eating smaller fish when it should be a baby pool full of quiet minnows.

Teddy stares at his feet, the loss surrounding him like a blanket. He has seen a lot in the last few months and I feel sad for him. It was bad enough having it happen to me at the ripe old age of sixteen, but I am better prepared. Teddy was babied quite a bit. I can't imagine him surviving something like this.

"How are you doing?" I ask him.

"Ummm...okay, I guess. I'm really, really tired, but it doesn't matter." He looks through the bushes at the alley in front of us. Something catches his attention and he stares intently down the street for a moment before he shakes his head. "I hate always being on guard," he says.

The moonlight lilts down in a blue haze and if you stare at anything too long, it could turn into anything. I look away and study the boy in front of me. He is dirty and grimy and in sore need of a haircut, which is almost funny, considering.

"Yeah, I know what you mean." I feel so tense. I might never stop trembling.

Teddy pulls in a gasp of air. "It just sucks, Ember." He turns his face away and sniffles, trying not to cry in front of me. "I just want everything to go back to the way it was. I liked my life the way it was. I was finally getting to do stuff. I begged my parents for a cell phone and they finally got me one a month before it all

70

happened. I had it for a whole month. I wish I had a time travel machine," he says, his voice trailing off wistfully.

The thought is intriguing.

"What would you do with a time travel machine?"

He wipes his eyes with the tattered hem of his t-shirt. "What do you think I'd do? I'd go back and drop a bomb on the bad guys before they could give everybody that virus."

"That's great, but how would you know who they were?"

"I don't know. Maybe I'd just bomb their whole country."

Wars have been started with that sort of thinking and I find my temper rising up until I realize where I am. "But then you'd kill a bunch of innocent people too."

"Yeah, well they probably died anyways with the virus, right?"

I think about this for a moment. He is right, but he's also very wrong. Is it okay to kill millions to save millions of other people? Is one person's life worth more than another's?

"Maybe. It's hard to say."

"What would you do?" he asks almost shyly.

I stretch and look up at the sliver of moon, peeking through the dark silhouette of the trees. It is the same moon that has been there since the beginning of time and it will be there well after we've both taken our last breath. It feels like the last normal thing left on our world.

"I'd go back to a few months before everybody started getting sick and I'd bring us all to a deserted island somewhere safe. Then we could all eat coconuts and work on our tans every day instead of dealing with this bullshit."

Teddy smiles when I say it, realizing that I'm only half serious. Honestly, his question unnerves me a little because I'm not sure what I would do if I could go back in time. I wouldn't know where to begin or what to change. If I could go back, would I just go a few months back? Or would I go back several decades and stop the devastation that led to this devastation? Or would I go back even further? There just wasn't a clear starting place. When did it all begin?

A yawn washes through me. I am too tired and fragile to think about it any longer.

"Are you tired?" Teddy asks, dismissing the bubble of silence that has grown between us.

"Extremely." As soon as I say the word, my body responds, and I feel the tremor return in the small muscles of my fingers. Now that the adrenaline has depleted, I am weak and trembling. "And hungry," I add.

I hear him root around in his backpack for a moment and then he presses something slim and cool into my hand. I run my fingers down the length of it, hearing the crinkle of the package, until my heart nearly shrieks with glee. It is a candy bar.

"Oh my God, Teddy. Where did you get this?"

Teddy shrugs. "I've had it for a while," he says simply, and I realize once again how little I know of this new Teddy. The old Teddy would have ripped the paper off and eaten it whole, barely stopping to savor the sweet warmth of the chocolate, not letting it melt on his tongue. This new Teddy has saved it for a special occasion.

I open it and hand him half.

I take a small bite and nearly moan. The caramel and chocolate coats the inside of my mouth with sheer Heaven and I hold it there, without swallowing, until I simply can't hold it any longer. I take another bite, forgetting everything except the taste of chocolate. When I am finished, I lick my fingers and then lick the inside of the candy wrapping for stray bits of chocolate. It is the best thing I've ever eaten in my whole life. I want to pull Teddy into my arms and hug him like a teddy bear.

"Thank you," I tell him and then remember that I have something to share as well. I fish around in the pocket of my jeans until I find the package of chewing gum. I open it and hand him a piece and then take a piece for myself as well. It is some sort of fruit flavor, raspberry maybe. The taste is strong, but sweet, mixing with the lingering taste of chocolate and making my mouth taste better than it has tasted in a long time.

We stand in the darkness, just chewing our gum for a moment while the crickets chirp and the wind whispers through the trees. It is such a simple thing, but it has become something nearly sacred. It is the end of something normal; something we once took for granted and never gave a second thought to. In our old world there would always be more gum and candy bars. They were lined up on the shelves of every grocery store in the country. All you had to do was plop a handful of change onto the counter and it was yours for the taking. Now, there were a finite number of them left, and when they were gone, they would be gone forever for us. If society ever restarted, they would probably worry about the big things first, like electricity and running water. Candy bars and chewing gum would be decades away, something we might never see again in our lifetimes. The thought is appropriately depressing. I put my hand in my pocket and cradle the pack of gum. It might as well have been a million dollars.

A thought occurs to me with the intensity of neon and firecrackers. The house that Teddy and Annie lived in was one of the nicest houses in town, maybe even the second nicest after you considered the Cooper House. Having been built in the early eighteen hundreds, it had a long history and was filled with secrets. It had been used as a hiding spot for runaway slaves. An underground tunnel ran from the garage across the street to the house, where a small room had been carved into the granite

73

earth. The entrance to the secret room and the tunnel were cleverly hidden behind a built-in book case, so it was nearly invisible unless you knew to look for it. Pictures of it had been featured in the local newspaper, but I doubted the bad guys knew about it. It would be a perfect place to hide.

"We can go to your house and hide in the secret room," I tell him, but he shakes his head.

"It's not safe. The bad guys have been in and out of the house for a couple of weeks now. I think they're using it as another camp because it's so close to the chemical plant."

His words sink in deeply. "So they are at the chemical plant." I take a deep breath and exhale with a sigh. "Have you seen what they're doing there?"

"No, but it's pretty easy to figure out. They're probably collecting the phosgene gas." Teddy's father also worked at Gordon Plastics, so he knew what the bad men could do with phosgene gas. It was something everybody in the area knew. It was drilled into us from birth.

It makes my heart feel heavy. If they're squirreling away the phosgene gas, then their plans are bigger than our town, maybe even bigger than the world. If guns and viruses aren't enough and they need poisonous gases, then their intent is pretty far-reaching.

"One of the houses at the base of the hill is on fire," I tell Teddy.

"Near my house?" he says, nearly coming unglued.

"No, on the other side of the hill, but if it reaches the plant, it could cause all that gas to release into the town." I remember my father complaining about the location. Phosgene is heavier than air and will sink down into the valleys before it dissipates. Since half the town is in a gully, we'd all be goners.

"We should probably get moving," I tell him.

He eases up from the ground. "Where you wanna go?"

I think of my sister's fair blond hair and the way she would wrap her whole self around you in a hug. We need to find a safe place to sleep, but I won't be able to rest until I've been to the one place where I need to go.

"The Cooper House," I say. We make it out to the sidewalk and then all Hell breaks loose.

10

We step onto the sidewalk as a vehicle careens around the corner, nearly pinning us with its headlights. I pull Teddy behind the large maple tree in front of the library and we watch the vehicle slow to a stop not far from where we are hiding.

I gasp as I recognize the vehicle. It is a brown Jeep Cherokee that is nearly covered with animal rights bumper stickers. It belongs to the dog catcher.

The dog catcher was a real character around town. When he wasn't working at the dog pound, he would drive around town looking for strays. We called him Creep in a Jeep because of the way he would sneer at us for no good reason at all. My mother used to consider him with the same expression she wore when my father belched at the dinner table.

"I wonder why someone who obviously hates animals so much works as the animal control officer?" she mused as we watched him snag a feral cat with a loop pole. The cat spun around madly at the end of the pole until he lifted it off the ground and let it dangle for a while, as if to teach it a lesson. My mother had pulled me away at that point, so I wasn't privy to the cat's eventual fate.

The man gets out of his vehicle and strides to the sidewalk across the street from us, obviously searching for something. He is dressed like a military man, complete with khaki shirt and cargo pants with his grey hair cut in a standard crew cut, even though he is old enough to be somebody's grandfather.

"Isn't that the dog catcher? What's he doing?" Teddy whispers to me.

"I think so. Just be quiet." We inch backwards and slip beneath the huge rhododendron bushes in front of the library. I hunch down until I am nearly sitting and find a gap in the bushes where I can peek out.

We watch the dog catcher inspect something on the sidewalk. I don't have a clear view of it, but it looks like a pile of rags. He kneels down and studies it for a few minutes before he stands up and peers down the street in the direction we were heading. As we are watching, another man joins him from the shadows.

"Who's that?" Teddy asks. I stare at the man, as a slow dawning comes over me. It's Henry Rivers. I nearly faint on the spot. Henry was my math tutor.

My father hired him to tutor me when I failed algebra. I'd been fearful, clearly imaging what a math tutor would look like. He would be thin and gangly, with thick soda-bottle glasses and a burbling red forehead filled with oozing pimples. His breath would smell like sardines and he would spit when he lectured at me, spraying me with the toxic debris lodged between his crusty teeth. I would learn nothing more than the concept of how long a minute could last.

I began dreaming of ways I could avoid this tutor. I would hide out at Annie's house, pretending to have forgotten, or perhaps I could stay after school and work on an extra credit project for English or biology. Or maybe I could simply hire someone to stand in and pretend to be me. The thoughts became wilder and more delirious as the days progressed. When my actual tutor arrived, he was nothing like I had expected. He was simply perfect. He was Henry Rivers.

I still think of his name with a sigh. He was almost as tall as my father, with skin that turned a golden brown in the summer and a body that was adept at any sport he fancied. His hair was the color of caramel, sort of blonde, but sort of brown as well, depending on the lighting and how it fell across his forehead. When he looked at me, all I could think about was how blue his eyes were. They were the color of a tropical pool of water, a color torn between blue and green, rimmed with black lashes that curled upwards naturally and made him all the more alluring.

He showed up that first day with a knock at the door that I refused to answer. I had parked myself at the dining room table where we would study, carefully positioning myself at the end of the table so he would be forced to sit on one side of me, but not beside me, where he could accidentally brush my breast with his hairy arm. I'd worn a shirt with buttons and had buttoned it all the way to the top so this tutor wouldn't be able to sneak even the slightest glance at my naked skin. I had a fresh yellow tablet of paper in front of me and a sharp number two pencil resting on top of it and I stared at it as I listened to the sounds of their voices in the entry way.

My mother opened the door and greeted him warmly, using that false-happy voice that she used with small children and church ladies on the phone. They spoke for a moment in lowered voices, probably discussing the thick-witted student he would be mentoring and all the difficulties I'd been having putting numbers together. Finally, I could hear the sound of my mother's heels on the hardwood floor as they made their way through the living room to the dining room.

"Henry, this is Ember," my mother said as though she were presenting me to him, the delight in her eye undeniable as she watched my reaction to this tutor, this *tutor*.

"Hey there, Ember," he said, barely brushing me with his gaze before he pulled a chair out and began arranging his tutoring materials. He made it clear from the very onset that he was here to work, plain and simple. If he noticed me, he never gave me any indicator of this. I was his student. We were there to learn math. Nothing else.

78

Lightning Strikes

We delved into equations and properties, sub-roots and numeric fractions. I followed his finger as he traced it across the paper, pointing to the things I needed to learn, but all I saw in the beginning was his finger and how his nails were perfectly arched. I watched his eyebrows lower as he concentrated on a problem, noticed the way he often twisted his lips to the side when he was perplexed, admired the way he smiled all the way through himself when something pleased him.

My grades improved, but only because I tried a little harder, trying to make him happy with me, wanting to bring out that smile that shone like the sun. I'd sit in my bedroom dreaming about him, writing his name in the margin of my notepads and then scratching it out so that no one would see it, finding songs that fit the way I felt about him. But as quickly as he came into my life, he was gone. My only mistake was telling Annie how I felt.

"Call him!" She threw her raspberry pink phone at me. "Just call him and talk to him. Ask him if he wants to come to my party on Friday night," she said, as though her world had anything to do with mine.

"No, I can't. He's not interested."

Annie rolled her eyes at me. "Maybe that's because he doesn't think you're interested." She took my hand and led me to the mirror. "I mean, what's not to like? Look at you. You have the most amazing green eyes. I could show you how to make them up a little bit, make them really sizzle." We looked at my reflection together, which only served to show me just how different the two of us were. Her auburn hair cascaded down her bare shoulders in a tumble of curls, framing a heart-shaped face with berry lips and wide blue eyes. I looked drab in comparison, with my brown hair and my faded Bob Marley t-shirt. I was someone the boys wanted to play baseball with; she

79

was someone they wanted to play baseball for. Some things would never change.

"No, that's not going to help. He's popular. He's good looking...he's..."

Annie swiveled me around and propelled me to the bed. She pulled the phone book out from under a pile of clothing and found his number in the student directory.

"I'm going to help you out a little here. He'll never know it's me." As she started to dial, a panic surged through me, hot and wild.

"Annie, don't." It wasn't the way I wanted it to go. I'd been so cautious with him, so careful not to make a total fool of myself. "Please, Annie...stop."

It was as though she never heard me; her mind was so fixated on solving my problem. She didn't consider how this would affect me if it went wrong; she could only see it as a remedy for my situation. Just wave a magic wand and everything will turn out like you wanted it to.

"Hello, Henry?" she started, and it all went downhill from there. She invited him to the party, flirted with him, and generally made a total fool of herself. When she got off the phone, her mood was much more sullen.

I turned away, not wanting to know what he said, wishing I could erase the last five minutes and start all over again. She'd ruined everything.

She touched my shoulder with a tentative hand. "I'm sorry, Ember. I shouldn't have done that."

"I told you not to do it."

She sighed. "I just thought that if you tried a little harder, he'd come around. I think you just give up too easily sometimes."

I simply came unglued. I flung her hand off my shoulder and turned to face her.

"You. Ruined. Everything." I stood up and began collecting my clothing off the floor, stuffing it into my backpack. "You have to understand that everything doesn't come easy for some of us. I'm not Queen Annie, born with a silver spoon shoved up my ass and a sparkly wand to make everything all sunshiny and beautiful. You've had it way too easy all your life. You don't know how it is for everyone else. You just think that since your life is so perfect, everyone else must be stupid to not have the same things. Well, let me tell you something, Annie. You got lucky. Boys like Henry Rivers don't look at girls like Ember Pain. They look at girls like you." I gave her one last scathing look. "I hope you're happy, because you have ruined my whole pathetic life."

I stomped out of her house, found my bicycle leaning against her garage door and rode off, my head pounding with anger. As it turns out, it was the last time I ever spoke to her.

"That's Henry Rivers," I tell Teddy. "He was my math tutor, once upon a time."

We watch as Henry joins the dog catcher at the curb.

I only have a handful of seconds to look at him, but it is enough to know that something is very wrong with Henry Rivers. It is like peering into a deep pool and finding flames instead of water. I cannot help but gasp.

Everything about him is different. If there is something familiar about him, it is his height and the placement of his features, but those characteristics are so slight and so diminished by all of the changes, I can barely find him beneath it all. He has become feral and dangerous. He reminds me of a wild animal, the sort of creature who would bite just for the sake of biting. He is no longer anyone's golden boy. Either he's

81

been affected by the virus or he's been affected by the situation. Either way, he's no longer the Henry Rivers I remember.

The two of them return to the Jeep. I lean forward and try to eavesdrop on their conversation. Henry isn't happy about something and is arguing with the dog catcher. I hear the word "cannibal" and my heart freezes.

"Did he just say 'cannibal'," Teddy asks me, and I shush him. I try to catch more of their conversation, but they get into the Jeep and drive away. I wait five full minutes before I climb out of the bushes.

"Let's go see what they were looking at," Teddy says, and I shush him again. I also want to see what they were looking at, but I want to make sure no one else is around first. The men talked about a cannibal. I want to make sure there isn't one around before I go parading down the street. I lead him to the maple tree and watch the street for another five minutes until I can hear the sound of the crickets chirping again.

"Okay. Let's cross the street. Stay low and run to that tree over there first." I point to a large tree near the curb. "Okay?" I ask and wait for him to nod. I have to wonder what he'd do if I wasn't there. He probably would have joined the two men at the curb.

I grab Teddy's hand and we dart across the street, making our way to the tree. Once the crickets resume their serenade, I edge out of hiding and walk a few steps closer to the curb.

Teddy reaches it first. "Ewww, gross!" he says a little too loudly.

I am ready to correct him, but then I see what he is looking at and the words simply vanish from my mind. It's a dead body.

11

The woman is on her side, her clothing ripped and tattered. Her blond hair pools on the sidewalk beside her, painted with blood. I remember seeing her around town, walking a tiny white dog. I consider taking her pulse, but it would be pointless. She is obviously dead.

"Where's her arm?" Teddy asks. The wound is jagged and bloody. The smell of coppery blood fills the air. My heart lunges in my chest. Before I can even answer him, I feel the bile rush up my throat. I turn and vomit in the grass behind me, the horror of what I've seen consuming me whole.

"You okay?"

I pull myself to a standing position and feel the world go brown at the edges. "I need to sit down."

We walk to the nearest house and sit on the steps. We probably shouldn't be staying in the area in case the cannibal comes back, but I'm afraid to move. If I start walking and faint on the sidewalk, Teddy's going to have to deal with my pale, limp body, and I cannot even imagine the consequences of that.

"Do you think the cannibal did that?" Teddy asks after a few minutes.

I take a deep breath and let it hiss through my lips. "Probably." The thought is nearly mind-numbing. If he'd caught either one of us at the library, then we'd be on the sidewalk instead of the woman. I take a few more lungfuls of air, until I'm assured I'm not going to faint, and then pull myself to my feet. "We need to get out of here."

We walk in silence for several blocks. I don't relax until we are further from the downtown area. By the time we've walked four blocks, the tremble eases out of my legs, and my mind begins wandering.

Teddy walks beside me, staring hard into the shadows instead of watching where he's walking. He trips over a lumpy root and nearly falls.

"Why do you think he does that?" he asks, making me jolt at the abrupt sound of his voice.

"Does what? You mean the cannibal?"

"Yeah. Why did he rip that lady's arm off when there is food everywhere?" He points at the row of houses. "I mean, if he's hungry, he could just walk into any of these houses and find all the food he wants. Why eat people?"

"I don't know. Something must have happened to him. He must have gotten the virus, and it scrambled his brains instead of killing him." As I say this, I think about Henry Rivers. He'd been affected too. It was evident in the way he carried himself and in the way he looked. I didn't think he was killing women and ripping their arms off, but he still frightened me.

"Do you think there are any more of them?" he asks in a tiny voice.

I don't want to scare him any more than he already is, but he needs to know the truth.

"There might be. We'll just have to keep our eyes open."

"Maybe we should get a gun," he says, and I feel my heart thud heavily at the thought. I've never even held a gun in my hands. I'd have no idea how to use one.

"Have you ever handled a gun before?" I ask, and he shakes his head.

"No. My mom was against guns. She wouldn't let my dad keep one in the house."

"My mom was the same way," I say with a sigh. "Maybe we can find bigger knives or something."

We continue walking, sticking to the sidewalk where the deep shadows hang like curtains. The residential area has been left intact and looks very similar to the way it used to look. Tall, winding oak trees line the residential portion of Main Street, giving the houses a bit of privacy from the relentless summer sun. Most of the houses are vintage hoity-toity Victorians mixed with stoic two-story colonials.

The windows on the houses are now as black as the night. The people who once lived there are now gone, and the houses are now just empty structures, waiting for time and the elements to eventually reduce them to rubble. If it weren't for the cannibal and the bad men, we could pick any house we wanted.

"Which house would you live in if you could just pick any one?" I ask.

He has been very quiet beside me. His face is turned downward as he watches the sidewalk ahead of him. He glances up and takes quick stock of the houses around him and shrugs.

"I don't know. None of them, probably."

"Why?" I ask.

He looks at me for a second, as if to see if I'm being serious. "Because they are right here in town, where the bad men are. They'd see me too easily."

"What if the bad men and the cannibal weren't around anymore? Which house would you pick?"

"I'd go back to my own house," he says as if it is a silly question. Maybe it is. I continue down the sidewalk.

I can't say I blame him. I'd like to go home too.

"Why do you think they kidnapped Elizabeth instead of...?" Teddy doesn't finish his sentence, but he doesn't have to. I've seen the bad men shoot people too. My guilt at letting them capture my sister nearly overcomes me for a moment, and I take a deep breath to suppress it.

"I don't know," I say, seeing Elizabeth's smiling, innocent face in my mind. Tears press at the backs of my eyes, and I blink hard to chase them away. "If I had to guess, I'd say they are keeping the children to train them."

"Train them to do what?"

"I don't know...to do all the things they don't want to do, maybe. Like cleaning houses, planting gardens, cleaning up, and stuff like that." I don't mention my theory on the breeders. Elizabeth is too young for that, but it doesn't mean they won't use her when she gets older. "I think they shoot the adults because most people would never stop trying to fight them. I know I wouldn't."

"Neither would I. Does that mean they will shoot us instead of kidnap us?" he asks.

"I guess that would depend on their definition of how old is too old. How old were the kids you saw being transported?"

Teddy shrugs. "I'm not sure. I couldn't really see them. I could just hear them crying."

"If you had to guess?" I ask.

Teddy kicks a stone on the sidewalk, sending it rolling end over end into the grass. "Elizabeth's age or younger, probably."

"That's what I thought." It makes me realize how lucky we've been so far. In the back of my mind, I thought that if they finally found me, they'd do the same thing with me that they did to my sister, but in reality, they'd probably just shoot me. It wasn't a very comforting thought. It makes the idea of trying to rescue Elizabeth even more terrifying than it already is.

"I wonder where they're keeping her at the Cooper House," I say out loud, not really expecting an answer.

"I dunno. They probably have her locked up in one of the bedrooms," he says, and I nod. It makes sense that they would use the small rooms upstairs to hold prisoners. They could lock

86

the doors and keep them inside. The windows were too high off the ground to jump from. I only wish I knew the floor plan better.

"Have you ever been inside there?"

"Just for a birthday party when I was in the third grade," he says. My hope grows for a moment. If he's been inside, he will know where the stairs are that lead to the upstairs and possibly where the bedrooms themselves are located.

"Do you remember much about the inside?"

"No, not really. They had the party outside in the back yard. I went in to use the bathroom, but that's all. Mrs. Cooper was trying to keep us all outside."

"Oh," I say, and the conversation dies very quickly. I don't know what I will do to rescue my sister. She is probably being guarded by men with machine guns and hand grenades, and all I have is a useless fourteen-year-old to protect me. I glance up at the houses we pass, wondering if one of them might have guns hidden inside, not that it would do us much good if we don't know how to use one. I can clearly picture Teddy shooting his own foot, and the thought isn't pretty.

Before I realize it, I am thinking about Henry Rivers again. I try to overlay the man I just saw on top of the golden boy athlete I once knew, and the image won't hold.

I think about what the newscaster said about how everyone was affected differently from the virus. Some people simply died, while some people lived, not suffering any effects. In between the two was a whole lot of grey area. It wouldn't surprise me if Henry had been changed by it. I mourn the loss of his old self as though he has died. I guess I should just be happy he is still alive, but I can't. I'm not sure how much of the old Henry still remains.

The moon slips out from behind the clouds, and the night seems suddenly brighter. The white porch railings gleam like teeth on the house beside me. A leaf flutters slowly to the ground ahead of us, reminding me that autumn is right around the corner. My shoe has come untied, so I pause to tie it before we continue on.

As soon as I rescue Elizabeth, there will be decisions to make and plans to deliberate over. Right now, it is simply about day-to-day survival. I hope we eventually make it to the planning stage. Something inside me panics a little every time I think about the winter ahead. I feel like I should be squirreling things aside and finding a warm place to hide during the cold months. I sigh at the thought.

The streets are quiet, and besides the occasional broken window or downed tree limb, the houses look as though their owners are just away on an extended vacation and forgot to pay someone to mow their lawn while they were gone. The smell of death lingers in the air, and I try not to think about what I would find inside some of the houses.

We hear the sound of an explosion in the distance and see the faint glow of fire peering through the quiet night. We turn to look and wonder about it for a moment, but then turn back and begin walking again. This is our world now.

"The bad men probably burned down another building," Teddy says.

"I wonder why they do that," I muse.

"I don't know. Because they can, probably." We walk in silence, thoughts jarring through my mind. As we pass one house, a light-colored cat jumps through a broken window and gives us a quick glance before disappearing into the shadows.

I hear a noise behind us, and I glance over my shoulder. Fear wraps cold fingers around my chest, making me suddenly breathless. Teddy looks up but doesn't glance behind us.

"What was that?" I whisper, as if he has the answer.

"I don't know." We walk in silence for a moment until the sound repeats. Every hair on the back of my neck stands at attention.

"It could be the cannibal."

The memory of the dead woman on the sidewalk returns to me in full color. I want to look behind me again, to see if I can catch a glimpse of our pursuer, but I'm afraid. If he sees me turn around, then he'll know that we are aware of him behind us. Then, he might just drop the pretenses and chase after us. Fear rushes through my body with a spike of adrenaline.

Teddy motions towards the silhouette of a large tree just ahead of us.

"Let's duck behind it and see if he passes us," he suggests, but all I hear is the word "if." What if he doesn't pass us? What then?

My heart pounds heavily as we come to the tree. We duck behind it as the sound of footsteps grows louder behind us. I don't like this. If we just stand here, he could just sneak up on us and grab us. A long row of evergreen hedges runs along the side of the property, so I grab Teddy's arm and pull him behind them. I point to the end of the bushes. If we can put some distance between us, then we might have a chance of losing him.

The hedges end at the side of a brick house. Wooden steps with a tick rail lead to a back door with a weathered floral wreath hanging from it. I am tempted to turn the doorknob, to see if it is unlocked, but I am afraid it will take too much time. If the stalker comes around the tree, it's possible he might look to his left and see us standing there. I pull Teddy onto the back lawn. We run, bent at the waist, down a concrete walk to a small white garage. There is a door along the side with a window, so I open it and haul Teddy in behind me. I close the door behind us and press myself against the wall. The sound of my heart beat has grown epic. It beats in my chest like a tribal drum.

After a moment, I realize I am still grasping Teddy's arm, so I lessen my grip. He yanks his arm away and rubs it as though I've had it in a vice grip.

"What now?"

I fan him away with my hand.

"Just be quiet. We need to wait."

The silence settles around us with an oppression I can feel deep in my soul. It feels like waiting, like being watched from somewhere afar, like counting the minutes until something monumental can happen.

Another boom thunders in the distance, and I wonder if it's the same house or another one. The sound is like a lead weight on my soul. The landscape we know is quickly being replaced by a war zone. By the end of the month, I might not recognize it at all. I take a deep breath and hold it in as long as I can.

The garage smells like greasy motor parts, with a faint tang of gasoline. As my eyes adjust, I can see a small white car just in front of us. It nearly consumes the entire garage, with just enough room to pass on one side. A work bench covered with random tools and gleaming, greasy parts lines the front of the room. I make a quick scan, hoping for a flashlight, but all I see are metal things, tossed without thought or organization onto the wooden table. It reminds me of my father's work bench in our own garage. My mother always chided him about his lack of organization, and he would just roll his eyes at her. "Garages aren't supposed to be neat," he'd tell her.

After several minutes have passed, I find the courage to tiptoe to the door and peek out the window. I am prepared for a hundred different scenarios to unwind, beginning with finding the cannibal pressing his face against the glass, smiling his evil little smile, but the window is empty. Outside, the lawn is quiet and moonlit with an opaque blue haze. A white shape materializes at the edge of the yard, where a picket fence marks the property line, and I nearly jump backwards until I realize it is the cat we saw earlier, picking his way along the weeds. He is probably hunting mice in the moonlight.

The air in the garage is stagnant and warm. The longer we stand there, the more difficult it becomes to even breathe. I imagine chemicals and gasoline drifting through the air in vapor clouds. A bead of sweat rolls down the back of my neck. I swipe my palm across my forehead and wipe it on the back of my jeans. We won't be able to stay here very much longer.

"See anything?" Teddy whispers behind me.

"No. Nothing." I scan the back yard once more, staring hard at the dark parts, but nothing else materializes.

"Think it's safe to go back outside?"

There is no clear-cut answer. I give the yard another quick inspection and shrug. "I hope so."

I open the door and the cool, sweet air rushes in. I just stand there for several seconds, doing nothing more than breathing and trying to purge out the smells of motor oil and gasoline that have permeated into my skin.

The lawn remains unchanged. No one jumps out at us, and nothing moves in the shadows. The sound of the crickets still filters through the darkness. I don't know if it is safe, but I'm pretty sure we're alone for the moment.

91

"Let's head down the alley instead of going back to the street," I suggest. Teddy presses close against me and we tiptoe along the wall of the garage to the alley. Silver trash cans sit at the curb, waiting for a trash pick-up that will never come. We step around one that has been tipped onto its side, spilling its guts onto the rutted street.

The smell of death grows stronger as we reach the end of the block. I can see something propped up against a garage wall ahead of us. As we get closer, the smell of decomposition is so strong, I can nearly see it hanging in the air. I pull the neck of my t-shirt up over my nose to block out the smell.

"Maybe we should go around the other block," Teddy says.

"That'll take too long. Just breath through your shirt, and we'll get past it quickly."

He covers his nose with his arm, and we pick up the pace. I know I shouldn't look, but I can't help it. I glance over at the garage wall as we rush past and see the silhouette of a man leaning against the garage wall. A trail of blood marks the wall above him, the door riddled with bullet holes.

"Oh God. The bad men must have executed him," I whisper, and Teddy touches my arm.

"Just don't look, Ember. They're all over the place. If you don't look, you can't see them."

It's almost like pulling the covers over my head to hide after having a scary nightmare, except for the fact that this monster will never go away. I don't know how long I can live like this.

The sound of my breathing seems louder than it should, and I close my eyes for a moment, trying to regain control. *In through the nose, out through the mouth,* my mother always told me, and I try this until I am calm again.

"Are you okay?" Teddy asks me, his brows pulled down in concern.

"Yeah. It's just weird seeing dead bodies all over town."

"I know it sounds crazy, but you get used to it after a while," he says. I'm not sure I believe him. I can't imagine ever getting used to the sight of dead bodies scattered around like old trash. I want to just take off running and not stop until the city is miles behind me. With every ounce of my being, I just want to climb back into my hidey-hole and wrap my grandmother's quilt around me and sleep until it all goes away.

We move along the next alley, putting another block behind us. The Cooper House is only another block away. I take a deep breath and try to calm myself, if nothing else for Elizabeth's sake. I need to be strong if I'm going to pull this off.

I peer through the darkness, half expecting to see the light from the building penetrating through the night. I thought the bad guys would have bonfires going in the front lawn and joyful music blasting from speakers, fired by generators, but the night is as silent as it was before.

"So what do you want to do when we get there?" Teddy asks as we pause at the edge of another garage.

"I don't know. I guess I just want to take a look and see if I can see her through a window." I haven't devoted much time to an actual plan. I just wanted to get there and then hope something came to me. "I thought we'd play it by ear. Does that sound okay?"

"Yeah, I guess so. I just don't want to get too close, okay?"

I squeeze his shoulder reassuringly. "That's fine with me. I want to get an idea of what we're dealing with. If it looks easy, then I'll sneak in and grab her, but if they have her locked up somewhere, then we can find somewhere to crash for the night and then make plans to go back tomorrow."

I am so tired. The thought of crashing for the night is alluring, lulling me forward step by step, nearly erasing the fear that hovers inside me like a giant balloon. I imagine us finding a house nearby, crawling into someone's unmade bed and pulling crisp, cool linens over our tired bodies, and sleeping dreamlessly until dawn's first light. I push myself onward, allowing the thought to carry me along. We make it down the next block without issue. If anyone is following us, I can't hear him.

We reach the block where the Cooper's Victorian resides. The houses are larger, spread out on larger lots. The younger Cape Cod and Ranch style houses give way for the older, lofty Victorians and Colonials, with wide front porches and long blacktop driveways. We are a dozen blocks from the downtown area, where the destruction is the heaviest. The houses that we pass look virtually untouched. We walk further down the block.

"It's right up here," Teddy says, motioning to the right.

I peer through the darkness, trying to find some hint of the massive structure gleaming in the moonlight, but all I see is more darkness.

"Do you see it?" I ask.

"No," he says, his voice puzzled. "It should be right there." He points ahead at the place where the house has sat for over a hundred years. The last time I saw it, Mrs. Cooper had red, white, and blue American flag runners along the porch to celebrate Memorial Day.

We edge closer, but pause at the end of the block. As we step out onto the street, the moon comes out from behind the clouds and provides us with our answer.

"Oh my God," I whisper. The smell of soot and ash waft through the air.

94

In the place where the house once stood is nothing more than charred timbers. The house has been burnt to the ground.

12

When our kitchen burned down so many years ago, the fire inspectors were not certain what actually caused the fire. They ruled it as faulty wiring, but I saw them staring at the long line of soot climbing the outside wall. It looked like a lightning strike, they agreed, but then stared up at the calm blue skies, where nary a cloud lingered, and couldn't make it work, no matter how they tried.

Elizabeth had been eight and I'd been fourteen, and we'd been getting ready for school. My mother had a meeting with a client who was commissioning a large garden sculpture for my mother to carve. She'd been nervous and edgy, misplacing her keys and spilling her coffee all over the floor in her haste to clear the breakfast dishes from the table. Elizabeth had wandered sleepily into the room, still dressed in her pajamas, even though we were supposed to leave in five minutes.

"Elizabeth, why aren't you dressed?" my mother asked, stopping in her tracks, a wet paper towel dripping from her hand.

Elizabeth crossed her arms over her chest and frowned so deeply, her eyebrows furrowed channels above her narrowed blue eyes. Her Clementine doll was tucked in the corner of her elbow, the white legs sticking out like strange appendages.

"Clementine doesn't want to go to school. She's sick!"

My mother closed her eyes for a moment, as if to quiet a surge of anger. I could almost imagine her chanting *calm, calm, calm* before she finally spoke.

"Elizabeth, Mommy really needs you to go upstairs and get dressed. We can take Clementine to the doll hospital after school and get her some medicine." I nearly chuckled at the thought of my mother's doll hospital, which was nothing more than a cardboard box in the corner of her studio. It held a needle and thread, an empty eye-drop bottle that had the words doll medicine written across the front in permanent marker, and a host of bandages and flesh-colored tape for small boo-boos that only Elizabeth could see. The doll hospital had saved us a number of times when Clementine took a spill. I could see from the dour expression on Elizabeth's face that it wasn't going to work this time.

"She doesn't need the doll hospital. She needs to stay home in bed and sleep. She's too tired to go to school."

My mother dropped the dripping paper towel into the trash and knelt down in front of my sister. I had to give her credit for her patience because I would have handled the situation much differently.

"Sweetheart, you know what I think Clementine really needs?" she said in a voice that was as soothing as melted butter. "I think she needs a new outfit. I know that always makes me feel better when I'm feeling a little blue." She pulled back and watched Elizabeth for a moment as the insolence curled away, moment by moment.

"I was thinking about going to Kimball's after work. They have some really lovely periwinkle fabric that would go really nicely with the new Venice lace trim I bought for your Easter dress. I might have a pattern that we could make a very nice dress for Clementine with. Are you interested? I'll even let you run my sewing machine."

The thought was like sunshine breaking through dark clouds. Elizabeth's arms uncrossed, and her eyebrows eased out of the scowl. She was on the very brink of agreeing to my mother's bribe when the worst thing of all happened. Clementine slipped to the floor and landed in the remnants of the coffee puddle. It was enough to send Elizabeth into a full-blown meltdown.

My mother closed her eyes for a moment and then glanced down at her watch. She'd already used all our time allowance, and we'd be late if we didn't leave right then. She looked at me with such weariness in her eyes I almost felt sorry for her before I remembered that this was something she'd brought upon herself. If she'd put her foot down when Elizabeth was two or even three, we wouldn't have been standing there having that conversation.

"Ember, just go get in the car. We'll be right there."

I yanked my backpack off the hook by the back door and shoved my arms in my jacket as I stomped through the house and out the front door, where my mother's car was parked. As I walked, I could hear the familiar strains of Elizabeth howling. Three minutes later, my mother pushed through the front door, half holding Elizabeth, who was still hanging onto the wet doll. My mother's pea coat hung off her other arm, dragging on the ground as she lugged my very heavy, very angry sister out to the car. As they reached the edge of the sidewalk, Elizabeth managed to slip from her grasp and ran back inside.

I watched my mother nearly collapse on the spot. The torment and angst transformed her face into something very tired and sorrowful. She looked as though she were on the verge of giving up, of just taking Elizabeth back inside, calling the school to tell them that both of us were sick with viruses, and retreating to her studio, where she'd play soft music and amuse Elizabeth with bits of colored ribbon and soft blocks of clay. I felt the anger rise up inside me, straight and bold. I needed to go to school. I had a history test I'd studied three hours for the night before and besides, we were starting our project in art class, and I was assigned to work with Michael Bellows, someone I'd been drooling over for nearly a year. Getting to work side by side with him on our volcano project was like winning the school lottery. If I was absent, they'd just give him a new partner, and I'd probably end up with Joe Konstantine, who picked his nose and ate his buggers and smelled like liverwurst. So, I did what I had to do. I honked the horn and gave my mother an exasperated look.

The give-up look faded from her face quickly. She straightened her spine and marched back into the house. She came back out thirty seconds later with a screaming Elizabeth beneath her arm. "I'll just bring her with me," she said, depositing my red-faced sister in the back seat. "Help her get buckled up, Ember," she said, and we were on our way. I don't remember seeing any dark clouds or gusts of wind appearing, but we'd barely gotten to school before the first fire truck roared down our street. These were the things that returned to me, softly and slowly, filling in the gaps and answering some of the questions. Elizabeth must have been responsible. All the signs had been there for a while. We just chose to overlook them.

A sob chokes in my chest as I stare at the Cooper House. A tear slips down my cheek, and I allow the sensation to roll through me for just a moment, letting the tears fall where they may. I don't know what to think.

"It doesn't mean anything, Ember. They could have just moved to another house and then burnt this one down."

I look at him, wanting to believe what he is saying, but I know better. Teddy doesn't know about the lightning.

I study the house for a moment. Portions of the stone foundation are visible in the moonlight, the stones gleaming through the soot in the places where the recent rain has washed it away. The stone fireplace rises above the ruins, still fully intact. My mother told me that Mr. Cooper would hang

Christmas stockings on the mantle every December and fill them with hundred dollar bills.

The house had stood there for over a hundred years, being devotedly maintained by a steady line of home owners for every year of its life. It never looked run down or old. Someone had always been there, repainting woodwork, replacing old windows, removing the rot, and rebuilding it better than it was before. It had survived high winds, tornado warnings, and blizzards, but now it was gone. Was Elizabeth responsible for it?

I remember her, sitting there perfectly untouched in the middle of my mother's party, surrounded by burnt grass smelling like charred rubble, and I feel a little better until I consider the other options. If she didn't do it, then someone else did. Tears press against the back of my eyes as I consider the possibilities.

I can't just walk away without looking.

"Where are you going?" Teddy asks.

"I need to look...to make sure," I tell him. I climb over the stone wall and wander around the ruins, lifting boards and pieces of wall board to peer underneath. After nearly an hour, I am on the edge of exhaustion and have learned nothing more than the obvious. Elizabeth was here, but now the house is gone.

"They probably just moved her to another house and then burnt this one down," Teddy tells me. "They like to burn things down. I saw flames a few nights ago coming from this direction, but they're always burning something down, so I didn't think much about it. Did you see the Laundromat?" he asks, and I nod. I think about the way they smashed the windows in my house. They are destructive. He might be right. It gives me a small measure of hope.

"Let's just get moving. Maybe we can sneak back tomorrow and look some more," I say with a sigh. I'm not sure what we will find. I'm not even sure I want to find anything. "No news is good news," my mother used to say, but it doesn't comfort me like it should. It just leaves me cold and empty inside. If Elizabeth isn't here, then where is she? Did she die in the fire, or did they manage to get her out before it got too dangerous? And where did they move her? The questions only serve to breed more questions, and my head hurts with the pounding thoughts. I just want to crawl up somewhere and let my weary mind chew on it for a while. I sigh again. As the air purges out of me, some of my resolve goes with it, leaving me weak and tired. I need sleep, and I need it now.

"I'm so tired. Can we find a house and bunker down for the night?"

Before Teddy has a chance to answer, I stop short. Something catches my eye on the sidewalk in front of the house. I bend down to look at it and feel as though the wind has been knocked out of me.

"What is it?" Teddy asks.

I pick it up from the sidewalk and show it to him.

"It's Elizabeth's hair ribbon, the one she was holding when the bad men took her."

13

"So what does that mean?" Teddy asks.

I hold the ribbon up to catch the gentle rays of the moonlight. The gold gossamer threads glow like firelight. I remember Elizabeth holding it in her hand as she darted away from me, directly into the path of the bad men. If she had dropped it on the lawn when they caught her, I would have found it later. It's very possible that she held onto it long after they kidnapped her. "I'm not sure."

I really want to get excited about it, but something holds me back.

"Are you sure it's hers?"

Take another look at it. "Yes. I'm positive." It's exactly like the one she had.

"So...if it's out here on the sidewalk, doesn't that mean that she's alive?"

I tighten my lips before speaking. "Maybe. I'm just afraid to get too excited in case it's nothing."

Teddy bumps my arm. "Oh, come on Ember. It's good news. Just smile and be happy about it." He takes the ribbon from my hand and studies it as though it has all the answers written within the threads. "This is crazy. Everything burnt up in the fire except for this one ribbon? She probably dropped it so you'd find it and know she's still alive."

His story is alluring. I want to believe it with all my heart. I only wish there were twenty more ribbons she could have dropped like bread crumbs.

"You really think so?"

"Yup. I do. How else would it have ended up here?" He points to the ground where we found it, and I find myself studying the sidewalk. Debris and hunks of blackened mounds cover the length of it. If the ribbon had been here before, it would have burned up. He might be right.

As we stand there, a shot rings out down the block and is followed by the sound of man shouting. It is enough to prompt me off the sidewalk and into the shadows.

"We should get moving. I feel too out in the open here." I tuck the ribbon in my pocket and start down the sidewalk. "So where can we sleep?" I eyeball the row of pretty Victorian houses in front of us. "Can't we just pick a house and be done with it?"

Teddy shakes his head. "It's too dangerous. They're up, buzzing around the streets as soon as the sun comes up. We'd be trapped inside the house until dark." He pauses and regards me for a moment, as though he is sizing me up.

"What?" I ask.

He shrugs, looking ten years older after all we've experienced. "I know a place. I'm just not sure how you're going to feel about it."

"I don't care. Just get me out of the city." I tug the strap on my backpack, which seems ten pounds heavier than it was before, and feel the muscles in my neck scream. I am so tired. I don't care where we go as long as it feels relatively safe. I want to get out of the city. We keep walking, and the more I think about the ribbon, the more it feels like it might mean something.

A heaviness settles around us as we put several blocks behind us. The events of the night are more than I've ever handled in my entire life, and I'm not sure how to keep going, how to keep putting one foot in front of the other. I'm not even sure I want to, but what other options do I have?

As the smell of death and soot eases and the normal smells of summer take their place, I find myself relaxing bit by bit until I can walk more than a few steps without glancing over my shoulder. At the end of the next block, Teddy stops.

"Ember?" he says, and waits for me to acknowledge him. "Can I ask you something?"

I glance at him, noticing the way he is still studying the ground at his feet, keeping his eyes deliberately off the horizon line, where a rosy glow tints the sky. "Yeah, sure. What?"

"Do you think of me as your friend?"

It is a strange question, coming after everything we've just lived through. My first inclination is to cuff him on the side of the head and start walking again, but then I see the look on his face. He gazes up at me with longing in his eyes, I can't be anything but sorry for him. "I think we're getting there, Teddy. We just need to stick together and have each other's backs, no matter what."

He seems pacified by my answer, and we walk the remainder of the block until he follows up on my words.

"If we have each other's backs, that means that we need to tell each other everything, right?"

I don't know what he means by *everything*. I'm certainly not going to share my innermost feelings with a fourteen-year-old. "What do you mean?"

"I want to know about Elizabeth and the lightning."

I stop short, shocked by the question. "How do you know about that?" As I say the words, the realization comes to me. Our mothers were friends and often shared details of each other's lives. It would make perfect sense for my mother to tell his mother about Elizabeth. He confirms it quickly.

104

"I heard our mothers talking about it. What does it mean, though? What can she do with it? Can she make it come down from the sky?"

"I don't know, Teddy. The two times I saw it, she just seemed to be there when it happened. I don't know if she made the lightning come or if it was just drawn to her."

"Why wasn't she killed by it?"

"I don't know. Nobody knows," I say. "Honestly, nobody even talked about it, but I know it happened. I saw it with my own eyes."

"So, what do you think happened back there? At the Cooper House?"

I think about the burnt timbers, the framework of the stone chimney poking through the mess, exposed to daylight for the very first time in its hundred-year history. I don't know what to think. If she had been able to call the lightning, then she might be alive. The ribbon gives me a glimmer of optimism. "I really don't know, Teddy. I guess we just have to hope for the best."

"Yeah, I guess so," he says.

We come to the edge of town, where the American Legion building stands at the end of the ball field, where children played little league for decades. Teddy shines his flashlight on the buildings in front of us. A long swipe of blood mars the white-sided concession stand, but there is no body to accompany it.

"Oh man," Teddy says, trailing the beam down to the ground. I wonder what happened to the body, but I don't linger on the thought.

We both shiver as we slip past it, keeping closer to the brick concession stand that sits beside it. Even with the flashlight, the space feels darker than pitch, and I hold my breath as we tiptoe through, hoping against hope that a door won't open and a madman won't pop out. Every dark space is an evil unknown, a place where we could wind up taking our last breath. As we come around the back side of the wall, we finally smell the body. Before I can stop him, Teddy shines his light around the corner, and we are treated to the sight of another armless person. This one is a dark-haired man. His clothing is shredded, and he appears to also be missing part of his leg.

"Dear God," I gasp. I grab Teddy's arm and pull him to the edge of the ball field.

We don't even talk about it, the image is so gruesome, but the thought rings through my mind like a metal ball on a pie pan. If the cannibal catches us, this is what will happen to us as well.

We pause at the edge of the ball field. Teddy turns off the flashlight and points to the cornfield that lines the park. "That's where we need to go."

I just nod, not having the emotional energy to do anything else.

Crickets and cicadas chirp and warble in the distance, as though everything is exactly the same as it was before. The air smells dusty and dry, tickling my nose, making me want to sneeze. I pinch my nose with my fingers to ward it off. The corn stalks rustle in the faint breeze, making a sound that is familiar but disconcerting. It could be the sound of the wind rustling through the dry stalks, but it could also be the sound of someone parting the rows.

We cross the space quickly but pause at the edge, where the stalks meet the grass.

Cornfields can be the best place to hide and also the worst. There is no way to walk through them without generating a

106

great deal of noise, which works for us but also against us. If there is anyone else in the field, we'll be able to hear them, but unfortunately, they'll also be able to hear us. I listen for several seconds until I'm confident that the noise we're hearing is just the wind.

"Okay, let's go in," I say, and he pauses, waiting for me to go first. "Come on, Teddy. I don't even know where we're going. You're going to have to lead the way this time."

I hear him sigh beside me as he steps in front of me. He passes through the opening between the rows and disappears almost immediately, swallowed by the stalks. I can hear him in front of me, the stalks making whispery sounds as he passes through each row. I close the gap and slip in behind him so we aren't making twice the noise.

When I was younger, the cornfields were a mysterious, delicious place to play. Annie and I would create rooms deep in the fields, where we would hide from the world and share our stories until we grew bored or hungry. If the farmer caught us, he would chase us out, yelling about the price of corn and how much we probably cost him by flattening six or seven stalks, but we didn't care. Almost getting caught was half the fun of hiding in the cornfield.

The corn ears have gotten hard sitting in the summer sun for so long. I pull several ears from the stalks and shove them into my jacket pockets anyways. If I can find some water, I might be able to grind them down to cornmeal and make Johnny cakes over a fire. It would be better than eating nothing, and my stomach is already grumbling, having thrown up the candy bar back in front of the library.

Teddy leads me through the field on a path he seems to know by heart. He doesn't slow down until we've reached the other side. The moon slips out from behind a cover of clouds and shines down on the landscape, blue and murky. Ahead of me, tombstones glisten in neat rows, looking like misplaced teeth jutting from the hard, cold soil. My heartbeat begins to quicken.

"Where are we going?" I ask.

He takes a deep breath and points to the dark end of the cemetery, to the one place I really, really don't want to go.

"To the mausoleum."

My legs tremble beneath me.

14

In our old world, a double dog dare was something you slung at someone when you wanted to watch them make a fool of themself. Turning down a double dog dare was the equivalent of walking around with "I'm a skuzzy pecker head" written on your forehead. It was something you just wouldn't do.

There were rules to the double dog dare, though, and boundaries you would never cross, even for the sake of a really awesome dare. You would never hurt someone on purpose. You would never do something that could land you in jail, and last but not least, you would never, ever dare someone to go into the mausoleum.

Some of the kids said that you could risk your life by even talking about it. You could draw the spirits in closer just by speaking their names. Other kids said that on warm summer nights, you could see the ghost wandering around the cemetery. The stories surrounding it were boundless.

I once spent an entire Sunday afternoon in the reading room of the library absorbing everything I could find on it. The mausoleum was built in the late eighteen hundreds by a wealthy businessman for his family. I can't remember his name, but I remember his essence. He was one of those guys who always needed to be the best and have the most. I am pretty sure he had been the first owner of the Cooper House.

When he died, he made sure that his body was laid to rest in a mausoleum. Being buried under the ground with all the other town schmucks wasn't something he was entirely comfortable with.

The only problem with his death fortress was the lack of security. Unlike six feet of earth, which is very difficult to move, locks can be picked and doors can be opened, which is exactly what happened. Having spent a lifetime flaunting his wealth, he was an easy target for looters in death. Within months of his burial, his tomb was invaded; his body was stripped of all its clothing and was unceremoniously dumped naked onto the floor. Sometime later, his coffin disappeared mysteriously. It was probably just kids playing pranks, but the thought was unnerving all the same.

His wife and all his survivors refused to be treated to the same burial and were buried nearby in traditional graves, complete with grave stones and six feet of nice hard soil separating them from the living world. No one is sure what eventually happened to the man's body. There isn't a grave stone for him beside his wife, and the mausoleum is empty, as far as I know. His spirit is said to roam the cemetery, looking for the looters. Everything else we've seen and experienced pales in comparison.

"You're kidding, right?" I ask.

He shrugs. "Can you think of a safer place?"

My shoulders pinch upwards in an involuntary heebie-jeebies shudder. "I don't know, Teddy." It is the creepiest place on the face of the planet. It doesn't get any worse than this.

He is quick to comfort me. "I've been there. It doesn't have any windows, so we can have our light on all night if we want to, and there is a door that locks from the inside."

"It locks from the inside?" I ask, and he nods.

"That is by far the most disturbing thing I've ever heard. Why would they do something like that?"

"I dunno?" Teddy answers as though I am actually asking for an answer.

I consider this for a moment, truly entertaining the idea of spending the night inside a stone grave where the ghost of a very angry man has been known to frequent. Then I think about the men with the black masks, the corpses with their missing appendages, and the cannibal pulling at my leg, and I remember another phrase my mother often used.

"Better the devil you know than the devil you don't know."

Teddy narrows his eyes at that.

"Don't ask. It made sense in my head."

Teddy shrugs and smiles. "It's not the stupidest thing you've ever said," he offers, and I smack his arm, lightly, just like old times. The moment serves to lighten the mood a little, which is something we both desperately need. If we are going to survive, we have to find some way to get past all the horrors that we witness.

I ruffle his hair and then catch him smiling to himself out of the corner of my eye. It is the smile a boy gets after a girl bats her eyes at him. It is the smile of anticipation. I have to wonder if he is hoping for something even more between us. In his eyes, we're nearly the same age, but in my eyes the gap is as large as a canyon. I think back to all those times when I hung out at their house, and I don't know how I could have missed it. He's probably been crushing on me for years. I make a mental note to be more careful with him. The last thing I want to do is give him false hopes.

We trudge through the cemetery, walking in single file through the long grass, being careful not to step on any graves. I can feel almost feel Desmond trotting along beside me, tail wagging and tongue lolling. I glance down, half expecting to actually see him, the vision is so complete, but all I see is the darkness.

"You know this place is supposed to be haunted," I say.

He doesn't answer me, pretending to be preoccupied with looking where he is stepping.

111

"The crazy old man who was buried there is supposed to roam around the cemetery looking for his body. Thieves broke in and stole it, you know," I add.

Teddy's spine straightens again, but he still doesn't comment.

"They say on especially dark nights, when the moon is hiding behind the clouds, you can see him actually standing beside the mausoleum."

Teddy swivels around, his face an angry mask. "Stop it, all right! I get it. This place is haunted. Who gives a crap?" He turns back around and starts walking again, his head tucked down. "I'd rather deal with ghosts than cannibals and terrorists anyways. At least ghosts don't try to eat you," he mumbles under his breath.

We reach the stone building and pause to absorb what we're seeing. It is about the size of a small bathroom, with tall stone walls covered with moss and streaked with black sooty lines. The name Walsh is emblazoned above the doorway.

"How are we getting in?"

"Just watch." Teddy kneels down in front of the door, the flashlight clamped between his teeth. He pulls an old skeleton key from his pocket and kneels down to jimmy it into the lock.

"Where in the world did you get that?"

Teddy pulls the flashlight from his mouth and hands it to me to hold. It is dripping with boy-saliva. I wipe it on the leg of my jeans with disgust.

"It's just an old key my mother had. She used to collect them. They're antiques or something." The lock makes a click, and Teddy jiggles the handle.

"How did you know it would work here?"

He shrugs. "I dunno. I just grabbed a handful of them and tried them, one by one, until one of them opened the door." As he says this, he turns the door knob again and it opens. "Voila!"

I clap for him, because it seems appropriate, and he takes a small bow.

"Thank you, thank you very much," he says with his very best Elvis imitation. I roll my eyes and then look past him at the gaping black maw that is the open doorway.

I shine the light into the dark hole that will be our home tonight. I think about the last person who spent the night here, and I shiver deep inside, where it counts the most. I have done a lot of foolish things in my life, and I've done some brave things too, but I've never done something that encompasses both so fully and so completely.

"Okay, let's get inside before someone sees us out here." I try to usher him in ahead of me, but he dodges my arm.

"No way, Jose. Ladies first."

"Youth before beauty," I counter, but he crosses his arms over his chest and doesn't budge. "Double dog dare?" I try, but he doesn't flinch.

"Like, who are you gonna tell?"

He has a point. A double-dog dare only works if you can tell all their friends what a chicken shit they were.

I sigh and push past him. "All right. I guess I'll have to be the brave one." I step through the doorway, but Teddy doesn't follow me. "At least follow me, okay?"

"I'm just giving it a minute."

I shine the light directly into his eyes and enjoy watching him flinch. "Why?"

"To see if anything gets you. Cause if it does, I'm running."

"Oh for crying out loud." I walk back to the doorway and grab him by the front of his shirt and haul him into the tomb behind me. If I'm going to die a horrible, terrifying death, at least I'm not going to do it alone. "This was your idea, by the way."

"I know. But that doesn't mean I have to like it, does it?"

He pulls the door closed behind us, leaving his question unanswered. There is something deep and meaningful behind his words. I don't want to spend too much time thinking about it. There's nothing about this new life that I like. Not one damn thing.

"So where's that lock you were telling me about?" I ask as I shine the light on the door. Teddy points to a brass knob just below the doorknob. I am stunned that a mausoleum would even have a doorknob on the inside, not to mention a lock. The thought is appropriately disturbing. Typically, once you go in, you never need to come back out again.

Teddy turns the knob and the lock engages with a heavy thud, locking us in for the night. There is something about the heavy sound of the lock engaging that comforts me, even though it probably shouldn't. I turn and shine the light around the small room.

"So let's check out this place." I sweep the light across all four walls, taking in the elaborate stone work and the ornate detail that went into something no one should ever see more than once. There are two oversized stone benches along opposite walls, anchored by pillars that must have taken months to carve. Doves and ivy are etched into the walls above the benches, making the room look more like a gothic sitting room than a burial chamber.

Teddy walks over with a proprietary air about him, as though he's going to give me a tour of his new find, and sits on one of the benches. "We can sleep on these."

"I think that's where the coffins are supposed to sit." I tell him, and he jumps up as though he's been goosed. He stares at the bench for a long moment, his face scrunched up in a scowl.

"Where did his coffin go?"

"I don't know. His grave was robbed not too long after he was buried, so somebody must have taken it. Hopefully, he doesn't visit us tonight looking for it," I add, just to make Teddy squirm.

"Which one did his coffin sit on?"

I don't know, but if human logic holds true, he would have probably have been placed on the right-hand side, with the spot on the left being reserved for his wife, who never utilized her space.

"Probably the left," I tell him in all sincerity, while simultaneously lying through my teeth.

He walks over to the right-hand bench and plops his backpack down as though he is selecting a bunk at summer camp. "Then this one is mine."

"Sounds good to me," I manage to say without smiling. I walk to the left-hand bench and sit down, not feeling one bit guilty for the lie. The stone is cold beneath my thighs, like a block of solid ice. I wonder if I will warm it up or if it will cool me down.

The design obviously had very little to do with the living. Dead people don't need warmth, so none had been provided. I am just happy they didn't installed stained glass windows, like some of the tombs I'd seen. The sanctity of four solid walls will allow us to keep a light on if we need it.

"Do you have your lantern?" I ask.

Teddy fishes around in his backpack, and for one terrorizing moment I'm afraid he is going to come back out empty-handed, but he smiles and pulls it from the pack.

"Yup."

"Then turn it on. I want to save the flashlight batteries in case we need them later," I say, trying not to imagine any of the reasons why we might need a flashlight inside a mortuary. "Do you have any more batteries?"

Teddy turns on the lamp, and the warm yellow light fills the room, almost like sunshine. He fishes around in his pack for a moment and pulls out two fat batteries.

"Just these. I found them in my mom's kitchen."

We were definitely going to need more batteries. "Have you looked inside any of the houses for more?"

Teddy makes the scrunched up face again. "I tried to go in once, but there were dead people inside. I got inside the door, and I smelled them." He looks down at his feet, telling me the rest of the story without needing to tell me. I'm not certain I could have gone inside either, at least not at first. Now it was becoming a necessity. I wonder if dead bodies eventually stop smelling bad.

My back aches from the heavy backpack. I unsnap the strap and let it slide from my shoulders, and the relief is immense. I roll my shoulders for a moment and then pop my neck. I drop the pack onto the bench, thinking that I will use it as a pillow later, if I can manage to sleep. My stomach grumbles again, and I eye Teddy's pack.

"Got anything else to eat in there?"

"Maybe, but shouldn't we be rationing our food?"

"Maybe, but I'm hungry now. We'll find more food tomorrow. We'll go and check out some of the houses and see if we can find anything," I tell him.

He continues to stare at me, probably wondering if I'm going to go inside the houses or if I'm going to try to force him to do it.

116

"We'll both go into a few houses. I'm sure there's lots of food. We'll empty our backpacks and bring back as much food as we can carry." I look around at our stone fortress. "We should be safe here as long as no one sees us coming or going. We'll just have to be careful."

Teddy pulls a granola bar from his bag and silently hands me half. I could have eaten the tiny morsel in one mouthful, but I stretch it out to three bites just to make it seem like more. My stomach grumbles at the prospect of food, but I have to tamp it down with a long swig of water from my bottle. I pass the bottle to Teddy, who begins to chug it.

"Hey there buddy. Take it easy with the water. Just think about it: if you have to go to the bathroom, you have to go outside into the cemetery to pee," I remind him. His eyes widen, and he hands me back the bottle.

"I wonder where they brought Elizabeth after the Cooper House burnt down," Teddy muses. I've had the same thought. I can't understand why they'd move away from such great digs, unless they had no choice. If Elizabeth burnt the house down with lightning, then they would have had to move. It also brings up an even bigger concern. If they saw her burn the building down, then they know about her capabilities. That would make her a valuable commodity. I can't even wrap my mind around it, it's so huge.

"I don't know. We'll have to give it some thought in the morning. I'm too tired to think right now."

"Me too." Teddy yawns and I soon finding myself following suit, having caught the yawn. I have the strange desire to know what time it is. A part of me still clings to the threads of humanity. Knowing the time of day has been one of the hardest things to relinquish. Time really has no meaning any more. You wake up when the sun comes out and you go to sleep when it gets dark, unless you have candles or a strong sense of bravery. I place my backpack on the stone bench and then lay down, using the backpack as a pillow.

"What do you think about all of this, Ember?" Teddy asks, and I turn to look at him. He has followed my lead and is laying on the stone bench with his head on his backpack. He is still barefooted and this bothers me again. All he will have to do is step on one rusty nail and it will be all over with. I make a mental note to find him some shoes tomorrow, even if I have to pull them off of a dead body.

"About what?"

"About everything," he says, his voice small and emotional. "How are we going to live with the terrorists always buzzing around and the cannibal trying to eat us? Where are we going to live? How are we going to get more food?" He pauses for a moment as if trying to find the courage to continue. "And Elizabeth. I know we need to find her, but how are we going to be able to rescue her when it's just me and you? What are we going to do?"

I take a deep breath and let it out with a sigh. He turns to look at me and we watch one another for a long moment. "I don't know. We'll have to work out a plan. Several plans."

The truth is, I have considered what we are going to do and I haven't come up with any easy answers. There is just so much we don't know. We don't know how widespread it is, how many of the bad men are actually around. Have they set up a temporary government? And do they have compounds in every town in the country? Our town was a natural choice because of the chemical plant, but how do we know where else they are? Are they in every state of the country? What about the rest of the world? I'd been taught that every culture had good people

118

and bad people and that good usually won out against evil. I never considered this. Not in a million years.

"How many of them are there, do you know?" I ask.

"I don't know. I just saw the news before it went out and they said they were in all the big cities. The reporter had blood dripping down her face," he adds and I nod. He must have seen the same news broadcast that I did.

"I saw that too. Then the station went dead and I didn't hear anything. I even tried the radio, but all I got was static."

I think about this for a minute. If the bad men and the cannibals are all over the world, then there wasn't much two kids could do about it. This life will always be about running and hiding. I don't know if I can handle a lifetime of that. The thought sends me spiraling downward.

I roll onto my side as the thoughts churn in my head. The stone is cold and unforgiving on my shoulder and hip bone. I see Elizabeth's face float into my mind and I close my eyes around it, feeling the guilt consume me whole. I should have fought harder for her. I should have at least tried.

Teddy shifts and sits Indian style. "You know what I'd like to do?" he asks, his face suddenly animated.

"What?"

"I'd like to find a way to steal their gas masks. Let them see how it feels to get sick and die."

His words are potent and I consider them, suddenly intrigued. "You know, that's a thought. A real substantial thought." I sit up too and swing my legs over the side.

"Substantial? What do you mean by that?" Teddy asks.

The ideas are coming to me in piggy-backs. "Well, just think about it. Some of them would be immune to the virus, just like us. But a lot of them would die if they got it, so they have to have the gas masks on all the time. All the time, Teddy," I say, punctuating the words to make sure he understands what I'm trying to tell him.

"So what do they do when they sleep?"

"Exactly." I smile. "They would probably need to take them off when they sleep. That is when they are the most vulnerable."

I imagine us sneaking into the compounds, stealing the gas masks and leaving them unprotected. But if we were going to take that risk, why not just mow them down with a hailstorm of bullets, like they did to our survivors? Why just take the passive route? As this question enters my mind, I wonder if I am capable of killing someone, if I could truly take another person's life.

"So, we could break in and steal their gas masks," Teddy says, growing more enthusiastic by the moment. I hate to deflate him, but reality is reality.

"It would never work. They'll have guards set up and men with guns. We'll have to get a gun of our own and maybe end up shooting people, or even worse, getting shot. We'll have to think of something else."

"Yeah, we could put something into their water or throw bombs through their windows." He sits up a little taller, his eyes wide with excitement. "What if we found a really sick, gross dead body and we threw it into the window?"

I roll my eyes. This is the problem with fourteen-year-olds. They still believe in comic books and cartoons. "No, we'll have to think of something else. That wouldn't work."

"Why not? Just imagine it, Ember. They probably take their gas masks off when they sleep. Imagine the looks on their faces when they woke up and there's this really gross, disgusting dead guy sitting there in the room with them."

120

"Who's going to carry the really gross dead guy into the room? I assure you, it isn't going to be me."

Some of the enthusiasm leaches from his expression.

"Maybe we could get a cart and pull him there."

"Teddy...honestly." I sigh. "Think about what you are saying. How in the world would we get a dead body onto a cart and then pull it past a guard with a gun, then pull it into a room full of sleeping men, and then get out again without being shot? It just wouldn't work. And besides, unless we also steal all their gas masks first, they'd just put them on and they'd be all set."

Teddy unfolds his legs and dangles them off the side of the stone bench. "Oh yeah." His voice is small again and I almost feel bad for stealing away some of his hope.

"Don't worry. There has to be something else we haven't thought about yet, but we'll find it. There has to be something." I watch him for a moment and he looks up and meets my eyes for a second before looking back down.

"Okay."

Another yawn finds me and carries me through the wake, like a wave in the ocean. "I'm tired, Teddy. We should probably get some sleep.

"Why don't you kill the lantern? We should be safe in here."

"I wish you wouldn't say that," Teddy says.

I pull my jacket around me like a blanket. "Say what?"

"Kill the lantern. I think there's been enough death around here to last us a gazillion years."

"Okay," I say and then close my eyes around the word *kill*.

Death has become more than just a word or something I will think about when I'm old and grey. Avoiding death has become a big part of my everyday existence, as common as brushing my teeth or eating breakfast. I linger on the word,

121

seeing it emblazoned on my eyelids until it spins around and around like a pinwheel. I reach into my pocket and finger the ribbon one more time before I close my eyes, allowing it to lift my spirits.

Sleep must have found me swiftly and fully, because this is the last thing I remember thinking before my dream world took over and began telling me stories about dead people. They were climbing over one another, like zombies in a horror flick, trying to get to me to eat my juicy flesh. Then, there were ghosts, drifting in and out of the cemetery, and madmen staring around corners.

One of them passes through the doorway and stands over me.

I open my eyes, ready to run for my life, and then I scream as I realize it is not a dream.

Someone is standing in front of me.

15

I jump to my feet with such force I knock the backpack off the bench. I find the ears of corn in my pocket and I smash them together in front of me. One of them makes contact with something hard and tangible, and the other swishes through the still air. I pull my arms back and swing again, and I see the person flee through the open doorway.

I blink and then blink again. Am I awake?

The door to the mausoleum is open. Moonlight pours through the opening, painting a silver rectangle on the floor in front of me. I watch it for a long moment, too terrified to move.

Teddy sits bolt upright.

"What's the matter?"

I cannot find my voice. I point one of the corn ears towards the doorway, my hand shaking.

The room is in shadows, the corners full of mind-numbing possibilities. Teddy flicks on the lantern and the shadows disappear, showing us nothing more than the empty room.

I spring from my bench and pull the door shut, knowing the light from the lantern must make our hiding place look like a lighthouse in the middle of the cemetery. I only hope it isn't too late, that someone hasn't seen us. My instinct tells me to run away, but I'm equally afraid of what is lingering outside. I twist the lock and then lean against the door, my heart pounding.

"What happened?" Teddy asks again.

"I'm not sure. I was dreaming about zombies and ghosts. When I woke up, someone was standing over me." I glance at the closed door and feel my blood run cold. "How would someone get in here? How could they have another key?"

Teddy looks down at the ground. "I didn't tell you everything."

"Everything about *what*?"

He glances back up for a second, his expression fleeting and fearful. "It might have not been a ghost. It might have been a real live person. When I first found the mausoleum, the door was already open." He pauses to let this information linger singularly before adding more words to the pile.

"What?" I nearly leap from my seat to throttle him.

"I don't think anyone else has a key, but they might be able to pick the lock," he says.

I lean down in front of the lock and inspect it. It is a fairly simple lock. Anyone with any skills in lock picking could probably get in easily. I think of Mr. McFarley. He always had a ring of keys hanging off his belt loop. If he was able to use one of them on the lock, he could get in anytime he wanted. My mind races with the implications. What if he comes back for more?

Teddy looks at me sheepishly, which he rightfully should. If he'd told me everything, I would have insisted we went somewhere else. We were lucky we hadn't been fricasseed already.

"I did go back to my house and get some of my mother's keys. That part is true," he says, watching my expression.

"And one of them worked," I say, repeating what I already knew. "So who opened the door?"

"I don't know. Every time I've been in the cemetery it's been closed. It was just open that one time."

I take a deep breath and let it out. "So either someone else has figured out how to pick that lock or there is a ghost who knows how to get inside." I realize I am still holding the corn ears. I set them down on the stone bench on either side of me, my fingers trembling. One of them rolls and then tumbles onto the floor with a thunk. I close my eyes and wish again that I could be back in my hidey-hole in my mother's kitchen with

Elizabeth, worrying about nothing more than canning
vegetables. There just isn't a safe place to hide. Even this place,
as despicable as it is, is not safe.

"What did he look like?"

"I don't know. It was dark. All I could see was his shape."

"Could you see through him?" Teddy asks.

I think about this for a moment. "No. He blocked the
moonlight." He was nothing more than a shadow across the
doorway, but he was solid. If he were a ghost, I would have
probably been able to have seen right through him.

"So it was a man and not a ghost?"

"Yeah, I think so." I swallow hard. "I hope so." And it
probably wasn't the cannibal either. If it were the cannibal, he
would have lunged on me instead of just standing there staring
at me. Either way, we needed to move on.

I sigh again, considering our new nomad existence. We'll
never be able to call anywhere home again. We'll have to
always keep moving, spending a night here and a night there.
We'll get comfortable somewhere, only to have to abandon it
later, always looking over our shoulders for trouble. The whole
thing almost seems pointless; the odds are stacked firmly
against us. It's just the two of us against a whole world full of
scary, freakish unknowns, of people who want to kill us and
others who might possibly want to eat us. I just want to curl into
ball until it all goes away.

Hot tears fill my eyes and I cover my face with my hands. I
hear the shifting of feet on concrete and then feel Teddy slide
beside me on the bench. He sits there for a moment and then
wraps his arm around me. The gesture is awkward, but sweet. I
pull my hands from my face and give him a weak smile.

"It's going to be okay, Ember. We'll find a safe place."

"Yeah, but what is safe? I thought this place was safe."

"I have another place near the train trestle. It's a shack back in the woods. Nobody ever goes there. We'll be okay." He pats my arm and I have to smile at his efforts. I remember another one of my mother's quotes.

"God only gives you as much as he thinks you can handle," I say.

"Yup, and he never closes a door without opening a window either," he says, and we both sigh. Thankfully we do not have a window to open. We sit silently for a moment.

I imagine us becoming a family of sorts, sticking together and looking out for one another like adoptive siblings. The hopeless feelings I'd had start to grow golden around the edges, turning into something warmer. If Annie were alive, she wouldn't believe I was capable of even entertaining such an idea. We spent hours planning ways to get even with her little brother.

A memory comes to me and I smile inside. Teddy was always such a good hider. On rainy Sunday afternoons, we'd spend them playing board games and also hide and seek, when we could get Teddy to play with us. He would always be the last one found. Always. It didn't matter where we played or who we played with. We could be playing in my very own house, which I thought I knew inside and out, and Teddy would climb into a laundry hamper or find a way to get behind the washing machine, and we'd be forced to ask him to please come out. He'd always have a smug grin on his face, knowing he was better at it than we were. All in all, although I would have rather had Annie as a companion, Teddy was probably my better option.

"So what's the plan?" Teddy asks.

"Let's wait until the sun comes up and then head down to the trestle. We can get some rest there and then head back into town and look for Elizabeth."

Teddy walks back to his bench and sits down, legs dangling. "You can sleep first. I'll keep watch," he offers.

"Thanks for the offer, but I don't think I'll be able to sleep."

"So, what do we do?" Teddy asks.

Before I can even open my mouth to speak, there is a very distinctive sound outside the mausoleum. Our intruder is back.

16

"Did you hear that?" Teddy whispers and I press my finger to my lips, hushing him. I motion for him to turn off the light. We have no way of knowing if the light is shining through any cracks or not. For all we know, there are holes all over the building, illuminating the entire area. I mentally kick myself for not checking it. I've made so many mistakes, it's a miracle I am still alive.

Teddy gets up and cuts the light. The room is instantly immersed in pitch blackness. I wave my hand in front of my face, but cannot see the movement. Fear creeps over me like a cold hand up my back and I close my eyes, trying to find the strength to push it away. I know what is in this tomb. I've seen every wall, every cobweb, and every bit of moss clinging to the concrete. There is nothing in here that can hurt me. Unless it's something that cannot be seen, my mind reminds me. My heart pounds a little harder and I stare wide-eyed into the blackness.

I can imagine clawed fingers flicking in front of my face, teeth gnashing beside my ear.

I hear a scraping sound across from me and then feel Teddy sit down next to me. I'm not sure if he knows about my fear of the darkness or if he is simply reacting to this newest level of terror, but I am thankful none the less. I find his hand beside mine and I squeeze it.

We sit in the silence and listen for sounds. I hear my heart pounding in my ears along with the steady inhale and exhale of Teddy breathing. Beyond that, the world is very quiet. It's too quiet. The crickets should be chirping, the cicadas should be singing, the night should be alive with sounds. Someone is out there.

I hear the noise again. It is the scuff of a shoe on concrete, the sound someone makes when they stop short. I imagine the cannibal lurking outside, smiling his evil smile, his weasel teeth pressed tightly together.

Come here little girl.

I want to show you my pet worm.

And then I think of the men in the black masks, walking through my house.

The thoughts swirl in my mind, pressing tightly against my sanity, pinching my frail sense of self, smashing against my courage like a log against a closed door. I wish I had a knife.

Could I do it?

Could I plunge my knife into someone's chest instead of allowing him to plunge his knife into mine? Could I actually kill someone? Teddy squeezes my hand and the answer comes to me very suddenly.

Yes, I think I could.

I press my mouth against Teddy's ear. "Be very quiet, but go get your knife and your flashlight. Okay?"

He squeezes my hand again in response and then slides away. I hear him rummaging through his backpack and then he returns to my side again. We sit there in the darkness for long minutes, listening to the sounds of the night gradually return. The crickets return first, followed by the cicadas.

"I think he's gone," I whisper.

"Then why are you whispering?"

I smack him because it seems to be the right thing to do. "Because, I'm not willing to bet my life on it, you idiot."

"That hurts," Teddy says in his best pretending-to-be-hurt voice. I smile in the darkness and am thankful for his company. There are a few moments when he is actually worth the amount of air he takes away from the rest of humanity and this is one of them. I am glad he is with me.

"So, what are we gonna do now?" he asks.

"I don't know." If we stay here, we'll be sitting ducks for the monster outside to return and pluck us from our stone soup bowl. But, if we leave, we are sitting ducks for anything else outside that wants to kill and eat us. There is no easy answer. "I think we'll be okay inside here for a while."

He begins to answer me, but is cut short by a loud thud. It is followed by an agonizing scream.

Teddy tightens up against me.

"What is that?" he whispers.

My hands begin to tremble and I press my eyes shut.

"I don't know."

The sound goes on for an eternity. The man screams and the sound is followed by another hollow thud. I imagine someone striking someone else with a club and then standing over him to watch him bleed.

"Noooooo…..don't!" the man's voice echoes.

There is another thunk and then the man is silent. I imagine him lying in the cool grass between two gravestones, staring up at the blanket of stars above while his life slips away from him. I want to do something so badly it rumbles inside of me like a live being trying desperately to escape, but I am also afraid. I did nothing to save Elizabeth when they came for her. Should I do something now for this man?

What could I possibly do?

I imagine slipping from the stone building, using only the moonlight to navigate, tip-toeing around each of the graves. They will glow like stubs of chalk in the moonlight and I will find more solace in the dark shadows between them than I will in hiding behind them. They will feel too bright, too noticeable in the darkness and I will avoid them. I will come upon the body of the man by accident, nearly falling over him because he will be closer than I thought he'd be. I'll catch my breath, holding my hand over my heart and I'll stand there and watch him for a moment, waiting for the rise and fall of his chest. After a few minutes, I might find myself brave enough to touch his wrist or the side of his neck to see if his heart still beats and after I don't find any signs of life, I might reach into his back pocket to look for a driver's license to see who he was, if he still carried a wallet.

"You think we should go out there and see if he's alive?" Teddy asks, mirroring my own thoughts. In our old world, it would have been the right thing to do, but now it is something else altogether. Right and wrong have somehow turned upside down and inside out. What used to be right could now be very wrong.

"I think we should just stay here. I don't think we could do anything anyways."

"I took first aid in the Cub Scouts," Teddy says, and I have a clear memory of him, standing in his mother's kitchen, wearing his navy blue uniform shirt.

"What did they teach you in first aid?"

"Umm...CPR, wound care, what to do if somebody's having seizures..." I imagine him ticking them off on his fingers as he thinks of them, his voice getting louder with every topic. "Splinting broken limbs, what to do if somebody gets bitten by a poisonous snake..."

"That's good. I get it," I say, cutting him off before his voice gets any louder. "That would be very helpful if one of us falls and breaks an arm or gets stung by a bee, but that man sounds like he needs an emergency room and I don't think there are any of those around here." The thought makes me appropriately anxious. It is one more thing that we used to take for granted but no longer have. It brings up so many what-if scenarios my head nearly spins. We will just have to be careful, that's all.

"Ember, what happens if one of us needs an emergency room?" he asks, as though reading my mind.

"Hopefully we won't. We'll just be careful and not take any crazy chances. Okay?" I say and feel beside me for his hand. I squeeze it, but he doesn't squeeze back. He is probably reliving every visit he's ever had to the emergency room and comparing them to the words I've just presented him with. Not too many emergencies could have been prevented by being careful. Things just happened sometimes.

"We'll be okay." I squeeze his hand again. "Besides, worrying about it isn't going to make it any better, right?"

He takes a deep breath and lets it out with a whoosh. "Yeah, I guess. It just sucks."

I nearly laugh, the nervousness trying to burble out of me. "Yeah, it does. It definitely sucks." I let a few moments pass as I absorb his words and replay them in my mind. If I allowed myself, I could spend a lot of time thinking about all the things that were gone from my life. I'd start with my friends and my family, then I'd tack on the big things, like electricity and running water, and then I'd take a huge eraser and remove the bad men with the black masks and we'd return back to our old life, where we once took all the simple pleasures for granted.

I stretch, feeling the pins and needles assault my legs. Sitting here isn't going to do us any good. As much as I don't want to move, it is time for action.

17

There is another thudding sound outside in the cemetery and we both stiffen.

"What was that?" Teddy whispers and I shush him again.

The crickets and the cicadas have grown quiet once more, leaving a huge wash of silence behind. I strain to listen, hoping that I don't hear anything else. If it is the man who picked the lock, then we are in very bad shape. I scramble to find a plan and come up with nothing substantial. We'll just have fight our way out, using surprise as our main weapon. It's not a great plan, but it's all I have.

I press my mouth to Teddy's ear.

"I need your knife," I tell him and wait for him to press it into my hand. The handle is cold against my skin, but it feels good. "Get your backpack and go stand beside the door. If he tries to come in again, I'm going to attack him and then we're going to run. Wait for my cue. Okay?"

He doesn't ask what my cue is and I'm thankful because I'm not actually sure what my cue is going to be. I'm hoping it will just be obvious.

It is a simple plan, but one that might work. It would be difficult to find something more complicated in a stone room filled with nothing more than air. We don't have much to work with. The stone benches are too heavy to pick up and the only weapon we have is the hunting knife. The only real thing we have that might save us is our wits. I push this to the forefront of my mind. We have to at least try.

I feel Teddy move past me to the right side of the doorway. Since the door opens outwards, he will be in the best position to run past the man and hopefully escape. It occurs to me that I also haven't told him where to go. We should have designated a place to meet in case we are separated. I want to tell him, but I can hear the sound of steps just outside the mausoleum and I'm afraid to say them out loud. It would be better if the man thinks we are sleeping. Maybe then he won't be as careful.

Unless it's not a man, my mind reminds me, bringing me back to the nightmares of my childhood. I can almost see him turning into a liquid mist and then slipping under the door like an envelope, where he will swirl above us until he is ready to attack.

"God, give me strength," I whisper under my breath.

I grab my back pack and slip my arms through the straps. I move to the left-hand side of the door, clutching my knife tightly in my hand.

I try to calm myself down, to find some semblance of myself under all the fear and the trembling. I remember something my mother once told me about one person making a difference. I'm sure she didn't ever intend for me to use it in this manner, but it comforts me anyways.

"I am only one," I whisper to myself. I imagine the earth floating in the vast sea of stars and constellations. The universe is infinite, bigger than I could ever contemplate, broader than anything I've ever known. It is larger than a drop of water in all the world's oceans, larger than a snowflake in a blizzard. Out there, somewhere, worse things are happening...and better things too. In a million years, none of this will even be remembered. I close my eye eyes, trying to imagine it.

I am only one, but I am also everything. If I die, some things will remain the same. The grass will still continue to grow, the wind will still blow, and the universe will still churn and birth new planets, where new creatures will evolve and grow, love and hate, devour and diminish, until they are as whole as they want to be. But the one that I am could mean the difference between a world with people and a world without. I cannot be

134

careless. People like me are becoming very rare; in fact they are growing downright extinct.

There is another sound outside. It is raspy and whispering, like the sound of footsteps walking through the tall, dry grass. It grows closer and closer and then stops just feet away from us. I feel the person standing just outside the mausoleum, trying to decide which option would be the most satisfying. He could either burst in and take us quickly, or he could play with us for a while, building our terror up to epic proportions. I tighten my grip on the knife.

I wonder who it is. I don't think he is the cannibal. He is too quiet, too calculating in his movements. If he were the cannibal, he wouldn't bother to sneak up to the stone building. He would have announced himself with a glorious anthem, singing my name loudly, trying to make me crazy from the outside in. I remember his terrifying thunderous steps on the library stairs. He had made no effort to be quiet then, so it doesn't make any sense that he'd suddenly be worried about making noises here. Noise was one of his favorite weapons.

I strain to listen for more sounds.

If it's not the cannibal, then who is it?

The bad men? Probably not. The bad men make hissing sounds as they breathe through their gas masks. This person is breathing the air normally, not worried about catching a virus. He is more worried about being quiet. Could it be someone like us, looking for a way to survive? The thought is warm and calming, but I can't trust it to be true. What if it isn't a normal person? What if it is someone worse? I think about all the prisons and jails in the world and imagine them emptying out, like rats deserting a sinking ship. If the virus didn't kill all the normal people, then it surely didn't kill all of the nasty ones either. I consider all the drug dealers and ax murderers, rapists, and pedophiles roaming the countryside, looking for more than just food, shelter, and water. Stumbling across us, so frail and unprotected, would be a dream come true for them.

The more I think about it, the more I am convinced. This person cannot be a good person. I think about the sounds of the man screaming for his life, the man who might still be bleeding to death in between the gravestones and I shiver. This stalker could be the same person who killed the woman on the street and the man beside the ball field. He could have been the person who was following us earlier.

The knob jiggles and I nearly come unglued. I stifle the gasp that nearly hisses from my lips and grip the knife as tightly as I can. I feel Desmond beside me, tensing as he sniffs the air, trying to determine if the person is friend or foe. I nearly reach down to comfort him before I remember that I can't. I almost wish he were still alive. I picture him, bristling with anger, ready to lunge through the opening and rip into the intruder, possibly giving us a chance to escape. As I'm thinking this, he growls very loudly on the other side of me, a sound so viscous and threatening, it causes the hairs on the back of my neck to rise.

It takes me a moment to realize it isn't Desmond growling. It is Teddy.

I nearly laugh with relief and am forced to cross my legs tightly to prevent peeing myself.

He stops the growling after a moment and I hear the sound of receding footsteps. Our intruder has left, having fallen for Teddy's ruse. I'm not sure whether to hug Teddy for saving us or to bean him upside his head for not warning me first. It makes me realize that I am very, very relieved and that I really, really, really need to pee. One more close call and I will end up wetting myself.

"You are...truly amazing." I pat him on the back. I can almost feel him smiling beside me.

"Thanks. The bad guys are scared of dogs. It was all I could think of."

"You told me they shoot them, but how do you know they're afraid of them?"

"I don't know for sure. I've just seen them do it," he says.

I think back to the first time the bad men came to my house and encountered my mother's little dog. Teddy might be onto something. If only we had a real dog. An imagined dog wasn't going to get us very far.

"I don't think it was a bad guy out there, though. Bad guys just blast everything with their guns. This might be the cannibal," I tell him.

"So what do we do?" he asks, and I give this some thought. We might be safe here, now that our intruder has run away, but it isn't something I want to count on.

"I think we should move on now while we have the advantage. It's probably not going to take him too long to realize we really don't have a dog in here with us."

"How would he know that?" Teddy asks, and I roll my eyes in the darkness.

"Because he was inside here a few minutes ago, standing over me, Dum-dum."

"How do you know it's the same guy?" Teddy asks, and my blood chills at the thought. I don't know. In fact, I don't know anything about our midnight caller except for the fact that he hadn't killed me when he'd had the chance.

"I don't, but I think it's a fairly safe assumption. Anyways, I have to pee, and I'm not going out there alone." I move towards the door, and put my hand on the lock. A tremendous part of me is afraid to turn the clasp. What if the man is still out there?

What if he only pretended to walk away? I hesitate a moment longer, my heart beat picking up the pace.

"It's okay, Ember. He's gone. I heard him."

I take a deep breath and try to flush out the anxiety. I hope he's right.

"Thanks. I needed that," I tell him and then turn the clasp.

The lock opens with a heavy snap and I turn the door knob slowly. Cool summer air drifts through the opening, smelling faintly of corn husks and sweet grass. The tomb had been stuffy and warm in comparison and I want to just breathe for a moment, enjoying the simple sensation. A mosquito drifts through the opening and buzzes near my ear. The sound of chirping crickets is very strong and it is enough to reassure me.

We step through the opening. Teddy is pressed so tightly against me; I can feel his sweaty skin sticking to my back. We walk to the other side of the mausoleum, to the place where the moon can't touch us, and we wait.

The sounds of the night surround us. We stand in the shadows for several seconds, listening for something that will give our intruder away. When we don't hear it, we move forward. I will get us out of the cemetery if it's the last thing I do.

I grab Teddy's arm and pull him along beside me, trying to stay near the dark edges of the cemetery, where the shadows of the forest can hide us.

The cemetery covers several acres of rolling hills, with graves planted eight feet apart. We are careful not to step onto the actual graves, where the bodies have been buried, even though there is at least six feet of dirt separating us. I'm not superstitious about walking over graves, I just don't think the spirits would take kindly to us trouncing on their final resting spot. It's one of those things you just don't do, no matter who

138

you are, especially when you've had the kind of day we've had. There's no sense in chancing it. We come to the north corner of the cemetery and I gasp. I'd forgotten all about the weeping Mary statue.

"Oh crap," Teddy whispers and stops in his tracks.

Ahead of us, silhouetted against the moonlight is Weeping Mary.

I can see her in the moonlight, looking skyward. The statue stands nearly eight feet tall with her arms open, palms up as though she is proposing a question to the heavens above, very similar to my mother's statue. Her face is tilted upwards, but her stone eyes are closed. Legend has it that she cries every year on the anniversary of her death.

Annie and I came to the cemetery once on her anniversary. It had been a cold and windy day, nearly turning our black umbrella inside out. We gathered the courage to walk through the cemetery, hanging onto one another tightly. When we finally found the massive statue, we'd been disappointed to find that her cheeks were as wet as the rest of her. The rain had started to lift while we stood there, huddled beneath our umbrella, but we didn't stick around long enough to see if she continued to cry. Ideas spawned in the comfort of your bedroom seldom seemed like a good idea once you took them to the cemetery. Sometimes just being able to say you did it was enough. Sticking around to prove a point wasn't on our agenda back then.

I can almost feel Desmond beside me again, brushing up against my leg, telling me a secret that only he can understand. I look down and find empty grass in the place where he should be, and I shiver despite myself.

Teddy presses up close behind me, holding tightly to my arm.

"Don't worry. I plan to give her a wide berth."

"Good."

We turn left and leave Weeping Mary behind. The night is still, the wind holding its breath against the blackness. Above, the moon paints the sky with a wash of blue and black, swirling together like an ominous Halloween landscape. The tombstones glimmer all around us.

I pull a deep lungful of air through my nose, smelling the earthy smell of the cemetery mixed with the dusty, husky smell of the cornfield. Beneath it is another smell that I don't recognize immediately. It is a musky, unclean smell. It is putrid and foul, the smell of feces, vomit, and unwashed flesh all rolled into one. I turn and sniff Teddy to make sure it isn't him before I take several steps forward. The smell is familiar, but I can't quite place it.

"What is that smell?" Teddy asks.

I hold my hand out for him to stay back. The odor grows stronger. It seems to be coming from the tombstone just ahead of me. I will take a quick look and then retreat before Teddy can see it too.

I step forward and nearly lose my balance.

"Oh my God," I breathe. It is the body of the cannibal.

18

I take a glimpse and turn around in horror. Bile rise up in my throat and I swallow hard.

"I wonder what happened to him," Teddy says, and I realize he has followed me to where the corpse lies.

"I think it's obvious, Teddy. His brains were bashed in with something. I'd guess with that," I say, gesturing to the bloody bat that is leaning against the nearest headstone.

Teddy starts to walk towards the bat, but then thinks better of it and stops.

I stare at the bat for a moment, stunned by the brazen act of simply walking away and leaving the murder weapon behind. The murderer didn't even bother to sling it into the bushes or drop it into a lake. I guess he probably realized that no one really cared any more. All the cops are gone, as well as the FBI and the crime lab technicians. I think about all the forensic labs sitting empty with their fingerprint kits and evidence bags becoming as useless as so many other things. Death has become just another thing, no different than a hangnail or an empty bottle of Pepsi or a thousand dollar bill.

"I wonder who killed him," Teddy says. As the words leave his mouth, he cranes his neck right and then left, as though he expects someone to jump from behind a tombstone. It is enough to snap me out of my daze.

"I don't know, but we can't assume that he's a good guy or that he's gone away. He could be hiding somewhere." I turn in a slow circle, checking the area for movement. When I don't find anything, I grab Teddy's arm and make a sharp right. I don't care if we walk directly past the Weeping Mary. I am not coming within twenty feet of that dead body again. I've seen too many movies where the woman has done this, only to discover that the corpse is not really a corpse. I am not in the mood for having my ankle grabbed, even though I know it is not possible. Men with their brains leaking onto the ground do not usually grab ankles, but I am still not taking any chances.

"Let's get out of here."

Teddy doesn't argue with me and allows himself to be led.

I am tired of being in a cemetery. My body is on the verge of simply giving out on me. I can feel it in the tremble of my legs and the lightheaded feeling in my head. I need sleep.

We move past the graves swiftly without incident, leaving them behind us like a bad memory, and then disappear into the thick forest of trees surrounding the west side of the cemetery. There are legends about the woods as well, but I have had about all I can take of legends. If something is going to get me, I wished it would just get it over with. I am tired of worrying about it.

"Aren't these woods haunted?" Teddy asks, looking wide-eyed around him at the wicked trees. Each one looks as though it could turn and grab us with its long clawed branches. Our feet crunch in the brittle leaves and we snap twig after twig until we sound like rice cereal popping in the silence. I give them a fleeting look, but dispel the shudder that would normally follow. I am just too exhausted to feel anything except numb.

"I don't think so. I think we're okay," I say, hoping to calm him down. Besides, I still need to empty my bladder. "Turn around. I need to pee," I order Teddy, and before he can even complete the movement, I have unzipped my jeans and am watering the haunted soil beneath my feet. When I finish, I don't feel better about our situation, but I can at least focus on moving forward.

"So...tell me about this place you're going to take me to. It's near Thomas's Trestle?" I am very familiar with Thomas's Trestle. Annie and I would go there and hang out sometimes. It was a teenager's paradise, a spot so far from the beaten path, the adults seldom bothered to follow us. We'd bring a six-pack of beer, stolen from my father's stash, a bag of Fritos, and an IPod with external speakers, and we'd be all set for the afternoon. We'd drink, eat, and dance to the music. Sometimes it would just be the two of us and other times, there would be a crowd. Some of the braver kids would jump off the trestle into the river, but we were never that foolish.

"You've been there?"

"Yeah, a few times, but I don't remember seeing a cabin."

"Have you ever jumped off of it and into the river?"

"Not in this lifetime. A kid from school named Danny Turner jumped off and broke his leg last year," I tell him, my voice trailing off. I remember the story making its way around our high school. I also remember thinking that Danny Turner was lucky to be alive after doing something so incredibly stupid. Not that it mattered any more. Danny Turner was probably dead now, along with the rest of my high school.

"Yeah, me neither."

"Tell me about the shack. I never heard about it," I say.

"That's because Steve and I built it."

I nearly groan, imagining pine boughs and random sticks piled together in teepee fashion. There will be a canvas tarp on the floor, moldy blankets, soggy boxes of crackers, and outdated girly magazines.

"You and Steve built a shack? Out of what?"

"Boards and stuff we found in his dad's garage." When I don't acknowledge him, he is quick to reassure me. "Don't worry, it's pretty nice. Steve's dad is a contractor, so Steve knows how to build stuff. He built this really cool tree house in his yard. It had electricity and Internet. He even had an X-Box up there. It was really cool."

"Wow." I'm thinking that we should just bypass the trestle shack and head to Steve's house, but I don't say this out loud. If the space were safe, Teddy would have already brought me there.

The woods are thankfully short in distance and we come out on the other side in less than ten minutes. We end up on a dirt road that leads out of town. By my estimation the trestle is two miles away. If we walk at our current pace, it shouldn't take us more than an hour. Hopefully Teddy's shack is ready for us to climb into because I am so tired, I'm afraid I might fall asleep while walking.

After a mile, I am satisfied that no one is following us. The land is flat and wide, becoming nothing more than a slip of earth beneath the vast, open breakaway sky. The stars above us are bright and plentiful, displayed in the deep black backdrop of the universe like diamonds on velvet. It occurs to me that no one has seen this sort of sky in hundreds of years, not since man polluted the darkness with artificial lights.

There are no more cities to drown out the perfection, no headlights of passing cars, no spotlights blazing across the darkness, advertising the opening of a new shopping mall. It is just this dazzling slice of perfection, on display in its original packaging.

Teddy is quiet beside me. I observe him from the corner of my eye, not wanting to pull him from his thoughts and cause him to start some inane conversation that I have no interest in participating in. I am enjoying the silence, but I am also proud of him. He is not the same boy I once knew, but then again I'm not the same either. We aren't the same kids who used to pour soda down the drain because it went flat or slept with teddy bears and nightlights in our wallpapered bedrooms. We have become whittled down until only a perfect effigy of courage

144

remains. When that wears thin, I wonder what we will find. What is buried beneath courage?

I feel bad for him. He's lost everything and everyone in his life, but worst of all, he's lost his future. He will never shyly ask a girl to dance at the school dance, he will never again get to gloat over an A on his report card, and he won't know the comfort of his mother's hand. I glance at him, hoping I can be enough. It makes me think of Elizabeth out there all alone, but I push away the thought before it can bury me.

"Hey, are your feet bothering you?" I ask, looking at his dusty bare feet.

He shrugs. "No. Not really. I like being barefoot. The bottoms of my feet are like leather." He lifts his foot and shows me, but I can see very little in the moonlight.

"We're really going to have to get you some shoes."

"Yeah, like where are you gonna find shoes? I don't see many shoe stores," Teddy says.

"I could have pulled them off the cannibal. He looks about your size."

He groans. "No way. NOT gonna happen."

Unfortunately for him, it might be the best way, but I don't tell him this. We walk in silence for a while.

I've given up a lot too and although I try not to think about it, the thoughts assault me anyways.

I'd never really had a boyfriend before the world ended. I'd had a few close calls, a few times when *almost* became a way of life. I'd meet a boy on vacation. We'd flirt for several days, almost getting to the point where he would work up the nerve to kiss me, and then vacation would end and I'd never hear from him again, even though he promised he would call. It would be another close call, but nothing substantial. Another *almost* I could put in my pocket like small change.

145

Unfortunately, though, even if I collected a pocket full of them, they still wouldn't add up to what I was hoping for.

By my sixteenth birthday, I was nearly delirious for romance. Annie had already had a slew of boyfriends, so many that she often confused them with one another. Did Jimmy have the birthmark shaped like the state of Florida on his stomach, or was it Jake? Which boy took her to fireworks down by the camp lake last summer? Adam or Michael? I would sigh and stare at myself in the mirror, wondering what was wrong with me. I was pretty enough, in a tomboy sort of way. I probably could have worn make-up, like Annie did, or sprayed myself with musky, sexy perfume and allowed my jeans to ride low on my hips. I could have laughed at all the boy's jokes, learning how to tilt my head in a way that made my hair tumble over my shoulder. I could have gotten blond highlights in my hair, whitened my teeth, and applied acrylic nails that were square and unnatural. I could have become someone altogether different and then I might have snagged an elusive boyfriend, but somewhere deep inside of me, I feared that in the process I would have lost myself instead.

"To be true to yourself in a world that is constantly trying to make you something else is the greatest accomplishment," my mother would tell me, again quoting Ralph Waldo Emerson. She had a book of quotes on her nightstand. I wish I could be back home to flip through them.

Be true to yourself. It seemed like a simple task because the easiest person to be was me, but who exactly was I? That was the million dollar question.

There was still so much I didn't know about myself. The layers of me were tightly wound and hidden from view, buried so deep I couldn't even begin to touch the core. I was so many things, but nothing at all. I was lazy about my appearance. I didn't even own a tube of mascara, hadn't bothered to get my driver's permit, and I often had evil thoughts about my sister and sometimes the rest of my family as well, before they died. I hoarded cookies in my room, not wanting to share them with anyone else, I stole my father's beer every chance I got. I sometime cheated on pop quizzes if the person sitting next to me was an honor student with clear handwriting. I popped my pimples, picked at scabs, and sometimes put my gum under my chair in class. If this was being true to me, I didn't see the point. Wouldn't it be better to strive to be someone a bit more perfect?

It hits me that everything I've looked forward to, everything I've spent my entire life preparing for, has now dissipated like dust in a wind storm. I will not graduate from high school. I will not go to college, and then find the perfect job. I will not meet the man of my dreams and have a white wedding in a quaint white church. I will not own a home, mow my lawn, and flip pancakes for my children in the kitchen while Aerosmith plays on the radio. And it's very possible that I will not ever see my sister again.

I don't realize I've been crying until I feel the tears fall onto my hands as I walk. I give Teddy a quick glance and see that he's simply trudging along, head down, nearly asleep on his feet. I wipe the tears away with the sleeve of my hoody, wishing I had a tissue to blow my nose with.

"Are we close?" I ask, and he looks up with a jolt.

"Umm...yeah, I think so. It should be just behind that line of trees."

He points to a shadowy bank of trees ahead in the distance. The land is so flat and low by the river it seems completely dwarfed by the sky above it. I close my eyes and breathe through my nose, noticing the salty brine of the water.

147

It smells slightly fishy, and my mind briefly touches on happier times, when the smell of the river was synonymous with fun and laughter. Now it is simply a large body of water.

The road makes a loop at the edge of the river and continues on around the bank to places I've never been before. I can remember riding our bikes out here, just throwing them down where they landed and running towards the water with nothing but glee in our hearts. It seems like a life time ago, almost as though it happened to someone else altogether.

"Follow me. The shack is just up here." Teddy says.

"Just a minute." I'm not certain why I do this, maybe a little voice inside my head is speaking just loud enough for me to hear, but I pull my flashlight from my pocket and turn it on. I aim it down at my dusty dirty shoes, to the dirt road beneath me. I turn and allow the light to follow the path that I've just created. Our footprints are laid out one after another, as easy to follow as a trail of breadcrumbs.

"What are you looking at?" Teddy asks me. I sigh and cut the light.

"Nothing," I tell him, hoping it's true. In reality, it might be the last mistake I have a chance to make.

19

I awaken to sunshine streaming through the cracks of the shack's walls. Dust motes float through the air, caught in the light like shimmering pixies. Beside me, on the bare dirt floor, Teddy snores softly, his arm thrown over his eyes to block out the sunshine. It's been a while since I've seen him in the daylight and I marvel again at how much he's changed. The flannel shirt he is wearing is blue, not green, like I thought it was. The arm of his shirt has risen nearly to his elbow and the fine hairs on his forearm glow reddish blonde in the sunlight.

I feel sluggish and lazy, as though I'd like to spend the entire day sleeping.

I wonder what day it is, what month it is even? July? August?

When it all ended, we only had four weeks of school left. The trees were just starting to leaf out and everything was still fresh and green. Every day a new tree would be fully leaved, when the day before it was naked and bare. The yellow forsythia had given way to the raspberry rosebuds and the white pear trees. Even the grass was growing long and silky, turning the green I dreamed about all winter long. On my way to school that morning, I'd caught a whiff of freshly cut grass and I'd closed my eyes on the school bus, savoring it as though it had been a morsel of chocolate melting on my tongue. *Summer*, I'd thought with a sigh, imagining a much different outcome.

The seedlings for my mother's garden had been sitting on the window sills, waiting for their Memorial Day planting. My mother was so structured in her routines. She was always fearful that if she planted before Memorial Day, an unexpected frost would kill off all her hard work. Two weeks after she died, I planted all her leggy seedlings into her carefully tilled garden. It seemed like a shame not to.

I try to figure out the month by the plantings. The tomatoes had really only started producing fruit a month ago, which was probably about six weeks after I planted them. I stare at the dust motes, floating through the air without worry or reason. August? It must be somewhere in late August. The days have become hot and dusty, the grass drying up to brittle stalks in the fields. The corn in the field near the cemetery had already hardened and the trees were turning a deep forest green.

I take a deep, meaningful breath. In our old life, at this time of the year we would be mourning the ending of summer. Our mothers would be planning a trip to the city for new school clothes, binders, and freshly sharpened pencils. We'd beg for new shoes as well and then nearly wear them out before school could even begin. We'd start to mentally separate ourselves from the thoughts of summer, of the water so warm and blue, of the long days spent doing absolutely nothing, of fireflies in the meadow at dusk

I sigh. If I could go back to my old life, I'd happily spend all summer in school as long as I had my family to go home to at the end of the day.

I roll onto my side and feel the twinge of a cramp in my lower abdomen. I am close to my time of the month, as my mother always referred to it. It was never a period or a menstrual cycle, always My Time of the Month, as though it should be printed on a calendar in italics with a rosebud beneath it. I have had two cycles since it happened. My mother's storage shelf has kept me properly outfitted with plenty of necessities, but now that I am away from home, I am not in good shape.

My sense of urgency increases with the thought. We need to head back towards town and find a house or two to ransack for supplies. Besides the needed batteries and tampons, we also need to refresh our food supply and find bottles of water and possibly some shoes for my barefooted friend. We can lay low for a few hours after we've found everything and then begin to hunt for my sister. I think about the fire burning near the chemical plant and increase the urgency in my mind.

"Hey," I nudge Teddy.

He comes awake quickly, nearly leaping to his feet as though he is being attacked by zombies. It is actually a good reflex to have. I compare his method of waking against mine. I usually wake slowly and lie as still as possible to assess my surroundings before I allow any outward signs of my wakefulness.

"Hey, hey, buddy. It's okay. It's just me," I say, and he looks at me with startled eyes, his expression frozen in panic. As his eyes focus and the last of his dreams sluice away, he visibly relaxes and slumps back down to the ground.

"Oh man, Ember. You scared the piss out of me." He stares into the dust as if collecting his thoughts. After a moment, he runs his hand through his hair and then looks around at the small room. "What do you think of our shack?" he asks.

"Nice," I say before I can say something closer to the truth. It is actually very far from nice. It is rustic and bare, nothing more than boards nailed together to keep out the wind and the sun. The room is smaller than the crypt we just left by nearly half, with low ceilings and a dirt floor. An old mattress is leaning against the far wall, smelling very strongly of urine and mildew. An egg crate full of old girlie magazines sits beside it for easy inspiration. I sit up and lean against the wall, feeling the rough boards press against my skin. I run my tongue over the front of

151

my teeth, feeling the thin film and taste of morning breath and then add tooth paste to my mental shopping list. I have not gone a day without brushing my teeth, and while it feels as though it should be my smallest concern, I don't plan on putting my personal hygiene on hold for the sake of anything.

"So, you wanna head closer to town and see if we can find some supplies?" I ask, and he watches me for a long moment before answering, probably considering the dead bodies we'll have to experience.

"Yeah, I guess," he says without much enthusiasm. He digs in his bag and comes up with two granola bars. He flips me one and I eat it in three bites, feeling the empty space in my stomach fill.

"Thanks. We'll need the energy." I think about how food has become something else altogether. It used to be a means of comfort, a way to stifle boredom, a social event. Now, it is nothing more than fuel for our bodies.

We grab our backpacks and step out into the sunshine.

I shield my eyes for a second and hold out an arm to keep Teddy from walking any further. "Just stand here a minute," I whisper.

A soft breeze ruffles through my hair, sending a stray strand across my cheek. I push it aside and really listen to the noises. Birds chirp happily in the treetops, welcoming the morning as they always do, and the river moves steadily with a low roar that is both comforting and annoying at the same time. After a minute I am relatively satisfied that we are still alone and I step away from the doorway.

"Wait here for a minute. I need to pee," I tell him. I walk behind the shack and squat in the tall grass, feeling the relief flood through me as my bladder empties. I pull my pants back up and walk back around the structure in time to see Teddy zipping his pants as well. He flushes red as he realizes I've seen him zipping, which is a far cry from the Teddy I used to know. He once peed in his mother's umbrella stand because Annie was in the bathroom too long.

"Don't worry, kid. I didn't see anything," I tell him, and he grows even redder.

In the sunshine, the shack looks much better than I thought it would. It has been built into the side of a hill, with only the door and the front section of the shack showing. Sticks and branches have been pushed up against it, shielding it from easy view. I take several steps back and give it some serious scrutiny. It's not bad, but it still falls short of the mark I was hoping for. With winter coming, we'll need somewhere with a fireplace. We might be able to rig the shack with a small fireplace or chiminea from someone's back deck, but I think we can do much better. After all, the world is full of empty houses. The real estate market has become a squatter's paradise.

The leaves rustle in the distance and I get the sensation that someone is watching us. I can nearly feel eyes boring into the back of my head, but when I turn, no one is there. I listen to the ambient noises surrounding me, not surprised to find the forest still and quiet. Not even a solitary bird chirps.

"I think someone is watching us," I whisper.

Teddy nods and scans the forest.

I stare hard into the woods, keeping my expression firm and angry, not allowing even a trace of fear to show through, even though I feel it down to the tips of my toes. My desire to flee is so strong, it is nearly combustible. My muscles tense with the urge to run.

Teddy stands beside me and watches the woods as well. "Who do you think it is?"

"I don't know." It could be anyone. We've seen what the virus has done to Mr. McFarley. It could have done the same thing to other people too. It's enough to propel me forward, wanting to put as much distance between us and the shack as possible.

"Do you think it's another cannibal?" he asks, his voice breaking.

I ignore his question, because even voicing it out loud is more than I can handle. "Let's just move on."

"Are you sure it's safe?" Teddy asks, still staring into the woods.

"I'm not sure of anything, but I'd really like to get as far away as possible. He might just be playing with us, but you never know."

"Good point."

We start walking towards the road, the sounds of our footsteps sounding like firecrackers as we get farther away from the roar of the river. I think about the possibilities. We've only seen two people so far, besides the cannibal and his victim. Could it be the dog catcher or Henry Rivers? As I think about Henry, a sigh washes through me.

I'd like nothing better than to find more people, but the thought is diluted with the prospects of uncertainty. Henry hadn't seemed the same as I remember him. He has become a hardened version of himself, someone I wouldn't trust immediately. The fact that he has joined forces with the dog catcher doesn't help either. Surely anyone as mean and vile as the dog catcher wouldn't attract normal people. Something must have happened to Henry. Maybe he's as bad as the dog catcher.

As we step from the shadows, the morning sun seems brighter and burns my eyes, turning my world temporarily brown at the edges. I close my eyes and try to blink it away. An image of Elizabeth comes to me so strong, so powerful, I nearly expect to open my eyes and see her standing in front of me. I imagine her in a room full of other children, waiting for what happens next, fear painting the room in shades of black.

I'll find you. I promise.

I send my words out into the wind and hope they hit their mark.

Elizabeth and I have always had a strong bond, despite everything. I don't know if she can hear me the way that I can sometimes hear her, but it doesn't hurt to try. I wish my father was still here. He would be able to help me figure this all out.

I think about the days following his death. There had been so much busywork to take care of. Neighbors and family friends stopped by, dropping off casseroles and meat loaves, saying things like "I'm so sorry," and "is there anything I can do for you?" while my mother held back the tears. I tried to ask Elizabeth about the lightning, but she'd just tucked her head into her chin, shielding her face with the curtain of her hair like she always did when she didn't want to talk about something.

"I couldn't help it," she'd said finally and then darted away. I wanted to talk to my mother about it, but her sorrow surrounded her like a fog. Parting through it to talk about the tragedy wasn't an option. If Elizabeth had killed my father, even accidentally, it wasn't something she was prepared to deal with. It comforts me a little to know that she'd at least talked to Teddy's mother about it. It confirmed my fears, but it also gave me something to consider. If Elizabeth were able to call the lightning, we might be able to use that to our advantage, as strange as it sounds.

Teddy is quiet for the first half hour of our walk and I'm thankful for the time to think. Sometimes when he prattles on, it prevents me from really thinking and I need this time to plot out our next move. We might have to break into several houses before we find what we need. We'll start with the first one we see. We will stand in the doorway and assess the situation. If the room looks lived in or if we smell even the slightest hint of death, then we'll just move onto the next house. I don't like the idea of stepping over gross, rotting bodies any more than Teddy does and I have no intention of being shot by a scared survivor.

"Do you think the person who is following us is the same person from the cemetery?" Teddy asks.

"Maybe," I tell him, keeping my internal litany to myself. If this stalker were the same person, did he kill the cannibal too? Did he bash his brains in with a wooden baseball bat and then shamelessly prop the murder weapon up against someone else's gravestone? Could it be Henry or the dog catcher? Worry fills me whole for a moment until I manage to blow it out with a sigh. I have to stay level-headed about this. Two people are now counting on me.

The dirt road is getting dusty in the strong morning sun and our footsteps stir the dust up, making it rise in a low cloud with every footstep. I have been so caught up in my thoughts, I haven't paid any attention to the road itself, and as the thought of someone stalking us grows stronger, I begin to analyze the evidence right in front of me. Three sets of footsteps lead down the road. I recognize my prints because there is a star on the bottom of my shoe. Teddy is barefooted, so his footprints are easily recognizable as well. The third set is much larger. I stop and kneel down to study them.

"What is it?" Teddy asks.

"Footprints." I point to the third set of prints. They look like boot prints, judging by the solid ridges. They remind me of the tan work boots my father used to wear when he worked out in the lawn. They had steel toes that he said protected him from chopping off his toes with the lawn mower. I don't know much about men's shoe sizes, but it is nearly three inches longer than mine.

"These are probably the footprints from the person who is following us," I say.

"Why would he be following us?"

"I don't know. Maybe he doesn't have anything else to do?"

"Yeah." He runs his finger through the dusty footprint, making a swirl design. "Maybe he wants to join us, but he's afraid."

It's something I haven't considered and I think about it for a moment. If he were a normal, sane person and he happened across us, wouldn't he just say 'hello' instead?

"Maybe, I don't know. I don't think we should let our guard down, though because what if he isn't friendly? What if he's just playing with us?"

"Well, yeah, but didn't he kill the cannibal for us?"

I hadn't considered that. The thought is warming, but I don't hold onto it for very long.

"That would be nice, but it's not something we should count on. We don't even know for sure that the cannibal killed those people we found. This guy could have killed everybody, for all we know. We still need to be careful." I stand up and rub my dusty hands on my black jeans, leaving a smear of dirt on each thigh. "Let's start walking, okay? I don't like standing out here in the open."

Teddy gets up and follows me without comment. The further we get from the safety of the woods, the more anxious I grow. If a car comes down the road, we'll have plenty of time to react, but nowhere to hide. We could run out into a field and hide, but that would be the equivalent of hiding behind a light post. There was very little chance we'd be able to pull it off.

I see a house in the distance. It sits at the end of a long driveway and as we get closer, I can make it out a little clearer. It's a small ranch- style house with yellow siding. There is a royal blue pickup truck parked in the driveway and a rusty swing set in the backyard. Seeing the swing set makes my stomach do a small flip-flop. I will have a hard enough time seeing a dead adult, but I know I won't be able to hold it all together if we find a dead kid. I shut down the thought before it can grow flesh.

"Okay, here's the plan. I think we should go in through the back door. That way if anyone drives by, they won't be able to see us. Once we get inside, we'll just stand in the doorway for a minute and see how bad it is. If it's bad, we won't go in, okay?"

Teddy nods. "That's Faith Eddy's house," he says, and then looks down at his feet as he walks. "She was in my class. She rode my school bus too. The bus driver always got really mad at her because she was never outside when he pulled up. He always had to wait for her."

I watch him for a moment wondering how he'll react to the body of a dead classmate. It makes me think of Annie and it occurs to me that I've never asked him what happened to her.

"What happened to Annie after she died? Did you bury her?"

He continues to stare at his feet as he walks. "Yeah. I buried her out in the flower garden."

I reach between us and hold his hand for several steps. "That's where I would have buried her too. She always loved your mother's flower garden."

A cold chill grazes my arm. I look skyward at the clouds hovering above us like puff of pure white cotton candy, floating in an impossibly blue sky. If there is a Heaven... is she looking down at us, thankful that we've somehow managed to find one another?

I think that the cold chill is her way of touching me, of making contact. I look down at the hairs on my arms, still standing upright even though the day is growing warmer. The ghosts must linger in this world, just like the thought of the small dog still trotting along beside me. This world has become so full of strife and turmoil, like static electricity burbling from the surface. When they died, the sudden atrocity, the wrongness of it all, might have shocked them and stopped them from continuing further. I imagine them, watching the white light of Heaven open up and then turning away, as though it is something that is not meant for them, at least not yet. There is so much they have left behind, so much to still settle back on the living plain, that walking through the light to Heaven feels like falling into your bed too many hours before your bed time. I smile up at the clouds. Everything is not okay in our world down below, but it is not ashes and soot either, at least not while there are people like me and Teddy still breathing.

I let the thought sink in for a moment before I answer him. "I think that people like you and me have a responsibility to survive. I don't know if we can do anything about the bad men, but I think that we have to at least try. I think that's why God left us behind," I tell Teddy.

"I know." He looks up at the clouds just like I've just done. "I think they're all up there watching us, cheering for us. My mom, my sister, your mom and dad."

I try to imagine them sitting together on a cloud, biting their fingernails as we tip-toed through the cemetery, but the image won't fully develop. I think that they are still lingering in our world, walking beside us, sight unseen, and I think they stay

159

with us until they are reassured that we'll be all right without them.

"Do you ever wonder why we're the only ones left?" he asks.

"Yeah. All the time."

"Yeah, me too. Sometimes I think it's for a reason...like, we're supposed to do something to save the world, like in those movies." He adjusts the strap on his backpack and shifts it to his other shoulder. "But other times, I think it's just my stupid luck. I never get sick. Everybody else in the family gets the flu, but I never get it," he says, glancing in my direction. "What about you?"

I have to think about it. I was prone to migraines, so it seemed like I was always sick, but I couldn't remember ever having a virus. "No, I don't usually get sick. That's weird," I say, noticing that we are almost to the driveway of the house. "You know, that's crazy because Elizabeth never got sick either. I remember my mother talking about what a healthy baby she always was...even in day care, when all the kids were sick all the time with runny noses, she was always healthy."

"I wonder if we are like...some sort of super humans," Teddy muses. I nearly laugh at his choice of words. I imagine us as gold-dipped robots, walking the earth with thunderous steps, shooting laser beams from our eyes.

"I don't know Teddy, maybe we are." I certainly don't feel like a super human. I feel closer to being sub-human, someone who would rather just crawl into a hole until it is all over with. I don't know if I have the courage to do any more than just survive, but I keep this to myself. There's no reason to drag my adolescent super-human friend down with me.

We reach the edge of the lawn and cut across to the back yard, being careful to only step on the bare areas of the lawn, even though our footprints are clearly laid out behind us. I look back to see the trail of them behind us.

"Stay here for a minute. I want to do something." I pull a branch from a tree, twisting it until it pulls clear from the limb. I run back to the road and use it to sweep our footprints away. I don't know how much good it will do, because anyone with any sense would simply look up from the footprints, see the house, and then know where we went, but it makes me feel better. For good measure, I walk back to the place where I began sweeping and I make deliberate steps, leading out into the other direction. It probably won't fool anyone, but at first glance it looks as though we've decided to walk out into the soybean field instead of walking towards the house.

I walk back to the house, sweeping the branch behind me to erase my footsteps.

"Good idea," Teddy says, giving me a thumbs up.

I look back at the road. "Yeah, I just wish I'd thought about it earlier." If our stalker was still hiding in the woods near the river, he'd have an easy time tracking us.

"Well, if he is following us, there aren't too many other places to go anyways. He'd just follow the road, right?"

"Probably." I tousle his hair and smile. "Thanks, buddy. I needed that."

He reaches up and tries to tousle my hair to return the gesture, but I dodge his arm. I don't want his sticky fingers anywhere near my hair.

"Hands off the hair," I warn him, and he laughs. It is a light moment, something we needed, something that will shore us up and give us the strength we need to tackle the next step.

I look up at the house in front of us, at the bank of dark windows that look down over the back lawn. A breeze washes across the lawn with a gust, making the swing on the swing set behind us move with a rusty squeal. I look back at it and wonder if it's really empty or if Faith Eddy is still swinging, watching us standing there in her back yard, while our hearts are beating a million miles an hour.

I look at Teddy, who is staring up at the blank windows, his expression unreadable.

"You ready?" I ask, and he just nods, not taking his eyes off the window.

"Then let's do it." I grab the doorknob.

20

At first I do not smell the dead bodies.

I stand in the doorway, holding the screen door open for Teddy, and try to absorb the feeling of the house without actually walking inside. I am braced for flight in case anything jumps out at me, my muscles tightly coiled.

The house is silent.

Gone are the typical sounds of a sleeping house, of the ticking grandfather clock, the soft whirr of the refrigerator, of the melodious sound of a radio left on in a teenager's bedroom. There is only the creak of wood as the house braces with the gusts of wind, the squeak of my rubber-soled sneakers pressing against the worn linoleum floor beneath me, and of my own pounding heartbeat.

"I don't hear anything." I turn to look at Teddy, to make sure he's okay with this. "Come on inside, but just stay by the door." I cock my head towards the window to the left of the kitchen door. "Keep your eye out this window to make sure nobody is coming down the road. You can be my look-out."

Teddy glances at the window, sees the view of the road, and then looks at the other end of the house, where there aren't any windows. I know what he is going to say before he says it. In another life, another time, he'd make a great cop.

"What about the other side of the house? What if somebody comes down the road from town?"

"I don't know. If someone sneaks up on us, I guess we'll just have to hide somewhere." I look around the room and see a door that probably leads to a basement. It is probably dusty and moldy and filled with spider webs. I'd really hate to have to resort to it, but it might be our best bet. "We'll just be quick in here and then we won't have to worry about it," I tell him, hoping I'm right.

Everything we need is hopefully right here in the kitchen. We will basically smash and grab, looting the house like common thugs until we've filled our backpacks.

I open the drawers near the back door, which seems like the most logical place for batteries, and find nothing but empty spaces. I open and close the rest of the drawers, finding nothing more interesting than playing cards and rubber bands. I grab the cards and shove them into my pocket, thinking that they might give us a good diversion later, and then move onto the cabinets. I find a half package of stale saltine crackers and few cans of vegetables. I shove them into my pack, even though they are heavy and packed with water. If we don't find anything else, they will be better than trying to sleep with an empty stomach.

"Vegetables?" Teddy whines from the doorway.

"It's all I found. You can look for other stuff. I'm going to go look for some shoes for you."

"Just make sure they aren't girl's shoes."

"Like, who's going to notice besides me?" I call over my shoulder. Teddy mumbles something, but I am too far away to hear it.

The house is a typical ranch design, which I'm thankful for because I'm familiar with the floor plan. On the other side of the kitchen is a living room, decorated by someone with a love for country. There is a newspaper on the coffee table. I lean over to read the date. It is dated May 28th and the headline reads "Massive Flu Outbreak Cripples the Nation."

I remember the day clearly. At that point the virus hadn't spread to our area yet, but rumors about it were floating around. I went to Wal-Mart with my mother that evening and we saw people walking around with paper face masks on.

"Isn't that a little overkill?" I asked my mother, and she shrugged. After suffering through the last flu virus, many people were becoming overly cautious. The next day, someone we knew from town contracted the virus after returning from a trip to New York. Three days later, his entire family was sick, along with every person he'd crossed paths with in the past five days. He died within a week and his family members followed suit days later. By the end of the following week, the majority of the town's population was either wheezing and coughing or were already dead and in the process of being buried.

I give the newspaper another glance. Someday, if the world ever picks up and moves on, it might be worth something, but right now it is worth the same amount as the coffee table it is sitting on, or the entire house for that matter. I leave it and move on.

On the mantle is a framed family photograph. In it, a pudgy brown- haired mother stands beside a balding, jolly-looking man. In front of them are two children, a brown-haired girl who is Teddy's age and a blond boy, who appears to be several years younger. I take a closer look at the brown- haired girl, Faith Eddy, and sincerely hope I'll never learn what really happened to her or her family. If I have my way, the house will be empty and we will leave, asking each other what we thought happened to them.

"Hurry up!" Teddy calls from the kitchen.

I nearly jump out of my skin.

"Okay, okay. Look for more food and quit worrying about me." I hear him sigh, which is followed by the sound of cabinets opening and closing as he looks for food. More than likely, he will come away with useless things like sour pops and gummy worms, but it will be better than nothing.

Ahead of me is a long dark hallway filled with closed doors. I stand at the end, wishing someone would have left a door open so that the light from the outside windows could light my way. As it is, the hallway looks like a long, narrow tomb. I glance back at the kitchen and living room, trying to gain some perspective on how long the hallway actually is, but I'm not sure. It could be anywhere from ten to twenty feet long for all I know. I just hope there isn't a bad man or a stalker standing at the end of it, waiting for me.

"Okay, here goes nothing." I start down the hallway, taking baby steps, my eyes open wide. I do not see the obstacle lying large and sticky in the hallway. I trip over it and plant my foot right in the middle of the goo.

"Oh, God." My heart lunges up into my throat.

I careen forward, pin wheeling my arms to keep myself from landing on whatever I've tripped over. As I fall into the wall, the stench of death surrounds me, the smell oozing and fermented. I press my hand against my nose and feel the gag of vomit attempt to lurch from my stomach. I swallow hard to keep it from making its way upwards and swipe my hand against the wall, looking for a light switch.

I flip the switch back and forth before I remember that the electricity is gone.

"Damn it." I fumble further down the hallway until I find a doorway. Hopefully the light from the window will be bright enough to illuminate the dark hallway. I'm not sure if I want to see what I've tripped over or not, but I definitely want to make sure there aren't four more of them ahead of me in the darkness.

I fling the door open and find myself looking into a girl's bedroom. It is pink and frilly, with gingham curtains, white high-gloss dresser, and a dollhouse filled with tiny furniture. A life-

166

sized doll is propped up on a pink canopy bed, staring back at me with empty eyes. I glance away and then realize what I've seen is not a doll. It is Faith Eddy.

I gasp, but I can't seem to stop staring. Her hair is matted into what little scalp she has left and her face reminds me of cowhide that has been bleached in the sun for months. Insects surround her, buzzing and wallowing in the goo that was once a little girl still dressed in pink and brown pajamas. The smell of her wafts through the doorway and gags me. It is so strong, it is almost visible. I swivel around, my stomach lurching once again, and find myself face to face with the object I have tripped over. It is the family dog, or what was left of it after he probably starved to death, sitting in the hallway waiting for his masters to come out of their bedrooms.

I feel something crawling on my leg and discover that my foot is covered in maggots.

"Aughh." I shake my foot, slinging the white larva against the wall, and run back down the hallway towards the kitchen. I no longer care if we haven't found any batteries, water, or shoes for Teddy. I just want out of the house, away from the stench of death. I want to run until my legs will no longer hold me, until the memory burned into my mind has lessened. I run into the kitchen with my hand pressed over my mouth, my throat choking.

I make it to the kitchen before my stomach finally loses the battle with my willpower. I try to reach the sink or at least the trash can by the back door, but I only make it to the cracked linoleum floor and I vomit all over it. I retch until my stomach is empty and only acids remain and then I dry heave until I feel as though I am going to turn myself inside out.

"Gross," Teddy says, and opens the door to fan the air.

167

"Get me a paper towel," I tell him, trying to hold my hair back out of my face.

Teddy is reaching for the paper towels when we hear the familiar sound of a truck pulling into the driveway. Foreign music blares from the speakers and then stops as the truck engine is shut off. Teddy and I are frozen in place. They will come through the back door in a matter of seconds.

"Oh my God," I gasp. There could not be a worse time.

I grab the paper towels and make a quick swipe at the floor, but it has splattered in ten different directions and would take me two full minutes to get it clean. I can hear their footsteps on the gravel driveway. There is nothing I can do to save the situation, to save us.

"Come on, Ember. We have to hide!" Teddy hisses.

Before I can pull him towards the front door, he has gone down the stairs.

"Shit!" I can't just leave him. I grab another wad of towel and race it across the floor, trying to mop up the smelly mess, knowing that my efforts are futile. Even if I get up enough of the mess, the smell of vomit will still linger. They will still know that we've been there and they will search the house until they find us.

This cannot be happening.

I make one more swipe at the vomit and then follow him, the wad of paper towels still in my hand. As I pull the door behind me, I hear the sound of the kitchen door opening.

Please, please, please, I whisper in my mind.

Voices chatter back and forth in a language I don't understand.

I move down the stairs slowly. Each step feels springy, as if the board is barely hanging onto the support, and I pray that they won't squeak. I step on the outward edges, rolling my feet to minimize the pressure, and make it all the way down without making a sound. I grasp the hand rail and look around quickly to get my bearings.

The floor beneath me is concrete. Light from two narrow windows at the far end of the room casts a faint glow into the long narrow cavern. It could be any basement in any house. A long line of shelves hold cast-off tools and coils of garden house. Boxes topple over in a corner, next to a sagging synthetic Christmas tree that is coated with dust. Cobwebs drape from the ceiling like garlands. I imagine spiders curled up in corners, watching me with hungry eyes.

I see Teddy hiding behind a hot-water heater and he motions for me to join him. I shake my head and point to the darker end of the basement. He has chosen a horrible hiding place. They'll see him the minute they come down the stairs.

I point at him and then point to the dark end of the basement again, but he shakes his head. My heart nearly breaks for him. He needs to find another spot. They're going to see him. I want to grab him and drag him to a safer place, but I don't have time.

Overhead, the floor boards squeak as the men follow my path from the kitchen to Faith Eddy's bedroom. By now, they will have found the family dog lying in the hallway and possibly the slimy trail of maggots still dribbling down the wall from where I flung them. I move to the dark end of the basement, taking small steps, willing my eyes to adapt to the darkness. I rake my hand through the air, combing through spider webs as thick as hair. Something twitches in my hand and I fling it in a panic, afraid of spiders even now, when they should be the least of my worries.

Please, please, please, I pray inside my head. Please let me live through this.

169

My foot finds a box. It shifts on the concrete with a sound that seems louder than firecrackers. I freeze, my heart racing madly. Above me, a door opens and then closes as they move down the hallway, looking for us.

I touch the box with my hand and feel my way around it, finding another larger box just behind it. There is a strong stench behind the boxes. It reminds me of the smell of a very old dog and I wonder if this is where the dog once slept.

I pat the ground and find an old quilt. It is caked with flaky dog hair and matted with dirt, but I don't have any choice. I pick up the corner and crawl beneath it, hoping that it will hold its worth as a good hiding spot.

Above me, the floor groans as the men return to the kitchen.

They must have found the vomit.

I hold my breath as the basement door opens.

Their voices are louder, amplified by the stairwell tunnel.

"Hello?" one of them says with a thick accent. They start down the stairs.

They reach the bottom and have a hushed debate in their own language. I don't know what they are saying, but I imagine it has to do with where they think we are hiding. They must know we are down here. It is only a matter of finding us. I hold my breath and press my eyes closed tightly and I pray.

Please, please, please. God, please.

I hear a scuffling sound at the other side of the room.

"Ah ha!" a man says, and then Teddy screams.

"Let go of me!"

There is a shift of feet on concrete as they pull him from his hiding place. They will sniff him to see if he smells like vomit and when he doesn't, they are going to hunt for me.

"Hello, hello?" the man says again, his voice growing louder as he moves closer to my hiding place.

My mind nearly shuts down with terror. What will they do to us? Will they push us up against the wall and shoot us, execution style? Or will they bring us with them to their camp? I can't believe that anything good will come to us after this moment. They will experiment with us and torture us endlessly until we long for death like we once longed for a full belly and a good night's sleep.

The smell of dirty dog is choking. A sneeze whispers in my nose, ready to expel.

The footsteps grow closer and a light flashes across me. I can see the pattern of the plaid blanket as the light shines through it. I have the insane thought that the blanket is the same plaid as Teddy's shirt. Blue, not green. The material is thinner than I first thought, and my body must be obvious beneath the covers.

"We will find you. Come out of your hiding place," the man says.

They whisk the blanket off of me. The bright light from his flashlight blinds me. I open my mouth to scream and then do the one thing I shouldn't do.

I faint.

21

Voices burble above me, blending and swirling like something liquid and unfamiliar. Their words do not have meaning and the tone is useless and meandering to someone like me who doesn't understand their language.

I drift away.

I struggle to find my way up through the thick sludge of darkness, but it pins me to the ground, keeping me fluid and incoherent. I drift again. Thoughts are like bubbles floating past me as I sink deeper and deeper. I think of my sister, so fair and pure. She is sunlight shining through the branches of a newly budded dogwood. She is the first snowflakes lighting on the tips of the pine boughs. She is the singing bird at dawn, joyful to simply be alive. I imagine her calling my name. Calling my name. Calling my name.

Ember, wake up!

Daylight brims above me, red instead of blue. It feels as though it is a mile away, shimmering like an elusive daydream, always farther away than it first appears. I try to pull my arms upwards and try to swim towards the daylight.

"Leave us alone," I hear Teddy say, and his words pull me closer to the surface with an invisible string.

I open my eyes with a flutter, letting in snatches of bright light, and then I come awake sharply, every nerve ending electrified, the dream sluicing away to nothing. They have carried me into the kitchen and have dropped me onto the floor into my own smear of vomit. I move stiffly and pull myself to a sitting position. There is a chunk of something mushy stuck to the palm of my hand and I flick it off, my stomach lurching all over again.

The two men stare down at me, smiling in a way that makes me want to crawl up inside of myself. They are dark-haired, with olive skin and scraggly beards. It's the first time I've seen them close up. Their expressions are blank, as though they've done this a thousand times and no longer look at us as fellow human beings. I come awake quickly now, the thickness thinning out to a normal consistency, the sleepiness wearing off swiftly. As I continue to look up at them, a dawning comes over me and my heart sinks. They are not wearing the gas masks. They must not need them now that all the sick people have died.

One of the men holds out his hand for me.

I pull my lip up into a sneer that I hope looks threatening.

"Go fuck yourself," I say, my voice sounding thick with sleep, and then spit on the hand.

He slaps me so hard my head snaps backwards. I can feel the ringing in my ears before I hear it. It spins around and around, like an old-fashioned top, whirling with colors until they all blend into one.

"Just do what they want you to do and maybe they'll let us go," Teddy pleads with me.

I glance in his direction and the spinning world slowly moves into place and locks down tight. I see that Teddy has been duct-taped to a kitchen chair. It's not a very good sign. If they planned to keep him as a hostage, they wouldn't have tied him to the furniture.

"They're not going to let us go, Teddy."

"You don't know that."

I don't know what he's trying to do, but now is not the time.

"Just shut up, Teddy. This isn't the time." I pull myself to my feet and back up until the wall stops me.

I am so dizzy, I fall to my knees.

173

My mind is screaming for me to make a run for it, but I can't leave Teddy.

I look them in the eye, hoping there is something human left in them. Maybe I can reason with them. Maybe they will realize we are just children and let us go.

"Please don't hurt us. We're just children. We're hungry and were just looking for food."

They stare at me with hardened expressions. They are dark and dangerous, dressed like assassins in their black-on-black uniforms and their penetrating stares. They look at me like I am livestock, beneficial but still disposable.

"I don't think they're going to hurt us, Ember, or else they wouldn't have tied me up," Teddy says. Before I can respond, one of the men narrows his eyes at me.

"Ember? Your name is Ember?"

I nod, wondering what this means. Why would they care what my name is?

They turn towards one another and discuss something in their language, their tones intense and urgent. One of them speaks into a radio and listens for the response.

There is no time for a response. As the man dips his ear towards the radio, an enormous explosion rocks the house.

The window in the kitchen blows inward with a hail of glass. Heat fills the room as shards of debris flies through the shattered window.

Teddy screams and rocks forward in his chair.

I dive under the kitchen table and pull him under with me, chair and all. Glass and wood rains down all around us.

The men kneel down, covering their heads with their hands. When it ends, they open the back door and run towards the site of the explosion.

I scramble from under the table.

174

"Hurry!" Teddy prompts me.

I tear through the kitchen drawers, but can't find a knife.

"Where's your knife?" I ask Teddy.

"It's in my backpack." He glances over his shoulder. His backpack is wedged between him and his chair.

"Dammit!" I turn and find the silverware drawer and dig until I find the largest knife in the drawer. It only takes me a few seconds to cut through the tape. Once I have an end, I rip it away from his skin.

"Owww, Ember. That hurts."

"It's better than a bullet. Come on." I push him towards the front door. If we can get through the door, we can run down the road and find a new place to hide while the bad men are preoccupied. We are halfway there when a man comes through the doorway and stops us.

I start to scream, but the man clamps his hand over my mouth. I stare at him wordlessly, understanding now who has been following us all along and who just came to our defense.

It is Henry Rivers.

22

If Henry recognizes me, he shows no signs of it.

"Come on. Move!" He grabs my arm and yanks me towards the doorway. I look down at his feet and find the same sort of work boots that had left the trail in the dusty road. He is the one who has been following us.

"Henry?" I ask him, and he pinches my arm a little tighter.

"Just move it." He opens the door and pulls me through it. Teddy grabs onto my other arm until we are a chain of people being led by a madman.

Henry leads us outside, where thick smokes rolls across the lawn. The smell is choking and thick with the pungent smell of burning rubber mixed with the thick smell of oil. I duck my face into my arm and try not to cough.

"Where are we going?" I whisper, but he pretends not to hear me.

I think that he is going to pull us down the road and away from the bad men, but he doesn't. He brings us to the corner of the house and motions for us to pause, his hand held up like a crossing guard.

I compress myself against the side of the house, feeling the smooth dusty siding beneath my palms. Teddy presses himself tightly behind me and I can feel the gallop of his heartbeat through his sweaty shirt.

Henry peers around the corner of the house. His fingers dig into my arm.

"All right. Come on." He pulls us towards the driveway, where the bad men's black Bronco is parked. It is one of those testosterone-laden trucks with big tires and lethal-looking roll bars. It has been painted flat black, a color that will not reflect light. Henry is looking at it hungrily.

I want to grab his arm and pull him away. How can he think this will work? We should be sneaking away as quietly as possible, trying to make our way as far down the road as we can before the bad men remember us. Henry moves forward and pulls us along behind him again.

We round the corner and I hold my breath, terrified.

The bad men are nearly lost in the smoke as they inspect the source of the explosion.

We take another step forward, and then stop. Henry makes a low shushing sound.

Something rumbles inside the garage. The bad men jump back skittishly as though they fear another explosion. They don't see us.

We move forward. I duck down behind Henry, using him as a shield. Behind me, Teddy does the same until we are like a Chinese box puzzle with each layer smaller than the first. If bullets begin to spew, I don't want to be hit and neither does Teddy.

Smoke is rolling out of the garage and the front wall hangs in shreds behind the thick black facade. The pickup truck that had been parked in the driveway is engulfed in flames, the windshield blown out and the tires burning freely, as if ignited by gasoline. It could be a scene from a war.

I try to wrench myself away from Henry, wanting to run as far as I can, but he has an iron grasp on my arm. He pulls us to the truck and motions for us to climb inside.

"Ember?" Teddy asks, and I just squeeze his hand. I don't know if I should trust this person, but I do not have many other options. I could run down the road and hope for the best, knowing very well that the next good hiding place might be a mile away, or I could follow this strange Henry and hope he knows what he's doing. He has one thing going for him. He saved us from certain death in the kitchen. For now, that is enough for me. We climb into the back seat of the Bronco as he hops into the front. I lean forward until I am between the bucket seats.

"What are you doing?" I ask.

Keys dangle from the steering wheel and he turns them, making the engine lunge to life. The men startle at the rumbling sound, twisting around with their mouths agape, twin looks of astonishment on their faces. One of them yells something at us, while the other reaches for his side mount.

"Get down," Henry tells us, but doesn't follow his own advice. He shifts the vehicle into reverse with one hand and pushes my head to the floor with the other. In seconds, we are propelled backwards down the driveway.

I hear several small explosions, which are followed by the hollow thunk of bullets striking metal. The men yell again and then the truck stops with a sudden jolt.

I ease up from the floorboard, fully expecting to find Henry slumped over the steering wheel with a bullet hole in his head, but am surprised to find him staring straight ahead, visibly unharmed, his hand gripping the steering wheel with pale knuckles.

"You want a piece of me?" he screams, the cords in his neck bulging outwards. "You want a PIECE OF ME?" The veins stand out at his temples and his eyes are narrowed down to slits. Danger wafts off of him in waves.

I do not know what he is planning to do until it is already too late to protest. He puts the truck into drive and he thunders back down the driveway to where the bad men stand in front of the burning truck. The surprise is so full-on, so sudden, they do not think to move out of the way. They continue to hammer us with bullets, but they are no match for the tremendous moving vehicle coming their way. Without pause or gasp, Henry rams into them, pushing them into the burning truck and smashing them into the garage.

The moment we hit, I make eye contact with one of the men and I consider for one moment that he is a person, as bad as he may be. He is still flesh and blood, with hopes and dreams and a beating pulse, until he is simply one less.

"YEAH!" Henry screams.

The impact is sudden and jarring. I am thrown against Henry's seat, my shoulder connecting solidly with the black vinyl. Teddy careens into the passenger seat, his knee knocking soundly into my leg. We strike so firmly, my teeth snap together and my head feels as though it has come loose from my shoulders. I only have two or three seconds to consider the moment before Henry hops from the vehicle and leaves us alone.

I rise up and peer over the top of the seat. Through the smoke, I can see the bloody remains of the man I'd made eye contact with, bent backwards over the charred and burning remains of the pickup truck. His arms are thrown above his head and the place where his midsection is supposed to be is nothing more than pulverized flesh. Fire is licking at his body, catching the edges of his shirt on fire. I turn away, feeling my stomach lurching once again.

"What's he doing?" Teddy asks, staring full-on at the gore and destruction as though it were nothing.

I look up to see Henry picking up one of the bad men's walkie-talkies. He shakes it, dusts it off, and then puts it to his ear. I don't know if it is working or not because his expression never changes, but he slips it into the pocket of his loose black jacket and makes his way back to where we wait.

179

He climbs in without a word or even a glance in my direction and puts the truck into reverse again. The engine revs with a loud animal roar and we rocket down the driveway.

He turns left towards the river. I am surprised by the direction, but I don't say anything. It is obvious that Henry has a plan.

We drive for ten minutes in total silence, the sound of my pounding heart keeping me company as we bump and thump along the rutted country road. I pull myself up off the floorboard and stare out the window, watching the scenery rush past. The mountains in the distance pass by in a blur. My thoughts are wild horses, running rampant. Teddy reaches over and touches my hand.

His eyes are wide and wild.

"Are you okay?" He stares at me for a few seconds and then slowly nods. He's probably not okay. I can see it in his eyes and the way he is sitting bolt upright, clutching the arm rest with his other hand. He is as shell-shocked as I am, if not more so. We've seen things in the last several hours that most people would never see in an entire lifetime. I begin to appreciate what people living in a war must endure. I wish there was some place where we could go and just feel safe for a little while.

I close my eyes against the thought, imagining green grass beneath me and towering oaks above me, their gentle leaves swaying in the slight summer breeze while birds chattered calmly in the distance. We would have a cabin with a fireplace and a storeroom filled with stolen food. In the evening, we would light a fire without fear of being seen and would play a game of gin rummy in the light of the flickering flames. Teddy would go fishing during the day and would come back with a handful of trout or bass and we'd fry them over an open flame, coating them first with cornmeal and flour to make them crispy

180

and delicious. I would tend to a garden, bringing a daily bounty of fresh corn on the cob and sugar squash. We'd eat until we were full and then sleep until we woke. And we'd have plenty of batteries to chase away the darkness.

We bump along the road and I open my eyes before I can fall asleep. I do not have very much control over this new Henry, but being asleep would give me less than nothing. I turn around to see a plume of dust behind us. In a little while it will dissipate and be gone and forgotten, but for ten minutes we are leaving a trail as obvious as neon arrows.

I lean forward until my mouth is level to Henry's ear.

"Where are we going?" I ask, but he pretends not to hear me. He has put on a pair of dark, wraparound sunglasses and stares out the windshield. Behind the glasses, he could be thinking anything and I'd never know it. If he didn't turn the wheel from time to time or adjust his grip on the steering wheel, I'd wonder if he were even awake. It very suddenly occurs to me that we've traded one captor for another.

It is hot in the truck, so I pull off my hooded jacket and tie it around my waist and then crack the window. A thin stream of perfectly dusty air fills the air and chases away some of the blistering heat.

We come to the curve in the road where the trestle shack is located and I think he is going to stop, but he only slows. He peers into the woods for a moment and then pounds the accelerator again, making the back end of the truck fishtail in the soft gravel.

"Hey, Ember," Teddy says, touching my arm to get my attention.

I look at him. He has something in his hand he is trying to give me. It takes me a moment to understand what it is until he flips it over and I see the familiar face of a clock, with hands

181

positioned at ten fifteen. The second hand sweeps around with steady ticks.

I couldn't be happier if Teddy had handed me a ham sandwich.

"Oh, Teddy. Thank you." I give him a one-armed hug, catching a quick whiff of fragrant unwashed boy, before I release him to his side of the seat. I take the watch in my hand and turn it over a few times. It is a standard Timex with both a battery and a manual winder, giving it an extended life after the battery has expired. "Where did you get this?"

He shrugs, which I'm learning is a Teddy Defense Mechanism to ward off undue praise. It is a gallant, no-worries guy-kind-of-thing. My father used to do it from time to time, telling us that he was happy to be the hero, but to not make too much of a fuss about it. Or more than likely, he enjoyed the fuss but didn't want to appear to be enjoying it.

"Did you find it at the house?" I prod.

He stares out the front windshield at the bleak, dusty road ahead of us. "Yeah. It was sitting on the kitchen table." He touches the watch. "Look at it, Ember. It has the date on it too."

I hold it closer and squint at the numbers. It is Thursday, August 26th. I gasp.

"Oh my God."

Teddy nearly jumps. "What?"

I touch his arm. "No, it's nothing. Relax. It's just that..."

"What?" he asks, and even though I don't want to make a big deal of it, I can't just drop the subject now. I sigh and give him a weak smile.

"It's my birthday the day after tomorrow. No big deal."

"Oh," he says, and it is the end of the conversation. It is my birthday, but it is also just any other day. If Teddy hadn't given me the watch, I would have never known. It is stunning to realize just how much has changed in one single year.

"Didn't we all go to the zoo last year for your birthday?" Teddy asks, as if reading my thoughts. I smile against the memory, even though I want to cry.

"Yeah, we did." I remember the warm sunshiny day and the hum of casual conversation as we drove the hour's drive to the zoo. Our mothers sat in the front seat, talking mom-talk, while we sat thigh-to-thigh in the back seat with Teddy in the middle hogging the space. Once we got there, all was forgotten. It was as though we'd stepped into another land, another place. A place where lions and zebras roamed and monkeys begged for grapes. I hadn't been to the zoo since I was a small child. I remember the heady smell of animal dung and the foreign sounds of exotic animals calling to one another, and the relaxing feel of having a bottomless day with no time limit. My mother said we could stay as late as we wanted to.

I wonder what happened to all the animals after all the people died. If we went there, would we find tigers and elephants roaming the streets, or would we find cages filled with death?

"How old will you be on your birthday?" Teddy asks, and I have to think about it for a moment. Age has become irrelevant now. I could be sixteen or I could be thirty.

"Seventeen." I close my eyes for a moment, imaging a world where I could be seventeen and it counted. "I'd have my driver's license by now." I think about my father and the way he'd been working on an old Jeep for me. He'd found it in the want ads and had spent a year toiling over it, putting on new tires and a new hardtop on it, rebuilding the engine and transmission until it purred like a kitten. He was getting ready to replace the old dry-rotted seats with new ones just before he

183

died. It had been sitting in his work shed ever since. I'd pacify myself by riding around the edge of the property on his old dirt bike when my mother wasn't around to see me.

"Do you know how to drive?" Henry asks very suddenly. His voice is so unexpected I jolt around in my seat, feeling as though my heart has lunged upward.

"Yes. My father taught me how to drive when I was fifteen."

"Good." He pulls over the side of the road and throws the truck into park. "You can drive for a while. I need to wrap my wound." I am not certain which part of his announcement shocks me the most: the fact that he wants me to drive or that he has a wound.

"You're hurt?"

He opens the door for me and I climb out.

"Yeah, it's nothing. I got grazed with a bullet." He lifts his shirt sleeve to show me a shallow gash running along the side of his arm. There is a perfectly round hole in the windshield. I follow the line of the trajectory and see a clean bullet hole in the seat behind him. I look into the back seat, and find a twin bullet hole through the seat where I would have been sitting had Henry not pushed me to the floor. The entire world becomes wobbly for a moment.

"Oh God. That would have hit me." I catch myself on the door of the truck and force myself to focus.

Henry glances at the back seat. "But it didn't. Consider yourself lucky and stop whining."

I stand a little taller and frown at him. "I'm not whining."

"Could have fooled me," he says. He comes very close to smiling before turning away.

I roll my eyes and begin rooting around in my backpack until I find something edible. I find the half package of saltine crackers. It's not much, but it will stave off the hunger until we can find something else.

"Hungry?" I ask Teddy and hand him a few after he nods. I try to hand a stack to Henry, but he looks at them as though I am trying to hand him a handful of dog turds.

"It's just crackers," I tell him, a bit irritated.

He stares at my hand for a moment longer before he turns to climb into the backseat. "I don't eat anything I didn't find myself," he says.

"Whatever." I swiftly divide the cracker pile in half and give some to Teddy. "More for us."

I shove a cracker into my mouth and spend a minute adjusting the seats and the mirror to my liking. Once I'm as comfortable as possible, I pull on my seat belt and meet Henry's eyes in the rearview mirror, or at least what I assume are his eyes behind the black wraparound sunglasses.

"Where to?"

He doesn't move an inch. "Just keep driving. I'll tell you when to turn."

We drive along the dirt road for nearly a half hour before he says another word.

"Turn here, at the next road," he says, finally. I glance behind me to see that he has torn off a piece of his shirt and has wrapped it around his bicep to stop the bleeding. I don't know a lot about first aid, but I believe that he will need to disinfect it before it gets infected. I don't share this information with him because it is evident that he doesn't care what I think. His arm can rot off for all I care.

I turn at the next road, which is an identical sibling to the road we were on. It just leads into another direction, away from the meandering river and towards higher ground where the vegetation is thicker. The houses we have passed are lifeless

185

and I have to wonder if they have been picked clean or if they contain any needed supplies. The cramps in my lower abdomen remind me that I am going to need tampons soon and I doubt that my new captor has any of those in his backpack. I imagine myself turning into a random driveway, taking matters into my own hands, but I can also imagine Henry putting his gun to the back of my head, so I just keep driving. I have to trust in fate at this point. It's all I've got.

The road begins to climb upwards, the passage becoming steeper by the minute. I look up and see the shadow of a mountain rising above me. The trees nearly swallow the road with a canopy of leaves and the temperature cools off substantially. I crack my window to let in some of the sweet fresh air.

We drive for another ten minutes before we come to a fallen tree across the road. I stop and put the truck into park, waiting for my next instructions.

"Okay kid, you get out and help me move the tree," he says to Teddy.

Teddy hops out without protest and they move the tree out of the way.

Henry returns to the vehicle and approaches my door.

"Scoot over. I'm going to drive now."

I move to the passenger's seat, happy to be relieved of my duties. Henry jumps in and moves the truck forward twenty feet and then jumps back out to move the fallen tree back across the road. I can't imagine it is much of a deterrent, but I am not about to question him. For all I know, there are wireless cameras in the trees, monitoring our progress, and booby traps hidden in the bramble. He seems so prepared, so self-contained; nothing would surprise me at this point.

We drive up the mountain, bumping through deep ruts and bottoming out on top of large stones that protrude through the road. We stop two more times to move trees from the road and one more time to add a large branch to a place in the road that had been clear before. It gives me pause for thought, because it is evident that once we get to where we are going, we are going to stay for a while. Panic rises in me as I realize I'm getting farther from Elizabeth instead of closer.

"Where are you taking us?" I ask, but he doesn't respond. "Henry, I need to find my sister. The bad men took her. I appreciate you saving us, but can you just take us back to town?"

He glances in my direction, his expression emotionless. "It's a little too late for that."

"Too late for what?" I ask, but he stills me with a raised finger.

He leans out the window, listening for something. After a moment, I hear a steady pounding. It reminds me of the sound of workmen building a house, of the sound of a hammer striking wood. Henry pulls himself back into the window and continues on.

"What was that?" Teddy asks me and I shrug my shoulders. I can't even hazard a guess and I am not asking Henry.

The truck rumbles up the final hill and we come to a clearing at the top of the mountain where the trees have been shaved away. It takes my eyes a moment to adjust, but when they do, I blink again, amazed at what I see.

"Do you see what I see?" Teddy asks.

I look to where he is pointing and I don't know what to think.

22

I nearly rub my eyes. Nearly a dozen people are walking around. They are mostly young, muscular men, but I see a woman in the group as well, which reassures me somewhat. The men are working on a project and are carrying lumber, hauling buckets, and talking to one another as they work. They look up suspiciously as we crest the hill, but then return to what they were doing as soon as they recognize Henry.

The area is a lodge or camp of some kind. It has a deep-rooted feel to it as though it has been hunkered down at the top of the small mountain for decades. A long brown cabin with screen windows sits at the edge of the clearing. Not far behind it is an A-frame building with no walls, only the long lines of a ceiling. In the middle of the clearing is a flag pole without any flags. In the near distance, I can see the peaked roofs of several other small buildings, hiding in the edges of the forest like deer peering into the meadow.

I am nearly euphoric. My mind simply cannot wrap itself around the vision in front of me and I want to laugh, cry, and shriek all at the same time. The people are buzzing around everywhere, working, building, and chatting as though the end of the world never happened. They don't glance over their shoulders with fear in their eyes or stay close to the edge of the woods, careful to keep an easy hiding place at hand. They don't seem to have any interest in us. For some reason, it reminds me of the Utopian cities of ancient lore we studied in Social Studies, where everything was perfect and harmony was a constant.

"Where are we?" I ask Henry, but he doesn't even glance in my direction.

"Just wait here," he says, and hops out.

Several people stop what they are doing and walk towards him.

I turn to Teddy. "Do you know where we are?"

"Yeah, this is Camp Montauk," Teddy says, as if I know what he's talking about.

"What's that?"

"It's a Boy Scout camp. I came here once for day camp."

I don't have to close my eyes to imagine it. I can easily picture the land filled with boys instead of adults, bustling about, setting up tents and organizing projects. I always wanted to be a scout, but the girl's version never seemed to have as much fun as the boy's version. Who wanted to learn how to roast pumpkin seeds or glue Popsicle sticks together when you could climb a mountain or kayak down a river?

"I don't like this, Ember. Something's not right."

I climb into the back seat next to Teddy. I reach down and hold his hand, ignoring the way it sticks to my skin as though he has been handling wet lollipops all day.

"Let's just see what happens. Surely Henry won't let anything happen to us."

"Who are those people?" he asks. "Do you recognize anybody?"

Henry is talking to two people. One is an older man with light grey hair and a full beard, and the other is an attractive younger woman, with shoulder-length blond hair. They glance in our direction, and I recognize the older man. Something inside me turns slippery and cold.

"Isn't that the dog catcher?" Teddy asks.

"Yeah, that's him." I think about how they were studying the dead woman on the sidewalk outside the library and wonder what is going on. Teddy's right, something isn't right. I can feel it in my bones.

"Just stay on your guard," I tell him, and he nods. I lean forward in the seat to eavesdrop.

"Why did you bring them here?" The dog catcher asks Henry. "Do the Hostiles know you have them?"

Henry shrugs. "I'm not sure."

"God damn it, Henry. Now they're going to be looking for us. You've put everybody in jeopardy."

Henry looks both dejected and angry at the same time. "What do you want me to do with them? Just leave them there?"

"You could have brought them somewhere else. I thought you were smarter than that."

The woman touches the older man's arm. "Denver, they're just children. I think he did the right thing. Henry and I will take care of them. We'll move them somewhere. Don't worry."

He bristles. "Don't worry about it? Don't WORRY about it? I don't see you busting your backside trying to keep this place safe." He looks towards us, his eyes narrowed down to slits. "They are going to have to go into the cellar until we figure out what to do with them."

My heart lurches at the thought of being thrown into a cellar. He might as well have said prison. I fear we are no better off than we were before. We're just in a different enemy camp. Henry glances at us, and then turns back to the man.

"If I hadn't taken them, the Hostiles would have gotten them. You really wanted that to happen?" Henry asks, his face reddening.

Denver throws his hands up. "Just keep them out of my way. We'll figure out something to do with them later."

I sit back in the seat with a thump.

"What did they mean by that?'" Teddy asks.

"I'm not sure, but...do you remember when the bad men asked if my name was Ember?"

Teddy nods. "You think Elizabeth told them about you?"

190

"I can't imagine any other way. But, why would they care?"

"What are we gonna do, Ember? I don't think these guys are very nice."

He's right. The concept that there would be more than one bad-guy camp scares me to the tips of my toes. "Just keep your eyes open."

After a minute or two of further conversation, Henry walks away without a glance back at us. He disappears into the brown building, leaving us to the mercy of the two new people. The dog catcher and the blond lady remain at the front of the Bronco, talking in hushed tones that I can't make out, their lips moving in avid conversation.

After a moment, the dog catcher shrugs and strides towards us. I feel my shoulders stiffen.

"I don't trust that man," Teddy whispers.

"Me neither."

A memory comes to me, like an air-blown wish. I remember a television program I once watched about how to survive scary situations; one of them had been about surviving a kidnapping. As he comes closer, I shut my eyes and try to force the memory. It comes to me bit by bit.

Rule number one: Attempt to thwart the abduction.

It is a little too late for rule number one. We had already been abducted when Henry found us.

Rule number two: Remind them you are a human being. Say your name as many times as possible.

The dog catcher stops in front of the opened door and pulls the front seat forward, making room for us to climb out of the back seat. He leans through the opening and frowns.

"All right. I need you to come on out of there and follow me," he says, his voice husky and raw. He is dressed in an olive t-shirt that has been tucked into military-style khaki pants with lots of pockets. A shark tooth on a faded gold chain hangs from his neck, making me wonder if he pulled it himself. He is scary. There's no doubt he is the man in charge of the camp. He looks like a retired military man, someone who does a hundred push-ups before getting into the shower each morning and then eats a dozen toddlers for breakfast.

"Where are you taking us?" I ask, hoping he will make eye contact with me, even for a second, but he doesn't. He glances around the inside of the Bronco as though he's looking for something.

"Come on, hurry it up."

I let go of Teddy's hand and climb out of the back seat. My feet hit the ground and I am treated to the same pins-and-needle sensation as before. I turn to grab my backpack, but he puts a hand on my shoulder.

"Leave the backpacks here."

I take a deep breath, wishing he would have overlooked them. I have a nice big kitchen knife tucked in my pack, along with several heavy cans of vegetables that could be used as weapons. I extend a hand to Teddy.

"Come on Teddy. Don't be afraid. It'll be okay," I say, giving him a secret wink so he will play along. Teddy pauses for a moment, giving me a blank, almost fearful look, and then the understanding washes over his face in a wave.

"But Ember. I am afraid. I've been hiding from the bad men for two months and now that guy brought us here. I'm so scared." He is a bit over the top with the dramatics and I want to roll my eyes, but I'm afraid he will take it the wrong way and do something foolish.

"I know, Teddy. I've been hiding from the bad men too and I'm scared too, but I'm sure these nice people are going to take good care of us. After all, we are on the same side, right?" I pause, wondering how much of our little play the dog catcher has caught. I'm not certain if there is even an ounce of compassion inside of him, but I have to try to find it. If he realizes that we are just children and we are afraid, maybe he will be kind to us. I can feel him standing behind me, his impatience growing like a dark storm cloud.

"Come on and hurry it up," he says again, this time with a sigh for good measure. "I ain't got all day."

Teddy climbs out and stands beside me. Before the dog catcher can close the Bronco door, I turn so that I am standing right in front of him. I cock my head slightly as though I've had a sudden insight.

"Hey, I know you. Weren't you the animal control officer?" I ask, wishing I had a positive story to share with him, like how he once saved my kitten from the jaws of a snarling dog. All I have is the bad story about the feral cat, but I don't think that will help my efforts any.

He glances up for a split second and I am rewarded with one perfect second of clarity. In that second, I see that he is still the same person he was before the virus. His eyes are bright and intelligent, not dazed and hostile. He might not have been a very good person before the virus, but at least he hasn't gone crazy. He was probably mean and power hungry before it all happened. The end of the world has only provided him with opportunities that he obviously cherishes.

"My name is Ember, and this is Teddy," I say, falling back to rule number two.

"I know who you are." He points towards the brown building "Head on into the building"

A smart girl would probably make a break for it. She'd put an elbow into the dog catcher's stomach, and then she'd run for all she was worth. I look around me for a way to escape, but don't see one that didn't end with him tackling me. Something from the television show comes back to me.

Rule number three: Pay close attention to your surroundings.

We walk into the brown building and find ourselves in a makeshift living room. The room is one big open area, with rustic log walls and pine board ceilings stained a hearty redwood color. Long rows of picnic tables fill the room, with the back half of the room set up as a kitchen. Food rations are stocked from the floor to the ceiling. I wonder if this is what Henry was doing when he found us, if he frequently went to town and raided abandoned houses for food and supplies when he wasn't snatching up children.

I stop when I reach the center of the room, waiting for more instructions. I am hoping that this is all a big mistake and he will lead us to one of the tables and provide us with a nice hot meal, but he does no such thing. He leads us to a hole in the floor, where the top of a ladder pokes through.

"Go on down there," he says, poking me in the back with his finger.

I pause, fear rushing through me. Once we are in the cellar, there will be no escape. Maybe I can catch him off guard and push him in.

He grabs my arm with a vice grip, as if reading my mind.

"Don't even think about it, sister. I could pick you up and throw you down there if I have to. Now, climb on down there like a good little girl," he says, giving me a slight shove forward for good measure.

I stumble and catch myself just short of the ladder. I flip him a dirty look before I remember that I shouldn't.

Rule number four: Avoid making an enemy of your captor

I should be polite and sympathize with him, letting him know that I'm on his side. The more comfortable he feels around me, the better my chances for release. I steady myself inside before turning towards him. I try to still the anger and replace it with a softer expression.

"I'll do whatever you want me to do. You don't need to push me. We're just scared, mister. We're just children," I tell him.

"Yeah, whatever. You're nothing more than Hostile magnets. Henry should have left you where he found you."

"What would the bad men have done with us?" I ask him.

He lowers one eyebrow. "That's what you call them? The Bad Men?" he asks.

"I guess. What do you call them?"

"We call them the Hostiles."

"What would they have done to us, if Henry hadn't rescued us?"

He ignores my question. "Get on down that ladder. I don't have time for this." He puts his hand on the small of my back and pushes me forward. I step onto the ladder. It seems important to do this, to let him know that I am compliant and willing to follow his orders and also, to remind him that I am a child.

I glance towards the door and see the blond lady standing there, watching us. The look in her eye is much softer, and I hope that my little performance hasn't been wasted after all. Hopefully she will help us when she gets a chance. It's obvious they are all more than a little intimidated by the dog catcher.

I climb down, feeling the temperature drop nearly twenty degrees as I reach the bottom. My jacket is still tied around my waist, making me glad I didn't ditch it when it got warmer.

As Teddy climbs down behind me, I take a few seconds to look around. The cellar is stale and sour. The smell of moth balls, combined with the stench of musty gym-bags, makes me want gag.

The walls are dark paneled, and the floors are concrete, covered with faded Native American print rugs. Clear glass blocks line the top of the long wall, allowing just enough sunshine to enter into the room without needing electricity to keep the space lit. Well-worn couches have been set up in the front of the room, while the back is filled with rugged wooden bunk beds. Meager light streams through the dirty windows, giving the room a brown- tinted glow.

Henry is at the back of the room, rooting through a green foot locker that probably came from an Army surplus store. When he stands up, I see that he is carrying an armful of blankets. He tosses them onto one of the bare mattresses on a bunk bed and moves past us, without a word. As he passes, I touch his arm.

"Thank you for the blankets, Henry."

He makes brief eye contact with me and for one split second, I see my old math tutor, the boy who would say "Try it again," with light in his eyes as I struggled over a complicated math problem. I give him the smallest of smiles, trying to hold his attention as long as I can.

"Can you also get us something to eat? Teddy and I are very hungry."

He yanks his arm back as though he's angry I have touched him.

"You've already gotten me in enough trouble. Just cool your heels for a little while until I figure this out, okay?"

His words surprise me and I find myself backing away. "I'm sorry. I'm just scared."

He turns. "Good. I'm glad you're scared. It's what keeps you alive." He pushes past me, leaving me to consider his words.

He is probably irritated that I made him remember the person he used to be, the person he left behind in the rubble of the old world we once lived in. Does he cling to this new persona because it is the only way he knows how to be in the new world, or does he claim this new Henry because he can't help himself? The virus might have churned his brains around and made him into this new version, but I have to wonder if it's possible to churn them back. The brief glimmer I saw in his eyes gives me hope. The old Henry is still in there somewhere. It just might take more than a touch of his arm to find him.

He doesn't look back as he climbs up, disappearing bit by bit until all I can see are the soles of his shoes. As soon as he reaches the top, the ladder is pulled upwards and the trap door is closed, shutting us into our dungeon.

Something shifts inside of me and I relax a little, even though I probably shouldn't. We are trapped in a cellar hole, but it is the first time in months when I haven't felt as though I were being hunted. I feel safe and secure for the strangest of reasons. It washes through me like a cold chill, leaving me languid and rubbery. I feel as though I could sleep for days.

Teddy begins walking the perimeter of the room. There is something very serious in the bend of his neck that reminds me of an old man. He leans down and touches his hand to the floor to balance himself, peers beneath a bed and then moves on to inspect a gap in the paneling.

"What are you looking for?" I ask.

"I dunno. Just looking, I guess."

I follow his gaze around the room, taking in the long line of bunk beds that create a U shape at the end of the room. If there

197

is an alternative escape route, it is very well hidden. All I can see are solid walls.

"Didn't you say you stayed here for camp or something?" I ask.

"Yeah, but they never let us down into this room. I just came for day camp. The older Scouts had tents outside. I think this is just for bad weather or something. You know, if they have bad thunderstorms or something, they let them come in here to sleep." He continues his inspection of the room, pausing occasionally to look under a bed or inside a foot locker. After a few minutes he returns to where I stand.

"Well?" I ask.

"Nothing. Just a couple of dust bunnies."

"That's not good."

He looks up at me. "How are we going to get out of here?" His eyes are little-boy wide.

"I don't know, but we'll think of something." I say, and he seems to accept this.

He takes a deep breath as if trying to calm himself. "Maybe we should try to get some sleep. You wanna take first shift?" he asks.

I stare at him for a moment as his words sink in. The things I've seen have almost made me punch drunk, giddy in a way that borders on hysteria, but I shut it down with a swallow. Teddy is right. We need to stay focused on the practical. We should rest while we can and it makes perfect sense for one of us to remain awake in case anything happens. I feel the world settle heavily around me once more.

"Yeah sure. You go to sleep. I'll keep watch," I tell him because I am the oldest and it feels like the right thing to do.

"Okay," he says, already moving towards the end of the room before I can finish my sentence. I watch him pat a few

198

mattresses until he finds one that doesn't send a cloud of dust upwards. He grabs a blanket from the pile Henry has left us and climbs in. Within seconds, I can hear the soft sound of his snores.

A feeling of emptiness and loneliness washes over me, making me feel lost and confused. A part of me wants to take full credit for the series of events that have led us here. Had I simply followed Teddy's lead, we'd still be camped out by the river, eating crackers and sardines, watching the lazy current of the water carrying driftwood around the bend.

I'd been determined to have more. I wanted batteries, better food, toiletries, and shoes for Teddy. Realistically, I probably could have gone without most of them and improvised the rest with things that were around me. I think a part of me will always long for the things I cannot have. It is the worst part of my human nature. It is the biggest thing that gets me into trouble.

I turn, to where the couches form an L at the front of the rectangular room. A large scarred black coffee table is centered in front of the couches and is filled with scouting magazines. They wouldn't be my first choice of reading materials, but they will do. I am suddenly as hungry for words as I am for food.

The magazine on top of the pile has a picture of a boy snorkeling on the cover and is dated for June, which seems ironic to me. By June, the majority of the world was already dead.

I flip open the magazine, ready to devour it cover to cover, and find my eyes watering in the middle of the first paragraph. Sleep finds me by the second article, whether I want it to or not, and in my sleep I find Elizabeth. She is calling to me in a way that makes me wonder if it is really a dream or not.

23

The dream is blue, lit from within by the glow from the hazy blush of sunlight streaming through the depths of the green-blue water. I feel the pressure in my ears from sitting on the bottom, looking up at a watery world I cannot inhabit for more than a minute at a time, and then I push off for the surface, regretful yet happy, and I realize that I am dreaming about Decker's Park.

Decker's Park was divided into two sections. One side of the park contained a moderate-sized amusement park, complete with Mother Goose themed rides and concessions. The other side was home to Decker Lake. My mother wouldn't bring us to the amusement park very often, claiming that the crowds and the noise gave her a migraine, but she would, on occasion, bring us to the lake.

On sweltering hot July days, we'd rise from our beds with the sheets clinging to our skin like onion paper and beg her to bring us swimming. There was usually some urgent project she needed to attend to and the answer would be "maybe tomorrow," but sometimes she would look at us with weary eyes and just give into our wishes.

One hot Monday in July we found ourselves on the right side of the question. The Beach Boys played on the speakers as we skipped across the hot sand, hopping from foot to foot, finding shadows and corners of beach towels to step on. My mother was behind us, lugging her beach chair, her face hidden beneath a giant straw hat and owlish sunglasses, saying "excuse me" and "so sorry" to all the people we trampled on our way to the perfect spot.

We found a place on the beach that was close to the water, but not too close to the action, a place where my mother could thumb through a magazine without getting sand kicked in her face from kids running in and out of the surf, but close enough to keep an eye on Elizabeth, who still couldn't swim by herself.

We'd tried to bring her to swimming lessons at the Y, but Elizabeth was unpredictable. Sometimes she would just glide through a situation, just rolling with the punches like any other kid, but other times she would find something completely intolerable and would dig her heels in until we finally just gave up. Swimming lessons were a part of the latter. My father had been harping on my mother to sign her up for months after seeing a sign posted on the grocery store's community bulletin board.

"With that lake in our front yard, we really need to teach her how to swim," he'd said, and my mother had turned away, like she always did when my father discussed something she wasn't comfortable with. She had tried to change the subject, but he'd been determined, wearing her down until she finally just picked up the phone and registered my sister for something she knew she wouldn't finish.

We'd shown up, after spending several days over-promoting the event with the same fake-happy voices we'd use to get her to the dentist, and she'd taken one look at the deep patch of ultramarine water and had furrowed her brows. We tried to lure her in, but she was unbendable. "Don't wanna," came from her lips, softly at first and finally evolving to a volume that silenced the room, causing mothers and children alike to turn their heads to see who's child was throwing the tantrum. My mother, exhausted from the efforts and shamed by the tisking from her peers, took Elizabeth by the shoulders and turned her around towards the door.

"I'll teach her myself," she'd said under her breath, just loud enough for me to hear, but no one else. I'd known better, even then at the gullible age of fourteen, that she would say this but never follow through with her good intentions. Elizabeth would continue to do what she wanted to do as long as she could find the right combination of exhaustion and embarrassment to ply my mother with.

We found a patch of sand near the lake and claimed it with our vibrant beach towels and then cast off our rubber-soled flip-flops with a kick and ran for the water as though we were drowning from air. We reached the water with a splash, the smell of coconut suntan lotion and the earthy tang of pond water filling our heads full of happy, endless-day thoughts.

"Watch your sister!" my mother called after us. I glanced up to find Elizabeth standing there in her pink Barbie bathing suit, her blond hair flying out behind her like a tattered yellow flag, her mouth curved into a soft pink smile. I parted through the bodies of children bobbing in the water until I found an open space, and I dove beneath the water, feeling the temperature of the water grow colder and colder as I swam deeper and deeper into the depths.

I swam along the bottom, pulling myself along with my hands until I found a place where I could just sit and stare up through the layers of water at the world I'd left behind. The sun shone through the water in shades of blue, because of the unusually pure clarity of the lake water. It was like staring through blue sea glass.

When I couldn't hold my breath any longer, I pushed off from the bottom and parted through the thin skin that separated water from air. The sunshine was hurtful after living for a moment in the tepid blue of the water world and I blinked. I wanted to dive back down to my serene world below, but I caught a glimpse of Elizabeth and my heart froze with sudden fear.

202

She was riding on the shoulders of a girl I knew from school, her face brilliant and smiling. In her hands my sister held a beach ball that was yellow, blue, green, and red, sectioned like an orange. I kicked my feet back and forth, treading the water because I couldn't touch the bottom, and kept my eye on her, praying that my friend wouldn't carry her any deeper.

"Mary Beth, stop! She can't swim!" I called, but my words were lost in the crowd of noisy, clamoring children. I dove beneath the water and swam fish-like towards them as fast as I could. When I rose through the surface, Mary Beth was gone, and in her place the beach ball bobbed on the surface.

I looked at the ball, knowing that somewhere beneath it my sister was probably holding onto her last breath of air. I dove down again, imagining her struggling to claw her way to the surface, feeling the pounding of my pulse in my every movement. I reached the spot where I thought she would be, but could see nothing except for silt, kicked up from hundreds of moving feet.

I surfaced, the perfect quiet of the water giving way to the thundering buzz of a hundred giddy children screaming in delight. I looked around, hoping to find her on someone else's shoulders, but it was impossible to pick her out in the crowd. She was just one blond-haired girl in a pink bathing suit among many. All I could see were arms and backs, moving in a flurry of kaleidoscope body parts.

The sky above me darkened in an instant, as heavy black clouds moved in like iron filaments drawn to a magnet. The lake grew silent for a moment as everyone looked upwards, and then exploded in movement. Children splashed their way to the shore, where their mothers were hastily shoving beach towels and sand toys into bags and packing up lawn chairs.

"Elizabeth!" I called and caught a glimpse of my mother rising out of her lawn chair, the magazine slipping off her lap onto the sand.

I looked back down at the water in front of me, praying for a miracle.

Thunder rolled with a heavy timbre and then the first lightning strike flashed high in the darkening sky. As I stared, four small fingers grazed the surface of the water, illuminated by the lightning, and I simply stopped thinking. I dove for her. It came as pure instinct, the way you automatically hold your hands out in front of you when you trip over a crack in a sidewalk, the way you blink at strong sunlight. I don't even remember taking a huge breath before going under the water. I just went, praying that it wasn't too late.

My fingers found her first, intertwining in the strands of her long hair. They floated like silk in the blue-green water, hiding her face from my view. I grabbed her under her arms and lugged her to the surface, panic flooding my mind. She grew limp and heavy as we broke the surface, and for one moment I thought I had been too late. I imagined life guards pushing on her stomach and breathing into her blue lips, while we cried and prayed. But then she did something amazing. She opened her bright blue eyes and smiled. Lake water purged from her lungs, cough by cough, until she was able to breathe again, and the world became ours once more.

"Ember," she said my name, reaching for my face with her small fingers. The sky above us lightened, moment by moment. By the time I'd made it safely to the shore, the blue skies were back in place and the sun was shining as though it had never stopped. The B 52's were singing about a love shack, and behind the music was the seismic roar of the Big Dipper roller coaster heading over the big hill.

204

My mother met us at the edge of the water, her hands fluttering uselessly at her sides as though she wanted to do something but wasn't sure what she should do. It was unimaginable that something like this could happen to us after losing our father. I staggered out of the water with Elizabeth's heavy weight in my arms slipping steadily towards the ground. By the time I made it to the towel, she was nearly on her feet, stumbling forward, unsure of how to walk, her mind still reeling from being under the water for so long.

"She dropped me," she wailed as soon as I laid her down on the towel. "She DROPPED ME."

My mother narrowed her eyes at me, needing to level the blame at someone. "I told you to watch her."

I started to protest, but realized the futility in it. If I'd been watching her, she wouldn't have ended up nearly drowning. My sister's wailing became louder by the minute, eventually drawing a crowd, who stood in a circle around us waiting to see what would happen next. My mother and I just dug in and silently began packing up our beach things, and we left, pulling my sister behind us like an anchor as she began screaming "I don't wanna leave," over and over, her words losing punctuation and clarity with every retelling. It was the last time we ever went to Decker's Lake. As I begin to wake up, I see my sister's face in my mind, older, like she was the last time I saw her, still dressed in the white nightgown my mother gave her for Christmas. She leans forward, smiling as if to tell me a secret, and then she whispers the words that bring me fully awake.

Come find me, Ember. Come save me again.

24

I awake with a start, still sitting upright on the couch with the scouting magazine spread out on my lap, opened to the page of the scuba diver swimming beneath the water. Elizabeth's name is on my lips, and for a moment I swear I can taste the pond water on my tongue.

I don't know how long I've been sleeping. I jolt around with a start, guilt filling me. I glance at the wall where the glass blocks rim the ceiling, but they give nothing away. They are exactly the same as they'd been when we first came down. Through groggy thoughts, I remember that I am now in the possession of a wrist watch, and I look down, only to find it has slipped around backwards on my wrist. By the time I twist it around, I am nearly in a full-blown panic. It is two o'clock. I've been asleep for two hours, at least.

I jump up as though I've been goosed and look for Teddy. For a moment, it is like parting through the surface of the water and finding Elizabeth in danger, the panic bursting inside my chest, but I am safe this time. The sound of his soft snores radiates through the room like a blessing. I relax a little, happy that nothing horrible has happened during my failed attempt at standing guard. I have been given a second chance, a Get-Out-Of-Jail-Free card, and a chance to redeem myself. I sink back into the couch and try to bring my pulse back down to an even cadence.

I think about the dream for a moment, wondering if it were a product of my imagination or something altogether different. It just seemed so real, so fluid in its details. I allow myself the luxury of simply remembering my sister for a few minutes, recalling the funny things she used to do and the mannerisms that made her unique. She was different in a way that defied words. It was almost like she was a product of sheer inspiration, part girl, part pixie, part delusion. There were times when she was as normal as any little sister, but other times when she did things that thoroughly defied logic.

I think about the lightning. After her second lightning strike, I'd scurried off to the library to learn as much as I could. I didn't think people could survive even one strike, but never two. It just didn't seem possible. But there in black and white came the story of a man who'd been struck seven times in his lifetime. I read with urgency, wanting to know why, but even a library full of books couldn't answer that.

Was there something in the chemistry of Elizabeth's body that drew the lightning? A woman in Minnesota reportedly became psychic after being struck by lightning and spent the rest of her life helping the police track down missing persons. Was this what happened to Elizabeth? Had the first strike changed her into something different, something that made the lightning return again and again? Or had she been that way from the very beginning?

Probably the oddest aspect of Elizabeth's lightning strikes was the absence of burns. Everything I read about lightning strike victims spoke about their severe burns and the way the bolt seared down the skin, leaving charred flesh in its wake. After the dust had settled, Elizabeth had been fine. My mother had brushed it off as if it hadn't happened, burying her head in the sand like she always did with issues she didn't feel equipped to handle.

Before I can think about her any longer, footsteps thump above me, and the sound is followed by the opening of the trap door. A ladder slides down into the room and feet quickly descend, barely taking the time to find footing on the slim black treads. It is the woman from earlier, the one with the blond hair who was talking to Henry and the dog catcher.

She glances at me and then searches the room until she sees Teddy still sleeping on the bunk. In her hand are two brown paper bags. She walks to where I am and hands them to me quickly, as though it's something she isn't supposed to do.

"Here's some food for the two of you. Eat it quickly, and I'll come back to collect your trash later." She glances fearfully over her shoulder at the trap door as if to make sure she hasn't been overheard.

"Thank you." I touch her arm. "Can I ask you a question?"

She pauses, uncertainty straining her features. She doesn't seem to have that craziness in her eyes like Henry, which gives me the smallest twinge of hope.

"Maybe. What?" she asks.

I could ask her a thousand questions, starting with why we were being held captive and when we were going to be released, but I can see it on her face that she probably won't answer them, so I go back to rule number two, but instead of trying to remind her that I'm a human being, I try to remind her that she is one too.

"What is your name?" I ask.

She almost smiles. I can see it in her eyes. "Heather," she says with a whisper. "My name is Heather." Footsteps sound above us and she startles. "I have to go. I'll check on you later. Make sure the boy eats soon."

She starts up the stairs, but I stop her.

"Heather?"

She bends so she can see me. "Yes?"

I hold her gaze for the duration of a heartbeat. "My name is Ember."

"I know." She gives me one more long meaningful look, as though she's trying to tell me a story with her eyes, and then she's gone back up the ladder.

208

I watch the bottom side of the trap door for an eternity, listening as the sounds of the cabin fade back into silence, wondering what is going to happen to us and how she knows my name.

The questions spur questions. Everything about Henry suggests that he doesn't remember me, that the virus in his body has erased all the memories from his mind. But, he must remember something or else Heather and the dog catcher wouldn't know as much as they do. I don't know if this is good or bad.

There was something in Heather's eyes that suggested that everything wasn't as civil and happy as it had first appeared. Was it Henry? Was he truly crazy, leading them through these post-apocalyptic times like a mad man with a vendetta? I imagined him as a warrior, crawling through the woods on his stomach as he stalked the bad guys, and then I consider the fact that he might have stalked us as well.

The thought is nearly mind numbing as I think back and recount every memory. I thumb through them, one by one, realizing that Henry had probably been stalking me since the moment I first arrived in town. I remember the sound of a stick breaking as I paused outside the hardware store. If it had been the cannibal, he would have just hauled me into the bushes like he'd done with the other woman. Henry had been following me from the very beginning.

Was it him who stood over me while I slept inside the mortuary? Why hadn't he just taken us then? I press my eyes closed, knowing the answer before it truly comes to me. He needed to kill the cannibal first. If he'd taken me then, the cannibal would have just followed us all. He must have lost us when we fled the cemetery and headed towards the river camp. It makes me appreciate my gut instincts. Somewhere deep inside of me, I'd known we needed to move on to a new hiding place, and by following that little voice, I'd managed to keep us safe a little bit longer. If I'd been smart, I would have also covered our tracks on the dusty road and might have prevented Henry from ever finding us, but I hadn't been quite that clever.

Hunger reminds me of the bag on my lap and I open it, my stomach growling appreciatively. There is a wedge of cheese, a package of freeze- dried nuts, a bag of Fritos, and a bottle of apple juice. It is the kind of lunch my mother would have packed me, hitting all the food groups, while making sure that my taste buds were kept happy at the same time. The only thing missing is a sandwich, and I mourn the thought, my soul growing hollow. It will be a long time before there are more sandwiches. All the bread in the world has molded and there isn't any bologna or honey-baked ham to slide between the slices either. I add these things to the growing list in my head of things that have become extinct, of IPods, air conditioning, cupcakes with cream filling, my mother's good night kiss. *Everything.*

I walk over to where Teddy is snoring and nudge him.

"Teddy, wake up. Chow time," I tell him.

He opens his eyes, ready for fight or flight again, his hands clenching into fists.

"What? What?" He finds his feet before his feet are ready to support him, and he sways backwards drunkenly until he catches himself on the bunk.

It strikes me how much this has altered his whole life. If he'd continued on the track he'd been on before the virus, he probably would have ended up weighing three hundred pounds, failing miserably at attracting members of the opposite sex, and eventually falling into a menial job with a menial salary. He would have met and married someone he wasn't attracted to, someone with the same afflictions and handicaps, someone

210

who nagged him to fix the hinges on the door, to take his shoes off for Christ sake when he came inside, someone who would cook him meatloaf and mashed potatoes for dinner and bake him a double-layer chocolate cake on his birthday. His life would have been a simple pattern of days, of pulling the daily Quote of the Day off of his desk calendar, of mowing the lawn on Saturday mornings, bowling with the guys on Tuesday nights, taking the kids to the movies on Fridays. He wouldn't have taken care of himself, allowing himself to eat whatever he chose, and he would have died by the age of sixty from heart failure. Now he is something different, and I cannot see his future no matter how hard I try. He might end up being a ninja, an engineer, or even a cannibal. His future is so uncertain, so unspoken for. He could end up being anything or nothing at all. It was hinged on thin air, waiting for the slightest of breezes to turn it the other way.

"They brought us some food." I hand him the bag and he stares at it for a long moment before he looks up at me, searching my face for an answer.

"What's the matter? You don't seem right," he asks me.

"I had the strangest dream," I say. The memory returns to me. I see Elizabeth's fingers poking from the top of the water, the smell of suntan lotion and briny lake water mixing like ingredients in a recipe.

"I dreamed about the day Elizabeth nearly drowned at Decker Lake," I tell him, and he nods.

"I know. I was there," he says. I am suddenly reminded that things are not what they seem to be, that time and experiences have been lined up like pin-straight dominos for years to bring us to this moment when we could topple them all over with one fell swoop. What were the odds that Teddy had been there that day?

25

The odds were actually staggering. Teddy and Annie usually didn't go to Decker's Lake. Annie preferred the town pool, where the chlorinated water was much cleaner and up to her standards. "Decker's has fish swimming around it in," she said as though she really meant lepers. The fact that they'd ended up at the lake was pretty unusual, coupled with the fact that out of acres of waterfront, they also happened to be sitting close to where we parked our towels and the fact that Teddy happened to be looking in our direction when it happened. It seemed very planned out, even though it couldn't have been.

Teddy tells me his version, from beginning to end, and I don't say anything until he's finished. He'd had been with his sister that day, fighting with her over who got the last Coke in the cooler. He'd looked up as the sky darkened and my mother screamed Elizabeth's name, knowing something horrible had just happened, knowing there was nothing he could do except watch it play out. By the time I emerged from the water with my sister in my arms, he had been shaken to the core.

I remain silent, not sharing my own truths with him. Something about it frightens me deeply. The skies had darkened in an instant as though she had called them. Had I not pulled her out of the water in time, she might have electrocuted a lake-full of children.

I walk back to the couch and plop down on the end, waiting for Teddy to join me. I hear the rustle of the paper bag and listen to him dig through the contents.

"Ember, do you think she called the storm that day?" he asks.

"I don't know. Maybe."

He studies me for a minute. "I think it's something she does when she's scared," he tells me. I stare back, remembering that he and Elizabeth were once friends.

"Did she tell you something about it?"

Teddy shakes his head. "I almost asked her about it once after I heard our mothers talking about it, but I was too afraid." He looks up and the fear in his eyes is real. "I mean, what if she really could call the lightning? What if she got mad at me and then struck me dead?"

I think about this for a moment. "I don't know. Maybe it's something she's learning to control. Maybe it's got something to do with the virus."

I don't know what else to say, so I fish the hand sanitizer from my pocket and I toss it to Teddy. He flips me a disdainful glance, but doesn't say anything. He squeezes out a puddle and wipes it into his skin and then tosses it back for me to use. I squirt some into my hand, appreciating the strong scent of alcohol, working it into the cracks and crevices a little more carefully than Teddy did. The last thing I need is to get sick out here, with no doctors.

I scarf down every morsel of food, barely tasting it as it heads towards my empty stomach. I don't consider that it might be the last meal I'll ever receive. I just eat it, appreciating all the tastes moving across my tongue, appreciating the way it quiets my rumbling stomach.

Teddy eats the cheese and the Fritos, but tucks the bag of peanuts into his pocket for later. He drinks half of his apple juice and then sets the plastic bottle on the coffee table and stares at it for a moment, as though he's contemplating another use for the container. I wonder if he is thinking of making it into a knife, and then I remember that Teddy might still have his knife.

"Do you still have your knife?" I ask.

213

"Yeah, I think so." He reaches into his front pocket and pulls out the folding hunting knife. It is the type you might use to peel an apple or cut the plastic off of wires. Not the kind you would use to save your life. I don't know what we will do with it, but it is nice to know we have it.

"Should we hide it somewhere?" I ask, thinking that the dog catcher or Henry might come back down and remember to frisk us. If we hid it in a mattress, they wouldn't be able to find it.

Teddy shakes his head. "I'd rather have it on me in case I need it. I don't think they plan to keep us here very long." His words surprise me.

"Why not?"

"Well, for one, there's no bathroom. They'll have to bring us up the ladder a couple times a day just to let us go pee. You heard the dog catcher talking to Henry. They really don't want us here."

"Good point." I sink back into the couch and consider it for a moment. Why are they afraid of keeping us?

"Why did the dog catcher say we were Hostile magnets? What would they want with us?"

"I'm not sure."

Teddy arches his eyebrows and then looks down at his lap. "It's just strange." His face is a clear reflection of his thoughts. He is probably thinking that they might have uses for sixteen-year-old girls and fourteen-year-old boys that we do not want to consider. All we know is that we are prisoners and our captors aren't necessarily friendly.

"Maybe Henry just wanted to save us out of the goodness of his heart," I offer.

Teddy rolls his eyes. "Like I believe *that*." He has a point. I don't know why Henry has saved us from one abduction, only to put us in another one. I wish he'd just drive us back to town and dump us.

"At least they fed us," I offer.

"Yeah, I guess." He is quiet for a moment. I know what he's going to say long before he says it. "Ember? What would the bad guys have done to us? What do you think anyways?"

We've been through this before and I don't understand why he's asking me. "I don't know, Teddy. Like I said before, maybe they need workers."

He looks at me with little boy eyes. "That's all?"

I shrug my shoulder and am honest with him. "I don't know. I really don't know." I ruffle his hair and attempt a smile. "One thing I do know is I don't want to find out."

I get up from the couch, depleted of energy from all the thinking. Sometimes it is easier to stop thinking and just stay moving. "Hand me your empty bag," I say.

He wads up the bag and tosses it to me like a basketball. It reminds me of the little hoop he had on the back of his bedroom door. He would shoot small foam basketballs into it, over and over again, shouting "score!" each time he sank one in, to the point where Annie would pound on the wall separating their bedrooms and scream at him to 'give it a rest.'

He joins me on the couch, sitting a little too close for my comfort. He is still at that age where he will be awkward with girls, but his intentions are growing clearer by the moment. I know what he's going to say long before he says it.

"Ember, I just want to tell you that I'm glad you're here with me. I know you probably still think of me as Annie's bratty little brother, but I think of you as my friend."

I stifle the sigh that wants to follow his words. We've been through a lot together, but I'll never be able to think of him as more than a kid. He's somewhat right in his analogy. I do still

215

think of him as Annie's bratty little brother, but he's slowly growing on me.

"Thanks, Teddy. I'm glad you're here with me too."

We hear the sound of a car pull up outside, followed by shouting.

I shove both bags into the edge of the cushions and run to the other end of the room, where the beds are pushed against the wall. A small cellar window is centered on the wall, providing us a view of the front area. Teddy and I climb up onto the bunk and look out. The window is covered with a layer of dirt. I wipe it with my hand until we can see.

"What's going on?" Teddy asks, even though his view is exactly the same as mine.

"I don't know. Just be quiet." A row of bushes have been planted along the front of the cabin, obstructing my view. The black Bronco is parked in the clearing in front of the cabin and several people have gathered around it, blocking our view with their bodies. After a moment, the crowd parts and a man dressed in black is pushed forward.

Teddy and I both gasp. It's one of the bad men.

His hands have been tied behind his back, and his face is bruised and swollen from an obvious beating. Henry walks behind him, looking as though he might simply self-combust. His anger is so prevalent, so near the surface. He is holding one of the bad men's walkie-talkies. The dog catcher is also with him, his brows furrowed in a scowl. He says something to Henry and then gives the bad man a push, which sends him stumbling forward, tripping and falling to his knees.

The moment is brittle. They make a semicircle around him and it could go either way, depending on who reacts first. I want to cover my eyes, but I can't stop staring.

"What are they going to do with him?" Teddy asks.

216

"I don't know," I say, but I fear the worst. They will probably interrogate him until they've learned everything they can possibly learn from someone who probably speaks very little of our language, and then they will be finished with him.

I feel the anger burble up inside me. This man and the people he belongs with have taken away every single thing I ever loved. They've taken away my mother, my friends, and my life. For every inventor of modern conveniences and machines and medicines, they are the un-inventors, bringing us back more than a hundred years. We are back to the days before the combustion engine, back before penicillin, before cars that can park themselves and books that can be read on reading machines. Because of people like him, we are all without our friends, our families, our mothers. He is the enemy. Plain and simple. If I feel pity for him because he is a human being in obvious pain, it is buried somewhere below all the rage. My hands knot into fists and I can't uncurl them no matter how hard I try.

Henry pulls the man to his feet and leads him towards our cabin. The dog catcher walks behind them, like a guard. Teddy and I shrink back into the shadows as they come closer, their legs blocking our view. Any one of them could simply lean down and peer at us though the glass.

Feet thump up the stairs and then across the wooden floor above us. I hold my breath, terrified they will throw him down into the cellar hole with us. But, then the sound of their feet stop and their voices grow louder.

I strain to hear their words, but they are muffled. I move closer to the cellar hatch and find I can some most of what they are saying.

"Can you hear anything?" Teddy asks.

"Shhhh," I hush him. I can hear Henry telling the dog catcher that it wasn't a good idea. I listen some more until I have the entire story and then edge back to where Teddy sits.

"They used the walkie-talkie that Henry took at Faith Eddie's house to find one of the bad guys out patrolling. They captured him to find out what he knows. The dog catcher wants to beat him to make him tell them where their main camp is, but Henry doesn't want to."

"They aren't going to throw him down here, are they?" Teddy asks, voicing my own fears.

"I hope not." The thought is terrifying. I can't imagine what we would do if that happened. We return to the couches and sit close together, trembling as we listen to the pounding footsteps above us. There is movement and the sounds of feet and chairs moving on the wooden floor. The sound of angry voices rises above the din, but I can only catch an occasional word. I hear the dog catcher's voice the most. Words like "what" and "where" burble to the surface.

"What are they doing?" Teddy reaches beside me to grab my hand.

"I don't know. I think they're interrogating him," I answer and then fall into silence, wanting to hear every possible word I can catch. It might mean the difference between life and death.

The voices rise to a crescendo as several people begin shouting at once. Feet scuffle on the floor above us again, and then there is a loud thump, as though a chair has fallen to the floor. Teddy leans into me, and I put my arm around him and pull him even closer.

"I think they're fighting over what to do with him," I tell him after I catch the sound of Henry's voice. It sounded as though he said, "Just let him go," but I can't be certain. Someone else yells "Stop it! Just STOP IT!" and it sounds like

218

Heather. I imagine them putting a gun to the bad man's head, demanding that he tell them all his secrets. He will be shaking his head, refusing, and this will drive them nearly insane with anger.

"Give me THAT!" another voice yells, which is followed by an explosion outside, in front of the cabin. It is a roar of tremendous proportions, similar to the explosion we'd heard at Faith Eddy's house. I can nearly visualize the black Bronco rolling with flames, parked near the place where we'd left it. I squeeze Teddy tighter, the fear worming a black path through my mind.

"What was that?" Teddy asks, pulling his face from the front of my shirt. As he looks wildly towards the front of the room, I can see that his face is streaked with tears. They run tracks through the dirt on his face.

"Sounded like an explosion." My mind races. What could have exploded? The Bronco outside? As the thought winds through my mind, I realize how dire our situation is. All of our guys are inside torturing the bad man. This must mean that other bad men might have followed them and are outside. Who else would blow up the Bronco? I jump up and pull Teddy upright. "Let's get closer to the trap door. I want to be ready in case we get a chance to get out of here." Surely Heather won't forget that we are locked down here.

We move on shaky legs to the front of the room. As we reach the couches, there is another explosion outside. It is followed by the sound of more angry voices coming from outside and the sounds of vehicles. It can only mean one thing. More bad men have arrived.

Another explosion rips through the front of the cabin and the entire structure rocks on the foundation. The window bursts open, sending a hail of glass into the room. Teddy and I cower together as glass rains down all around us.

"What do we do?" Teddy asks, his voice high and shaky.

Smoke rolls in rapidly. I can barely see to the other end of the room. Panic fills me. If we try to push ourselves through the broken window, we'll be captured by the bad men. If we stay and hide, we'll die of smoke inhalation.

I pull Teddy close, thinking that it might be the end for us. I say a frantic prayer in my head and then a miracle happens.

The trap door opens and the ladder descends.

"Hurry!" Henry shouts.

Teddy and I jump up from the couch. As we scramble towards the trap door, I bump into a table, knocking it over and spilling a stack of books onto the floor. I stop short as I nearly slip on a book.

"Oh my God." I feel a tremble in my fingers as I reach for it. The words come to me in an instant:

"Her hair was as orange as a sunny surprise.

She had rosy cheeks and a gleam in her eyes.

She loved sunsets, orange lollipops, and golden birds on a line.

Everyone called her Clementine."

It's Elizabeth's Clementine book.

26

Henry's fingers latch tightly onto my arm. I have only two seconds to react. Instead of reaching down for the Clementine book, I reach behind me and grab the front of Teddy's shirt, pulling him along behind me as we are whisked into the din above.

Thick sooty smoke fills the room, erasing all detail.

"Duck down," Henry yells.

We crouch down beneath the roll of smoke and scramble towards the door.

I nearly trip over something. I scream as it comes into focus.

It's a dead body tied to a chair. It must be the bad man they were interrogating. Blood pours out of his head and pools onto the floor. I feel it beneath my feet, sticky and wet, and my stomach reels.

"Ember!" Teddy calls out, before breaking into a coughing fit.

I latch onto him tighter, my fingers weaving into the front of his shirt.

Seconds later, we burst through the door and find ourselves in a war zone. Black smoke fills the air, coming from a burning vehicle that is lodged into the front of the cabin. Voices fill the air as bullets whizz past us.

Another black truck is parked near the entrance. Bad men lean around the doorways with guns in their hands, spraying bullets at us. The men from Denver's camp shoot back, using the corner of the cabin as cover.

Flashes of firefight glint through the smoke. A bullet zips through the air beside my ear and I duck, long after the bullet has already passed.

"Around here," Henry says, leading us around the corner of the cabin to the edge of the hill. There is no time to think, only to react. He pulls us down a steep incline. We both slip on the dry leaves and slide until we can stop ourselves. Metal sparkles through the trees ahead of us.

"Hurry, Henry. They just came over the hill behind you," a voice says ahead of us. As we get closer, I see Heather waiting beside two off-road motorcycles.

She pulls me towards her motorcycle. Henry grabs Teddy's arm and leads him towards the other bike.

"You ride with me," he tells him.

Teddy looks at me with wide eyes. "But Ember."

There isn't time to think this through and I don't know who to trust. All I know is that Teddy and I are being separated and I don't like it.

"Teddy, listen to me." I hold his gaze as long as possible. "I only cry once a year on my birthday," I tell him, hoping he understands my secret message. If we can break free, we will meet at the Weeping Mary statue the day after tomorrow, on my birthday.

He nods, tears flowing freely down his face.

Henry jumps on the motorcycle and Teddy rushes to get on behind him. I don't have the chance to watch them because Heather is pulling me towards our bike. She hops on and fires it up with a practiced thrust of her leg. The machine roars as I climb on behind her. I barely have a chance to latch my arms around her waist before we rocket away, sending a flurry of dry leaves into the air behind us. I tuck my head into the hollow between her shoulder blades, feeling the rough corduroy of her shirt against my cheek. My heart pounds heavily in my chest.

We follow a worn trail through the forest. It runs sideways along the hill and then turns sharply in the opposite direction in

222

a zigzag pattern running down the steep decline. I tighten my grip and dare to look behind us, to see if the bad men are following us. I catch a quick glimpse of green leaves and tree trunks and then a bump jolts me back into place. If the bad men have been following us, they would have been forced to give up after a while unless they have motorcycles of their own. After several more minutes, we make our way down the hill to a straight trail that runs beside a wide stream. Ahead of us, Henry and Teddy are nothing more than a speck.

Inside, I am bewildered and terrified. I don't understand what was going on at the cabin and why Henry and Heather bothered to rescue us, when it was evident that we were nothing more than prisoners to them. The questions only breed more questions.

I fall into a silence inside my mind and just watch the landscape pass by as I digest it all. If God is here, He is not helping. I don't understand how any of this can be happening. I think about a sermon I'd once heard at church and the memory returns to me in full color, as though it is something I should pay attention to.

Elizabeth was never reliable enough to bring to church, so she had always stayed home with my mother, while my father and I endured the hour-long service. It had always felt senseless and pompous to me, sitting in an overly warm room filled with perfumed old ladies and half-dozing men, listening to Someone Important tell us how we were supposed to live our lives. Typically, these same people would cut us off in the parking lot as we left. If we accidentally brushed carts at the supermarket later in the week, they would blatantly ignore us. We were only nice to each other when we thought God was looking, I guess.

I tried to complain about it, but my father had given me that knowing look and told me that I'd understand one day. It

223

seems unfortunate now, because I'd really hoped to one day understand the logic behind his statement, but that day will never come. Being polite and forgiving people was part of another time. Now, we simply do what we have to for survival.

The only part of the entire hour that actually interested me was the ten-minute prelude the minister always used to work into his sermon. Usually it was a topic that we were familiar with. He'd use it to lead into a dull story about the Bible. I don't remember most of his stories, but the one I do remember rises up in my mind.

The preacher had asked us what we'd grab if our house was on fire. People held up their hands, like school children, waiting to be called on. One man said he'd grab his wallet. Another woman said she'd look for her purse. It took several more people before the minister got the answer he was looking for. One woman looked at the others as though they had totally lost their minds and told him she'd grab her family, that everything else was replaceable.

This makes me wonder why Heather and Henry had grabbed Teddy and me. With food and water at such a shortage, they should have grabbed a handful of food off the shelf, or at least reached for a weapon to protect themselves with. Instead, they grabbed us. It sends a chill down my spine.

I don't have long to ponder it before we reach the end of the trail. A small walking bridge crosses a burbling stream. It is the same sort of stream that runs through my back yard, the same sort of stream that Elizabeth and I would wash our dishes in and pretend to explore. Heather turns onto the bridge, and I am only allowed one quick glimpse down at the rushing water before we are back onto solid land.

The bridge leads to a parking lot, where hikers once met at the trail head, eager to climb up the trail to the top of the mountain. A brown sign with slots for trail maps sits at the entrance and I consider how useless it is now that all the hikers are gone. Inside my head, I begin repeating the Lord's Prayer, trying desperately to hold on to my sanity.

Heather pulls on the throttle and we nearly do a wheelie out of the parking lot. Our tires grab onto the blacktop with a squeal and we lean into the turn. As we zip along the blacktop, I can't see Henry ahead of us and I panic for a moment until I see the flash of his red brake lights in the distance. We move along for miles upon miles, trading one highway for another until we are so far away from my home I can no longer feel its pull.

We take a turn onto a highway that is both familiar and oddly catastrophic at the same time. Low rolling fields stretch miles in every direction on either side of the black two-lane road, making it look like a dividing line between the umber and green. The sky above it seems vast and liquid, the color a deep periwinkle blue that could never be replicated on paper. As we turn a corner, the fields give way to tall evergreens, which erase the sky and crowd the road, turning it into a different place altogether.

The road is eerily empty, except for a handful of vehicles abandoned along the side. I imagine the drivers pulling over to rest for a moment, the effort of driving becoming too much. I try not to look too closely at them, not wanting to confirm my suspicions that many of them might have ended up as coffins. I have collected enough images of dead people to last a lifetime.

We pass rows of houses, set in lines near the roads. Dark green grass grows high in the shadows, looking silky and tender. It is the kind of grass you could hold between your finger and thumb and blow on, making a sound that tickles your lips.

Ahead is a brown wooden sign that says "Decker's Park — 10 miles ahead." My thoughts run rampant.

I consider the dream I had. I can nearly feel the bubbles tickling the side of my face as I rose to the surface, pulling Elizabeth's heavy body behind me. The world suddenly seems so carefully calculated, as though nothing in this life has ever happened by accident. It has all been part of a larger plan, a step that leads to another step and another step, until all the individual steps have been forgotten, yet leading to a destination that truly matters.

Ember. My name is written in the air, coming to me clearly from nowhere.

I close my eyes and I see Elizabeth, smiling into the sunshine, her yellow-white hair hiding most of her face from view. She turns to me and the sunshine fades.

Her hair parts from her face and I can see her eyes, serious and searching. Words flit into my mind, one at a time. I feel them come to me as clear as messages, real and undeniable, yet ghostly invisible. They take my breath away and make me question everything I've ever trusted to be right and true.

The first word is *love* and it appears on pink gossamer ribbon, exactly like the one in my pocket. I feel such a sense of sorrow wrapped around that one word. It nearly breaks my heart.

I see her again, briefly this time, as though the effort is too much to endure. It is draining her, leaving her empty and spent, and her hand falls to her lap like a wounded butterfly. *Clementine* she says, and I know without knowing that it will be the last thing she will say for a while.

I open my eyes and realize that miles have passed since I closed them. I reach into my pocket, feeling Elizabeth's hair ribbon. The one she'd been holding when the bad men took her away from me.

226

"Clementine," I say to myself and think about the book I found on floor of the cabin. For reasons I cannot explain, I know that I will need to return for it.

27

We pull into the parking lot at Decker's Park and slow to a stop as we approach the main entrance. A large wooden sign stretches over the opening with bright blue letters spelling out Decker's Park, where fairy tales come true! It feels a bit surreal to be here.

It is not difficult to envision it as it had been before. The memories snap back quickly until all that is missing are the people. I can see us sitting in my mother's Volvo, waiting in line behind several other cars, my mother complaining about the ten dollar parking fee. My sister and I would be leaning left and then right to get a glimpse of the Ferris wheel or the Big Dipper roller coaster, trying to think of ways to convince my mother to bring us to the amusement park instead of just to the lake.

We cruise through the entrance, slowing as we come to the sign. I don't know why we are stopping here, but I'm hoping that Henry has a plan in mind. As they pass through the entrance ahead of us, Teddy turns back and makes brief eye contact with me. He looks scared.

We come to a fork in the road and Heather pauses. One direction will lead us to Decker's Park, where the amusement rides are located and the other road will take us to Decker's Lake, where we used to swim. Henry and Teddy turn left towards the park, but Heather veers right towards the lake.

I watch them disappear around the corner, feeling that sick sensation grow stronger.

"Shouldn't we stay together?" I ask Heather, but she doesn't answer. Instead she pulls up to the paved parking lot and turns off the engine. She gets off the bike and lifts her arms above her head and rolls her neck until it makes an audible crack.

"I need to stretch for a minute," she tells me, as though nothing monumental has happened to us in the last hour. "Don't worry," she tells me, apparently seeing the panicked look on my face. "The Hostiles have no idea where we went. We lost them on top of that mountain. We'll be safe."

I hope she's right. I look around, feeling as though my old world and my new world are colliding before my eyes. Decker's Lake looks just like it did the last time I was there, minus the people of course. It is nothing more than a broad sweep of land, tapering off to a wide blue lake at the bottom. A no-frills concession stand sits at the top of the hill. It's just a square metal structure with poured concrete floors that are perpetually sticky underfoot from years of spilled sodas. The building is open on three sides, with picnic tables filling the space inside. Every summer, a hornet would start a nest under the rafters and the maintenance man would have to knock it down.

I climb off the motorcycle and stretch my legs. My shoelace has come untied, so I bend to tie it. Heather waits for me, watching me quietly as I fumble with my laces. My fingers are trembling so badly, I drop the bunny ear twice before I finally get it into the hole. I stand up and feel as though I am still moving, even though I'm not.

"Let's take a walk," Heather says. I nod, content not to feel the vibrations rumble through my body any longer.

"What about Henry and Teddy?" I ask.

Heather shrugs. "They'll join us if they want to. Henry probably just wants to check out the park in case there's anything there we can use. We took off without grabbing any food or water." As she says this, I turn to look up the hill, where the top half of the Ferris wheel rises above the trees.

229

I check my watch. It is only 4:30, but the heat of the day is still sweltering. I can feel the sweat dripping down the back of my neck, making my head feel woozy. I need to get out of the sun. Heather must be thinking the same thing, because we both move towards the building and step into the shade under the roof, where it is at least ten degrees cooler.

I look around, feeling a sense of the familiar rush through me, filling me with pure longing and loss. The sensation is so strong; it nearly brings tears to my eyes. It is a place I knew well. I almost expect to smell the mouth-watering aroma of freshly grilled hamburgers lingering in the air, but I can't catch even the faintest hint of it now. I tilt my head and look up at the ceiling, where strings of white Christmas lights weave through the tangle of weathered pine rafters. Years ago, the pavilion was used for weekend rock concerts. I'd been told that at night, when the band set up at the far end of the room, the lights almost looked like stars in the heavens, but during the day they just looked cheap.

"So, what is this place?" Heather asks me. She must have grown up somewhere else to not know this, but I don't question her.

"It's Decker's Lake. We used to come here swimming every summer." As the words leave my lips, I feel a cold chill climb my spine and my gaze is inadvertently drawn to the lake.

The last time I was here was when Elizabeth nearly drowned.

I close my eyes and the pull of the memory is so strong, it ripples through me with a tremble. The wind whispers through my hair with delicate fingers, smelling very briefly of coconut suntan lotion, and the music lilts through my mind like a ghost. I can nearly see my sister's four tiny fingers graze the surface of the soft blue water. I open my eyes and push my hand into my pocket to touch Elizabeth's ribbon and I sigh as it all washes away in an instant. I don't know what to think.

There is so much going on. It seems important to me to consider everything. The Clementine book I saw in the basement of the Boy Scout camp couldn't have gotten there by accident. It's possible that another Clementine book ended up on that table, but not one that had Elizabeth's name written in red crayon on the front cover. It seems to be the answer to everything. She must have been in the basement at one point. Had she been rescued by Henry too? I glance at Heather, wondering if I can trust her with my questions.

The wind ruffles through my hair and I turn around to put my face into the wind. Out of the corner of my eye, I catch a glimpse of something black moving along the horizon. Heather follows the line of my stare.

"Oh shit," she says.

"What is it?" I ask.

"It's a black Bronco. Come on," she says, barely giving me a second to digest her words before she is flying back to the motorcycle. "We need to find Henry."

As I run, I glance up to see the black truck cresting the far hill, nearly a half mile behind us. They will be upon us in a matter of minutes, maybe seconds.

Heather hops on the motorcycle.

I feel as though I am paralyzed, watching the bad men get closer and closer. I imagine them coming to a grinding stop, spewing gravel behind them and bullets in front of them.

"Come on!" Heather shouts at me and then gives the kick-start another thrust. It sputters hopefully for a few seconds, but then falls back to silence. She tries again, but nothing is happening.

231

I finally find my feet and run to where she is standing over the red machine. Steam is lilting off the engine and the smell of burning oil drifts to my nose. I don't know a lot about motorcycles beyond the old dirt bike my father let me ride on occasion, but I know that something is wrong with the engine. It shouldn't be smoking as much as it is.

"What's the matter?" I ask. She glances behind us again.

"I don't know. It won't start."

"We need to get out of here." I watch the black truck grow even closer. Panic twists around me, tighter and tighter, the trembling in my legs growing stronger by the second.

She kicks it again, but it won't start. "Come on, come on!" She glances over her shoulder at the approaching truck, alarm etched clearly in her features.

"Shit." She presses her eyes closed, her knuckles fisted. Finally, she opens her eyes and takes a deep breath. "You used to come here swimming. Do you know a place where we can hide?" She jumps off the motorcycle and begins pushing it towards the open structure.

I glance behind me as we slip under the roof and back into the shadows. I don't think the bad men have seen us, but I wouldn't bet my life on it. I press my fingers over my racing heart as panic fills my veins.

"I don't know," I whisper, wracking my mind for any nook or cranny that will conceal us, and then the answer comes to me with a suddenness that explodes inside of me. "Follow me."

"Where are we going?"

"Quick. Hide the bike in the men's bathroom and then follow me. There's a hole in the fence behind the concession stand that leads up to the park. There are a million places to hide there."

232

"And we can find Henry," she adds, already pushing the motorcycle towards the men's room. She thrusts it through the door and drops it with a heavy clunk that doesn't seem very practical, considering we might need it later. I don't have time to consider it though. The bad men are almost right behind us.

"All right, let's go." I grab her hand and pull her across the concrete floor.

We slip around the side of the building in the loose gravel, sneaking glances behind us to see how close they are. I see a flash of metal, glinting in the sun near the entrance to the park, in the place where the parking attendant collected money.

"God, they're close. Hurry!" Heather says.

"Through here." I lead her through the thick undergrowth behind the building to the eight-foot chain link fence that surrounds the park. I quickly find the broken section and hold it open for her to climb through.

After Heather crawls through, I follow her. I am careful to lower it exactly like I'd found it and then we race up the short hill to the backside of Decker's Park.

We come up behind the Peter Pan swing ride. It sits eerily idle in the middle of the graying hardtop, the swings swaying gently in the breeze. It's not hard to imagine children hanging onto the chains and swinging their legs as they wait for the ride to begin. A red column rises nearly a hundred feet into the air, with a small lookout basket perched halfway up. A fading replica of Peter Pan stands in the basket, a long scope pressed to his ceramic face. A bird has made a nest in the hook of his arm and the tufts of straw poke up into his face.

I slip past the ticket booth, where a sharp-voiced woman used to sit, handing out tickets while she simultaneously talked on her cell phone. A coil of red tickets snakes across the counter, the front portion faded a pale pink by the relentless sunshine.

"This is creepy," Heather whispers.

I nod, feeling cold chills running down my spine. I can almost feel the anticipation lingering in the air as though the park might burst to life at any second, with lights flashing and carnival music blaring at full volume.

Ahead of us is a walkway leading to the other amusements. Faded teddy bears look at me with solemn eyes from the rafters of the ring toss game. We pick up the pace and nearly run. There is no sign of Henry and Teddy.

"Henry, where you?" Heather mumbles to herself, as we pass the looming carcass of the gigantic Ferris wheel. Grass and vines have poked through the broken asphalt and have climbed nearly halfway up the support columns. One of the buckets teeters in the wind and I can easily imagine a small face peering over the top.

I strain my eyes, taking in the landscape ahead of me, but I don't see any sign of them.

"I don't see them. They must have gone out the back exit."

Heather shields the sun from her eyes and peers behind us, in the direction where the bad men were. "Then we should probably find a place to hide.'

Behind us comes the sound of a man shouting.

I look up and the options are very limited. There truly is only one place where we can go. I lift my shaking hand and point ahead, towards the Haunted Tunnel.

"We can hide there," I say, wishing I could take back the words.

234

28

I take a deep breath and allow it to fill my body. It will take the threat of bad men to make me go down there, but there aren't any other choices. Either we take the unknown risk or we stand here and face certain death.

I pause at the entrance and try not to shudder, but my legs are like rubber.

The opening to the Haunted Tunnel is an enormous clown's head. His mouth gapes open, making a doorway that we must walk into. There is something very wrong about the clown. He is the kind of clown who will slip into your bedroom at night and sit in the corner, waiting for you to wake up and notice him. His red hair is faded from the sun, but his evil blue eyes are nearly electric in their intensity. They look down at us, watching us pause before we slip through his opened jaws.

Heather quivers beside me. "I hate clowns," she whispers.

I nod, watching the edges of his mouth for any sign of movement. "Yeah, me too."

We slip through the entrance, pausing in the shadows to gather our bearings. The smell of mold lingers in the air. The floor beneath our feet is sticky and cool. As we walk forward, the temperature falls several degrees, reminding me that we are actually going underneath the ground. I untie my sweatshirt from around my waist and slip my arms into the sleeves, but the goose bumps remain.

Our footsteps echo against the concrete walls and we both consciously slow down to lessen the noise.

When I was ten, Annie double-dog dared me to walk through the tunnel with her. A green-faced troll jumped out at me and terrified me to the very core of my being. I haven't been back since.

"You think there's a good place to hide here?" Heather asks, sounding unconvinced.

"Yeah. I have a place in mind." I don't tell her about the troll, because it doesn't make sense that two of us should be searching the shadows for his return.

The tunnel grows substantially darker ahead of us. I pull my flashlight out of my pocket, but discover the batteries have died. With a sigh, I tuck it back into my pocket. Heather pulls a small penlight out of her pocket.

"Maybe this will help a little bit." She turns it on and shines it on the ground ahead of us, where it makes a small spot of light. The concrete is dotted with blown debris. Leaves and soda lids, candy wrappers, and food containers litter the floor like dirty confetti.

We come to the first turn. The walls grow narrower and we are forced to walk single file. If I remember correctly, the tunnel is only fifty or sixty feet long, looping around and coming out at a separate exit. I press my hand against the wall and follow it like a blind woman. It brings us around in a loop and then opens up into a room filled with mirrors.

"Crap." I'd forgotten about this room.

Heather shines the flashlight around the room and all we see are hundreds of representations of ourselves, looking very shell-shocked and wild-haired.

"How are we going to get through here? Do you know the way?" she asks with a shaky voice.

I look around at the hundreds of Heathers and Embers, my stomach clenching appropriately. And then it comes to me. "Look down at the floor."

On the floor at our feet is a path of dirty footprints. We follow them, moving quickly toward the next room. I try not to look up at my startled image, but it feels like being turned loose in a world of doppelgangers. I almost expect one of them to stand up straight and start walking towards me with an evil gleam in her eye.

"Through here," I say, wanting to put some distance between us and our reflections.

We come through a doorway and find ourselves in a pitch dark room full of glow-in-the-dark tombstones. I nearly groan out loud. After being in a real haunted cemetery, this one is nearly laughable, with its painted tombstones and cheesecloth ghosts that hang from the ceiling with fishing line.

"What room is this? A cemetery?" Heather asks.

"Yeah. I think something comes out of the wall over there when people walk through." I point to the darkness where I believe there might be a fake wall.

"Is there anywhere we can hide here?"

"I don't think so." I lean against one of the tombstones and inadvertently cause an animatronics ghost to pop up from behind the grave. The motion is so abrupt, we both let out short shrieks of surprise. I slap my hand over my mouth, wishing I could take it back. If the bad men didn't know we were down here before, they certainly are aware of it now.

"Come on, we need to find a hiding place quick," I say and pull Heather onto the next room. A fake yellow moon glows against the back wall and the ceiling is painted with metallic stars that catch the rays of the flashlight and send sparkles around the room. We are in the troll room.

I hear something rustle in the far corner. It is the sound of claws against paper. I imagine the troll sitting in the corner, licking the wrapper of an old cotton candy cone, watching us grow closer and closer and closer.

I lock my knees together to keep them from shaking. I'd like nothing more than to turn tail and run back out the way we came, blowing past the tombstones and mirrors until I reached daylight, but I don't take the chance. Down here, everything is make-believe scary. Outside, it is the real deal.

"There might be a place to hide in here," I say.

Her fingers tremble against my back, giving her fear away. "Are you sure this is safe?"

I peer ahead of me, seeing nothing but blackness.

"I hope so," I say, feeling my stomach clinch with pure fear.

There is something very illogical about hiding in the Haunted Tunnel. It is a place most people would run away from. It is dark and creepy, but unfortunately it's the only place I can think of. As the thought crosses my mind, I hear the sound of footsteps echoing behind us.

"Hurry! They're coming," Heather prompts me, and we move deeper into the shadows.

I hold my breath as I hear the sound of the men's voices grow louder.

The floor beneath our feet becomes softer as the plywood turns to carpeting. It muffles our steps as we inch through the room. I take another step and I realize how foolish this could be. Anything could be down here. Anything at all.

The thought rattles through me and I sniff the air, trying to detect the trace of dead bodies. It smells musty, with a slight tang of mildew, as though the carpeting has gotten wet and never thoroughly dried, but there is no trace of death in the air. I reach out in front of me and find a large upright object that is smooth beneath my hands.

I let out a small involuntary gasp and pull my hands away.

"What?" Heather whispers and turns her flashlight in my direction.

A sharp-tooth troll blocks my path. She shines the light around the room and we are confronted with dozens of his relatives.

"Let's go back here." I pull her towards the far corner.

I cannot hear the bad men any longer, but that doesn't mean they aren't lurking just outside the entrance to the mirrored room. I start forward toward the back of the display, terrified I will step on something that will make a large noise and give us away.

Please, God, please.

The terror rolls through me, hot and powerful, and I clamp down on it.

If I can't do this, we're both as good as dead.

I close my eyes for a second, but I am no calmer than I was before. I force myself to move forward, swiping the air until my hand comes in contact with another plastic troll. I nearly scream as I touch it.

We maneuver around the plastic statue and tread deeper into the room. The smell of mildew is much stronger. The floor beneath my feet is spongy, as though it might break through at any moment. I sweep my arms in front of me and my fingers graze something hard and unyielding. I yank my arm back with a start and barely stifle a scream.

"What? What?" She shines her light in front of us. I see the outline of a small house.

"It's a troll house," I say, as the memory of the room returns to me. It might be our best option.

I pull her around the corner and fall to my knees, so I can crawl into the small doorway. The beam of Heather's small flashlight shines ahead of me, jolting upwards as she moves. I catch a quick glimpse of a pile of burlap lying on the ground, almost in a man-sized shape. I swallow the lump in my throat and reach to touch it. As I do, the blanket shifts, and a small rodent runs out.

I jerk away with a hitch of my breath and watch the rat disappear into the darkness.

"What it is, Ember? Talk to me," she pleads.

Be brave, be brave, I tell myself and reach out again and pull the burlap up off the ground. Beneath it is a pile of straw. I nearly melt into the ground.

"Nothing. It's just a pile of straw and a piece of burlap." I press my hand against my pounding heart and close my eyes again, seeing bright spears of stars behind my eyelids as the adrenaline spikes through me with jagged edges

Behind us, comes the distinct sound of footsteps on concrete.

Heather puts a hand on my arm, as if in question. The sound of footsteps grows louder and closer.

I listen to the darkness, straining to pick up any hint of sound.

"In here," I tell Heather and move further into the doorway so she can follow me.

I wait until she has crawled in beside me and I cover us with the thin blanket of burlap. I take her hand and squeeze it tightly just as the sound of footsteps echo into the troll's lair. The bad men have arrived.

The footsteps grow louder and a flashlight is swept across the room. It lights up the other side of the troll's house and shines through the burlap, which is pressed close to my face. I close my eyes again and for a moment I am simply gone inside of myself.

It feels like a dream, but has the texture of real life. I feel the cool wind against my skin, brushing my hair against my arm in a place where my hair has never brushed before. I glance

240

down to find that my hair is now longer and blonder. It looks like a curtain of pure sunshine. I try to move again, to touch it, but find that I don't have control of this body. I am only an observer, along for the ride.

Elizabeth, I think, and I feel my face smile in response.

Yes.

Where are you? I try, but she doesn't answer. Instead, she shows me something she thinks I should know. The air shifts with a pop, like air under pressure, and we are suddenly standing outside in the crisp night air. The air has the smell of wet sheet metal and I understand the night she is showing me.

In my world, I had been sitting on a milk crate outside my parent's house, watching the storm roll in from the east, just moments before the bad men pulled into the driveway. In her world, she'd been somewhere else.

Her eyes gaze out at the street in front of her, taking in the lavender Victorian across the street. She watches it for a moment until the knowledge grows inside of me and I know exactly where she stands. She turns and her hair wraps around her body like a silky cape. She is standing in front of the Cooper House.

I gasp, surprised beyond belief to see it standing there in its untouched glory. The walls are not crumbled ashes and the fireplace doesn't loom over the wreckage like a watchful sentry. It is solid and beautiful, just like it had been before the fire destroyed it. The tattered flag banners dangle from the porch, waving in the moonlit breeze.

"Where is she?" a voice thunders and I don't know if it is a voice inside my head in Elizabeth's world or outside my head in the tunnel. I try to turn, to look, but I can't react to either. I am a hostage inside Elizabeth's body. I cannot move unless she allows me to move. There is a sense of the familiar, of

241

Elizabeth's need to show me something, whether I want to see it or not. The stubborn insolence washes through me like blood.

She looks towards the sound of the voice and a man comes running towards her, speaking in his native language. I feel her mouth move into a smile. As he sees her, witnesses her beatific smile, something in him is abruptly altered. The angry scowl slides from his face and his eyes take her in as though she were an apparition, glowing in the moonlight. He drops to his knees in front of her and whispers something under his breath that sounds like a prayer.

He mouths the words softly and I do not know if he is calling to his god or if he is calling to her. He is otherwise motionless, trapped by pure rapture. Above us, the sky thunders and growls, like a beast prowling across the sky, growing closer by the moment.

A single raindrop falls onto the sidewalk between us and the man. The sound is like the slap of a bare hand on concrete and is quickly followed by another and another. She opens her arms wide, sweeps her fingertips to the sky. A drop of rain pelts against her finger and another grazes her arm, but she doesn't move. She holds the pose like the statue in my mother's garden.

The man is joined by another man and he too drops to his knees before her. It is clear in an instant that they don't want her to use as a slave or for medical experiments. There is something more about her. Something that both intrigues and frightens them and they are afraid to let her go.

Elizabeth. I whisper her name inside my head and it collapses like a popped bubble. Noise roils downward, turning the world inside out with a white-hot flash of burning light. There is no need for further thought, only pain and that searing hot light. I feel it move through me, through us, like a spear of pure molten lava, the hottest of metals stretching through my

242

veins, making them bulge with pressure. The world outside my body is suddenly white, sparkling with the reflection of raindrops sizzling into steam. The smell of burned metal is so strong, so prevalent; it fills my body with the taste. I feel it on my tongue and in my eyes. It stings, hot and burning, making me feel as though I'm melting where I stand. And then it is gone.

I find myself standing in front of flames. They move, possessing arms and legs and voices that scream words I cannot understand. I watch them run away from me, waving their flaming arms and I smell the odor of their flesh cooking in the heat. There is no fear, no remorse, only the wondering, the wondrous wondering. The moment when ignorance becomes knowledge and knowledge becomes power. I watch the men run down the street until they fall within themselves and burn to ashes in a pile.

In front of me, the house burns as well and I watch it for a moment, thinking what a loss it is. After a moment, Elizabeth turns and I see the street behind me. I feel a quiet tremble run up my spine and I see the man standing further down the street, safe from the danger, bearing witness to all she's done.

I watch his face, capture the moment when his gaze is torn from the burning house to the sight of her, standing untouched in front of it. I see the knowing in his eyes. He moves towards us and I am unafraid because his is a face that I know very well. He is Henry. Ember's *Henry*. My *Henry*. One thought overlaps over the other. Her thought and then mine softly following like an echo.

Henry goes to her and she lifts her arms to be picked up and then the vision fades from the outside corners inward, like a slow faint, burning the corners of my vision. Blackness closes in on me, squeezing the sight of him down to a small dot of light. Rapidly, the smell of burning flesh is replaced by the smell of molding carpeting. When I open my eyes again, all I see is light brown burlap and I know what Elizabeth is trying to tell me.

I know.

29

Heather is shaking me and whispering my name.

"Are you okay? Ember, answer me."

She slaps my cheeks gently and shines the flashlight in my eyes.

It takes me a minute to focus on her, to comprehend where I am. I feel groggy and tired, as though I've been sleeping for hours. The light is painfully bright and it brings me around quickly.

I lift a hand to shield my eyes. "What?"

"Oh, thank God." She falls back on her heels and places the flashlight on the ground beside her. Soft yellow light fans against the wall.

I think about the dream, about watching Elizabeth from the inside, feeling the fire lick through my body, yet leave me untouched. It comes to me with a gradual knowing. It is the kind of thought that builds slowly because if it came too quickly, it might hobble me with the pure breadth of its intensity.

It's true. My God, it's true. I want to laugh, cry and scream at the same time.

Elizabeth is communicating with me. She just confirmed everything I had suspected about the Cooper House fire. She burnt it down with lightning.

The thought is powerful and nearly unbelievable. I don't know how or why, but it is true. She can actually call the lightning now.

I pull myself up and sit against the wall. The burlap blanket rests on the floor beside me and I use it to cover my legs. I am suddenly cold, so cold I feel as though ice is surging through my veins. I am also tired. It makes me wonder if I had been in a state that is deeper than sleep. I almost feel as though I could actually have been dead for a few minutes. The blood pumps through my veins now with urgency and I can feel myself growing warmer by the moment.

"How long was I out?"

"Not long." She watches me for a moment, her light eyes taking me in with careful inspection. "Does this happen often to you?" There is a strong hint of concern in her expression, in the way she pinches her lips tightly together. For one brief moment, she reminds me of my mother.

She makes a hum of acknowledgment, making me realize that I make her a little bit nervous. I can't blame her. I wouldn't want to be saddled with someone like me either, someone who was prone to falling into dead faints. It would make survival much more difficult.

"I don't think so. I don't know," I say, not knowing how much I can trust her. I look towards the tunnel stairs, to the place where I heard the men just before I lost consciousness. "Where did they go?"

"They went back down the tunnel. They've been gone for about ten minutes." She pulls a bottle of water out of her pack and hands it to me first. I take a deep swig and hand it back, feeling the liquid absorb rapidly into my system. After she takes a drink, she sits back and just looks at me. In her expression, I realize that she is earnest and giving, the kind of person I would want for a friend, especially now.

"Maybe we can just stay here until they go away," she says, and then studies me. "I guess you probably have questions."

I nod.

She takes a deep breath and lets it out with a sigh. "Before all this started, before the virus, I mean...I was a sophomore at Boston University with Henry. We met in physics our freshman year and have been dating for a year now. I'm originally from

Iowa," she says, which explains why she didn't know about Decker's Park.

I find myself thinking about Henry and how much he has changed since the last time I saw him. "Why is Henry the way he is?" I ask.

She looks down at the ground and traces her fingers along a strip of fraying carpeting. "I'm not sure. I think it has something to do with the way the virus affects some people. It outright killed some people, like my parents and all of my friends, but it didn't touch me or you. Henry is somewhere in the middle. It made him a different version of himself. It took away some of his sweetness and made him more aggressive. When he found me hiding in my dorm room, I barely recognized him." She looks up and smiles. "It actually took me a while to finally trust him, but then again I've seen a lot of zombie movies."

We both smile softly at the thought because it would have been so unbelievable in our old world, but here in this new world, it is something that could happen. After seeing the cannibal, I'd believe anything.

"We saw someone else like Henry, only worse," I tell her and then explain our narrow escape from the cannibal. When I finish, she is giving me a knowing look.

"I know about the janitor. Henry had been following him for a few days before he happened upon the two of you." She looks up at the ceiling. "Henry and Denver become...obsessed, I guess you could say. They've been hunting the cannibal since they first saw him."

She runs her hand through her hair. "I keep hoping he'll come back around. He used to be such a sweet man..."

I touch her hand. "He was my math tutor. I remember how he used to be."

247

She nods with a smile as though this isn't new to her, but doesn't elaborate.

"Why are the bad men killing some people, but keeping others alive?"

"I'm not completely sure. We talked about that," she says. "We think they're taking the young ones to train them."

"How do you know that?"

She arches an eyebrow. "We watched them for a while and it seemed like they were only kidnapping the young ones," she says. "Henry thought they were probably taking them to some kind of boot camp, where they'd train them to be Hostiles."

I look down at my lap, thoughts of my sister coming so strong they are nearly suffocating. I imagine her in a training camp, not understanding, not complying. How long will they keep her if she isn't trainable?

"They took my sister, Elizabeth."

She squeezes my hand. "I know they did, but I think they learned not to mess with her. I think she's okay."

I look up, shocked. "What do you mean?" I think about the Clementine book in the basement and realize that Heather has known this all along. Elizabeth was at the Boy Scout camp at one point. I wonder if Henry rescued her shortly after she burned down the Cooper House. Is that what my sister was trying to tell me?

Heather meets my gaze, openly curious. "I think you know what I mean. Henry was there when she made lightning burn down that big mansion, the Cooper House." She studies me for a moment, waiting for my response.

"I was never really sure, I mean, not really..." Honestly, I've been avoiding the thought since the day she electrocuted my father in the pond, making me nearly as bad as my mother. It

248

was just so strange. I mean, how do you wrap your mind around something like that?

"How does she do it? How does she make the lightning come out of the sky like that?"

I sigh. "I don't know, to be honest with you. She's been struck by lightning twice that I know of. I was there both times," I pause as the memory lilts into my mind. "She just sat there and the entire world lit up and then when it was over, she was still just sitting there perfectly untouched. I didn't know what to think. None of us did. My mother wouldn't talk about it and we just sort of tried to pretend it never happened. I guess not talking about was easier than admitting the truth."

"But it doesn't surprise you that she can make it happen? That it didn't just happen?"

"No, not really, I guess." I think about the day by the pond, when she electrocuted my father after getting angry with him. "I think she's been getting better at it for years. They must have made her very angry and she finally figured out how to control it." This gives me a pause for thought. "Is this the reason why Henry stole her from them?"

She frowns. "How do you know about that?

"I saw her Clementine book in the basement of the cabin."

"Oh." She studies her lap. "Henry didn't rescue her for that reason, you know." She looks up, her eyes weary with worry. She plays with the flashlight and twirls it around in her hand, sending wild shadows up the walls before setting it back down so we could see one another again. "He remembered her from when he was your tutor. He just wanted to do the right thing, like he did with you and Teddy."

"So, why did he save us and then bring us to the Boy Scout camp?"

"It's complicated. I don't know how to explain it, Ember. Henry wanted to save you because he remembered you. He didn't want you to get killed. You might be too old for them to retrain."

I stand up and stretch my legs for a moment. It is all too unreal, too easily explained, but yet it doesn't quite fit. It is like a puzzle piece squeezed into a spot where it doesn't belong.

"Why was he so mean to us when that man threw us down into the basement at the camp?" I remember the way he stalked away after turning us over to the dog catcher.

"He had to listen to Denver."

"The dog catcher?"

"Yeah," she says with clear distain. "Denver had his own ideas of how the world was supposed to work. He wanted us to start a new society and at first, it seemed like a good idea, but after a while we started to see a side of Denver that we didn't like." She gets up from the ground and dusts the straw and dirt off her jeans. "He had this idea that we could set up a new society and start all over again, once we killed all the bad guys, of course."

"How did he plan on killing the bad men?"

She rolls her eyes. "With brutal force, I would guess. At first, he was really nice to us. He fed us and gave us a place to sleep, but after a while, he started showing his true colors. He's nothing more than a dictator. Everything has to be his way." She turns and I can see the anguish in her face. "He beat a man nearly to death because he took an extra package of crackers. We just knew it was a matter of time before he had us all locked in cages like animals. We were actually trying to escape his camp when the bad men came up. That's why I had the motorcycles hidden behind the cabin."

She looks away into the distance, as though she is caught in a memory. I watch her for a moment, imaging her as the pretty college student she must have been before the world ended. With her blond hair and classic features, she could have been a model. There was something more to her, though, than the pretty girl looks. She had depth and integrity. She fed us when we were hungry. The thought makes me think about the book I saw under the couch.

"Heather?" I wait until she looks back at me. "What happened to Elizabeth? Where did she go after she left the Boy Scout camp?"

Heather pauses. "Henry told Denver about what he saw her do at the Cooper House and Denver wanted to use her. I think he thought that if he could make her create the lightning, then he could wipe out all the Militant Camps pretty quickly. He had a big problem with her, though."

I know what she's going to say. "Let me guess. Elizabeth wouldn't cooperate."

"Pretty much. They were trying to find a way to get her to do it on command, but they never came up with anything. Henry got tired of watching it. He was worried that Denver would push it too far. He took her one night and was going to relocate her somewhere safer – somewhere Denver didn't know about, but the bad guys ambushed him while he was driving and stole her back. He was nearly killed in the process."

"How'd they get her back and not get electrocuted? Didn't she call the lightning?"

"No. After Denver figured out that he couldn't manipulate her, he started drugging her to keep her asleep. She couldn't call the lightning when she was sleeping." She runs her fingers through the front of her hair. "I'm not proud of it, but it was the safe thing to do. We didn't know what she was capable of and we didn't want to get her mad at us. We woke her up several times a day and fed her, so she never went without food. She just slept."

She stops short, her attention drawn to an abrupt noise at the end of the tunnel, near the exit. A slow glow of light trickles down the tunnel, growing brighter and brighter, as it sends dancing shadows along the walls.

"Oh dear God. They've set the building on fire."

The world tilts on its edge for a moment and I feel my stomach roll with nausea. I jump to my feet and am immediately rewarded with a lungful of smoke. I duck back down below the billowing smoke, to where the air is still breathable.

"What are we going to do?" The panic laces through me, hot and wild.

"We have to run through it. There's no other way out," she tells me.

"But, what if the bad guys are still there?"

Heather gives me a look of exasperation. "Would you rather die of smoke inhalation?" She shakes her head and doesn't give me a chance to respond before she is heading towards the exit.

She pauses and ducks down low beneath the smoke. It will be difficult to get through the burning building and then find a clear path outside, but she is right. There isn't another option. I run to where she pauses.

"All right. Let's go. Just stay low and hold your breath," she tells me.

We move through the rest of the tunnel, ignoring the coffins full of vampires and the werewolves standing with snarled muzzles. As we reach the exit, we can feel the blast of heat. Smoke and flames fill the space where the exit used to be.

As we pause, a timber falls from the ceiling and lands several feet in front of us, sending a fan of sparks into the air.

Heather ducks her head and runs towards the entrance, with me close behind. We reach the doorway without issue and nearly fall into the open, clean air. There is no time to celebrate our escape, though. A group of bad men linger near the other end of the building, near the flaming clown's head.

"Shit," she says, grabbing my arm. She pulls me back into the cover of smoke, where we are momentarily hidden. I hold my breath for as long as I can, but I can't hold it for more than a few seconds. I take a small breathe and begin coughing immediately.

"We have to get out of this smoke," I whisper in between coughs. I'm trying to be quiet, but I can't stop the coughing once it has gotten started.

Heather darts a glance back at the place where the bad men had been standing and then pulls me around the back of the building, where a walkway separates the Haunted Tunnel building from a row of restrooms and water fountains.

"Hide in the bathroom in one of the stalls. I just want to see how close they are." She says this and leans around the corner of the building. As she does a shot rings out.

I gasp and my hand finds its way to my mouth. Heather looks at me for one lucid moment, her eyes wide and blue, a round hole marking her forehead, and then she falls to the ground in a lifeless pile.

"Oh my God, Heather," I cry. Shouts ring out from around the corner.

I step backwards into the restroom, gasping so hard I can hardly breathe, drawing in more smoke that clogs my lungs. I press my mouth against my elbow, in the way my mother taught me and muffle the sound, while my mind spins out of control. All I can see it the perfect hole in Heather's forehead as I watched the life drain from her body.

Oh my God. Oh my God. Oh my God.

I will be next if they find me.

30

I blindly find a stall, my hands roaming around in the darkness until they land on the wall. I follow the wall to the end, where a bank of stalls is tucked against the far wall. I slip into a stall as far down the wall as possible and then sit on the back of the toilet with my face pressed into my hands, gasping the clean air until I begin to hiccup.

Heather is dead.

A sense of total and utter shock washes through me, leaving me nearly limp. Flashes of thoughts run through my mind, mindless and panicked. I don't understand how it could have happened. She rescued me. She should have made it through this experience and gone onto live her happily ever after. The tears break through my resolve and for one quiet moment, I simply sob into my hands. It is too much. Too much. And now Heather is dead.

"I'm sorry. I am so sorry," I whisper into the air.

If it hadn't been for me, Heather might have found a better place to hide. Even if she had gone down the Haunted Tunnel, she wouldn't have been so foolish as to lean against a tombstone and cause a spring-loaded ghost to pop out. She'd be sitting here on this toilet, wondering what she should do next instead of emptying her blood onto the sidewalk outside.

The smell of smoke brings me back.

I need to get moving.

"Okay...I can do this." The words give me enough strength to open my eyes and gather my courage. I wipe my face with the bottom of my shirt. I feel for the roll of toilet paper, wanting very badly to blow my nose, but I know that the sound might give me away.

I drop my hand back to my lap and I listen for sounds of the bad men. I don't hear anything. I make myself wait until the heat of the burning building begins to warm the tiles behind me. It is enough to propel me forward. If I don't leave, I will burn to death inside the rest room.

My heart thuds as I slip down from the back of the toilet. I open the stall door and tiptoe to the entrance. I press my ear to the door and hear nothing more than the roaring of the fire. Maybe they've moved further away.

I push the door open an inch and observe the small slice of the world outside. My eyes water from the smoke and as it parts, I can see a portion of the red tilt-o-whirl ride across the walkway and part of the bright blue ticket booth beside it. I push the door open a bit more and peer out the doorway. The park seems eerily quiet. Nothing moves. It is as though everything is frozen in place, waiting for the world to resume again. A small grey bird flits down from a branch and begins picking at something on the ground near Heather's hair.

A drift of smoke rolls around the edge of the building, causing the bird to flutter off again. Hopefully the bad men have abandoned this part of the park for the moment. They are probably walking around from building to building looking for me. I need to put as much distance between me and the park as possible. I hope Henry and Teddy have already done the same.

"All right. It's now or never," I whisper.

There is a fence just behind the tilt-o-whirl ride and it is short enough for me to climb. If I can make it there, it will lead me back out to the side road that parallels the park.

I say a quick prayer in my head and then bolt forward. I nearly trip over Heather's body, lying just outside the doorway and I feel my stomach lurch up into my heart. Full blown panic fills my veins and I just run.

My thoughts turn to a blur as my feet pound the asphalt. I run as hard as I can across the walkway and past the ride, hoping against hope that the bad men don't see me. The thought becomes a mantra that I repeat with every footstep.

Please don't see me.

Please don't see me.

Please don't see me.

I sneak a glance over my shoulder. They are near the rest rooms, very close to where I'd just been. They have their backs turned.

It's now or never.

I bolt across the tall grass to the fence. A steep hill is in front of me and I tackle it with every ounce of fire in my body, knowing that it is the perfect backdrop to highlight my fleeing body. If they turn, they will see me. All they'd have to do is point their guns in my direction and pull the trigger and I will be as dead as my friend.

My lungs are filled with liquid lead. I will my body to continue moving.

Ten more feet, eight more feet, five more feet.

I crest the hill, wanting nothing more than to collapse in a pile, but I can't. I lodge the toe of my shoe into the chain link fence and scramble up. I reach the top and simply fling myself over, landing in a pile in the soft, warm grass. I'd like to lay there for a while and catch my breath, but I don't take the chance. If the bad men saw me, they are probably heading my way.

"Keep moving," I tell myself.

I look up and nearly crumble with relief. The road ahead of me leads to a subdivision filled with houses. I pick myself off the ground and run for it.

One of my friends from school lived here somewhere. The school bus would drop her off at the entrance to the subdivision and I'd watch her walk, head down, down the street while the bus continued on. My breath becomes ragged and pain tears through my body, but I pick up the pace. I am too close to give up now.

Fifty more feet.

The houses are laid out like gifts to me and I am uncertain which one to choose. Each house is nearly identical to the others, simple brick squares with two-car garages extending off the sides. Tall brittle grass grows limply in the front yards, giving them the distinct look of neglect. I am almost delirious with relief.

The first house has two cars parked in the driveway, which seems like a bad omen to me. I am desperate to find cover, but not desperate enough to endure more dead bodies. The horrendous image of Faith Eddy sitting in her bed like a rotting doll comes to me and my stomach curls around it. I use every ounce of energy left in my body and I sprint to the second house on the left.

My hands are sweaty and tingly as I grab the doorknob. I register the sudden flash of cold metal beneath my palm at the same time I realize that the door is mercifully unlocked. I push the door open and feel the cool air inside the house rush out at me.

Thank God.

I glance behind me to make sure the bad men aren't following me. Thick smoke pours into the sky. By morning, the entire park might be burned to the ground. I can hardly breathe.

I try not to think about everything that has just happened. I push it back into the furthermost recesses of my mind and just focus on moving forward. With trembling hands, I grab the heavy front door and push it closed. When I hear the reassuring sound of metal against metal, I just stand there for a moment, leaning against it in the darkness. The house smells musty and stale, and is deeply soundless. My ears begin ringing and I can feel my heart beat pounding in my temples.

It takes me a long moment to catch my breath again. I try to pull my mind away from the vision of Heather's face, but it keeps returning to me. I feel the loss like a hollow gap in my soul. I think about all that she was and all that she went through just to make it as far as she did. It seems like such a tragedy that she is gone. Now there is one less of us.

"Heather," I whisper her name again, just for the sound of it and wish for a moment that I could have known her better. She gave her life for me. I wonder what Henry will say when he learns about it.

I hear the sound of a truck on the road outside and I freeze, waiting to see what it will do. It will either grow closer as it pulls into the driveway or trail away as it continues down the road. I remind myself that there isn't a reason for them to have seen me. They didn't see me climb the hill and I was careful as I ran towards the houses, keeping the bank of trees between us, but the bad guys often had a sixth sense about them. They seemed to know where to look and where to search. Sometimes it almost seemed like they had an advantage over us. Maybe it was just due to practice. Human nature probably made us react in similar ways and it was only a matter of following the obvious patterns.

The truck sound grows closer as it comes to the subdivision. It pauses for a long moment, stopping in the same place where the school bus always stopped, making my heart pick up the pace. I can imagine them sitting there, at the end of the road, looking up the street, searching for me, wondering.

Had they seen one person running up the hill towards the amusement park or had they seen two? If they have searched the entire park, then they know there is no other place I could have run to. There aren't any other hiding places within miles. If they're smart, they'll now I have to be here somewhere.

A small panic rips through me as I realize that I ran across the yard instead of running up the driveway. I probably left a trampled-down trail through the overgrown lawn.

I hold my breath, looking around me, trying to find a place to hide that won't be the first place they look.

31

The truck engine revs loudly and then continues down the road, the sound of the engine growing fainter until it is gone completely. The moment becomes as brittle as glass, translucent and fragile. I could go into two directions, depending on my inner will. I could either collapse into a heap beside the door and just break down into a thousand pieces, or I could take one step forward into an uncertain future. I lift my foot, but am hesitant to put it back down.

Every nerve ending in my body is on fire and I tremble uncontrollably. I want nothing more than to just quit. It would be such a relief. It would be a tremendous liberation, just to let go. Just lie down and be done with it.

I am so tired of running and hiding, of always looking over my shoulder. I could find a bottle of pills and eat them like candy, and then find a comfortable place to wait for the end. I imagine the relief, the warm arms of salvation reaching out for me, drawing me to a place where pain and suffering are not in existence. Even if there is not a Heaven, I'd be happy with nothing. Nothing would be Heaven compared to this.

Her name comes to me in a heartbeat and I feel the swift pull of guilt.

Elizabeth.

I close my eyes and see her face, so trusting and pure.

Ember, come find me.

She calls to me in a way that isn't natural. I can feel her as though she is within touching distance, smiling shyly, her eyes bright and blue.

You can't give up now.

I open my eyes after a moment, knowing that I have to be strong. I very simply cannot leave her alone in the world. I'm all she has and she is waiting for me to rescue her.

With a sigh, I push away from the door. I try to shake off the doom and gloom that has settled so heavily on my shoulders. I'm not sure what to believe. Either I'm quickly losing my mind, or Elizabeth is learning how to communicate with me telepathically. I think back to that day by the lake and remember her voice echoing through my head, but if I dig deeper, there are other instances as well. Things I chose not to consider.

When Elizabeth was six, she'd been outside playing in the yard by herself. My mother was working in her studio and had asked me to please keep an eye on her. For most six-year-olds, this would be a major task in itself, but with Elizabeth, it was even more time consuming.

I had been sitting on the sofa, eating cheese puffs and watching an old sit-com rerun on TV. Elizabeth had been playing on the lawn with a slew of Barbie dolls. She had spread a pale pink blanket on the grass and was dressing and redressing her dolls, selecting their clothing from a mammoth pile she'd unceremoniously dumped in the middle of the blanket. I could hear her singing softly to herself and used that as a monitoring tool, considering myself very lucky she was occupied with something. Every few minutes she would stop singing, so I would lean up from the couch and look out the window to make sure she was okay.

I must have gotten distracted by the television, because the next thing I knew, Elizabeth was screaming. I jumped up and looked out the window. The dolls and clothes were scattered across the blanket, but Elizabeth was gone. She screamed again and then I heard her again, very clearly in my mind.

Ember! Bad dog! Bad dog!

I jumped off the couch and ran out the front door, my bare feet pounding on the wooden deck, my fingers leaving orange spots on the doorframe from the cheese puffs. Elizabeth was standing at the edge of the lawn, her arms raised over her head, as a large black dog jumped all around her. I took a deep breath, feeling relief pour through me. It was just our neighbor's over-enthusiastic dog, hoping for someone to play with. He wouldn't hurt her. I whistled and called the dog.

"It's okay, Elizabeth. Blacky isn't going to hurt you."

As soon as the dog came running, I grabbed his collar and held him until my sister could run into the house. I stood there for several long seconds, wondering how I'd heard her when she'd been so far away. Somewhere in the back of my mind, I must have touched on the truth, but it was harder to digest than a simple shrug, so I went with the shrug and didn't think about it again until the incident by the pond.

I shake my head and step further in the room. In front of me is a living room with nubby beige couches and tall wooden bookcases filled with hardback novels. I take a step towards a doorway that must lead to a kitchen. The house is a moderate-sized ranch design, larger than the one Faith Eddy had lived in and better equipped.

Framed paintings hang on the wall. I touch one and feel the brush marks on canvas, something my mother taught me to tell the difference between a painting and a print. It is a pretty scene of an ocean wave crashing over a rounded brown rock, but it is as useless as any other thing. The most it could be for me would be firewood. I have no room for hopeful scenery, no need for decorative burdens.

I find the kitchen. Several bowls rest in the sink drainer, waiting to be put away. I imagine a couple living here, washing the dishes and rinsing them under the stream of water before leaving for work. A series of windows line the back of the house, letting in a subtle drift of late afternoon sunshine. It will be dark soon, so I'd better hurry, I remind myself.

Very foul smells radiate from the refrigerator, so I give it a wide berth. The cabinets are stocked full of portable, nutritious food though, so I am happy. I find power bars, granola bars, saltine crackers, squares of chocolate wrapped in silver foil, trail mix, and dried apricots. I squirt a handful of hand sanitizer into the palm of my hand and rub it in carefully before I stuff a handful of apricots in my mouth. I nearly cry as my salivary glands tighten at the taste. It is the best thing I've ever tasted, I think until I take a bite of the chocolate and it becomes the best thing I've ever tasted. I polish it off with a swig of warm soda from a can and feel the belch climb swiftly up my gullet.

The simple sensation of burping nearly brings a smile to my face. It has been a long time since I've been even remotely capable. Burping is one of those things that belong in our old world, something I had nearly forgotten about. I take another swig and feel the second burp build in my stomach. My mother would sometimes playfully rank our burps, unless of course we were out in public. Then, she would narrow her eyes at us until we said 'excuse me.' I take another swig and produce what I consider to be a 'seven' before moving onto more important issues.

I find a small flashlight and a package of batteries in the drawer beside the back door and I put those in my front pocket. I stuff the rest of my pockets full of food, but realize that I left my backpack at the Boy Scout camp. I will really need to replace it so I can bring more supplies with me. The food in my pocket will only last me a day or two. If I have a backpack, I can survive for much longer. I look down the hallway at a bank of closed doors and feel the nervousness return to me with a pounding heartbeat. The soda burbles uncomfortably in my stomach.

I take a deep breath and let it out in a sigh. I can do this.

There weren't any cars parked in the driveway, I remind myself.

Unless they parked their cars in the garage.

The thought makes me stop in my tracks. But there isn't any smell, I remind myself.

There wouldn't be an odor if the doors are closed.

I think of Faith Eddy and the horror washes over me, immersing me whole. I don't want to see another dead body. I really don't.

"You can do it," I say out loud.

I force myself to take a step down the hallway. I need tampons. I need them and they could be here, just inside one of those doors. I try to determine which door would be the bathroom. Surely the first room on the right. It would make obvious sense. I have my hand on the doorknob.

Unless it is the doorway to the basement?

I pull my hand away as if it has been stung. The basement is a place where bad things could be lurking. I imagine another cannibal leering just on the other side, smiling a hideous, lecherous smile, his pointy teeth glimmering as he salivates at the thought of me. He would probably find me to be tender and tasty, like a Twinkie, only larger.

"Stop it!"

My words echo down the hallway, sounding loud and strange. It is enough though. It pulls me out of my self-induced panic and allows me the courage to reach out for the doorknob again. I twist it and push the door inward with one movement before my mind can convince me otherwise.

The room is dark and I stare hopelessly at it for a moment until I realize that I have possession of a flashlight again. The thought whoops through me with elation and I pull it out of my pocket, feeling as though I've won the lottery. I turn it on and find myself looking at a small half bath. The cabinet below the sink contains an unopened box of tampons.

Hallelujah!

I root through the medicine cabinet and find ibuprofen, bandages, throat lozenges, and stomach aids. I pull them out and line them up on the counter and stare at them as though they are bars of solid gold. I will definitely need a backpack. I turn back to the doorway and to the other unopened doors in the hallway.

It isn't as difficult this time. Spurred by my success with the one room, I run down the hallway and open all the doors, chasing away the shadows by allowing the light from the windows to permeate the house. The house is empty of people, just as I had hoped it would be. The owners must have gone away and died somewhere else. Thankfully, they didn't have any pets locked away in a back bedroom. I have the entire house to myself.

I find an old blue backpack in a hall closet, wedged on the top shelf between a bowling ball bag and a sewing machine. I pull it down and dust it off, happy to find it empty and ready to be filled with treasures. I sprint back to the bathroom and toss in the medications and tampons, and run back in to add a roll of toilet paper to the mix. It will feel like Heaven compared to the leaves and handfuls of long grasses that I have been using. The thought makes me wistful for a bath. I lift my arm and take a whiff, sampling the stale smell of my own sweat.

Cleanliness is next to Godliness, one of my mother's phrases returns to me, making me realize that it has been days since I've thought of her quotes. They used to be as familiar to me as my own breath and I'd clung to them for months, letting them help me get through the madness, but now they have been reduced to mere memories.

I open the closet door in the master bedroom, hoping the women who lived here was close to my size. If she were obese or really tall, I'd be forced to stay in my old, smelly clothes and I am anxious for something clean against my skin again.

The closet is divided into his and her sections. The first section belongs to him. It is filled with dark suits and crisp white shirts. Shiny black and brown shoes are lined up along the bottom. A tennis racket and a tube of balls rest on the shelf above the clothes, next to a faded Monopoly game.

I stare longingly at the game. If I had more room, I'd take it with me. I can easily imagine Teddy and myself sitting around a campfire somewhere tossing dice and groaning as we missed the Free Parking square. It will have to remain here, though. I have too many other necessities that need to come first. I could always come back and replenish my supplies, but I hate to gamble on something so important. I will take what I need and leave the rest. If I can come back, I will gather more supplies, but if I can't, I will have the essentials. I move onto the second half of the closet.

I hold my breath as I open the door and smile as I see the neat rows of clothes that are very close to my size. I take a glimpse at the tag on a pair of jeans and see that they are the size I used to wear. When I slip them on though, they are loose and baggy. I wonder how much weight I've lost. I add a belt and cinch it in nice and tight.

I remove the flashlight and the pack of chewing gum from my jeans pocket and stuff them in my new pockets, then ball up my old clothes and stuff them under the bed where they won't be seen. I add another pair of jeans and several well-pressed t-shirts into the backpack on top of the medications, feeling the luxury of having a second set of clothing. I move onto the dresser and shop for clean underwear, socks, and a bra that is a cup size too large. In the nightstand, I find a bottle of sleeping pills. My fingers linger on them, dark thoughts returning to me. I should pull my hand away before the temptation overcomes me, but I find myself moving forward, grasping them between my sweating fingers.

Take them, a voice whispers in my mind and I curl my fingers around the bottle, not knowing if it is my subconscious or something else that is guiding me.

I check the windows and then pull the blinds. I will sleep in the closet, I've already decided. Even though there are several beds at my disposal, I don't trust my surroundings to allow myself to be so blatantly visible. I pull a blanket out of a linen closet and a pillow from the bed and line the floor inside the closet like a nest.

Before I climb into my hidey-hole for the night, I return to the kitchen and fill the backpack with more food and bottles of water, matches, candles, and add a long, sharp knife from the butcher block holder. I turn on the water and am delighted to hear it sputter and then spurt a solid stream of water into the sink. I fill up several pans and light the gas stove to allow them to boil.

I light several scented candles and pour a bit of lavender bath bubbles into the cold water. I make several trips back and forth to the kitchen and add the boiling water until the tub is tepid, but not cold, and then I disrobe and climb in.

The simple luxury of taking a bath brings tears to my eyes. The mixed scents of cinnamon from the candles and lavender from the bubbles lilt through the air, giving me one solid minute of normal. If I block out the memories, this could be a moment from my past, of slipping into my mother's bathroom and indulging in one of her favorite pleasures.

I wash my hair with expensive shampoo and conditioner and even shave my legs with a razor I find parked at the edge of the tub. I close my eyes and just float for a while, thinking of nothing but the solitude of water touching my clean body. When the water turns cold, I rise and dry myself with a thick terrycloth towel. Once I've dressed again, I add the shampoo and a clean towel to my backpack, even though they are luxuries that I should leave behind.

I return to the kitchen for another meal as the sun is setting low on the horizon. I watch it for a moment, relishing the dazzling colors mixing together, touching my soul with grace and serenity. It is a sunset that Heather will never see and I think of her cold, still body lying on the sidewalk where she fell. The tears find me again and I give into them for several seconds until I am able to find my center again. I have to stay strong for Elizabeth. With a sigh, I return to the closet, where I fall into a dreamless sleep.

32

I come awake in the closet with a start. It is still dark outside and I focus on my breathing for a moment just to gather my bearings. It takes me several seconds to remember where I am and as the knowledge returns to me, so does the memory of Heather's death. A sob catches in my throat and I hold onto it, allowing it to purge through my soul. I feel the loss as though she were a relevant part of my existence, as though I've known her forever. In many ways, it doesn't matter that I barely knew her. Her death is one more death piled onto the deaths I've already suffered. It brings back the pain and makes the other deaths fresh again. I feel them pressing on me, weighing me down.

I would stay in the closet forever if it weren't for the pressing needs of my body, urging me up.

My feet hit the familiar coolness of the tiled kitchen floor and it feels like being back in the past, minus the electricity and people. I carry my flashlight into the dark bathroom and reluctantly begin to mull over my options. The future is such a cloudy, murky fog hanging in front of me and I can't see through it to know where I need to go. With every ounce of my being, I just want to stay here, eating all the wonderful food and feeling the comfort of being in a home again, but the other part of me knows that I need to leave. Guilt is a strong motivator for me and I know that I can't just abandon my search for my sister. Besides, if I find Teddy and Elizabeth, we can always return here and live for a while.

I relieve myself in the bathroom on an actual toilet and marvel for a moment over the ability to flush and have my waste carried away without effort. I did not have to dig a hole in the ground and then cover it with fresh dirt and leaves, I just flushed and it all went away. This will only last for a while. I don't know much about the public water system, but I can't imagine it will run forever without power or people to maintain it.

I pause at the mirror over the bathroom sink, taking in my somber appearance and my too thin face.

"So, what happens next?" I ask my reflection. I cannot imagine the future that awaits us. Even if I am successful, there is everything else to consider. We'll always be running, always be looking over our shoulders, always be searching for the basic necessities we need to keep us alive.

If we outnumber the bad men, we might have a chance of taking back our planet. It is just as simple as that. Unfortunately, we are all scattered, hiding from the world in our cubby holes and abandoned houses, terrified of being discovered.

I don't have any idea how we are going to get rid of the bad men. Teddy and I had thought about taking away their face masks, but this is no longer an option since we saw them without masks at Faith Eddy's house. The virus probably dies within a few days if it doesn't have a host to support it. The bad men must have figured this out already, hence the lack of gas masks.

"Back to the drawing board," I tell my reflection with a sigh.

I find my way into the kitchen to begin packing my backpack.

Besides the normal stock pile of rice mixes, pasta mixes, and canned foods, I also find freeze-dried meals intended for camping. I feel as though I have won the food lottery. I pull a package of teriyaki chicken and rice mix out and dance around the kitchen with it for a moment until I discover a packet of lasagna with meat sauce and I dance around with it. There is chicken ala king, macaroni and cheese, sweet and sour pork

271

with rice, and beef stroganoff with noodles. I run back and retrieve my backpack and fill it with my top five favorites. This will give me nearly a week's worth of dinner meals until I need to come back and refill my pack.

As this thought comes to me, I realize that I have already made my decision without realizing what I was going to do. I close my eyes, allowing the thought to wash through me. It is the right decision. I need to find Teddy. Tomorrow is my birthday and I told him I'd meet him at the Weeping Mary statue, so that's where I need to be.

I finish packing and then pause at the front door, giving the house one last longing look before I head out. It has been a necessary refuge and I feel better for having stopped. I have caught up on my sleep, eaten my fill, and probably smell much better, thanks to the bath and clean clothing. The only thing I am missing is the sense of satisfaction that should accompany all of those things. I won't feel anything good until I've found my sister.

I close the door behind me and feel the metaphorical moment deep in my soul. I have closed one door and am standing on the threshold of another. Now that I've made my decision, there will be no turning back. I am no longer bumbling along, searching for the basic necessities and trying to survive. I now have a purpose and I feel like a warrior heading off to battle.

I stand on the stoop for a moment and simply observe the small slice of the world that is spread out in front of me. The land is softly arched, like earth spread over the bottom of a bowl, with an abundance of grass, soil, and trees. I am amazed at how utterly quiet the world has become. Airplanes no longer drone across the skies, painting white lines against the powder blue. Trucks and cars no longer hum along the highways. The power lines don't buzz with electricity and houses don't purr when the air conditioners kick on. There is no chatter of children playing on their lawns or dogs barking in backyards. People don't call to one another and telephones don't ring inside empty houses. There is just a perfect mantle of silence.

I sigh and step out onto the lawn. The long grass blows softly in the breeze and I am careful to only step in the places where it is the thinnest so I don't leave a trail. I find my way back to the intersection of the streets and I pause. If I turn right, I will head into town. If I turn left, I will head back towards Decker's Park.

I take a deep breath. Sometimes doing the right thing isn't the easiest path.

I take a long look to the left, to where the town is waiting for me and I sigh. It will have to wait a little bit longer. I need to go back and bury Heather.

I return to the garage for a shovel and a length of bright blue tarp and then head back down the driveway. Sometimes I wish I weren't the good guy, always doing the right thing. Being a bad guy seems so much easier.

32

I stand over Heather's grave, my arms like leaden appendages, and my face awash with tears. I should really say something. I have only been to one funeral and all I can remember is the incessant crying, the black suits and the touch of a hand on my shoulder over the loss of my father.

I try to imagine my mother standing beside me, helping me and then the words come easily. With a shaky voice, I recite the Lord's Prayer because it is the only prayer I know. As the *Amen* escapes my lips, I close my eyes and silently thank her for all that she was and for all that she's given. And then I thank her for giving her life so that I might survive. I turn with a heavy sigh and walk to the men's restroom, where the motorcycle waits for me.

There is no clear way to separate the two events, Heather's funeral and my escape. One simply follows the other the best way it can. I give the motorcycle a moment's examination, trying to make sense of it.

It is a machine that was meant for off road. There are no headlights, only a number plate that has been left blank. It looks as though it were stolen straight from a dealership, having belonged to no one and this pleases me for the strangest of reasons. I am tired of stealing, tired of removing things that belonged to people who have died. There are times when I feel like nothing more than a thief, a grave robber at best, but this feels like something else. Heather would have wanted me to have it, even though it really wasn't hers to give.

I slide onto the seat and put the bike into neutral.

I am thankful that my father took the time to teach me how to ride his old dirt bike when I was younger. It is another one of those things that simply is falling into place as though there is a higher purpose. Sometimes it all feels like my destiny has already been determined.

I start the bike on the first attempt, defying all sense of logic. I try not to consider what might have happened if the bike had started this way yesterday, but it's hard not to linger on. If it had started, Heather and I might have made our escape. We could be sitting with Henry and Teddy, marveling at our luck. I sigh deeply and then move on. It's all I can do.

I pass by yesterday's scenery backwards, taking in the rolling green hills and the tall whispering pines from the opposite angle. I pass the houses, with grass growing long and tall in the lawns, with limbs scattered on the roads, of leaf-covered cars in driveways, waiting patiently for their owners to come outside and take them for a ride. Wild rabbits flourish in the undergrowth, hopping through gardens and lawns without worry. I see the murmuring sky, filled with flimsy clouds that are a new kind of normal, and then for one brief second, I see my sister's face, smiling the shyest of smiles.

Ember. I hear it echo in my head as loud as real words.

"I'm coming, Elizabeth," I tell her, and for the first time, I believe it's true.

The Boy Scout camp is empty. The burned-out Bronco sits in its own pile of ashes. It is nothing more than a black skeleton, surrounded by rubble that is no longer recognizable unless you look really closely. Tires have burned away, as well as the steering wheel and the entire interior of the vehicle, leaving a shell full of ashes. It smells sharp and hurtful, the smell of burning rubber and spent fuel mixing with char and soot. There is some symbolism here, but I push it away before it can take hold in my mind.

The cabin hasn't fared much better. The entire front of the structure has been blackened and all the windows are blown out. I am surprised to find that it didn't burn to the ground. The smell of charred wood is overpowering and sickening. I try to breathe through my mouth to keep from smelling it.

Beads of sweat pop up on my forehead and trickle down my temples and I swipe at them before they can run down my face. The air on the top of the mountain is cooler, but still very warm in the direct August sunlight. I step around the back of the cabin and find refuge in the shadows, where the air is much cooler. I think about Teddy. It doesn't seem that long since we were here, being pulled along by Henry.

A part of me wishes for Teddy's imaginary time machine. I would go back, if I could, and tell myself something that would stop the madness before it could begin. We wouldn't stop at Decker's Park. We would just keep riding until we came to the stopping place where Teddy and Henry might have spent the night and I wouldn't be here all alone with tears staining the front of my shirt.

I have the strongest need to find Elizabeth's book. I don't know precisely what I will do with it, but the urge to come here and find it was too strong to resist. Something in the back of my mind nags me to press further and look deeper. I push the red motorcycle into a clump of bushes and cover it carefully with a fallen limb, so it can't be seen, and then make my way into the cabin.

The inside of the cabin is remarkably intact and it only takes me a minute to get in, grab the book and get back out again. I give the dead man a wide berth, not giving in to the urge to glance down at him as I pass. I retrace my path back out to the golden sunlight with the book cradled protectively against my chest.

276

I carry the book down a trail to a clearing, needing a moment to collect my thoughts. The air is much cooler here, smelling of pine and pollen instead of ash and charred wood. I take a deep breath through my nose and try to clear away all of the memories. It is peaceful here, a place where nature can open up and allow itself to be fully appreciated. I can easily imagine a troop of Boy Scouts sitting in a circle, learning how to tie square knots on a length of rope or start a fire with flint and stone. I sit down and am getting ready to look at the book when I hear the sound of a truck approaching the camp site.

I duck down behind the log and peer through the leaves in time to see Denver get out of a truck. Two men climb out behind him and they begin moving around the campsite, collecting tools and supplies.

"Hurry it up, guys. I'd like to be out of here in ten minutes tops," Denver says.

I slip the book into my backpack and ease further back into the shadows.

The men work for nearly double the ten-minute time limit, carrying boxes of food to the truck and loading them into the back. When they have finished, they pause at the edge of the clearing, near the truck.

"So what are you gonna do about those kids? We really need that girl."

"I don't know. I guess we gotta find them first," Denver says.

"Where do you think they took them?"

"I don't know. Not a clue. We'll have to spend some time tonight looking around. We can start..."

They move closer to the cabin, but their voices are too faint to clearly hear, so I edge from my hiding place and slip closer. I need to know more details. Are they talking about

Teddy and me? Why would they feel they needed me in particular? What makes me so valuable? Or is it Elizabeth they're talking about? I reach the edge of the pine grove and slip behind a stand of saplings.

"Strangest thing I've ever heard..." one of the men starts to say and then hushes the others. "What was that?"

"Shhhhh..." Footsteps crack through the underbrush, coming towards me.

I catch a glimpse of them through the trees, looking in my direction as though they've heard something and I am nearly frozen with fear. I need to move, but I don't see any easy escape routes. I could run through the woods, but they would quickly overtake me. If I stay where I am, they will find me in a matter of minutes.

My only choice is the motorcycle. It's just fifteen feet away. I can see the gleam of the handlebars through the tree branches. The men are only thirty feet on the other side of it. If I can get to it in time, I might have a chance of outrunning them through the woods. I just need a little more space. What I need is a distraction. If they are looking in one direction while I am running in the other direction, then I might have a chance.

I search through the leaves at my feet until I find a good-sized rock and chuck it as hard as I can. It doesn't land where I want it to, but it is still on the other side of the clearing. If they take the bait, I will run for it.

Denver holds up his hand to quiet them. They move forward, step by step, edgy and cautious.

When they have moved to the far edge of the clearing, I make my move. It's now or never.

I bolt from my hiding place and move quietly through the woods towards the motorcycle. I steal a glance behind me to see if they have noticed me and am thankful to see them still peering into the bushes.

I lift the bike from the ground and push it towards the back of the cabin, where the trail runs down the mountain. If I can get it there in time, I can coast it down the hill and start it while it's moving, giving me a head start.

As I reach the edge of the cabin, I hear someone shout. I look behind me.

"There she is," a man shouts, and they all come running for me.

34

I find the path much easier than I thought I would. The first man rounds the corner of the cabin as I'm throwing my leg over the seat.

"Get her, Denver," one of the men shouts.

I look back to see the dog catcher closing in on me.

I push off with my legs, holding in the clutch. The motor catches almost immediately and the engine roars to life. Denver is only five steps behind me when I press on the throttle and leave him behind.

I am nearly all the way to town before my heart returns to a normal pace. I have won the battle, but I am not even close to winning the war. Now that they know I'm around, they will be fervently looking for me.

It is too early to arrive at the cemetery, but I don't know where else to go. I push the motorcycle down the gravel walkways, avoiding leaving tire tracks on the grass. The sky above me has turned ominous and grey, as though it is trying to provide an appropriate backdrop to my feelings. A black crow lands on a tombstone and calls out, as if warning me.

I have a clear view of the town from the top of the hill. My eyes automatically search out the hill where the chemical plant sits, a ticking time bomb. The fire that had been burning at the edge of town is no longer visible. It must have burnt itself out, but it doesn't mean it still isn't a danger. I sigh and turn away because there's nothing more to consider for the moment, except for the things I must do next.

By the time I reach the stone mortuary, I am winded. I open the door and park the bike inside behind the slab where Teddy had slept.

I turn the latch and feel much better having a locked door between me and the outside world, even though I probably shouldn't. It wouldn't take much to get in if someone wanted to badly enough. I just have to hope that no one knows where I am. I stow my backpack on the stone bench I'd claimed before.

I prop my flashlight up on the stone shelf on the back wall. A fan of amber light splays up the wall, highlighting the strings of cobwebs that dangle down from the ceiling. My fingers tremble as I pull the book out of my backpack.

I stare at it for a long moment, thoughts running through my mind.

Elizabeth went through stages. When she was four or five, she loved anything to do with princesses and when she turned eight, it was Clementine. She carried the doll everywhere and made sure my mother read her the book every night before bed. If my mother forgot, Elizabeth became inconsolable and would keep the house up for hours as she cried and cried. My mother would sigh and then say, "Okay, Elizabeth, but only one time," and they'd read it twice, at the very least.

I flip through the pages, seeing the familiar story, hearing my mother's voice lilting in my mind. I don't pause until I get to page 38. When I do, I simply stop, and the breath is knocked out of me.

In the story, Clementine is getting ready for bed.
"The day has been fun, the day has been great,
But the ticking clock says it's getting late.
It's time to go where dreamland reaps,
It's time to close your eyes and go to sleep."
The words 'go to sleep" are underlined in purple crayon. I press the book to my chest and close my eyes.

I think back to the day when the bad men came to the house and I hid in the kitchen cubby hole. They walked around the house and threw cans of food through the windows, but they must have also been there for another reason. I remember the Clementine doll that had disappeared off the dining room table. They must have come to the house for these items. Elizabeth must have insisted on it.

My mind spins with the implications.

There is more going on than what I can see with my eyes. I feel Desmond beside me again, coming to me at the important parts. I squint down at the place where he should be and I open my mind to all that there is to hear.

The wind whispers through the cemetery trees and the birds chatter to one another as though it is any old day. Thunder rolls softly in the distance, working slowly up to something. The thought comes to me and I am breathless in its wake.

I wasn't imaging it. Elizabeth has been sending me messages. I think back to all those times when I've heard her voice in my mind. I would hear only a word or two before she faded away, but she has full reign while I sleep. Just as she has been learning to control the lightning, she is still learning to harness the capability to communicate with me in my mind. She can send me short message when I am awake, but she is much more effective when I am asleep.

I don't know why I haven't understood this before. Maybe I didn't trust that it was truly Elizabeth. Maybe I thought it was just a dream, but it is clear to me now. She did it when I fainted in the haunted tunnel. She did it when I fell asleep in the basement of the cabin. I sigh and shake my head. Six months ago, I would have laughed at the thought, but anything is possible now.

"It's time to close your eyes and go to sleep," I say out loud, remembering the sleeping pills I pulled from the medicine cabinet.

Everything is beginning to make sense to me now. It is like a bank of fog lifting in my mind. When I first saw the sleeping pills, I felt a strong urge to bring them with me, even though they were about as practical as packing a curling iron or high-heeled shoes. They weren't something I needed, but I trusted in my instincts and took them anyway. Now I realize that I might have not been doing these things all on my own. Elizabeth had been leading me from the very beginning. It was probably planned from the moment I fled from my family's house.

I retrieve the bottle from my backpack and shake two small blue tablets out in my hand. They look like tiny robin's eggs nested in the palm of my hand. I roll them back and forth for a moment and consider the ramifications.

Falling asleep in broad daylight in the middle of a cemetery isn't a safe thing to do. I take a deep breath and let it out slowly, feeling the oxygen rush through my body. Before I can change my mind, I pop the pills into my mouth and wash them down with a swig of water. Someday, when the world is whole again, I hope someone remembers the small terrifying steps it took us to get it there.

I lie down on the stone bench and close my eyes. It should take me thirty minutes to fall asleep, but it doesn't. I fall asleep in an instant with the smell of my sister surrounding me like a hug. She is waiting for me, there on the other side and it doesn't take her long to tell me everything I need to know.

35

I consider for a moment how circular everything has become. Things that were once presented to me with a sense of importance have now escalated to life or death matters. Everything has a purpose, a plan. If I neglect to pay attention to the details, I might miss the one thing that could save all of our lives.

There are so many *what ifs*. Had my father not taught me to ride a motorcycle, I couldn't have made it back to town. Had Elizabeth not written her name on the cover of her Clementine book when she was eight, I wouldn't have known without a doubt that it was hers.

I only hope my instincts are on target. Elizabeth has actually shown me very little. She has shown me flashes that aren't so dissimilar to the lopsided drawings she hung on my mother's refrigerator with plastic alphabet magnets. She's shown me sleepy puppy dogs as often as she's shown me the scowling faces of the bad men who keep her. She's shown me a room full of children being shuffled onto a big green Army truck and her remorse at being the only one left behind. She's shown me smiling men handing her cookies and she's shown me the pretty pink blanket they've given her to cover up with, the one with the purple stars that I recognized in an instant. She has shown me a bedroom with glow-in-the-dark stars on the ceiling and posters of handsome boys on the walls. She has shown me a pink rhinestone bag filled with makeup, carpeting that is as blue as the ocean, and the mountain of stuffed animals that fill the bed where she sleeps. She has also shown me things between those snippets, things I couldn't have known otherwise and those things make all the difference.

I think it's only natural to question myself, but I have to trust the feelings inside of myself. If everything that is happening to me is truly destiny, leading me down a path, or just a product of my imagination, I have no choice but to follow it. The only thing I do know for certain is that Elizabeth is leading me. I can feel her touching my mind like a feather. With everything else, there is doubt. Here there is only truth.

Once I wake up, I fix myself a quick meal. The beef teriyaki isn't great, but it's tremendously better than the stale crackers and granola bars I've been eating for days on end. I eat the entire packet and then lick the inside of the foil until it is clean and shiny.

Thanks to my foray at the subdivision, I have some basic necessities that make my second trip to the mortuary more enjoyable. I have a small flannel blanket to keep me warm and ample batteries to feed to my flashlight. Most important, though, I have a plan. It burns through me with such promise; I can nearly taste it on my lips.

My muscles ache from digging Heather's grave, so I swallow a pain reliever tablet and hope it does the trick. In several years, all of the remaining tablets will be gone, and we will have nothing left to ease our pain. My only hope is that maybe it isn't as bad as it seems. Maybe there are more people out there like me, people who can rebuild and start the world all over again. It is a nice thought and it follows me into my dreams before I even realize I've fallen back asleep. I awake several hours later, while it is still dark outside and then I begin my plan.

I walk across town, taking my time and sticking to the shadows where I can't be seen. I no longer worry about stepping in the worn places in the grass. If my plan holds true, I will no longer need to. There will be a certain freedom that will be returned to us.

285

I try to imagine the world without the bad men. I try to remember what it felt like to walk down the middle of the street in broad daylight without worry or hesitation. If we have the chance, we can rebuild what we lost. People will begin to bury the dead and then fill the houses again. Someone will figure out how to bring back the electricity, the medicine, better methods of communication and we will slowly begin to reconstruct our civilization again. None of it can begin until they are gone, though. It is the first step.

Unfortunately, there can't be a bloodless way to go about this. They've already set their mark on us, on everything we stand for, and they've cut us down to our knees. What we need is a miracle.

They believe very strongly in their faith and whether or not they care to admit it, they are also very superstitious. They might not avoid walking under ladders or breaking mirrors, but they do avoid things that have brought them misery in the past. Elizabeth has shown this to me in my dreams.

She is a bit of a mystery to them, an enigma of impossibilities and propositions that defy logic. She is only a child, yet she is able to reach out into the heavens with her mind. She is soft and sweet with eyes as blue as the sky, but she can throw a tantrum that comes complete with thunder and lightning. They aren't sure what to do with her, but then again they aren't sure what to do without her. And one thing is for certain, even if they aren't capable of harnessing her, of controlling her ability and using it to strengthen their hold on us, they certainly don't want us to have it instead. What they fear is that we'll be able to use her in ways they cannot. So, instead, they simply keep her away from us.

They have been keeping Elizabeth asleep. After witnessing her deadly lightning show at the Cooper House, they came to realize that a sleeping Elizabeth was a safer version of the blond-haired child they were so taken with. I can't say that I blame them. I think back to the morning by the lake and how she struck our father down for simply losing his temper and this makes me nervous. What will happen to us now that she's aware she has this power? Will she use it on me the first time I make her eat her green beans? Will I eventually succumb to the same sordid measures the bad guys are currently using to keep her under control?

I don't know. I am not even sure how they are keeping her asleep. More than likely they are putting sleeping pills into her food or beverages. Elizabeth simply cannot turn down a frothing cup of hot chocolate. If they knew this, they'd be all set. Keeping her sedated would be easy for them as long as they played by her rules. What they don't know is that she is actually more dangerous when she is asleep than when she is awake. When she's awake, she is capable of calling the lightning, but when she is asleep, she is able to call me.

There is more to it, more to all of it. It is not simply about Elizabeth. It isn't even about me and my quest to bring back my old life. It is the calm that used to reside inside of me, that small part of me that I was never really aware of before. It is the hum of boredom on an endless Saturday afternoon, the way I could lie on my back on the green, green lawn and contemplate the clouds passing overhead, the way I could simply walk down the middle of the street and think about what flavor of ice cream I would buy at the grocery store. Now everything is mixed up, turned upside down and inside out. Fear has filled the spots where tranquility once lingered and terror blankets the rest with a constant presence.

I've come to realize that I hunger for *calm* almost as much as I long for love. I want a sense of family, warm hugs, and the

287

sharing and caring that comes easily to people who are happy together. Love isn't something you search for and then capture, something you lasso and then hover over with a twelve-gauge shotgun, protecting it from looters. Love is something that is simply there. It floats freely in the atmosphere. It is in the air. It is in the water. It is in every pore of our being. It is ours for the taking, provided we learn how to tap into it.

I think about my sister, with her bright eyes and her smile that reaches all the way through to the core of her and I think about Teddy, shyly sharing his candy bar with me even though he could have eaten the entire thing himself. Then, I think about Heather, who gave her life for me. And I also think of Henry, who is important to all of us in his own way. It's all love. It's just different flavors. Somehow through the tragedy, I've found the one thing that my life has always been missing. It is enough to fight for, of that I'm sure. Is it enough to die for? I close my eyes for several seconds, allowing the thought to truly take hold. It just might be.

I finally reach my destination. It is a place I know well. I have spent many nights here, sleeping in tents on the lawn, sampling makeup in the bathroom, playing hide and seek with my friends. It is the second largest house in town. It is Teddy and Annie's house.

36

I find Elizabeth quickly, but that is the easy part.

I start in the garage on the other side of the street, finding the hidden wall that leads to the secret tunnel once used to hide slaves, then later whiskey. I follow the tunnel under the street and into the belly of the basement. The basement smells of dusty mold and nearly makes me sneeze. Long silky cobwebs dangle from the ceiling, making me think of spiders and dead insects. I allow the door to close behind me and feel the cold wrap itself around me like a blanket.

I stand in the gloom and just listen to the sounds of the house for a moment. The house is quiet. Instead of the tick and hum of the old massive furnace that is planted in the center of the room, there is nothing. No other sounds fill the gaps or even try to take the place of the old sounds. There is just nothing. It is deadly still, something that feels as tangible as the cobwebs brushing against my face.

I find the back staircase at the end of the basement. The wooden stairs are grey from decades of neglect. Back in the days when the house had actual servants, the stairs had led to their living quarters. I tiptoe up them, mindful of squeaking treads. Annie and I knew each stair by heart. Sometimes Annie and I would sneak down them and escape outside. We'd slip into the darkness and simply walk along the darkened streets at midnight, marveling at the sky full of stars or the way the town slept so soundly and so deeply. I miss her in a way that squeezes my soul.

Elizabeth is in Annie's old room, which is at the end of the hallway, the first door I come to as I reach the landing.

The hallway is dark, lit only by the afterglow from the lights downstairs. I can hear the voices of the men speaking occasionally and the slight rattle of papers, as though they are reviewing paperwork. It is possible that they are planning a second attack to rid themselves of the rest of us, but this isn't something I'm privy to. I only know what Elizabeth has shown me and all she has shown me so far is the blanket on top of her bed, which was something I gave Annie for her sixteenth birthday last year. It is the sole reason why I know where to find her.

I make my way to Annie's door, acknowledging the pink sign that says Annie in cursive script, something we made together in her backyard one summer. I have a matching one that says Ember on my own door.

I push the door open, bracing myself for a squeal of hinges which will surely give me away, but it is mercifully quiet. The door opens silently as though it has been recently oiled. I slip in and close the door behind me, smelling the familiar perfumed fragrance of Annie's room. I could close my eyes and imagine myself climbing into bed with Annie during a sleepover, sharing secrets and dreams about our futures. As my eyes adjust to the moonlit room, a sob hitches in my chest.

Elizabeth.

She is lying on Annie's bed, under a mound of covers. A black blindfold is wrapped around her eyes and her hands are attached to the brass bed frame with shining steel handcuffs. An IV is connected to her arm with a long thin tube, dripping medication into her veins, drop by drop, keeping her asleep.

I walk to her side, the enormity of the moment bringing tears to my eyes. I see her in my mind, smiling shyly, peering around a doorframe with some sweet secret held tightly in her fisted hand. I see her running across the yard, pulling a red balloon behind her, the sheer delight in the movement, the way it simply follows her without question, consuming her, filling her with pure glee. I see her the day she came home from the hospital, all pink and small, the whirl of white blond hair corkscrewing off the top of her head like a pinnacle. She has always been more than us. She has always been something better, untainted and prevailing, like Eve in the Garden of Eden, the first of something the world has never seen before. We'd had been so consumed by looking at the things she wasn't that we missed the things she was.

In this moment, as I stare down at her, tied to the bed, sleeping a dreamless sleep, I realize that she is our fate. There is a reason why the bad men have kept her here. They saw it too. They felt the pull of her, stronger than an ocean tide. If there is to be a future, she is at the heart of it. She is at the heart of us. She is our hope. She is everything. Completely and truly.

With every breath in my being, I want to wake her and hold her in my arms and tell her that everything is okay, but I can't. Everything rides on this one moment. I gather my strength around me like a cloak and I turn my back to her and I leave. Tears stream down my face, but I push them away. There is work to do first.

37

My watch tells me that it is my birthday. I am now seventeen years old. In our old world, I'd be thinking about my last year in high school, the year I'd spent my entire life pining away for. There would be senior pictures, the senior prom, senior skip day, and finally graduation. It would be the year I'd finally rise to the top of the crowd before being expelled out into the wide wonderful world of adulthood. Instead, it is this.

It is a lifetime of scrounging for food, while trying to avoid dead bodies, angry men with guns, and cannibals who want to eat us alive. It is bathing in cold water, wearing clothing that doesn't belong to us, and always living in fear. I sigh because there is nothing else I can do.

The moon is high and bright in the sky. It lights the night with blue hues, making it seem like muted daylight. Shadows splay out from trees, tattooing the sidewalk with lacy patterns.

I find my way back to the cemetery without issue. I've learned how to walk quietly in the shadows and to listen for every noise before making hasty movements. I find that my fear of the dark has faded into a distinct memory. I now prefer the dark. It's a place where I can hide without being seen.

As I walk past the Weeping Mary statue, I think I see a small shadow ahead of me, darting between the tombstones with his nose pressed to the ground.

"I'm sorry," I tell him, and I am. What I did to him was unforgivable, but I'd do it again if I had to. "I'm sorry," I tell him again, just to be sure he heard me.

Just after our mother died, Elizabeth and I were out in her garden pushing bark mulch over the bare dirt, trying to make it look nice. This had happened at the very beginning of everything and I was still stuck in the outer loop of my learning curve. I'd given everything great thought, but I'd never considered that the men might actually come to our house until they actually did. I didn't know they would be looking for us. We'd barely finished spreading the mulch when we heard the sound of tires on gravel and loud foreign music.

Elizabeth started to run out onto the lawn to greet our visitors, but I held her back. If they hadn't blared their foreign music, I might have done the same thing, but something told me to hang back and assess the situation. The only things we knew about the men were that they were from another country and that they wore gas masks to protect themselves from the air-borne virus. We'd learned that much from the news before they took over the television stations.

"Wait, Elizabeth. I think they are bad men." I pulled her back around the corner of the house to the edge of the woods where they couldn't see us. We hunched down in the shadows behind a bank of leafy ferns and watched the silhouette of the house through the leaves. Desmond stalked around the yard, the hair on his back standing up.

Desmond had always hated strangers with a vengeance. He'd bark at the mailman from the confines of the house, nearly tearing window blinds from windows. If the UPS man dared to come onto the porch, he'd nearly dig a hole through the door, trying to get to him. My father always joked that nobody would ever break into our house as long as they were accompanied by a delivery man.

I imagined keeping him around for company, not because I was a huge fan of dogs in general, but because he reminded me of my mother and I knew she'd want us to take good care of him after she died. That day, when the men came back, everything changed though. He nearly cost us our lives.

As the men came around the corner, he'd started barking at them like he would have done any other stranger, hopping

293

stiff-legged like a stuffed footstool, bouncing stupidly across the lawn. The men had frowned, almost fearfully, and one of them had pointed the gun at him.

Elizabeth had stiffened beside me and I quickly put my hand over her eyes.

"Don't look, sweetie. Look down here at the ground and count the pebbles. When we're done, we'll take the pretty ones down to the stream and wash them. Maybe we'll make a bracelet out of them."

For once in her life, Elizabeth did what I asked her to do, but my mother's faithful companion didn't comply. He continued barking madly at the men. One of them fired off a hailstorm of bullets at the dog, catching him in his thigh. He yipped, a sound that tore through the still air and echoed in the valley. Elizabeth put her fingers into her ears and began to hum softly.

I watched wide-eyed as Desmond did the one thing he knew to do. He headed down the broad expanse of the lawn to the bank of ferns where we hid, still barking and yipping madly. He was looking for his humans to protect him. As he reached us, the men stared harder into the forest, probably wondering where the dog had gone, maybe even touching on the truth of the matter and wondering if he were retreating to his hidden masters. I stroked his fur and ran my fingers down his flank to the place where he'd been hit with a bullet. It was bad. He needed surgery and antibiotics. He'd probably die within a few days if it wasn't attended to.

The men took several steps towards us and Desmond began to growl again. If I let him continue, he would have raced out of the hiding place snapping and snarling at them, before darting back to me for protection, giving us away.

294

"Desmond...no," I closed my eyes and whispered softly to him, but his growls only grew louder. I took a deep breath and did what I needed to do until the growling stopped. Tears fell down my face as I let his limp body fall to the ground and I told him I was sorry a thousand times in my mind, like a cadence coming from deep within my soul. I prayed to God to take care of him, prayed to my mother to forgive me and then prayed for the men to continue on. It was, I believe, the first time I truly prayed.

The men stared into the bushes for a long moment and then thankfully continued on with their search of the house and property. After they left, I buried Desmond beside my mother in the flower garden. I told Elizabeth that he'd died from his gunshot wounds because it was better than admitting the truth. I'd rather her believe a lie and let her believe that he died a hero trying to protect us than tell her the bloody truth. I'd bring that little secret to my own grave one day.

I retreat into mausoleum and wait for morning. At this point, everything depends on Teddy. I just hope he comes through.

38

Morning comes far too early, and I spend a few minutes thinking about the dreams I've been having. They are senseless and full of color and pictures, sounds, and scents. There is a white angora bunny wearing a purple cat collar hopping through green clover. There is pepperoni pizza, fresh from the oven. And then there is a bad man holding a gun, frowning. I have a flash of the night Henry tried to move her from the Boy Scout camp to a house in the woods, but it makes very little sense considering she was drugged at the time. All I see is Henry running, leaving my sleeping sister behind in the truck. My dreams have become so vivid lately, it's almost as though I'm leading a second life in my sleep. I imagine it is due to Elizabeth's influence, now that she knows she can take over my sleeping world. I wonder how anything can ever be normal again.

If I'm able to rescue her, how will we be able to move on with our lives? I'll constantly be pulling her indoors, away from the sounds of vehicles, hoping she'll listen to me one more time. The thoughts roll through my head like thunder and for one brief moment, I consider just walking away and leaving her, but then reality returns to me. I can't do that. She's my sister. I feel the light and love of her surround me and fill me with yearning. I have to save her.

I have to.

I pull myself up off the stiff, cold bench and open the door, allowing the golden sunlight to pour in. It is warm against my skin, bringing with it the dusty scents of the cemetery. I step outside and raise my hand to shade my eyes from the blinding sunlight. It takes my eyes a moment to adjust.

The cemetery is as quiet as it should be. There is nothing but muted bird song and the sound of leaves feathering against each other in the lofty treetops. It is a large cemetery and I can see for miles from my vantage point at the top of the hill. The green, shaggy land gives way to a grey road that separates the cemetery from the cornfield. Beyond that, the slumbering town glitters in the morning light. I glance at the chemical plant on the hill and sigh. A bumble bee lurches slowly past me, stopping to land on a faded plastic tombstone floral display, before ambling off, disappointed.

I have nothing but time on my hands now. I cannot rescue Elizabeth on my own. She is too heavy to carry and she is handcuffed to the bed. I will need at least one other larger person and a heavy set of bolt cutters. Even then, there are other dangers to sort out. I will have to figure out how to get her out of the house without the bad men knowing I've stolen her. What I really need is a good backup plan in case Henry and Teddy don't come back, but I can't seem to come up with one.

I need to find something that the bad men are afraid of or something that will distract them. I think about Teddy's idea of pushing a really gross dead person into the house, and I find myself smiling, despite everything.

It comes to me as a surprise that I miss Teddy. I miss the way he'd ask me endless questions, hanging on my answers as though they were the word of God, waiting for me to make the next move forward, hoping so sweetly that we can be friends.

"My friend," I whisper with a smile. I hope he's okay and that Henry has kept him safe. I remember the way Teddy had given me half of his candy bar, and the thought makes me warm inside.

My stomach growls thinking about the chocolate, so I go back inside the mausoleum and pull the hand sanitizer from my pocket. The solution inside has gotten watery and squirts out rapidly when I use it now, almost like a squirt gun. I have to be careful not to squirt the walls of the mausoleum with it. Once I'm satisfied that my hands are clean, I root around in my bag until I find something suitable for breakfast. It is only a power bar and a cup of applesauce, but it fills me up and brings me energy, two things I will need to get through the morning. I try to remember the old days when meals were planned around a clock, when we'd actually look at our watches and eat a meal because it was noon. We'd pull frozen delicacies out of the freezer compartment in our refrigerators and pop them into the microwave for a minute or two until the food came out delicious and steaming. Now food comes with more effort, like everything else in this new world.

I wonder what will happen in a few years, what we'll do to survive. Food is still plentiful because it has only been several months, but what will happen when it starts to run out? Will we travel from town to town, raiding their resources and then moving along when we've depleted them? Or will we learn to live from the earth, growing gardens and hunting for our meat? Neither prospect sounds very appealing. I wonder how long it will take before I stop wishing to have my old world back. The hopeless thought that fills my mind feels like just another shade of fear.

We have a long cold winter ahead of us and it bothers me more than a little that I don't have a good plan in place. I should be gathering firewood and stockpiling necessities, like food and candles. When the snow comes, I will be forced to stay inside so I don't make footprints that can be followed. I try to imagine doing this with Elizabeth in tow and simply can't. She will want to go outside to make a snowman and I won't be able to stop her.

I walk back into the mausoleum and sit down on the bench. I close the door behind me and turn on my small lantern. I roll

298

over onto my back and pull the blanket over myself and fall back asleep. Elizabeth finds me immediately, filling my head with dreams.

She is an angel, one of many who have come to my aid.

I see them, standing as straight as statues in my mother's garden.

There is Aphrodite, the goddess of love, who marks the resting place of my mother, who prepared me for this in her own way, with her love and her quotes. There is my father, who looks at me with pride in his eyes. Beside them, Annie stands with her hands in her pockets. And then I see Desmond, the smallest angel of all. My mother had another quote she used. It was an old Egyptian proverb and seems fitting somehow.

When the Angels arrive, the devil leaves.

I only hope it's true.

Elizabeth watches me in the dream, standing high on a platform, her arms stretched wide if reaching for the Heavens. I can feel the sun on my face, riding lower in the sky as though it is September or October. Tears stream down her cheeks because she is sad, but she stands straight and tall, a different Elizabeth than the one she'd once been. She is older somehow, carrying the weight of the world in her expression. Behind her stands Henry. She turns to make eye contact with him and doesn't turn back around until he has nodded his approval. I am happy to see that she is listening to someone.

Bad men crest the hill in front of us, their black guns held out in front of them ready to mow us all down. She waits until they get closer and then she closes her eyes in concentration. We reach for her and then touch her with outstretched arms, feeling the protection of her aura gather around us, keeping us safe. And then it happens. She almost glows in the darkening light, her arms reaching higher and higher. Dark clouds move in like the sweep of a paint brush and then the world is washed clean with blinding light. It means something, but I cannot decipher it. Before I can consider it, my eyes flutter open and I realize that the blinding daylight is coming from the waking world. Someone has opened the door to my mausoleum.

I sit bolt upright, my hands moving quickly into fists.

37

"Happy birthday!"

I blink several times, trying to come awake. The dream had been so vibrant; I cannot distinguish it from real life. I nearly flinch, thinking I'm about to be struck by lightning.

"Teddy?" I ask, squinting into the light. Behind him in the doorway is the silhouette of another person. He shifts and rests his arm against the doorframe and I see that it is Henry. I feel as though a thousand-pound weight has been removed from my shoulders.

"In the flesh," Teddy says, trying to be cool. "We didn't see you at the Weeping Mary statue, so we came here."

I don't give him the chance to say anything else. I bound from my bench and wrap him deeply into a hug. He is sweaty and smells even worse than he had before, like a combination of unwashed boy and pork rinds, but he is alive and breathing. That counts for a lot.

I pull away and look at him. He is still wearing the same shirt he'd been wearing several days ago, but there are now shoes on his feet, which I assume is Henry's influence.

"Oh my God. I can't believe you're here." I feel the tears press against the backs of my eyes and I want to hug him again, but I hold back, not wanting to look foolish in front of Henry. I glance up at Henry and we briefly make eye contact. He seems the same, but it's always hard to tell with him. The virus has changed him into someone I don't know, someone whose actions I can't predict.

I study him for a moment, softly remembering him as someone who once set my heart on fire. Even despite the long unkept hair and the roughened edges, he is still very attractive, with his chiseled jaw and his sultry blue eyes. He makes eye contact with me, holding my gaze for a long, languid moment and I feel myself respond, ever so slightly.

"Are you okay?" he asks.

I nod, not knowing what to say, how to respond.

He leans into the room and looks around, taking in the sight of my backpack on one stone bench and the motorcycle leaning against the other. I know what he is about to ask me long before opens his mouth.

"Where's Heather?" he asks and meets my eyes again.

I stare at him for several seconds, feeling the familiar sensation of grief and guilt rush through me. I remember her, fierce and strong, racing against the wind and then I remember her, lying on the concrete sidewalk with a perfectly round hole in the middle of her forehead. A quiver takes hold in my legs and works its way up my body until I am forced to sit down again.

"She didn't make it. They shot her at the amusement park." I take a deep breath and dig deep. "I buried her near the lake," I tell him because this is something he should know. I don't want him to think of her lying dead and cold on the ground, where she will be picked apart by wildlife. I want him to imagine her beneath the ground with a blanket of stars above her.

As I say these words, Henry watches me for a moment and I can see the emotion running close to the surface of his face. His eyes water over and his shoulders tighten before he abruptly turns and walks away.

His reaction makes me wither inside. The tears I've been holding back stream down my face as I stare at the space where he'd just been. Heather had been his girlfriend, someone he clung to during the cold nights, someone he might have confessed his deepest fears to when he needed to lighten his load. Having her gone so suddenly must feel like half his soul being ripped cleanly away. It wasn't my fault, but I still feel responsible somehow.

"I'm sorry, Ember." Teddy presses against me in an awkward hug, trying to be something he's not to me.

I stand up and wrap my arms around him, squeezing tightly anyways. There is so much we've both lost, so much we'll never have again and it really hits me that we are now down to three. It seems like such a small number when you compare it against the whole wide world. Every time we lose another one of us, humanity's chances grow slimmer. I pull away and ruffle his hair, not wanting this moment to leach any deeper into my soul. It's better to cast it off before it can go too deep.

"So where have you been?" I sit down on the bench again, feeling the cold stone through my jeans. Teddy removes his backpack with a sigh of relief and plops it onto the other bench.

"Ummm. I don't know really. We ended up at some big white farm house." He sits down beside his backpack and looks around the room. I sigh, realizing that if I want to learn anything, I am going to have to drag it out of him.

"How long did you ride …until the sun went down?"

"Yeah, something like that. We stopped at an old gas station and Henry smashed the vending machine with a rock. We filled up our backpacks with food." As he says this, he reaches for his backpack and roots around in it for a moment before coming out with a candy bar. "I got this for you."

He tosses it to me casually and I catch it one handed.

"Thanks, Teddy. That was really nice of you." I tuck the candy bar into my bag. "So did you two stop for the night somewhere?"

"Yeah, we stopped by some river. I wanted to sleep inside of a house, but Henry didn't want to. He said he'd rather be outside so we could be ready to leave if he needed to."

303

"And then you went to the farm house?

"Yeah. That's where Henry said we're gonna live for a while. We're gonna have our own camp."

"So why did you come back? If you drove all that way…"

Teddy's gaze flits to the doorway of the mausoleum. "Henry wanted to come back. When you and Heather didn't show up at the farmhouse last night, he got worried…I also kind of begged him to come back. I told him that you wanted me to meet you here today, that I really, really needed to be here." His words trail off and he looks down at his feet, letting me know without saying it that he'd probably fought hard to get Henry to come back.

"Well, I'm glad you did. I was getting lonely here by myself," I say with a small smile. The moment drops off into a stilled quiet. Teddy finally breaks the silence.

"Hey, I got shoes," he says excitedly. I can't help but smile again.

"Yeah, I see that. Nice!" I don't ask him where he got them because it's pointless. Judging by the scuffs, he probably pulled them out of somebody's closet, trying not to think too hard about the person who had worn them last.

"Hey, guess what?" I ask him, the excitement leeching into my voice.

"What?"

I pause several seconds, feeling an even wider smile creep across my face. "I found Elizabeth."

"You did?" He springs from his seat. "Where?"

"You'll never guess it in a million years."

"Where? I don't wanna guess. Just tell me."

A shadow appears across the doorway, darkening the room. Henry is back.

"You found her?" he asks, sounding far more interested than he should. I try to shove back any romantic notions I might be developing for him and force myself to reconsider his motive. He knows about Elizabeth. He saw her call the lightning in front of the Cooper House. I wonder if he has come back for more than he's admitting to. Elizabeth is the greatest weapon imaginable. He might want to use her like everyone else does.

"Yeah, I found her. She's at Teddy's house, handcuffed to his bed."

Teddy nearly bursts at the seams. "My house? She's at my house?"

"Yup. I used the secret tunnel to get in and I walked right up the back staircase."

Henry shifts in the doorway. "How did you know where she was?"

I look down and study my hands. There is so much to tell him, but so much he won't even begin to believe. I can feel the time running out. The end is growing closer and closer. A big part of me doesn't want to trust this Henry, but I don't have any other options.

"I just knew. I had a dream about her and I saw where she was."

They don't question me about it. After everything we've been through, it would be pointless. Thankfully, they both just nod.

Henry runs his hand through the front of his hair. "We'll have to check it out and get a plan together. It's not going to be easy," he says, sounding more like the old Henry.

"Yeah, I know." I look down at my feet. It seems like an impossible task and I can't imagine how we'll be able to pull it off, just the three of us.

He looks at me and nearly smiles. "Don't worry so much," he tells me and for several seconds he is the old Henry. I only hope he knows what he's talking about.

38

We consume an unfortunate dinner of pork and beans before we leave the cemetery. There are some foods that are better for recon missions than others and beans are not one of them. We start off with Henry in the lead, Teddy following in the middle and me trailing behind, but I switch this around after growing tired of continually encountering Teddy's smelly flatulence.

"Good God, Teddy. Put a cork in it."

"I can't help it," he whines.

Henry gives Teddy the evil eye and then turns back around. "Next time, I think we'll just have the pork and skip the beans," he says, and I chuckle softly to myself, warming to him little by little.

He is softening around the edges enough that I am starting to remember him again as the person I used to know. I find myself slowly beginning to trust him again.

Teddy has been quiet all day, silently watching us interact. Every time Henry touches my arm, I can see Teddy watching and I have to wonder if things are going to get complicated between the three of us. My mother always said that two's company, but three's a crowd.

We are quiet again as we make our way through the cemetery, with the words that need to be spoken growing as heavy as sand in our shoes. Henry has discussed his plan with us and I've shared the layout of Teddy's house with him, but I can't imagine a scenario that will work successfully. Once we reach the edge of the corn field, he finally breaks the silence.

"I've been listening to the Hostiles on a two-way radio," he says, and I remember him going back to pick it up off the driveway after crushing the wild-eyed man with the Bronco. "What do they talk about? Can you understand them?" I ask.

Henry doesn't answer me, but holds up a hand and gestures for us to follow him deeper into the corn field where we can't be overheard in case someone is near.

 We slip through the endless rows, the sounds of the husks whisking against our arms filling the silence. It sounds as loud as firecrackers to me and I am afraid, but Henry continues forward as though he doesn't hear the enormous amount of noise we're making. He needs me more than he realizes he does.

"We should be a little quieter," I suggest. "We're making a lot of noise." As I say this, our group automatically slows down. "So what do they talk about?" I ask him again. This time he stops and looks back at me, almost startled as though I've awaken him from a dream.

"I can understand a little of what they're saying, but not a lot. I picked up a book at the library...," he says, and then stops short.

A dawning comes to me. Henry was outside in the shadows when Teddy and I came out "You were there that night that Teddy and I were there," I say, astonished.

"Who do you think scared the cannibal away?"

"I thought he ran away because I stabbed him."

Henry smiles, the corner of his mouth hitching up in that mischievous way that reminds me of his former self. It makes me almost giddy to see that so much of the old him has survived.

"Believe what you want to. He was on my list and I needed to take him out before he killed anyone else. There aren't enough of us left as it is."

I couldn't agree more, but I keep this to myself.

"Why was Denver trying to catch the cannibal?"

He shakes his head. "I'm not sure, really. He had it in his head that he needed to get that guy out of the picture. It must

308

be due to all those years he spent picking stray dogs off the street. He said that McFarley was a loose cannon and he didn't want to take any chances with him. He was probably worried that he'd stumble into our camp and take off with one of our people. I'm not completely sure. Denver has his own agenda."

I am so full of questions, I nearly burst. I know so very little about the bad men.

"What did you learn about the bad men? Are there lots of them? More than just the ones here in town? Are they here because of the phosgene?" I shoot off questions in rapid-fire sequence. I would probably ask even more, but Henry grabs my arm and squeezes it, making me realize my voice has risen above a whisper.

"Shhhh...keep it down. Yeah, there are a lot of them and yes, they are collecting the phosgene gas. They are the same crazy men who blow up embassies and shoot down airplanes. They've been planning this for years. They've set up camp in every city and large town on the entire East Coast of the United States. They're moving from east to west, setting up camps and taking care of the survivors." He releases my arm to make a sweeping motion with his hands. "They're making a clean sweep. A *cleansing.*"

"What are they doing with the children?" I ask, thinking of Elizabeth's dream of all the children getting loaded onto green trucks.

"We're not completely sure. The best we can figure is they're moving them to a central location for training. Right now, they have the ones from this area in Springfield, but as they move further west, they'll move them too. They keep talking about Yellowstone, so I'm assuming that the Yellowstone National Park is their goal for a headquarters."

I gasp, feeling my heart sink. We'd been to Yellowstone once on vacation. The area was vast and wide, with plenty of room to build compounds. "Why Yellowstone?"

Henry looks down at the ground and scratches his head. "I don't know for sure, but I'd guess it has something to do with nuclear power plants. Wyoming is one of the handfuls of states that don't have any. I think they finally realized that when they removed all the people, they set loose some major demons. The power plants will be melting down any day now as the cores run out of water to keep them cool. Once that happens, radiation will be released into the environment. Wyoming is in the middle of several states without reactors. It's where I'd go if I had a choice."

He touches my arm again and I shiver despite myself.

"That's not the worst of it, Ember. This is bigger than any of us every imagined. Denver said the virus has reached other countries too. It won't be long until the entire world is infected."

I feel his words fill me and imagine the world as an empty hull. There will be others like us, but we will always be outnumbered by the bad men.

"Do they have bad men sweeping through other countries too?"

He cocks his head up to stare at the stars, so infinite and vast. "Some. There are a lot of them. You can't even imagine. Their country has been spending the last twenty years working on building their ground forces, hoping for an advantage like this. They stole the virus from a government lab. We're not sure how, but they must have had somebody on the inside."

"Why? Why would anybody do this?" The question is preposterous and there's no way Henry can even begin to answer it, but I feel it inside me wanting to escape.

310

Henry sighs and releases my arm. "They call it the Mitnah. In their language, it means a test or trial to separate the good from the bad. The group that released the virus has convinced several other countries to either help them or be culled from the herd, so their numbers are growing. It's bad, Ember. It's really bad."

When I don't respond, Henry squares his shoulders and moves ahead again. His words run through my head like the buzzing of bees. Somewhere in the back of my mind, I thought the British Army or the French National Guard would show up on the shore of the Atlantic Ocean and help us regain control, but it's not going to happen if they're suffering the same fate that we are facing. The thoughts swirl and burn in my head and I shut them down. Hopefully there will be more time to think about this later. I need to stay focused on the present. I need to think about my sister.

We reach the edge of the cornfield and he pauses, holding up his hand to keep us silent. Teddy presses against my back and I can feel the tremble in his fingers. This is more than a practice run and we can both feel it. We might only have one chance to get Elizabeth and we can't screw it up. It looms ahead of us heavily.

"Be quiet for a second and just stay here. I think somebody's following us." Henry says this and then disappears into the darkness, leaving Teddy and me to fend for ourselves. Visions of cannibals and bad men crowd my mind and I find myself reaching back to grab Teddy's hand.

"Where'd he go?" Teddy whispers.

I want to shush him, but I'm afraid to even make that much noise. I step backwards and move us back into the cover of the cornfield a little deeper, pushing Teddy behind me as I move.

311

We move several rows back to a place where we can see out, but still remain hidden.

We have come out at a different place. When Teddy first brought me to the cornfield, we had entered it by cutting through the Little League ball field near the American Legion Post, but now we have come out several blocks further down the street. In front of us is an empty lot, filled with high grass and beer cans. It's where the homeless people used to hang out. They'd set up a campfire ring in the middle of the lot and would sit around a small fire, laughing and drinking until the police found them and chased them off. Annie once joked that with all the alcohol that was spilled in the grass there, if someone lit a match it would probably burn to ashes in three seconds flat.

As we stare into the muted moonlit scene, our eyes slowly adjust to the lighting. After a few minutes, I can see further down the street, down the trim row of one-story houses. Heavy trees line the walks, deepening the shadows and giving the pale grey streets a brighter contrast. Somewhere in the distance a dog barks and it occurs to me that I haven't heard that sound in many days. Teddy said the bad men didn't like dogs and I wonder if they've gone out of their way to shoot most of them.

"Who do you think is following us?" Teddy whispers.

"I don't know." It probably wouldn't be a bad man. He'd just blast us with bullets and be done with it. It wouldn't be another survivor. I would think they would see the group of us and call out to us. Single people wandering around would be scary. They could be cannibals or people otherwise affected by the virus, but a group of survivors would have a greater chance of being normal, I would imagine. That leaves nothing but bad things for me to consider. If someone is following us, they can't be up to anything good.

Henry returns to us a moment later, appearing out of nowhere with ninja silence. I jump when I see him and stop myself short from screaming. I am wound so tightly, I might explode if handled incorrectly.

"What'd you see?" Teddy asks, wide-eyed.

"Nothing," Henry says, in a way that makes me think he is holding back something. It is very possible he has a good idea who is following us, but doesn't want to scare us, which only serves to scare me more. Henry doesn't get too freaked out about much, but it is apparent that he is shaken by what he knows. "Let's move on," he says, loud enough for both of us to hear, but then moves close to me and whispers in my ear. "Keep an eye out behind us, but be discreet. Okay?"

I nod and then pull myself away from him. "Let's just get going," I say, wanting to get farther away from this danger that might be following us. If it comes up behind us, I will be the first one to encounter it.

We step out of the cornfield, but stay close to the edge, where the shadows can hide us. We are carrying nothing more than a few simple tools and knives for protection. I wonder why Henry hasn't gotten us guns. If he is carrying one, he is keeping it hidden. As far as I know, all he has is the heavy hunting knife he carries on his hip in a leather holster. As these thoughts bang around inside my head, Henry sidles up next to me and presses his mouth close to my ear.

"Do you have a weapon on you? A knife or something?"

I jump as though goosed. "Yeah, I have a knife and Teddy has one too. Why?"

"Do you know how to use it?"

The question unnerves me more than a little. I am a seventeen-year-old girl who lived a sheltered life in a house

313

with two parents and a sister. Of course I don't know how to use a knife. "Not really," I tell him, and he sighs.

"That's too bad, because you might need to. I should have worked with you today." He pulls a knife out of his holster and holds it in his fist. "This is how you hold it. It gives you the best leverage." He holds his hand out to show me. "You just get in close and go for a soft spot that will do the most damage. Okay?" he waits for my nod before putting the knife away again.

"You think I'm going to need to use it?" I ask, the tremors coming on stronger.

He darts a glance over his shoulder at the darkness behind us and it is apparent that he is looking for someone. "We're being followed. I'm not sure who it is, but I have a pretty good idea." Before I can grill him on this, he moves back to speak with Teddy, probably giving him the same knife instructions he has given me.

I am back to that familiar guessing game: who is the stalker. It can't be a bad man because he would have already blasted us full of holes. It wasn't the cannibal because he was dead. That left two options: it's either Denver's group or someone altogether new.

I wait until he finishes with Teddy and move close to him.

"Do you think it's the dog catcher, Denver?" I ask.

"It might be," he says and moves away, leaving me with nothing else to go on. If I don't know what to do with a knife, I'm not sure how I can possibly be ready for an attack by a former military man. I will just have to hope that he goes for Henry and not for Teddy or me.

We continue our trek across town, sticking to the shadows and stealing glances over our shoulders. It isn't until we've made it within a half block of Teddy's house that our suspicions are finally confirmed. We turn the corner and Henry pulls us behind a house.

He holds his finger up to his lips, silencing the questions I want to ask, and points down the street, to a place where the moonlight touches the sidewalk. As we watch, a group of men appear at the end of the block, guns in their hands. They cross through the moonlight, obviously looking for us.

39

A thread of anxiety laces through my veins. I don't know if Henry is having the same thoughts that I am, but this situation cannot get much worse. The people who are following us probably don't know the score. They know that Elizabeth is a potential weapon because Henry has already shared that information with them. But, they don't know that Elizabeth is being held hostage at Teddy's house. If we stop to fight them, as foolish as that would be, we'd do nothing more than draw the attention of the bad men, who will simply shoot us all dead. But, if we just continue along, they will follow us to Teddy's house. Once they see the bad men's camp, they'll know for certain where Elizabeth is and they will kidnap her before we even have a chance to get in the back door.

When I was younger and I got into a difficult situation, I would wish for a magic wand to make everything go away, but now I find I am wishing for a gun. I don't know if I am capable of shooting someone in cold blood, but I'm not sure that I'm not capable of doing it either. So much has happened to me in the last few months, I am not the same person I once was. I don't know if my mother would be shocked or proud if she could see me now.

I touch Henry's arm and he nods.

"Back here," he whispers, pulling us deeper into the shadows.

We slip further and further into the shadows until we reach the shrubbery surrounding a house. I can't see very much of the house, but remember it from earlier times as being Mrs. Lackey's house, my third grade teacher. She used to sit on the front porch reading romance novels, her tiny jeweled glasses perched on the tip of her nose and a cup of tea sitting close by. She had a big orange tomcat that would sit on the top step,

Lightning Strikes

swishing his tail back and forth as he watched the birds flutter in the trees. I asked Annie once why the cat never left the porch, but she just shrugged, telling me that I noticed the weirdest things.

Henry latches onto my arm and pulls me around the side of the house. I grab Teddy until we make a chain again. I don't know where we are going, but it's better than just standing there waiting for trouble to happen.

"Stay here. Don't move," Henry says, and then he is gone.

"Where'd he go?" Teddy asks, as if I would actually know this.

"I don't know, Teddy," I breathe in a sigh.

I hear the sound of footsteps growing closer, so I pull Teddy behind a large shrub at the corner of the house. We crouch down until the bristly branches poke into our faces. The ground smells very strongly of urine, probably from Mrs. Lackey's cat, and I find myself covering my nose with the front of my shirt. We hold as still as possible and try not to shift our feet in the dry leaves beneath us. The night grows still and cold, surrounding us like a blanket until the sound of footsteps grows closer and closer. I catch a glimpse of a shadow in front of the house and my blood runs cold. They know we're somewhere close. It's just a matter of finding us.

"Where'd they go?" one of the men whispers.

"They're probably hiding like the chicken shits they are," says a voice that sounds like the dog catcher. He doesn't even bother to whisper. In fact, I get the feeling that he wants us to hear him.

In some ways, Denver and his group are no better than the bad men. They want the same power and authority. They want control of everyone. I'd be willing to bet Denver was a school yard bully, pushing down the smaller kids and stealing their lunch money.

The group pauses only twenty feet or so from where Teddy and I are hiding. As they pass, I can see the silhouettes of four people with large rifles dangling by their sides. They look like military men, the kind of people who open beer bottles with their teeth and think nothing of crawling through the cold mud for eighteen hours to reach a destination. They are not the kind of people that two kids and a semi-crazy man should mess with, especially considering we are armed with nothing more than kitchen knives. Teddy squeezes my hand and I pray that neither of us will choose that moment to sneeze or cough. If we do, the heavily armed men in front of us will just lace us full of bullets.

A slim shadow passes at ground level in front of us. As it darts though a beam of moonlight, I see that it is Mrs. Lackey's orange cat. He pays no attention to us, but hops up on the bulkhead of the house next door and prepares to leap into a broken window above it. I watch him for a moment, feeling my anxiety grow. If the cat makes a noise, the men will be drawn closer to where we're hiding. I hold my breath and listen to the sound of my pulse echo inside my head.

The men stand there for an eternity, just staring into the shadows. Finally, they move forward. "Let's get moving. They're probably up ahead," the dog catcher says, and the group moves away from the front of the house.

Teddy starts to stand up, but I hold him tight. I'm not going anywhere until Henry gets back. For all I know Denver is trying to trick us and is standing just on the other side of the neighbor's hedges waiting for us to pop out of our hiding spot.

My anxiety grows. I hope Henry comes back soon.

The night is unnaturally quiet, as though it too is waiting for something to happen. I wonder if the bad men have a pit fire

318

going in the front yard at Teddy's house and are sitting around it, trading war stories while they plot how to take over the rest of the world. Our little town must have been very easy for them. I only hope that if we can't stop them, someone else can. It doesn't seem fair that they could really win, not after everything they've done. My mother always said that good guys finish last, but I hope she's wrong, at least this time.

I try to envision the scenario. As they walk closer, Denver's group will eventually see the bad men's camp. If they stick around, they very well might see us sneaking in the back way.

Our original plan is now impossible with Denver standing on the other side of the street. I can't access the garage and secret tunnel with them so close. Our backup plan has too many complications surrounding it, too many ways that things can go wrong. What we need is a distraction, something to bring the bad men out to the front of the house just as Denver's group shows up. Then they can shoot each other to their hearts' content, while Teddy and I walk in and grab my sister. As I am thinking these thoughts, Henry reappears beside us, holding a propane tank from someone's gas grill.

"Let's go. We need to hurry," he says.

I take a deep breath and hope against hope that his plan will work.

40

Teddy's old neighborhood is filled with lofty Victorians. They are the kind of houses that have wide wraparound porches with blue ceilings and white wicker sofas and swings hanging from chains. The lawns are deep and green, shaded by rambling two-hundred-year-old oak trees. They are spaced close enough together so that neighbors could toss a friendly wave to one another as they meandered down their brick sidewalks to collect their morning newspapers from the curb, but far enough away to allow for some well-needed privacy. Luckily enough, I know this neighborhood better than any other neighborhood in town.

I feel a tremble come over me as I wait for Henry to begin.

A small hill separates Teddy's house from the house next door. A long green privacy hedge runs along the top of the hill, essentially splitting the two yards. Henry will sneak along the hedge, undo the cap on the propane tank and roll it down the hill and into the bonfire, where it will catch on fire and make a tremendous explosion. By this time, Teddy and I will be inside the house, releasing my sister from her handcuffs with the bolt cutters I have in my pocket. Henry will meet us shortly after and help us carry her out and through the hidden tunnel in the basement to where he has an escape vehicle stashed.

We slip across the street and cut through the lawns behind the houses, arriving at Teddy's house ahead of Denver's group. The moon parts through the thin veil of clouds and I see them checking out the other houses further down the block, probably still looking for the three of us. They pause at the house beside Mrs. Lackey's house. Her cat must have tipped something over inside the house, making a loud enough noise to draw the dog catcher's attention. When this is all said and done and we make it through alive, I will bring him a can of tuna to thank him for being so clumsy. I tuck my head down and move on.

As we close in on Teddy's house, I can see a light from the bonfire. It glows warm and bright, sending long flickering shadows up the trees. The wood pops, sending several embers of ash high into the air where they glow like fireflies until they finally burn out. As I study the area, I can begin to make out the shape of several men, milling around in front of the fire, weapons held slackly by their sides.

"Look," Teddy whispers, pointing at the men.

"Yeah, I see them." And I see their big shiny guns as well, but I don't mention this to Teddy.

"Let's keep moving," Henry says, nudging us ahead of him. I grab Teddy's hand so I can keep him close, and we crouch down and slip into the back yard like a pack of burglars.

The stars above us burn bright and cold and the sliver of moon hangs in the sky like a nightlight, lighting our way. We reach the backyard in less than twenty steps. My heart pounds.

I glance up at the back of the house and find Annie's bedroom window, pushing aside the flurry of memories that try to assault me. This has always been a happy place for me and now it has become a prison. I can imagine music drifting through the window, her shadow dancing past the white curtains like a ghost. Henry touches my arm, reminding me to move forward again.

"Why's it so dark?" Teddy whispers, and I shrug.

If I didn't know better, I'd think the house was vacant. Why would the bad men congregated in the front yard, around a bonfire, instead of sitting inside? They could be running a generator, enjoying all the modern conveniences that were denied to the rest of us. If they were really smart, they'd have security lights set up around the perimeter of the house at the very least. It doesn't make any sense. Something in the back of my mind worries about this, but I don't know why. Hopefully if it's important, it will come to me in time.

Henry motions for Teddy and me to move back behind the bank of bushes.

"I want the two of you to hide back here for a few minutes. I'm going to throw this propane tank into the bonfire for a distraction. When you hear the explosion, run to the back of the house, to the old service entrance. You'll get the spare key if the door is locked, right?" he asks.

We'd gone over the plans time and time again at the mortuary. Teddy's mother had hidden a key in a flower pot beside the door. If the door was locked, I would use that to get in with.

"Yeah, I will."

He watches me for a moment, as if assessing me. "I'll meet you inside at the back stairs in just a few minutes. Be quick, okay?"

He doesn't wait for my answer. He turns, leaving us with the cold prospect of the job ahead of us. I watch him cross the yard, the pit of my stomach growing bitter and small.

It sounds like an easy plan, but there are just so many things that could go wrong. If we succeed, the bad men will be blown to bits by the propane tank and we'll escape with Elizabeth, but if we don't succeed, the consequences could be enormous.

If we are caught, the three of us will probably be executed on the spot and Elizabeth will be whisked away without hope of ever being rescued. They will march her from city to city, frying their enemies into dust. I try to imagine how they will force her to call the lightning if she doesn't want to. Then it comes to me with a rush of fear. Maybe things aren't as they seem.

322

They need us to control Elizabeth. They need *me*.

"Oh my God, Teddy. This is all a trap," I start to say, but the words die quickly as a shadow passes in front of us.

"Well, well, well. Look what we have here," says a man with a thick accent. He grabs us by the back of our necks and pushes us across the lawn.

41

I am so stupid. We walked right into a trap.

The house wasn't lit up because they were lying in wait for us. They must have sentries set up at the perimeter of the property and probably saw us the minute we crossed the street. All they had to do was wait for us to come to them.

They knew we'd come because they have Elizabeth. They have probably been planning this since they found out that Elizabeth had a sister. They knew they couldn't make her call the lightning without a very good reason. It's why Denver was looking for me too. They want to use me to get her to do what they want.

The man pushes us ahead of him, his gun leveled evenly at the back of our heads.

"Move!" he says. His voice is loud enough to carry and I'm not sure whether to be relieved or worried. If Henry has heard him, then he might come to our rescue, but if Denver has heard him, he might use it as a distraction to go find Elizabeth. When we first saw Denver's group, I foolishly thought they were looking for us, but in reality they were probably doing the same thing we were doing: looking for Elizabeth. I am angry at Henry for not thinking this through a little better. I look around, trying to catch a glimpse of him, but I don't see him. If he is still around, he is well hidden. I just hope that he hasn't suffered the same fate.

"What are you going to do with us? We're just children," Teddy asks in a loud voice and I nudge him with my elbow. We are well past the point where hostage tactics are going to work. They don't care that we are just kids. They don't even see us as actual people. We are nothing more than tools to them.

The bad man shoves the gun into Teddy's back, causing him to protest with a yelp.

"Ouch, that hurts!" he says, a little louder than necessary and it finally dawns on me what he is doing. He is trying to let Henry know what is going on.

"You don't need to put the gun in his back," I say, calling out even louder and the bad man moves the gun from Teddy's back to mine, striking me with enough force to bruise my skin. I bite down on the pain and remain silent, not wanting to give him another reason to hurt me.

What we need is a miracle. I close my eyes for the duration of a heartbeat and I wish for one. If I've ever wished for anything in my life, it is not with the brevity that I now wish for this.

Please, please, please, I pray, and then the strangest thing happens.

A shadow darts across the lawn in front me. It is small, the size of a house cat or small dog. I hear the sound of panting and my heart grows wings.

"Desmond?" I ask and am answered by a high bark.

The bad man turns toward the sound of the bark and it's is all the time I need. I pull the knife from my belt. I gather every ounce of courage. The moment of truth is finally upon me. Without another second of hesitation, I sink the knife into his throat and then we run like hell.

42

An explosion rocks the still night air with a thunderous boom. It is followed by the sound of men screaming. Henry's propane tank has exploded.

I don't wait to find out what has happened in the front yard and I don't think about the fact that I have just killed a living, breathing human being. I don't even wonder if the dog in the yard was just a neighborhood stray or if my mother's dog was somehow still protecting me. I simply grab Teddy by the arm and bolt across the back lawn towards the service entrance. I yank on the door handle and am relieved to find it unlocked. I won't need to waste time searching for the spare key. I grab the doorknob, feeling the cold metal beneath my hand. It opens silently on well-greased hinges and we step inside like intruders.

The house is dark and quiet, giving away nothing, not even a shadow. I want to rush in and scramble up the stairs, taking them two at a time, until I reach the landing, but I need to be a quiet. I have fallen for one trap. I do not plan to fall for another one. It's very possible there is another man hiding in the shadows, ready to grab us.

I pull the door closed behind Teddy and move through the small utility room. Teddy's mother once used it as a mud room. The wall nearest the door is lined with cabinets and hooks where they once hung their coats. A tray on the other side of the door held shoes and boots. I am careful not to trip over it.

We tip-toe through the utility room and as we reach the hallway, where the stairs branch off, I can see the light from the bonfire through the window. The explosion has set the giant oak tree on fire and the leaves sparkle and hiss. Men scream and I hear the sound of guns blasting. It is possible that Henry has timed this just right, catching both Denver and his group at the same time, introducing them to one another in the confines of the front yard. If the plan plays out correctly, they will shoot each other dead and all of our worries will be over. If the plan doesn't play out correctly, then we will have two angry groups trying to kill us.

We reach the stairs. There are twenty stairs altogether. There are ten steps up to the first landing and then ten more to the second floor. The fourth stair squeaks, so I step over it and pull Teddy along behind me so he does the same. We reach the landing and move up the second set of stairs to the second floor.

The second floor sports a long balcony, which overlooks the main staircase. The hallway is dark, lit only by the firelight flickering in from the first floor windows. All of the doors along the hallway have been closed. If someone is hiding in one of the rooms, they will have to open the door to reach us.

I pause in front of Annie's door, almost afraid at what I will find.

What if I open the door and the room is empty?

They could have moved her. They might have seen me leaving the night before and relocated her. I might open the door expecting to see her and find a bad man in her bed instead. As I lean over the bed to pull back the blankets, he will jump up and grab me. I take a deep breath.

"Just go in. Hurry!" Teddy hisses in my ear.

"What if she's not in there? What if there's a bad man there instead?"

"Then we push him out the window," he says, and I nearly laugh. It is so outlandish, so like Teddy, it breaks me out of my panic.

"Okay. You can be the one to push him. I'll rescue Elizabeth."

He touches my arm. "Deal."
With that, there is only one thing left to do.
I open the door.

43

Moonlight pours through the window, painting the room full of soft blue light. I see Elizabeth immediately, the soft profile of her face traced by the glow of light. I feel as though I am walking into a dream. The moment becomes fevered and yearning, stretched tightly through raveled emotions and heartache until it is so taut it might break into a million pieces. I have spent the past month longing for this moment, this juncture in time when I can finally separate myself from the incessant worry and fear over my sister's fate. Elizabeth is safe.

Now that I am here, able to rescue her, I am rooted to the spot. A rush of emotions moves through me, sending goose bumps up both arms. I am sorry for allowing the bad men to take her. I am angry at the way she is chained to the bed. I am sad because I've missed her, but most of all I am simply happy to see her.

"Elizabeth," I breathe her name.

She turns her head and gazes at me with sleepy eyes. Her arms are chained to the brass bed frame at either corner, making her look like a messiah on a metal cross. The IV that had been connected to her wrist now lies limply on the bed beside her, having been disconnected and possibly forgotten hours ago. It is another miracle that we needed.

As she recognizes me, she pulls against her chains, her eyes bright with excitement.

"Ember! You came! You came to get me!" she cries, her voice far too loud, far too dangerous in the still of the house.

I cringe, my heart nearly lunging out of my chest. I glance at the door, waiting for it to crash open.

She is dangerous, as wild and unpredictable as a flash of lightning in a warm southern sky. Life without her would undoubtedly be easier. I'd have a much better chance at survival without her. I could put aside the constant worries and finally rest. But, when I look at her, it all comes together into one shining, perfect moment. She is Elizabeth and I can't live without her.

I rush to her side, wanting to give in to the overwhelming need to simply wrap her in my arms and hold her until I've had my fill. Instead, I manage to separate myself from the emotions and do the one thing I've come here to do. I pull the bolt cutters from my pocket and I free her from the handcuffs.

She springs up from the bed and is into my arms a second later, pressing wet kisses on my cheeks, chanting my name over and over again.

"Elizabeth." I hug her close to me, feeling the warmth of her small body, feeling her arms wrap around me, her tiny fingernails digging into the soft parts of my arms. She is still dressed in the white cotton nightgown my mother gave her for Christmas last year. It glows in the moonlight, making her look exactly like an angel.

"Let's get out of here," I tell her, and she smiles, her eyes bright through the tangle of her hair. As we move to the center of the room, Teddy steps out of the shadows and she squeals with delight at seeing him.

"Teddy BEAR!" she leans away from me, trying very hard to get to Teddy. She already weighs more than I can easily carry and the extra movement nearly sends me to the floor with her. I clamp my hand over her mouth, my heart taking great lunges.

"Shhhh...Elizabeth! You need to be really, really quiet or those bad men are going to come up here and shoot us." She pulls again, as though she doesn't hear me and manages to lunge out of my arms. She falls to the floor with a thump, not having used her legs for the past few days, if not weeks. Her muscles have become slack and underused. She has probably been kept unconscious except for meals and bathroom breaks since she burnt down the Cooper House. She crawls to where Teddy stands looking down at her, a mixture of horror and surprise etched on his face.

I'm not sure what to do. Elizabeth's rescue is everything I feared it would be. She is wild and uncertain and will certainly give us away before we even have a chance to escape. If I can't find a way to control her, she will be our death sentence. I am halfway across the room to collect her when Annie's bedroom door opens.

I gasp, rooted to the spot. I am expecting to see a bad man standing there with a gun pointed at my head, but instead I see Henry. Relief floods through me as I take in the sight of him, standing strong and confident in the doorway. He slips into the room and stares down at Elizabeth, frowning.

"Elizabeth. Stop it! Right now!" he says with the deepest of voices. It is the voice of authority, something she needed to hear a long time ago and she responds appropriately.

She lets go of Teddy's leg and peers up at Henry. For a moment I think she is going to tumble into a category five level temper tantrum, but she doesn't. He seems to have a calming effect on her. She crawls back to me, tossing one cautious glance over her shoulder at him as she moves.

"Pick me up, Ember," she says, her voice sweet and shy again.

I lift her up and settle her on my hip like we used to carry her when she was five, even though she is now close to sixty pounds. I won't be able to carry her for long.

The moment has gone on long enough. Any longer and we risk being detected. Henry must realize this as well because he shifts towards the door.

331

"All right. Let's get out of here." He opens the hallway door and peers out before leaning back in. "Okay, here's how it's going to go. Teddy, you're going to lead us down the back stairs to the basement. Ember, you carry Elizabeth and follow him and I'll bring up the rear. If you see anyone, duck down and hide. Don't try to fight them, not while we have Elizabeth. Got it?" he asks and waits for our nods of consent.

Teddy opens the door and steps into the hallway. I pull Elizabeth close to me and follow him. We are halfway through the doorway, when she leans away from me with a cry.

"Clementine!" She stares at her bed, where the doll is half buried in the covers. I know from past experiences that it will be a losing battle if we don't return for her. Elizabeth will scream and cry until we either go back for the doll or are shot dead by the bad men.

Henry starts to protest, but then turns back to the bed to snatch the doll up. He hands it to my sister, nearly shoving it into her outstretched arms, the look on his face undeniably impatient. Elizabeth beams brightly and presses the doll to her chest with her free arm.

"It's okay Clementine. We're safe now," she says, and then pops her thumb into her mouth and stares up at him with wide blue eyes. For a moment, I watch him weighing the options in his mind as he considers everything we are going to risk by having her with us. If he leaves her, he still has a chance at survival. If he brings her, he risks everything.

I understand what he is feeling. There is something very intoxicating about Elizabeth, about the way she can look at you. It makes you forget the tantrums and the screams and consider blue skies and kittens, and sweet butterfly kisses planted one by one on your cheek. She is so innocent. And yet, she is also the

332

key to everything. With a sigh, he puts his hand on my back and gently moves me forward.

"We need to hurry. We don't have much time." At the sound of his voice, we are jarred out of the moment and we rush forward into the hall. Elizabeth tucks her head into the hollow of my shoulder and I can smell the scent of her, filling me with sunshine. We tip-toe down the hallway to the back stairs. At the bottom of the landing, Teddy hesitates in front of the hidden doorway to the basement.

"Go Teddy!" I hiss in his ear, but he holds up a hand.

"I hear something down there. It sounds like..." he starts, but doesn't get to finish his sentence. A man comes up the back staircase towards us.

It's Denver.

44

"Thanks for finding the girl. Nice work!" he says to Henry.

Henry glares at him, the cords on his neck protruding stiff and tight.

"Just let us go, Denver. We don't need this."

"Let you go? You gotta be off your rocker, pal. I'm not going anywhere without the girl. She's a real firecracker. I can put her to good use."

I imagine him, keeping her in a cage, hauling her from town to town to eliminate the enemy. I glance back at Henry again to see his expression, hoping that he will do something to stop this. He is staring Denver square in the face, the heat nearly rising off of him in wafts, the pulse in his temple standing out against his pale skin. He takes a step forward, jostling me into Teddy as though he's forgotten I'm even there.

"I don't know why you'd want her. You've seen how unpredictable she is. These guys couldn't even handle her. They had to keep her unconscious to control her." Henry says.

The dog catcher laughs. "Yeah, but they didn't have Secret Weapon Number Two, now did they?" he says, looking at me. "I'd guess that little Miss Elizabeth would do anything to keep me from hurting her big sister, now wouldn't she?" he says, sending chills down my back.

If Henry doesn't do something, then I'm going to have to. I weigh the risks. I don't see a gun in Denver's hands, but it doesn't mean that he doesn't have one close by. If he is a trained military man, it will only take him a second to bring me to my knees. What we need is another distraction. I would knee him in the crotch, but Teddy is in the way. I only have one potential weapon left.

I reach into my pocket and feel the small container of hand sanitizer. When I'd used it earlier at the mausoleum, it had squirted out in a stream, almost like a squirt gun. I pull it from my pocket, flip the lid and take a deep breath. If it doesn't work, he might just shoot me where I stand. Before I lose my nerve, I hold it up and squirt him directly in his face.

His reaction is predictable. He screams and claws at his eyes.

Henry doesn't waste the moment. He grabs onto my belt loops and pulls me backwards, with Teddy right behind us.

"Hurry!"

Another explosion rocks the house, sending a blast of scorching air towards us. The house nearly rocks off its foundation and smoke floods through the hall. I nearly stumble with the weight of Elizabeth still on my hip. Teddy steadies me, keeping me from falling and we move towards the front door and into the thick black smoke. Elizabeth tucks herself into the front of my shirt, coughing.

"Hold your breath, Honey," I say, and she squeezes me tighter.

We run down the hallway and into the living room. Through the choking smoke, I see the blaze of orange flames engulfing the front of the room. A large smoldering tree limb protrudes into the room from the oak tree out front. It catches the sofa on fire, the flames racing across the fabric and finding their way to the love seat beside it.

Henry finds the front door and wrenches it open. Cool air rushes into the room, further fueling the fire. It lunges upward and outward, roaring as loudly as a mad man, catching curtains, walls, and furniture on fire in an instant. We nearly fall out of the door, still latched onto one another.

My lungs are filled with the choking smoke and I can't stop coughing. My eyes tear and I gag, trying to pull fresh air into my body. We stumble out into the front yard, which has become a war zone of fire and destruction. The fire from the propane tank has ignited one of the Broncos and it burns freely on the lawn. Thick smoke rolls in waves. Wounded men are scattered in the wreckage, blood pouring from their flesh. I don't know where to go, where to run to.

"Let's get to the garage across the street. There's a truck there," Henry says.

My ears are ringing from the force of the explosion and I can see his mouth move, but can barely hear his words. Everything feels as though it is happening in slow motion.

Henry waits for me to move, but my feet are rooted to the ground. Everything that has happened to me rushes through my head and I feel numb all the way through. He touches my face and moves my head until I am looking at him.

"It's going to be okay," he tells me, the look in his eye kind and gentle, like the old Henry.

It is enough to snap me out of it. I follow him into the middle of the yard and then the worst thing in the world happens.

A truck full of bad men pulls up.

45

The bad men pull to a screeching halt in front of the house and five angry men pour out, their guns pointed at our heads. They are evil, looking demonic in the firelight glow. It is clear from their expressions that they have lost touch with reality. They will kill us just because they can, because it makes them feel more powerful.

As we stand there, frozen to the ground, things quickly go from bad to worse. Denver bursts through the doorway behind us. His eyes are red from the hand sanitizer, and his expression is anything but friendly. Several of his men step from the shadows, making the reunion complete.

It is a bad situation, as bad as it can possibly get. If we aren't killed by gunfire as they attempt to shoot each other, we will be taken hostage by the victor. I hold my breath, my heart pounding.

Perhaps ten seconds separate us from instant death. I look at Henry and see that he is staring intently at Elizabeth. She is still tucked into the crook of my arm, the Clementine doll cradled in the crook of her arm, a mirror of us. She is looking upwards at the darkening sky, her eyes narrowed in concentration.

"Now, Elizabeth. Now," Henry says, his voice gentle.

The moment is poignant, filled to the brim with so many emotions; I can't even begin to count them. The world presses down on us, holding its breath. Waiting.

And then it happens.

Elizabeth reaches out her hands to Henry and Teddy and the instant they touch her, the world surrounding us turns white.

46

Inside the strike, the world is hush quiet and soft to the touch. It smells like sulfur and gunpowder, an odor so strong it coats my tongue with the taste. There is no pain, even though there should be blinding heat and searing flesh. Instead, there is this unbelievable calm, this sense of rightness, as though everything is systematically and very carefully being put back into its place. When it ends, my eyes are blinded for nearly thirty seconds and my ears are ringing, ringing, ringing.

I slip to the ground with the weight of Elizabeth still on me and I swear I see the angels march by, one by one. They line up, two deep and then three deep until there are so many of them, I can no longer find the ending of them. I see my mother and father and then I see Annie arching her eyebrows. Others join them, smiling at us as though they'd been watching us all along. They radiate nothing but pure gratitude and peace.

Desmond darts across the front of the group. His nose is to the ground and he disappears as quickly as he came. My eyes begin to tear as they all fade softly into the rolling smoke as though they were never there to begin with.

Elizabeth takes a strand of my hair between my fingers and rolls it back and forth. After a moment, I finally remember to breath.

47

We climb into one of the bad men's Broncos and simply drive away, leaving all the death and destruction behind us like a bad memory. I can almost see the ashes blowing in the wind, kicking up a tail of dust in our wake.

I take a deep breath and watch it fog up the window. I'm leaving the town I grew up in, leaving behind everything I've ever known. I think about my house and of the hidey-hole with my grandmother's quilt inside it, just sitting there being slowly eroded by time and weather. I imagine the house finally falling into itself, becoming nothing more than a bump in the forest. Small animals and insects will quickly claim it, burrowing into all of our most prized possessions and ruining them forever. Everything I've ever known is now lost to me. As my eyes well up with tears, I feel the press of a small hand into mine.

I turn to find Elizabeth silently watching me.

Elizabeth.

My heart fills will love in an instant and I smile at her, drinking her in.

I'd always thought of her as an inconvenience, someone who came along and took up my parent's time and attention. Everything had always revolved around her and her moods. If Elizabeth didn't want to do something, then none of us got to do it. I hadn't been able to look past that to see the goodness of her until she'd been removed from my life. Now I know. I can replace all the things that I've lost, but I can never replace her.

We drive for several more minutes, climbing the rise of the Berkshire Mountains until we are nearly touching the stars. I find the Big Dipper and remember the days when I would lie in the tall silky grass with Annie, staring up at the stars and talking about boys. It seems like it could have happened in another lifetime.

After a while, we reach a summit. Henry finds the turn off here where tourists used to park to take pictures and pulls over. He kills the engine and the silence surrounds us like a promise. At first I'm not certain what he's doing, but then I remember that we still have unfinished business to attend to.

Henry glances back at us, taking us all in one at a time until his eyes settle on Elizabeth.

"You know what you need to do, right?" he asks.

He looks out the window and she follows the line of his gaze.

The chemical plant looms in the distance, lit up with a soft glow from the generators. Men walk around the building, collecting the poisonous gas canisters they will use against the remainder of the survivors. After a moment she nods.

We climb out of the truck and walk to the edge of the road, where we have a clear view of the valley. The town nearly sparkles in the moonlight, the shell of something that is long dead. I can see the flat roof of my high school and the steeple of a church pointing towards Heaven. It could be another town altogether now that it has lost its life.

Elizabeth stares into the distance and the sky rumbles, the energy surging through the air like something I could scoop with my father's fishing net. Before I can even take a breath, a sheer bolt of lightning rips through the combustible sky, striking the chemical plant with a roar. The explosion turns night into day and the hill becomes alive with fire.

We are too far away to hear the screams. All we can see is the orange ball of fire growing larger as it rips through the remains of the plant. The explosion is followed by several more

340

until the night becomes quiet and the building burns to the ground.

Elizabeth finds my hand again and I squeeze it tight, the mixed emotions of happiness and sadness filling me to the brim. Teddy walks to my other side and takes my other hand until we are a chain. I glance behind us at Henry, who is still so much of a mystery to me. He meets my eyes, the hint of a smile playing on his lips. He is so handsome, my heart nearly breaks.

This new life will be rough. There will not be any clarinets and super glue, no new digital music downloads, no twenty-four hour grocery stores, at least not for a while. But, there is this.

There is this.

The End

To My Readers

If you enoyed *Lightning Strikes*, please recommend this book to others on Goodreads, and also log onto the site where you purchased it to leave a positive review. Every positive review brings me closer to my dream.

About the author...

Joni Mayhan lives in Massachusetts with her well-loved pets and nearly grown children. When she's not writing, she is a seasoned paranormal investigator, spending her weekends in dark places with her best friends, talking to shadows. A hopeful romantic, she is also a confessed Facebook addict, enjoys reading other people's novels, eating pie in diners, and has spent most of her life working in the pet industry. She also hates pickles, spiders and negative people, but that's another story altogether.

Please check out my web-site: Jonimayhan.com or email me at Jonimayhan@gmail.com.

Keep reading for a preview of *Ember Rain*, the second book in the *Angels of Ember Trilogy*, which is now available on Amazon.com.

Ember Rain

By

Joni Mayhan

Chapter 1

The nightmare comes to me in the middle of the night, during the time when I should be curled on my side, dreaming of blue skies and meadows. I feel it melt into me, like a languid outer skin, covering me whole and then sinking into me slowly.

The house is dark and silent.

At first I think I must be trapped in a tomb, the darkness is so perfect.

I turn down a hallway, feeling the walls with my sweaty palms. I don't know where I am, but a certain familiarity lingers and I can't put my finger on it. It feels like something I've lived through, or maybe a prophetic glimpse of my future.

"Hello?" I call out. My voice echoes down the hallway.

Something crackles and I turn with a gasp to see an apparition appear at the end of the hall. It is silky and transparent, casting a hazy glow of white light down the corridor. Panic rises inside of me, and I begin to tremble, starting with the small muscles in my fingers.

I watch it warily, hoping it disappears as quickly as it appeared. Everything I've ever read about ghosts suggests that they don't want to be seen. This one seems to have other ideas. It begins to slowly drift towards me, growing brighter and brighter until I have to shield my eyes. The trembling moves down my body in a wave.

It's going to be bad. Really bad.

I can feel it in my bones.

God help me.

"Henry!" I call out, knowing he's always within shouting distance, but my voice echoes uselessly down the hall.

I reach into my mind for my sister, calling her in the wordless way we often communicate, but there is nothing.

"Teddy?" I call, but don't hear an answer.

The apparition begins taking shape slowly. Pure red fear rushes through me and I am rooted to the spot. I can't move until it is nearly a yard away from me, lingering just out of arms reach. Its face begins melting, changing from one face to another. It happens so quickly, I can barely recognize one before it becomes something else.

I see my mother, my father, Annie, and then Heather. Then it changes to a series of people I've never met. One is an old lady with a school teacher's face, who turns into a small blond-haired girl, then an old man with wild white hair, before disappearing altogether.

I break the paralysis and turn, seeing a set of stairs appear in front of me. They lead down to a basement that is darker than soot. My breath catches in my throat, and every cell in my body begins quivering. I do not want to go down there.

I jolt back around, but the hallway has vanished behind me.

In the distance, I hear the sounds of children screaming. I pivot in a circle, trying to pinpoint the sound, but it seems to be coming from all around me. When I turn back to the stairs, the darkness has been replaced with fire.

Make it rain.

I have no idea what this means.

I search for the source of the voice, but all I see is darkness. I turn back towards the flaming stairs, and I know without knowing that I must go down there. It's imprinted on my brain like a tattoo.

I imagine a room filled with corpses, reaching for me at the bottom. I see them bloody and mutilated. Some are missing arms, others are missing legs, and some have been eaten alive. I'll get to the last stair and the steps behind me will fade away, trapping me in their tomb forever. They will reach for me with their clawed talons, pulling me into their death beds, making me one of them forever and ever.

Make it rain.

I take a step. The heat is unbearable, rolling towards me in waves of red and yellow. Charred embers line the walls like a gateway to Hell. I take another step, and the stairs give out completely.

I begin to fall, fall, fall until I awake with a start.

"Ember?"

I open my eyes to find Elizabeth staring at me, her curtain of long blond hair pushed behind her ears. Her eyes are serious and worried. It's not often I have nightmares, but I've been having a lot of them lately. I push away the dream and smile at my sister.

"I'm okay. I just had a nightmare."

She props herself on her elbow beside me on the thin cot. The bed is barely big enough for one, but she doesn't want to sleep alone, so we've just made it work.

"Is it the same dream about the stairs and the fire?" she asks.

I take a deep breath to steady myself. I want to tell her something that won't frighten her, but I don't want to lie to her either. Telling the truth has become essential to our survival.

"Yes. It's the same dream."

I've had it for five nights in a row now, and each time it becomes clearer and clearer. I have picked it apart, section by section, but I can't find any hidden meaning behind it.

"It's just a silly dream," I tell her, trying to fake a smile. "It probably doesn't mean anything." As I say this, my mind turns inward, remembering the sounds of the children screaming.

Each night I've had the dream it has progressed a little further. The first night, I was in the dark hallway and saw the phantom appear before I awoke. The next night it grew closer, progressing night by night, until I finally wake up falling. It's almost enough to make me not want to go to sleep at night.

"What happens after you step onto the stairs?" Elizabeth asks, mesmerized by my dream.

I feel my heart begin to pound just thinking about it.

"I fall," I say simply, wondering what it means.

Elizabeth looks at me with the earnest expression of a ten-year-old and smiles. "Maybe tomorrow night you'll grow wings and fly," she says, her blue eyes twinkling.

"Maybe," I say, but I don't feel very confident about it. With my luck, I'll probably plunge into a pit full of flesh-eating corpses.

I roll over and look across the basement, searching for Henry.

"He already left. He didn't say where he was going, but he's probably out hunting for supplies," she says, reading my thoughts like she often does.

346

I rise from the cot and stretch, feeling my muscles gr
from the hard unforgiving mattress, and make my way ov
the box where I keep my things.

As I pull on a t-shirt and jeans, I try not to think about my
dream, but the images haunt me regardless. It feels prophetic
like something that hasn't happened yet.

I hope I'm wrong.

Chapter 2

My mother had a book of quotes in her lavender-scented
nightstand drawer. The book was thick with love blessings and
life lessons, and she had a knack of picking just the right one for
every situation. It was as though she could tap into my internal
thoughts and find the perfect quote to mend my inner wounds
like a Band-Aid and a kiss. She would read one to me every night
before she tucked me into bed. It became sort of a ritual for us,
and I miss it more than I miss the electricity and running water
that has also been taken away from me.

"Ember, here's a good one," she told me towards the end
of our lives together.

I'd been in her bathroom, looking for a tube of antibiotic
ointment to put on a paper-cut that stung like a knife wound,
weeding through tubes of lip ointment, furry hairbrushes, and
boxes of sample-sized toothpaste, frustrated that my mother
wasn't better organized. I could have literally bled to death in
the clutter.

"What?" I said a little sharply.

"Every exit is an entrance to somewhere else."

"Yeah, okay...thanks, Mom," I said, and then went back to my pursuit of ointment. When I look back, these are the times I regret the most. I wish I had spent more time listening to her, because it's all I long for now.

I try to imagine what life would be like if she were here to make all the decisions for me. I would be able to plod through, following closely in her shadow instead of blazing a trail all by myself. I am lost most of the time, making choices I am not fully capable of making, and then living with the ramifications for the rest of my life. I wrap my arms around my body and try to remember what it felt like to hug her. The memories are fading like ghosts in the daylight.

A stray hair blows across my face and as I swipe it away, I catch Henry out of the corner of my eye, swinging an ax as he chops wood. He is tall and lean, the blond in his hair coming out more and more as he spends his days working outdoors. His skin has been kissed by the summer sun, glowing across the beautiful planes of his body, defining each muscle with a thin sheen of moisture.

There is something about the bend of his neck and the tilt of his chin that makes me think that his mind is a million miles away. Sometimes I wish he would let me inside, and other times I'm happy to be without the knowledge. As long as I don't know for certain, I can fill the gaps with my own version of the truth.

Once upon a time, Henry had been my math tutor, someone my father hired to help me bring my failing grades back to a comfortable level. I'd been dreading his first visit, imagining him as a troll-faced academic, one of those boys who alternated between finding summations and flicking buggers, but I'd been surprised. Henry was no troll. He was one of those boys you loved to hate. He was beautiful to look at, good at everything, and was adored unconditionally by everyone. He had the prettiest girlfriends and the shiniest cars. He could spout love sonnets as easily as he could figure the sum of *x* over *y*. After the virus, he's become something else, and I'm not certain which version of him I like the best, the real or the imagined. He's different now. I can't really explain it, but he has hardened, as though all the soft boyish parts of him have turned to granite overnight.

He swings the axe again, making direct contact with the piece of wood sitting on a chopping block. The sound echoes through the valley, and I catch myself looking around, to make sure no one has heard this.

It has been nearly six months since our civilization came to an end, since the terrorists released a virus that wiped out the majority of the population. Since then, we've been confronted with the bad guys who hunt us and the cannibals who want to eat us. We are always running, always looking over our shoulders.

My sister comes out of the kitchen door, dressed in the long white gown she found in one of the houses we raided for supplies. It is too large for her, billowing around her bare ankles and nearly tripping her as she comes down the stairs.

A sharp gust of wind crosses the open area between us, rippling the tall brown grass and kicking up a small cloud of dust before it finds her. It is too cold outside to be barefoot, but I've learned to back off and let Elizabeth make those decisions herself. After a minute, she gathers the dress with one hand and sits on the second step, her attention focused on Henry.

I watch her, wondering, always wondering. There is more to Elizabeth than what meets the eye. We've all become a little cautious of her, now that we know what she's capable of.

"Where's Teddy?" she calls to me and I shrug. Teddy was my best friend Annie's younger brother. I once thought of him

349

WITHDRAWN *Joni Mayhan*

as the demon spawn who stole our Barbies and read our diaries, but things have changed since then. Now, Teddy is simply one of us, a member of our strange motley family.

Since we've settled down in the white farmhouse, Teddy spends long hours by himself. He has taught himself to hunt with a crossbow, and he often rewards us with bloody, dead carcasses we are supposed to get excited about eating. For me, meat comes in a package from the supermarket, without a face or a mother. If I can't have that, I'll eat everything else that is left in the world, even if it's just canned beans and wild asparagus.

"He's probably out hunting," I tell her, and she absorbs this information by wrapping her arms around her shins and resting her chin on her knees. Elizabeth doesn't like the hunting either. As my words trail off, a shot rings out in the distance.

Henry lowers the axe, and we all stare in the direction of the shot. My heart freezes in my chest like a lump of lead. The shot is followed by the sound of a truck engine and the bray of joyful music, trademarks of the bad guys who hunt us.

"Everybody in the basement, now!" Henry screams, and I find myself rooted to the spot.

"What about Teddy?" I ask.

Henry continues to stare off into the distance. "He's on his own this time."

I feel a shiver run down my spine, knowing that the bad men wouldn't just shoot a warning shot before coming to find us. They must have been shooting at something.
I only hope it wasn't Teddy.

350

Sutton Public Library
P.O. Box 544
4 Uxbridge Road
Sutton, MA 01590

CPSIA information can be obtained at www.ICGtesting.com
Printed in the USA
LVOW10s1717220913

353565LV00005B/230/P

9 781482 768930